Lola found herself shaking her head. "We only have part of a song."

"My mind goes where my mind goes." Dylan picked up his guitar and strummed a portion of the melody they'd worked on the day before.

"That works in rock music, I'm sure, but music for a movie is different." They had specific time periods to fill, action to cover.

"I know," Dylan said, "but this is where I was heading. I throw a lot of stuff out there and I'm a great editor."

I can't work this way, Lola thought, trying to control the panic. *He's all over the place.* Her approach was more structured, more linear.

"Are you okay?" Dylan asked, concern in his tone.

"I'm fine." *I think*, she thought.

"You look anxious."

"I can do this," Lola said firmly.

"Are you sure? I don't know if I need to call a doctor, thump you on the back or get you some bourbon." His gaze moved over her.

He'd tied his blond hair back into a ponytail. He wore torn, faded jeans and a band T-shirt. A small gold stud in one ear caught the light. Everything about him shouted rebel, yet he was polite, articulate and paternal.

She took a deep breath, calming herself as best she could. "I have a hard time… My process is more… I just can't work this way."

Jackie and Miriam have been writing partners for twenty years, though some days it feels like forever. Jackie is a spontaneous writer and Miriam is the planner. Despite such diverse approaches to writing, they have managed to achieve a balance between their unique styles. Jackie is creative, passionate and dedicated. Miriam is focused, thoughtful and detail-oriented. Jackie loves dogs and thinks she doesn't have enough of them. Miriam loves cats, though currently, she is catless. Between the two of them, they work hard to bring their stories to life.

Books by J.M. Jeffries

Harlequin Kimani Romance

J.M. JEFFRIES

Seductive Melody &
Capture My Heart

H **HARLEQUIN**® KIMANI™ ROMANCE

ISBN-13: 978-1-335-00586-1

Seductive Melody & Capture My Heart

Copyright © 2019 by Harlequin Books S.A.

The publisher acknowledges the copyright holder of the individual works as follows:

Seductive Melody
Copyright © 2019 by Miriam A. Pace and Jacqueline S. Hamilton

Capture My Heart
Copyright © 2019 by Miriam A. Pace and Jacqueline S. Hamilton

Recycling programs for this product may not exist in your area.

This edition published by arrangement with Harlequin Books S.A.

For questions and comments about the quality of this book, please contact us at CustomerService@Harlequin.com.

Printed in U.S.A.

CONTENTS

Jackie:
I want to dedicate this book to every musician
and singer, from Beethoven to Public Enemy
to Billie Holiday and Johnny Cash.
You made my existence a life worth living.

Miriam:
I'm basically tone deaf, but I do hear Cher and I love
her. This book is dedicated to Cher, who lives her life
her way. May we all find a little Cher inside us.

SEDUCTIVE MELODY

J.M. Jeffries

Dear Reader,

Music defines the soul. For Dylan Ward, music gave his life purpose; for Lola Torres, it's ingrained in her DNA. Their diverse musical approaches will set them on a journey that will not only challenge them, but inspire them. They must both learn to merge their styles so they can allow passion to flow through their lives. As different as they are, music provides them with a harmony of love.

Best,

J.M. Jeffries

Prologue

Tall oak trees swayed in the breeze. Despite the cold drizzle, the cemetery was peaceful and calm. April in Portland was cool and damp. A sea of black umbrellas surrounded the plain white canopy covering two gleaming bronze caskets.

Dylan Ward braced himself against the grief that surrounded him. He couldn't believe his brother and sister-in-law were dead, the result of a collision with a drunk driver on a dark, rainy night. Anthony, eight years older than Dylan, had been so full of life and his wife, Yvonne, had been Anthony's best friend. Dylan found it hard to think of them as dead. He kept expecting Anthony to jump out of the bushes and yell, "April Fools!" But the day wasn't a joke.

Dylan held his niece's and nephew's hands. Fair-haired like his brother, Emma looked dazed. At seven years old, Emma probably didn't really understand what was happening. Ten-year-old Justin looked angry with his mouth pressed tightly closed and his eyes downcast. He refused to look at the caskets. He'd refused to talk or even make eye contact with anyone.

The loss of his only brother left Dylan bereft. One moment had changed everything and now Dylan felt very alone. He'd idolized his older brother and adored his sister-in-law.

The solemn ceremony came to an end. The final words of the prayer faded away into the breeze. People approached Dylan, the children and Dylan's parents as they stood beneath the canopy and stoically accepted the offered condolences. Dylan tried to be gracious, but he couldn't seem to find words of any kind. Yeah, they'd be all right, but for the moment the pain of the loss was too great to process.

Dylan felt a hand on his shoulder. He turned to face his manager.

Max Gunther was a slender man of medium height in his mid-thirties with squinting eyes and dark brown hair already receding. "Do you need a few days to help get the kids settled with your parents?"

For a second Dylan was too surprised to respond. Why did everyone assume his parents had been appointed guardians to the two children?

"Not going to my parents," Dylan replied. "They're coming with me."

Justin and Emma were being hugged and petted and looked so lost his heart ached for them, and he didn't know how he was going to cope as their new parent. He hated to uproot them from Portland, but he lived in Los Angeles. He detested taking them away from what was familiar to them, but he had no choice.

"I'm their guardian," Dylan explained.

"I have two kids, a wife and a nanny," Max replied. "I can barely keep up. This is going to affect your life, you know. What was your brother thinking?"

Offended, Dylan said, "I'm sure he and his wife were thinking I'd make a pretty good parent." Did everyone think he was useless because he'd chosen not to follow his parents into their law firm? And why did Max think it was okay to insult Anthony's memory by suggesting he was irresponsible to let Dylan care for the kids?

Max frowned. "How are you planning to balance your career with parenting?"

Dylan didn't know, but he could see Max was worried about his own bottom line. Dylan and his bandmates had formed their rock band, Calamity, when they'd been sophomores in high school. They'd had enough raw talent to turn a small regional rock band into an international sensation in a few years through persistence, lots of energy and plain stubbornness.

"We just finished a tour," Dylan said, "and we aren't planning another album for another year or two. I can take some time off."

"B-B-But what about your band members?" Max stuttered. "What are they going to do while you're—" Max glanced at the children who were now with Dylan's parents "—babysitting?"

"They have their own lives and some side projects."

Dylan had always encouraged his friends to look at other avenues for their talent. "They're not going to be unemployed." His bandmates had already said they understood.

Dylan glanced around the crowd of mourners. His mother, with Emma and Justin by her side, stood talking with a woman Dylan recognized as his brother's assistant at the law firm. His mother still looked stunned. His father stood by himself, looking remote and angry.

His parents had always been aloof, more interested in their law careers than anything else. They'd told him more than once how disappointed they were over his life choices. He'd barely graduated from high school and then decided against college. In a family of lawyers, his decision had not been popular. The only classes he'd excelled at were English—because he'd known he wanted to write songs—and music. Anthony had been the only one to encourage him to follow his dream.

"You can't just stop being Dylan Ward, front man for the band." Max glared at Dylan as though everything were his fault.

"Calamity will survive." Dylan believed that with no reservations.

"Then hire a nanny."

The fact that Max was being so unsympathetic was more than just irritating. It didn't bode well for the future, especially his lack of understanding of any obligations beyond Dylan's music. He couldn't throw away his niece and nephew. Anthony and Yvonne had trusted him to take care of them.

"They just lost their parents." Dylan tried not to

sound impatient but he gave Max a cold stare trying to control his anger. "Did you think I was going to just toss them in my house and get on with my life?"

"A lot of parents do exactly that." Max glanced at his Rolex watch. "What about Yvonne's family?"

"She grew up in foster care," Dylan said icily, now expecting no sympathy from Max. Here they were at his brother and sister-in-law's funeral, and all Max wanted to talk about was how inconvenient their deaths were. Yvonne had once told him foster care was truly difficult for orphans, but he didn't expect Max to care about that.

"Dylan, I don't want to tell you how to live your life…"

"This is not the place, Max," Dylan warned.

Emma tugged at his sleeve. "Uncle Dylan."

He smiled down at her, wanting to gather her in his arms and keep her safe. "Max, this discussion is over." He knelt down on the damp grass and smiled at his niece.

"What's going to happen to Justin and me?" Emma looked so lost and forlorn, Dylan's heart broke.

"You and Justin are coming to California to live with me," he said. "I hope that's okay with you."

Emma gave him a sweet smile. "Can we go to Disneyland every day?"

He kissed her on the forehead. "If that is what you need, we will."

Chapter 1

Six months later

Lola Torres sat at the end of the long conference table, trying not to be intimidated by the two producers, John Milles and Bobby Ramirez, who'd hired her to write the musical score for their new animated movie. John and Bobby were the new golden boys in the entertainment industry. Each one was in their mid-thirties, and in the last ten years they'd produced four animated movies. Two of those movies won a number of awards. Between the two men, they had seven Oscars.

Bobby was a small man with a round belly. His light brown hair was thin with a comb-over trying to cover an early onset bald spot. John was the athletic type with muscled arms and shoulders and thick thighs. His hair was already iron gray, making him look years older than he actually was.

The conference room had blinding white walls with boring abstract art and pristine white carpeting. At one end sat an elegant cherrywood sideboard with a silver carafe of coffee, ceramic cups, creamer and sugar pot, along with serving dishes of tiny appetizers. They'd brought her into their office probably hoping she'd be intimidated by the opulence. Most of their meetings had been held over meals at restaurants. Producers liked to lunch and do business, because it killed two birds with one stone and was tax deductible. This did not bode well.

Lola tapped her fingers against the surface of the table, the melody in her head repeating so she wouldn't forget. Her thoughts looked like musical notes, and tunes bombarded her mind constantly. She wished she'd brought a notebook so she could write the melody down; otherwise it would loop through her thoughts continuously.

"This is a big project, Lola," the producer John Milles said, his tone slightly condescending. "Frankly, we're worried about your ability to handle it."

She could do this job. She tried not to scowl at the man. From the moment she could talk, she'd been hearing music in her head. "Of course, I can handle it. I'm looking forward to the challenge." The music in her head grew louder with the escalation of her stress. And this was her chance to show what she could do.

John Milles and Bobby Ramirez had founded their small, independent production company when still at

UCLA, specializing in computer-generated animated movies. Several high-profile studios had complimented them on the creativity of their last movie. And who could ignore all those Oscars?

"It's not that we don't have confidence in your ability…" John said, his voice hesitant.

And so it begins, she thought. Because she was only twenty-six with just a few highly visible musical credits, they doubted her. She didn't understand. She'd already won her own growing shelf of awards. If they thought she wasn't capable, then why hire her?

"And we do like the samples you sent, but we thought—" John gave her a wide, fake grin "—well, maybe a cowriter."

Irritation spread through her. She didn't want to be annoyed, but she was. The last time she'd collaborated with another writer, a disaster had occurred. She didn't want a repeat because she valued her reputation too much. But she'd already signed the contract and, while she'd read the provision allowing them to ask her to work with other musicians, hadn't expected them to enforce the clause. She was a professional. She could do this. Her record spoke for itself.

"We want something edgier…" John said.

She never understood what *edgier* meant. From Los Angeles County High School for the Arts, she'd progressed to Berklee College of Music in Boston for a bachelor of music in film scoring. She'd already scored two Japanese anime movies and two TV shows and written dozens of songs and commercial jingles. She was eminently qualified for their needs. Did they doubt her because she was a woman?

She tried to be philosophical. If they wanted her to work with someone, she could do that as much as she loathed the idea. "Who did you have in mind?" If she wanted this job, she would have to be flexible.

John nodded at an anonymous assistant who'd been hovering near the door and staying out of the line of fire. He opened it and motioned to someone outside her view. A tall man entered dressed in jeans and a black Henley shirt. She stared at him, feeling a new pounding in her heart.

Oh, my God. Dylan Ward. They wanted her to work with Dylan Ward. She started to hyperventilate. Someone poured her a glass of water and she gulped it down. Dylan grinned at her and she melted back into her chair too stunned to react. For a moment she wanted to scream like a fangirl but contained herself.

He sat down in the empty chair next to her.

"You're writing music for a children's animated movie?" she asked in surprise. This man had proved his cred already. "Why?" He was a star in his own right and didn't need to be a cowriter on anything. And he was too handsome to be real.

"I'm trying new things." His voice was deep and sexy and she almost melted into a puddle of groupie goo.

John added, "And he's going to do Little Wolf's singing voice."

"What happened to Paul Sanders?" she asked.

"Mr. Sanders has a little problem not conducive to

a children's movie," John said smoothly without elaborating.

"I don't want to know." She resisted the urge to cover her ears. She'd heard rumors about Paul long ago.

"Me neither," Dylan said with a suggestive half laugh that sent shivers up and down her spine.

"Unfortunately," John said, "I do know and I don't want to ever have to deal with it again." He frowned. "So do you two think you can work together?"

"Yes," Dylan said.

"Of course," Lola said even as dread filled her. She wanted to gush like a groupie because this was Dylan Ward and who wouldn't want to work with him, but she needed to be cool, considering how thrilled with the opportunity. She wanted to whip out her iPhone to show him all the Calamity music on her playlist, but that would be a little too fangirl. She wanted to take selfies with him and post them to her Facebook, Instagram and Twitter accounts, but *stalker* was not a term that would look good on her résumé.

He was more beautiful in person than on his band's album covers. His hair was a gorgeous shade of reddish blond pulled back into a neat ponytail and his eyes were so light a gray they were almost white. He had golden California-sun-kissed skin. He was as lean and slim as the surfers she used to admire at Venice Beach.

"I knew you two could work together," John said, a satisfied tone in his voice. "You've both looked at the storyboards and read the screenplay. I know you're going to compose an awesome soundtrack."

Lola smiled as best she could. "I'm ready to get to work."

Dylan rubbed his hands together with a swift glance at her. "Me, too."

John stood. "I'll let you two get to know each other a little bit."

Dylan glanced at his watch. "How about some lunch?"

Lola grinned at him. "I know a great place that serves an amazing lunch."

He studied her for a moment. "I'm hoping you are talking about your parents' restaurant."

So, he knew about them. Had he researched her? "You are so lucky the restaurant is only two miles from here." She rose and led the way out of the conference room, down the hall, out into the lobby leading directly into the attached parking structure.

"I'll follow you," Dylan said as she walked to her Camry.

She nodded.

Luna el Sol was only half-filled with the lunch crowd. Neither of her parents were there. Her father had another commitment and her mother was helping a friend. Several diners glanced at her as she passed and she nodded at those she recognized. A couple diners looked surprised when they saw Dylan.

The hostess seated them in the section reserved for her family and separated from the rest of the diners by a low wall filled with plants that partially obscured them from the rest of the room.

A few heads turned to watch them. A couple of women smiled invitingly at Dylan and held up their smartphones, but he ignored them. He probably had women falling at his feet all the time.

A waitress approached with a basket of bread. Lola ordered iced tea and Dylan ordered a soda. For a moment they stared at each other awkwardly. She had no idea how to talk to this amazingly sexy man with such kissable lips.

"I love the music you did for the *Tokyo Rock* movie," he said.

"I just finished the score for the second one. Who knew you're a fan of anime?" That surprised her. He didn't seem the type to be interested in anime, but then again she'd never expected her very serious oldest brother, Matteus, to like anime, either.

"Not until my nephew turned me on to it. He's ten and there isn't an anime anything that he hasn't seen or read. I plan to take him to the next convention in San Diego."

"I've been a fan for years and I loved working on those movies. I even went to Tokyo and met the voice actors, the screenwriters and the book writers. I took several months and immersed myself in the culture. I had a great time." She'd had more than a great time. She'd even learned to play several native instruments.

"I've been to Tokyo on tour, but never longer than a couple of nights. I'd like to go back just to do some touristy stuff."

"Let me know. I have a friend who lives there and

she'd be happy to show you around. She's good at the cultural and the silly."

"The waitress didn't bring menus," he said with a slight frown.

"Do you trust me?" She loved when she could surprise people with the variety of food that wasn't always on the menu.

He studied her. "I'm going to have to."

She grinned. The waitress returned with their drinks and Lola ordered two *pastéis*.

"What are *pastéis*?" he asked, mangling the pronunciation slightly.

Should she tell him or let him discover it for himself? "All I'm going to say is that tomorrow you'll need to schedule some extra cardio."

He laughed. "I'm not on tour. I don't have to worry."

He had a nice laugh, low and sexy, that sent little tremors down her spine. "Please. Please don't tell me you're going to let yourself go to wrack and ruin. Your fans would never forgive me."

He chuckled again. "My days of touring are going to be limited for the next few years."

She wanted to ask why, but it really wasn't any of her business. "I understand if you don't want to answer, but I'm curious. Why take on working with me, when I'm relatively unknown, to score the music and the voice of *Little Wolf's Journey*?" He was big enough to work the project on his own. Maybe she shouldn't have asked. Celebrities were very protective of their privacy. Even the most mundane piece of information could be misinterpreted. "I'm sorry, I overstepped my bounds, but if we're going to work together…" If she'd had time, she would have researched him on the internet to see if something popped up about new directions he was taking, though separating truth from fiction had its own challenges.

He seemed to hesitate and then shrug. "My brother and his wife were killed in an auto accident six months ago. I took over as guardian for my niece and nephew and they need a parent who stays home. Right now, they're still grieving and need me to be here. And a seven-year-old girl and a ten-year-old boy need things." Deep pain showed on his face.

A mix of emotions flooded her. First, sympathy. Lola's heart went out to him, though she wasn't about to admit she hadn't known. She didn't have time to keep up on Hollywood gossip. Six months ago she'd been deep in a project and when she was that engrossed she seldom came up for air, much less for a news flash. In fact, she would have forgotten her own birthday, if her mother hadn't started sending her reminder texts the week before. She was a little obsessive-compulsive when working. "I'm sorry for your loss."

She was sincerely sorry for his situation. Trying to be a parent to his niece and nephew couldn't be easy. But, she still felt a little wounded that he thought he was taking a step back—even down—to work with her.

He shrugged. "I'm learning the parenting thing and I'm not going to learn it on the road."

Their waitress returned with their food. She sighed a little, sadness in her eyes, as she placed his plate down in front of him. Lola didn't blame her. But she still felt anger at the producers because they didn't think she could handle the johis was the biggest opportunity she'd ever had. She couldn't flub it, no matter how attracted she was to the man who would be her cowriter.

How could she prove herself capable if Dylan received half the credit? Hollywood was still a good-old-boys' network and giving this job to a woman and then partnering her with a man was very telling. Dylan had won several Grammys. If their musical score got any notice, he was the one who would get all the credit and she'd be shuffled to the sidelines. She hated herself for her whining, but she couldn't help feeling slighted.

Get a grip, she told herself. She would get through this. She was fuming on the inside, but on the outside she would be the consummate professional. Her mother always told her honey catches more flies than vinegar. She was still at the start of her career, and she couldn't afford to alienate anyone. She needed more honey.

"But why this project?" Lola knew she was being unfair by continuing to press him, but wanted an answer.

"No one was prouder of me than my brother," he said, "but he didn't let his kids listen to my music. He called it 'music with an adult content.' I want to write music my niece and nephew can listen to and be proud of."

Her heart melted a little. He was doing this for his niece and nephew. How sweet. Music was Lola's whole world. She listened to all forms as often as she could. "Your brother sounds very conscientious."

"He was. I spend a lot of time negotiating with the kids, but I need to get to the point where they don't know I'm negotiating."

She should introduce Dylan to her mother. Grace Torres had raised seven children and made parenting look effortless. Yet, Lola didn't want to be too friendly with Dylan. He was going through some bad stuff, but he didn't need to take over her parade. She needed to make it clear from the beginning they were equals in this relationship.

"Right now, the only thing I have going for me as a parent," he continued, "is that money isn't an issue. Other aspects of parenting, like researching school districts and children's programs, made me feel like I'm from another planet. I even hired a nanny."

She had a mental image of a sweet young thing in tight jeans who didn't know a thing about kids. "How did you do on hiring a nanny?"

He looked away, then shook his head. "For the first one, I went typically male and hired someone pretty to look at, and when I found her in my bed wearing her birthday suit, I panicked. Sam, my bassist, is the only one in the band married with kids…"

"So you asked him?"

"Of course not," Dylan scoffed. "He wouldn't have known the answer. I asked his wife and she pointed me at an agency specializing in nannies."

"So does your current nanny come with sensible shoes and clothes?"

"She could've doubled as a bodyguard," he replied artlessly, "but she knew how to be a nanny. She home-schooled the kids after I brought them back from Port-land and stayed until we moved to Pacific Palisades and settled into our routine. Then she quit and went back to England to work for the royal family."

"At least you knew she was good enough that they wanted her."

He nodded. "And I decided not to hire a new one."

"How's that going for you?" Lola knew it must be tough parenting alone. With both her parents working, she'd watched them juggle their schedules to make time for their seven children. When one parent was on the road, the other stayed home. Her father opened Luna el Sol so he'd be home all the time while her mother was on the road as a backup singer for some of the top names in the music business.

"I don't know how parents parent." A small sigh of frustration escaped him. "One minute I'm the good guy and the next minute, I'm the monster under the bed."

"You must have your hands full." She took a bite of her *pastel* and tried not to sigh at the heavenly taste the custard tart left on her tongue. Her favorite tastes were vanilla and cinnamon. She sipped her iced tea, wanting to know more about him but wanting to make it clear she expected to be treated as an artistic equal, despite his greater star power. "So, how will you also take on a monumental project like *Little Wolf's Journey*?" Surely he could live off his past success. He didn't need to insert himself in hers.

"I can stay home with Emma and Justin, and still work. I have a full recording studio in my home with soundproofing, the latest in digital equipment and editing software. I can work from home and I'm hoping you'll consider working there with me."

"Of course." She intended to be flexible no matter what. No one was going to call her a crazy diva.

"What instruments do you play?" he asked after several minutes elapsed and he'd eaten most of his *pastel.*

"Whatever you need when you need it." She prided herself on her abilities.

With one eyebrow raised, he said, "I'm not sure what you mean?"

"When I was scoring the anime movies I learned to play a Japanese koto and a *mokugyo.* That was fun." And she'd loved every minute. The challenges of mastering new instruments stretched her as an artist and added depth to her music.

"What are those?"

"A koto is like a zither. And a *mokugyo* is a drum-like block of wood shaped like a fish and used with a stick to create a melody."

He looked a little confused. "That sounds...complicated."

Complicated, yes, but these men had hired her, and she'd been fully committed to the work, to producing music that fit the project. "The anime producers were impressed that I wanted it to have a cultural feel with modern sensibilities—their words, not mine. I got the job and they liked the first score well enough to hire me for the second movie." She didn't intend to sound smug, but she knew she did. "Along with those instruments, I play the usual—piano, guitar, flute—and a few odd instruments, like a zydeco rubboard—or washboard, depending on who you talk to."

Again a look of confusion crossed his face.

"It's like a washboard that fits over your shoulders." She pulled her phone out of her purse and showed him a photo of the instrument.

"That's interesting…" His voice trailed away while he continued to eat. "Before you turn me down…"

"I didn't turn you down," she objected.

"You didn't look too convinced. Just come to my home and look over my studio. I'll arrange to have any instrument you feel you need brought over if you agree."

She nodded. "Okay. How about tomorrow?"

"Come for lunch. I make a pretty mean sandwich."

Chapter 2

The meeting with Lola Torres did not go well. Even though she'd been agreeable and said all the right things, he sensed she wasn't happy from the tip of her hair to her ankle.

Dylan had been surprised to learn he would be collaborating. At first, he'd thought he was creating the musical score on his own. He'd looked forward to it, to making his mark in a different part of the industry. After meeting Lola, though, any disappointment at the cowriting arrangement evaporated; he'd been fine with her. She was talented, if her versatility with instruments was any guide. She certainly was lovely with her Rosario Dawson looks, though her hair was shorter and her eyes a darker brown. She definitely wasn't hard to look at.

He'd intended to go home after their lunch, but found himself parking in front of his best friend and bandmate's house. Dylan had an hour before he needed to pick up Emma and Justin from school, but first he needed advice.

Sam Delano and Dylan had been friends since eighth grade. When Sam answered the door, he didn't ask one question, just stood aside and let Dylan in.

He sat down. "Where's Elise?"

Their house was a one-story ranch on the eastern edge of Brentwood overlooking a golf course. Elise's favorite colors were dark gray and red, but the red was a subtle accent in the living room with its white walls and gray furniture. Even though three lively children lived in the house, not one toy was in sight. Dylan knew they had a playroom at the back of the house, off the family room.

People thought rock bands lived exotic, chaotic lives. The truth was more mundane. Sam liked to golf. Most mornings, after the children left for school, he'd be on the course.

Sam laughed as he sat down. "I didn't tell you my news. Elise found a job."

"Is she modeling again?"

Sam had met Elise when they'd done a concert in Paris. He had fallen in love with her at first sight. Elise had been a bit elusive, though, letting him chase her until she caught him, as Sam often said. Dylan knew they were happy.

"She's working with the Girl Smart organization."

"Girl Smart?" Dylan vaguely remembered hearing something about it.

"It promotes education for girls all over the world. You know Elise is rabid about women being given equal opportunities."

"Do you, uh, need money?" Dylan asked cautiously. He hadn't thought that taking a break from touring for a few years would put the other members in jeopardy financially. They had a steady income from album sales and they all had their own side projects.

Sam shook his head. "You don't need to worry about any of us. We've never taken a break for this long before, and now that I'm spending more time at home being house dad, which I'm totally loving, Elise decided to get out in order to save our marriage or, as she announced, she would file for divorce after she knocked me over the head with a baseball bat. So, I'm home being daddy with the two best people in the world, my kids. We go to horseback-riding lessons, soccer practice and Girl Scouts. I'm looking forward to cookie sales in February."

"Courtney, Sydney and Ashley are pretty lucky to have you for a dad." Dylan didn't think Emma or Justin felt the same way about him.

"We have playtime 24-7. I'm enjoying every minute of it. I'm not going to think about anything. You take as long as you need, because I have three girls who look at me like the sun rises and sets with me every single day. I used to think groupies were an ego boost, but nothing like three daughters who think I'm perfect."

"My niece and nephew don't think that way." In fact,

Emma had told him bluntly he'd been more fun before he'd become both mother and father to her.

"That's because you have to be both parents. Courtney and Ashley think I'm just another playmate that occasionally has to be obeyed. And Sydney thinks I'm the best. I'm so loving this."

"Yeah," Dylan said. He wondered if the other guys felt the same way. He knew Ben Faulkner was taking some college classes to finish his music degree, and Wally Carleton was producing an album for an up-and-coming young singer making the transition between tween star and adult.

"It was a bit bumpy the first few months," Sam continued. "But it's nice having this peaceful quiet. And I enjoy being a house husband."

Dylan felt relief. He knew he'd upset the apple cart, and he worried Sam, Ben and Wally would resent what he was doing. They had all made their plans and eventually they would get back together. In a few more years they'd be back touring, though probably on a more abbreviated schedule, but still touring. Dylan's responsibilities would be growing as Emma and Justin got older.

"How did your meeting go?" Sam asked.

"Interesting." The doubt in his voice hung in the air.

Sam's eyebrows rose curiously. "In what way?"

Dylan took a moment to phrase his words. "I met the other composer, Lola Torres."

"Any relation to Grace Torres?"

"Her daughter." He'd known of her before meeting Lola. Good backup singers had reputations.

"Anyway, she says she's thrilled to work with me."

Sam's eyes narrowed. "But…"

"Her body language is a whole different message." And then some, he thought. Resentment had been buried deep, but he could see it in Lola's eyes.

"Keep on talking," Sam said.

"She's not what I expected." She was disciplined, eager, and dedicated to her music.

Sam chuckled. "I don't know about Lola Torres, but her mother did the backup vocals for Devil's Road's third album and I sat on the drums. Grace brought Brazilian food, wooed us with her charm, did her vocals in one take and made us all look like we were still in an elementary-school band and we didn't know one key on the keyboard from the other.

"Three years ago, I went to a Cher concert and Grace was singing backup on stage and Cher acted like she had Jesus with her. She's pretty much sung backup for everybody from Tony Bennett to Foo Fighters. If genetics count for anything, Lola has greatness…and professionalism.

"Lola's written some beautiful music. She won an award for that little indie film, *A Force of Habit*. The film wasn't too great, but the music was absolutely amazing."

"She doesn't want to work with me," Dylan replied.

"The producers threw her a curve ball. Give her a moment," Sam said. "This is like someone saying, 'Dylan, you're pretty great all by yourself, but we're going to have Dave Grohl help you with your vocals.'"

Dylan thought about that for a moment and nodded. "Yeah, I'd take a statement like that a little personally."

Then he smiled. "I will admit, looking at her face day after day will be compensation for her resentment." That thought cheered him up.

Sam said, "She's pretty to look at, and you're going to do what you need to do even if she snarls and bites you. Which reminds me, Elise's birthday is Sunday and the girls bought her a puppy."

Dylan stared at Sam. "You are kidding me." He looked around. Elise's house was pristine. Dust was afraid of her. "What did you get her—a miniature poodle or some other purse puppy?"

"Hell, no. We went to the pound. Ashley and Courtney picked out an akita-Rottweiler-German-shepherd mix. Sydney wanted a poodle mix, but was voted down. This puppy is going to grow up and weigh a hundred pounds or more." Sam looked so pleased, Dylan had to look away or he'd break out laughing. Elise was never going to forgive him.

"I hope the puppy matches the furniture." Dylan knew the puppy was the girls' idea because they wanted one. He hoped Elise wasn't too shocked.

Sam waved a hand. "Elise will be fine. And you'll be fine with Lola. Even if you two hate each other, you're going to turn out something great. No one in the band is angry with you because we all know you need to score this movie as much for Emma and Justin as for yourself."

Dylan warmed with appreciation for his friends' support. They knew he wanted the movie to be a bonding moment for him and his niece and nephew. Despite his worry about the upcoming collaboration with Lola, he had friends who had his back.

Lola sat at the kitchen island in her small Hollywood Hills home, waiting for her brother Sebastian. Like her, he was the only one who liked to jog and they met several mornings a week to run in the hills. A cool breeze flowed through the open French doors that led to her redwood deck and backyard.

Her two-bedroom cottage was perched on the side of a hill overlooking the city. Higher up the hill the houses became progressively more expensive and larger, places where prominent movers and shakers in the entertainment industry could prowl their domains and survey the less prestigious properties below.

She'd kept her decorating to a minimum, with Stickley furniture upholstered in pale yellows and blues, watercolors from an artist friend on the walls and polished wood floors. She liked color on the walls, and each room was a palette of natural green bringing nature in like an extension of her backyard. The yard itself was a jungle of large flowering plants and towering trees jammed together around a tiny gazebo overlooking the canyon behind her. From one side of her yard she could see the H-O-L in the famous Hollywood Hills sign, and from the other side of her yard she could see down to Mulholland Drive winding its way through the city.

She nursed a third cup of coffee while she wrestled with the problem of working with Dylan Ward. She tried to dampen her anger, but her feelings were definitely hurt. The producers, John and Bobby, didn't trust her despite her résumé, which they had said was truly impressive.

She could do edgy. No, really, she could. They needed to give her a chance, but instead they'd saddled her with a rock star who'd almost won her over with his cute story about his niece and nephew and the sadness of their parents' deaths. She'd come close to understanding his motives, but this job was hers. She'd worked hard to get to this point so early in her career and she felt as if she was being deliberately sidelined. Her name on the movie would be overshadowed by Dylan's.

Lola had known music would be an integral part of her life from the moment she could hum a tune and bang little songs on her mother's piano. Every thought, every move since she'd graduated from Berklee had been calculated to get her to this point.

Sebastian entered through the open French doors and silently headed straight for the coffeepot, poured a mug, stirred sugar and cream into it before sitting down across from her. He'd dressed in his usual jogging clothes: black shorts and white T-shirt with crosstrainers on his feet. He was the second oldest of her brothers. They had always been close. The twins, Daniel and Nick, had each other. Matteus, the oldest brother, had always been close with Nina, her sister, which left her with Sebastian. Her youngest brother, Rafael, seemed happy without a confidante, being the most self-contained of all the siblings.

"Wow! You are looking glum this morning." He reached for a croissant, took a bite before asking, "What happened at the meeting yesterday?"

"I don't want to talk about it," she half-growled.

Sebastian laughed. "That is Lola speak for you want to spill your guts."

Like her, he was tall and lean limbed with long dexterous fingers that were perfect for the tricks he'd perfected over the years, eventually leading him to a membership and employment at the Magic Castle. He'd tried to teach her card tricks over the years since her fingers were like his, but she had never been interested.

"I want to get our five-mile run over and head to the nearest mall for some retail therapy." A new pair of shoes always made her happy. Though, considering the latest blow to her confidence, two pairs of shoes would be better.

"You really want to confide in your big brother." He put his elbows on the table and leaned toward her. "Tell Dr. Sebastian everything."

She reached for a croissant, took a bite and then a sip of coffee. She drew a breath and everything just spilled out—her anger, her sense of betrayal, her feelings about Dylan Ward and her struggle to stay professional. He nodded in all the appropriate places, made sympathetic noises and once even patted her hand.

Silence eventually fell. She gazed out the kitchen window. Hummingbirds had gathered at the feeders she'd hung from the roof edge, and she watched their tiny fluttering bodies as they competed for food.

"That sucked the fun right out of your day, didn't it?" Sebastian laughed at her.

"And my tomorrow, my next week, my next month and all the time I'll have to spend with that man."

"That man," Sebastian said with a wry chuckle, "is pretty talented."

"I didn't say he wasn't."

"Not as talented as you," Sebastian said.

"Stop trying to stroke my ego." She batted at his arm.

"And therein lies the difference between men and women." Sebastian took a second croissant. "A man would never tell anyone to stop stroking his ego."

Lola couldn't help it. Laughter bubbled up in her. Sebastian always made her happy. "Just stop it. I want to be an angry, bitter woman."

"You know what mom would say—"

"Which," she interrupted, "is why I'm not talking to her."

"So walk away."

"Are you kidding?" Lola said aghast. "Not only did I already sign a contract, but this is the opportunity that puts me where I want to be in the music industry. I want to be in the Musicians Hall of Fame, I want a star on Hollywood Boulevard, I want…" She stopped, uncertain what else she wanted.

"You'll get those things." His voice was soothing. He knew her so well.

Lola covered her face. "I just don't know how I'm going to work with him. One minute I want to punch him in the face and the next I want to turn into a puddle of groupie goo. He's accomplished a lot of the things I want to accomplish and he's only a couple of years older than me."

"Is the J word involved here?"

"I'm not jealous of Dylan Ward," she said firmly.

How could her best brother think she was jealous? Did he think her so petty?

"Are you sure?" He gave her a long searching look. He was a handsome man and she wondered where his forever love might be hiding.

She explored her feelings more deeply. Not jealousy. "I'm resentful and I don't want to be. That's going to hamper the way I process music." *Resentful* wasn't quite the word, but it would do. Resentful at the producers who'd put her in this awkward situation, working with a man she admired when she didn't want to be working with anyone.

Sebastian sipped his coffee. "Let's go for a run. Jogging helps clear my head." He stood and settled a hand on her shoulder. "You're a professional. You're going to do the best job of your life and in ten years when you're at the top of your profession, this is just going to be a blip on the radar of your life. Maybe even a good one."

"So says the man who spends his life playing with cards."

"Do you know how much I made for a week in Vegas?" She shook her head. "Enough for my new shoes?

"Enough to buy Daniel a new Bentley."

Their brother Daniel was all about cars, though that interest had been tempered recently after having gotten married on New Year's Day, on a Rose Parade float no less, to a woman who specialized in float design. Now he was looking at a chunk of real estate in Pasadena to build a new house on for the family not yet conceived.

"Come on," she chided him as she beat him to the door. "Try to keep up."

He chuckled as he followed her, and soon they were enjoying a quiet jog that did end up settling her thoughts.

After her run, she showered and dressed for her lunch with Dylan at his home. He'd texted the directions to her phone and she plugged it into her car's GPS, ready to face this collaboration head-on.

Chapter 3

Pacific Palisades was an upscale neighborhood just east of Malibu. Lola's new sister-in-law, Roxanne who was married to her brother Nick, lived in Pacific Palisades and, as it turned out, only a mile from Dylan's home. Which meant if things got tough, she could stop by for a cocktail with Roxanne's grandmother, Donna, who always had margaritas in the blender.

Dylan answered the door wearing jeans, a loose-fitting T-shirt and bare feet. His hair was free and flowed over his shoulders in a red-blond cascade that made her want to run her fingers through it. She almost reached up to push a stray tendril away from his forehead, but stopped herself before she gave in to the impulse.

"Wow," Lola said as he walked her through the wrought-iron front doors and into the living room.

"I never expected you to have this type of taste." She wasn't certain what a rock star's house would be like, but she didn't expect something so traditional and so beautiful.

"I bought it fully furnished. I'm not much of a wood person. At first, I had all these plans for changing the furniture, but the longer I lived here, the more I liked it. I did make some changes so that it was more kid friendly, and I did make over the guesthouse as a studio, soundproofing and installing recording equipment."

He led her through the house, out the patio doors and along a walkway skirting the pool. She loved to swim but her small lot was not large enough. And she would hate to cut back her garden.

The guesthouse was a two-story structure. He opened the door and she stared at the selection of instruments hanging on the walls. Two dark blue sofas faced each other in the center with several matching chairs at both ends. A bar dominated one end and an open doorway led to a galley kitchen on the other side. A stairway along one wall led to the second story.

He led her through the living room to the studio beyond, which sent her pulse into an uproar. She looked around at the recording equipment separated from the sound room by a thick glass wall. The sound room was set off to one side with microphones placed at equal intervals and a Bösendorfer piano in the background. She tried to tamp down her envy. This was the recording room of her dreams and put her own little guest bedroom-studio to shame. Her fingers itched to sit down at the Bösendorfer, which she was certain was in perfect tune.

He dabbed the corner of her mouth. "A little drool right there."

His touch enflamed her. She didn't usually like strangers to take that kind of liberty with her, but there was something about the way his skin felt on hers that excited her.

She found herself beaming as she stepped into the sound room and went to open the piano. "It's hard not to be jealous." Maybe working with him wouldn't be such a hardship. She could learn something and she got to play in musician heaven.

She ran a hand over the smooth finish of the piano and tapped a key. A clear tone sounded and it was perfect.

"Play something," Dylan urged. He sat down on the end of the bench.

She sat down with a smile and cracked her knuckles, kneading the joints. She leaned over the ivories and with two fingers rapped out her version of "Chopsticks."

For a second, Dylan looked surprised, then almost fell off the bench laughing. He sat at the other end of the piano and started his own version of "Chopsticks," harmonizing with her, taking the pulsing rhythm into a bluesy riff, then a waltz tempo and finally a rollicking ragtime-like syncopation. She kept up with him, even pushing him into some of the variations. Laughter bubbled inside her as they grinned at each other at the cadence.

Her hands fell away from the keyboard. Silence fell over the room.

"Not bad. Unexpected, but nice," Dylan said. He finished off with a quick flourish and turned to look at her.

"Speaking of unexpected…" He smiled at her. "Do you want to talk about it?"

"About what?" She pretended to play innocent.

"I know you're not happy working with me." He stood and led her back into the living room.

"I'm fine," she said, keeping her face as blank as possible. She wasn't a good liar.

He opened a small refrigerator behind the bar and pulled out two glass bottles of water. He handed one to her. The container was ice cold and one sip was so refreshing she almost guzzled it all down, unaware of how thirsty she'd been until this moment.

He sat down across from her. "Sure, you are. I know if I were in your shoes, I wouldn't be. Being asked to work with a co-writer."

"I'll admit, I wasn't happy at first, but I'm going to do the job." If for nothing else, just to work in his studio.

"You can't be creative if you're miserable."

"I'm not miserable." She glanced around and gestured at the room. "Who could be miserable here? This is the Taj Mahal of music studios. Your studio makes my tiny home studio look like a slum." She paused. "I'm flexible. I can work anywhere, even in the center of the intersection at Hollywood and Vine with tourists looking over my shoulders and breathing down my neck." When she and her brother, Nick, had been kids, they'd head to Hollywood Boulevard and he would dance to music she'd composed for him. They'd made good money and the memory brought a smile to her face. Nick had used his money to keep his car running, and she'd saved hers because she'd already had Berklee in her sights.

"Good."

"And you?"

"On-the-job training made me adaptable. I learned to work on a leaky, drafty, old school bus on our first tour, breathing in road fumes and eating greasy diner food. We were sixteen and Sam's father drove."

"So you're saying…what?"

"I'm not fussy, either," he said with a frown. He pushed to his feet and walked into the small kitchen. He opened the fridge. "Come on, lunch is served."

Dylan sat at the square bar-height table. He poured water into glasses filled with ice and watched as she tucked into the roast-beef sandwich. He'd always enjoyed being in the kitchen. Something about food and music went together. When he was stuck on an idea, he cooked. He wondered if she was the same.

"Do you like to cook?" he asked, watching her add extra mustard to her sandwich. Knowing her family's love affair with food made him a bit self-conscious about his lunch offering. They were only sandwiches.

"I'm afraid that gene passed me by. I'm the world's worst cook."

"I don't believe that."

She laughed. "I'll call my mother and you can ask her." She started to reach into her purse.

"That bad, huh?"

"I was making hard-boiled eggs one day and I had this tune running through my head I couldn't seem to get rid of. I forgot I was cooking and didn't remember until the fire alarm went off. I had to throw out the pan. There was no salvaging it." She took another bite of her sandwich and nodded. "Good."

"My grandfather taught me to cook." His grandfather had loved being in the kitchen. In fact, when he'd married Dylan's grandmother, she couldn't make anything except angel food cake. His grandfather taught her to cook and she'd turned into a dynamite chef, but she was happy to relinquish the kitchen whenever she could. "Music is like cooking. You put all these different flavors together and you come up with a masterpiece."

"Music is more like a jigsaw puzzle for me. You keep putting the pieces together until they fit and make a complete, coherent picture."

He found himself nodding. "Okay, so we see things differently. That doesn't mean our music won't mesh."

She pursed her lips. He could see her thinking. "Our backgrounds are so different."

"Yours is more classical. I see that. I have to admit, I'm a bit jealous that you had so much formal training and I learned as I needed to."

Her eyebrows went up in surprise. "Why are you jealous?"

"Because you not only have the education to do this job, you have the talent, and I approach music from the position of being self-taught. You know structure, harmonic theory. I just know what I hear. If someone gave me a complicated score, I'd struggle trying to follow it."

She sat back in her chair and studied him. He was struck again by how lovely she was, how calm and composed despite her reservations. "Considering the number of albums that went platinum, I don't think your lack of education has inhibited you."

"But—" he found himself frowning "—everyone in the band contributed. I may have planted the tree, but Sam pruned, Wally watered, and Ben sang until the tree bloomed."

"I'm an avid gardener, so now you're speaking to me in a language I understand."

Silence fell between them. She finished the last of her sandwich and took her plate to the sink and cleaned it before he could protest.

She sat back down across from him. "Where do you see the music for Little Wolf going?" Her fingers tapped a rhythm on the tabletop. Her gaze seemed to turn inward and Dylan knew she was listening to music in her mind. Ben had that same look when a lyric was generating.

The movie had been on his mind for days. "The movie opens with Little Wolf as a cub and ends with him as a full-grown adult wolf. So, we have to generate music that reflects his childhood, his teen years and the adult he becomes because of his experiences."

"We're going to write something fun, something serious and then something mature." Her fingers stopped their restless tapping. Her head tilted and she closed her eyes.

"And something to reflect the culture of the Cheyenne medicine woman he dreams about."

"I can hear the drums in my head."

Excitement filled him. He gently took her hand and led her out of the kitchen and back to the studio. Instead of the Bösendorfer, he sat down at an electric keyboard. She sat next to him on the bench, turned on the keyboard, activated the drums and lightly pressed the keys. "Something like this."

The sound of the drums filled his head, and he heard the tapping of feet on hard soil and the delicate sound of fringe swaying with seashells and elk's teeth hitting each other.

He lost himself in her music, watching on a nearby computer screen as the notes materialized from a music-scoring software program attached to the keyboard while she tapped away at the keys. He didn't realize so much time had passed until his gaze focused and he realized Emma and Justin were staring at him.

"Hi," Emma said. "We're home from school. I don't like riding the bus. Can I have a snack? I'm hungry."

Justin stared at Lola. Slowly the dazed look from her face faded, and like him she came back to the present to gaze in surprise at the two children.

Dylan gave Emma a hug. "This is Miss Lola Torres." He gestured at her. "Lola, this is Emma and Justin."

"Hello," Justin said, his voice containing a touch of suspicion. "Are you our new nanny?"

"No, silly," Emma stated. "She's too pretty to be a nanny like Miss Edith."

"Oh," Lola said with a grin. "Thank you."

"Can I have my snack now?" Emma said, turning back to Dylan, her dark blue eyes searching his face.

"I'm hungry," Justin announced.

"A snack and a chat," Dylan said. "I'll be back in a minute," he said to Lola.

He started to take Justin's hand, but the boy shrugged him off and headed out of the studio. Emma smirked cheekily at Lola as she tucked her tiny hand inside Dylan's.

In the kitchen, Dylan poured milk into two glasses and handed each a banana. "You should be nicer to my guest," he told Justin gently. "You sounded angry, and that can make people uncomfortable."

Justin glared at him and shrugged. "Is she your girl-friend?"

He had no girlfriend, not with two children to take care of. Before they'd come into his life, he'd indulged in every perk a rock star could get. And these two had put a crimp in his social life because he was trying to act like an adult. He'd taken them to a therapist who specialized in children's grief. Justin had refused to co-operate while Emma had understood her time with the therapist was all about Emma.

"She is working with me on the musical score for *Little Wolf's Journey.*"

Justin peeled his banana, tossed the peel in the trash compactor and walked away, leaving the compactor open. Dylan tried not to frown. Emma, with a girlish flourish, tossed her peel in and closed the compactor and turned it on. She kept her huge blue eyes on Dylan as though saying, "Look at me. I'm being a good girl."

Dylan couldn't help but give her his approval. "Thank you, Emma."

"Thank you, Emma," Justin mimicked in a squeaky, mocking tone.

"Don't be such a poophead," Emma said with a chirpy smile.

"We don't use language like that," Dylan chided when he really wanted to say "You go, girl." She was as cute, charming and manipulative as any seven-year-old girl could be and she knew just how to get her way. "Do you two have homework?"

"Yeah," Justin said.

Emma simply nodded, her mouth full of banana.

"When you're done with your snack, start your homework. Miss Lola and I have some more work to do."

Justin shrugged. Emma skipped out of the kitchen and into the living room where she grabbed her back-pack and brought it back. "Mrs. Morgan says you have to quiz me on my spelling words."

"I'll do that after dinner." Dylan left them in the kitchen, returning to Lola.

Lola sat where he'd left her. She'd plugged in the headphones and was still working at the keyboard, though every second she'd stop and write down a few notes on a nearby music notebook. Sometimes it was scribbled words, sometimes chord names, sometimes what looked like hieroglyphics but what he knew were some shorthand musical notations for repetitions and patterns.

When she saw him, she removed the headphones and looked at him, waiting.

"I apologize for Justin's behavior."

"No need," she said quietly. "He's just a kid."

"He's not adjusting well." Dylan didn't mean to sound desperate.

"Have you tried grief counseling?"

"He goes twice a week and does nothing. And Emma knows that those hours are Emma time and takes full advantage." Emma kept nothing to herself. If she was sad, she'd announce it. When she was angry, Dylan had no doubt about her feelings. She let everyone within striking distance know how she felt.

Lola chuckled. "Men are taught to be stoic and women are taught to deal with their emotions early on."

"Justin's a little boy."

Lola shook her head. "He's learning about being a man by watching you." She pushed back from the keyboard after turning it off. She added her sheet of music to the pile of music Dylan had already printed out. "How do you handle your grief?"

He studied her. "I don't have time to worry about grief. I have two kids to raise and a musical score—"

She held her hand up, stopping him. "You've pushed your grief down deep inside yourself and you keep it so bottled up tight you're radiating dysfunction."

He stared at her. "What do you know about grief?"

She smiled at him. "My brother Matteus lost his wife a few years ago to cancer. He did the same thing. He pushed his grief down so tight I knew that one day he'd explode."

"Did he?"

"He exploded all right. Matteus is a cop and he was chasing down a murder suspect. Matteus almost beat the man half to death. He ended up on six months' administrative leave with instructions to get his head back on straight before his bosses would let him back on the job. If he couldn't do that, he would be retired."

Dylan didn't know how to deal with his sorrow. Six months after the funeral and he still missed his brother, missed his sister-in-law. He'd had to push those feelings to the background, though, as he dealt with Justin and Emma. Considering how he felt, he knew Emma and Justin were really suffering, but he felt helpless to support them when he couldn't help himself.

He didn't know what to say.

"I need to be going," Lola said. "I'll see you tomorrow bright and early."

"Not too early. The kids don't have to be to school until 8:20." He drove them most mornings, and occasionally picked them up, but usually they came home on the school bus.

"I'll see you in the morning around 8:45."

He nodded, holding the guest house door open for her and followed around the pool back into the main house and out the front door. He stood in the doorway, watching her get in her car and back out of the driveway, wishing she'd stay longer so he didn't have to deal with his niece and nephew alone. Something about her presence, her empathy, made things easier.

Chapter 4

Lola attacked the encroaching weeds around her roses. Her mother sat in the gazebo, a glass of sangria on the table next to her along with a wedge of brie and crackers.

Grace Torres liberally spread cheese on a cracker and took a bite. "If you had some jalapeño jelly, the brie would be perfect. I could have brought some if you'd asked."

Lola leaned back on her heels and smiled at her mother. "Sorry, Mom, but I forgot to tell you I was out." If not for her mother, her refrigerator would be filled with takeout.

"Your Peace rose is looking a little dehydrated."

Lola glanced at the rose. "I had an infestation of mites again. The roses take a while to bounce back."

She grabbed her trowel and gently raked the dirt around the base of the rosebush. She worked fertilizer into the soil. When she was done, she'd turn on the drip watering system and the fertilizer would get to work, helping restore her roses to prime health. Not that they weren't healthy. Her garden was always a riot of color and she loved every flower, every bush and every tree in it. Especially her Japanese maple in the corner behind the gazebo.

"How did things go on the first day of your new job?"

"What did Sebastian say to you?"

Grace tried to look innocent. "What makes you think Sebastian said anything to me?"

"Because you gave him the glare of truth and he broke under the strain." Lola trimmed a spent rose.

"I do no such thing."

"Fibber," she joked. "You can sniff out intel like a pig sniffs out truffles."

Grace grinned. "I do love my truffles. And I resent being compared to a pig."

Lola burst out laughing. "Pigs are intelligent. I like pigs. George Clooney had a Vietnamese potbellied pig and told people it was the perfect pet." She tossed the faded rose into the mulch bucket. "What did Sebastian say?"

"Only that you're working with Dylan Ward." Grace fanned herself with her hand. "He's hot."

"He's young enough to be your son."

"I'm not dead," Grace said. "And you know how I love musicians."

Lola shook her head. "I admit, he's pretty to look at."

"How is he to work with?"

"We only worked a couple of hours today and wrote a portion of something. Amazingly enough he was very nice, which makes it harder to feel annoyed being stuck working with him."

"My," Grace said after a long sip of her sangria. "What a conundrum."

"You're my mother. You're supposed to be sympathetic to your daughter. Your sarcasm is unattractive."

Grace smiled. She took a delicate bite of her brie-laden cracker. "Your whining is unattractive."

Lola sighed. "I'm not whining. I foresee me doing all the work and him getting all the credit."

"As a backup singer for so many years, I didn't get a lot of credit, but I did get the reputation of being a solid performer, which has kept me working to this day. I'm still turning down jobs. Singing is wonderful, darling, but as long as your name is spelled correctly on the check and it clears, you're doing good. You're being paid for what you love to do."

Lola still didn't like the sense of resentment inside her. "I just can't help feeling the producers don't trust me to do the job."

Grace frowned. "Number one, you're a very talented musician and writer. The producers wouldn't have hired you if they thought you weren't right for the job. Number two, the producers respected you enough to pair you with someone of equal talent. You have a good reputation in this business, and maybe Dylan wanted to work with you."

Lola stared at her, openmouthed. "What?"

"My darling daughter, you are one of the most talented songwriters to come along in a while. Don't you read your press?"

"You told me not to." In fact, Lola actively fought not to read anything about herself.

"Wow. I'm a much better mother than I thought." Grace sat back with a benign smile. "Well, I read your press and I think Dylan Ward wanted to work with you. The two of you have a lot to learn from each other. Take advantage of this opportunity."

"What would Dylan learn from me?"

"A lot. He doesn't have an Emmy or a Clio award. You have both. And with him in the picture, your music could easily get more notice than those anime movies you did. Enough notice to garner an Academy Award nomination."

Lola paused in her weeding to think. "I'm not pinning my hopes on such a rarified achievement."

"Yeah, right," Grace said with a laugh. "Like you haven't been dreaming of a star on Hollywood Boulevard since you were four years old. I still have the star you and your dad made out of concrete."

"And it's still in the backyard where you can walk all over it?"

"Lola Torres, pity party of one," her mother half sang. "Your table is ready."

"Ouch," Lola said. She left off weeding and went to sit next to her mother. She poured herself a glass of sangria and took a cracker.

"If your mother can't be honest with you, then who can?"

"You're supposed to be on my side."

"I'm on your side, but that doesn't mean I can't be honest with you."

Lola patted her mother's hand. "I know. I just needed this conversation." This was the great Torres version of the pep talk. Lola had finally found her fight. "Thank you. You're good, Mom."

"And you are a good daughter, my darling."

"I'm glad I've gotten this all out of my system. That man has a lot on his plate."

Grace gave her daughter a curious look. "What do you mean?"

"He's dealing with some heavy stuff with his brother and sister-in-law having died and being handed guardianship of his niece and nephew. They are a handful and he's still grieving himself. I think he feels like he's drowning. How did you manage seven children?"

"I had help in the beginning. Your *avó* was a treasure."

Lola had distant memories of her paternal grandmother. Mostly of her grandmother reading to her in Portuguese and not understanding a word, but loving the lilting tone of her grandmother's voice. Eventually, she'd learned Portuguese so she could read to her grandmother.

"If Avó had had her way, there'd be more little Torreses than just you seven."

Lola smiled. Her father was the third of five children. Except for her *avó* and an aunt, along with her father, everyone else had stayed in Brazil. Avó had wanted to see the world and spent years traveling whenever she could, until she'd had a stroke and went into an assisted-living facility. Lola still missed her grandmother. Sometimes, she'd go to the cemetery with a bouquet of flowers from her garden, read a children's book in Portuguese to her grandmother and play her flute.

"So you're telling me I will get through this. I'm talented. I will survive."

"In a nutshell," Grace said. "Now, how about more sangria?" She held out her glass.

"How much did you bring?"

"Enough to get both of us through till Sunday."

"You already wrote the lyrics to the tune we worked on yesterday!" Lola stared at him, stunned, in the studio. They weren't finished with that melody. She didn't like being hemmed in by what they'd put on paper so far. Creativity was crazy like that. You had immense freedom…until the first notes were written down. Then they confined you to structure. They'd not finished building that structure.

"The first and second verses are always easy," Dylan said, his tone nonchalant. "*Moon* and *June* and *soon* and *boon*. And then you get to the third and fourth verses and you end up with *loon* and *bassoon* and *buffoon*."

Lola found herself shaking her head. "We only have part of a song."

"My mind goes where my mind goes." Dylan picked up his guitar and strummed a portion of the melody they'd worked on the day before.

"That works in rock music, I'm sure, but music for

a movie is different." They had specific time periods to fill, action to cover.

"I know," Dylan said, "but this is where I was heading. I throw a lot of stuff out there and I'm a great editor."

I can't work this way, Lola thought, trying to control the panic. *He's all over the place.* Her approach was more structured, in a more linear fashion.

"Are you okay?" Dylan asked, concern in his tone.

"I'm fine." *I suppose,* she thought.

"You look anxious."

"I can do this," Lola said firmly.

"Are you sure? I don't know if I need to call a doctor, thump you on the back or get you some bourbon." His gaze moved over her.

He'd tied his reddish-blond hair back into a ponytail. He wore torn, faded jeans and a Led Zeppelin T-shirt. A small gold stud in one ear caught the light. Everything about him shouted rebel, yet he was polite, articulate and attentive.

She took a deep breath, calming herself as best she could. "I have a hard time… My process is more… I just can't work this way."

He drew back from her in surprise. "How do you work?"

"In a more linear manner."

"You mean like A to B to C."

"That's where I'm comfortable."

"I know I'm more unstructured, but if we're going to work together, we're going to have to find a middle ground." His lips twitched. "I, surprisingly, do understand. Ben is like you. He likes to work on one project at a time, from start to finish, before he moves on to the next one."

"I like working in a straight line. I feel like I'm always moving forward. The melody gets stuck in my head and until I've written it all down, I can't get rid of it and move on."

"I tend to thrive more on the chaos. I write a bit here and a bit there and in the end the song just comes together."

She jumped out of her chair and started to pace the sound room. "How are we going to work together when our approaches are so different?"

"First of all, we have a common goal." He watched her move back and forth across the small room. "We have to keep that in mind all the time. Even though we have different directions on how to get there, we do have a final destination and we each have to learn to be flexible."

She sat down again and took another deep, calming breath. "Okay."

"And it's all right if we panic, but we don't need to panic yet. We've got weeks to work on this. We have plenty of time."

All he was really doing was adding to the pressure rather than relaxing her. She rubbed her forehead. "All right. Where do you see what we wrote fitting into the overall plot of the movie?"

"I think this tune works for the dream sequences Little Wolf has of the shaman."

Lola nodded. She felt that same way. They had copies of the storyboard that she had taped to the wall, needing to see the storyline in its linear sequence. The script lay open on a stool. She'd read it a dozen times and had scribbled notes in the margins on what she thought the music would be like at each point—gentle or fierce, fast or slow, major or minor. Broad strokes that outlined the structure.

"All right. Let's work out this song and see where it takes us."

He grinned at her. "Let's do this."

She tapped the melody out on the keyboard and his baritone floated out over the sound booth.

"Dream yourself into being.
You control your fate.
Be who you are.
It's never too late."

A shiver went down her spine at the haunting lyrics. "This is definitely Lona's song." She found herself joining in, harmonizing. Her fingers flew over the keyboard. They stopped throughout the session to quickly work out awkward phrases, to tweak harmonies, to enhance the song's climax, each of them seeming to know when the other wasn't happy with a sequence. It was as if they were one creative mind together. When they finished, she found herself smiling. "Which dream sequence do you see this melody for?"

"The first one. We're setting up the relationship between the Cheyenne woman, Lona, and Little Wolf."

Lola glanced at the storyboard. There were two stories. Lona's story of her clan's flight from the encroaching of the white man on Cheyenne ancestral lands and Little Wolf's fight to survive.

"I need a sandwich," Dylan suddenly said.

"What?" Lola had been so deeply immersed that she had no idea of how much time had elapsed.

"I'm hungry. The kids are going to be home from school soon and tonight is back-to-school night."

"You don't sound like you're looking forward to it." She glanced at her watch. They'd been working for almost six straight hours. How had that happened? She glanced down at her notes and the snatches of melody.

"I'm not. What do I say to the teacher, the other parents?" He looked panicked.

Lola patted his hand. "I can help with that if you like. My brother, Nick and my sister-in-law live a couple of streets over and they love it here. I'll ask Roxanne to help you navigate Pacific Palisades. Donna Deveraux, her grandmother, knows everyone."

"Donna Deveraux," Dylan said. "She's with the welcoming committee. She brought me a basket of goodies and stuff when I first moved in. And she included some of the best double-chocolate-chip-and-peanut-butter brownies I've ever eaten. She told me she made them."

"From what I understand, Miss Donna has seduced whole neighborhoods with her cookies and brownies."

"Maybe I should take some with me tonight." He sounded hopeful.

"On second thought, I have a better idea," Lola said. "Take my mother. Grace is an old hand at back-to-school nights. She will make sure you ask all the right questions. I'll call her."

The sound of a slamming door and running feet interrupted them. Emma and Justin burst into the studio like a hurricane.

"Uncle Dylan," Emma cried. "Look what I got today from my teacher." She held up a paper with a huge red star on it and the word *excellent* written underneath. "She said my math was perfect. Hello, Miss Lola."

"Hello, Emma."

Dylan dropped to his knee and hugged her. Justin stood away from them looking sullen. "How was your day?"

"Whatever," Justin said. He turned away. "I have homework." He stomped out of the studio without a backward glance.

"I'm hungry," Emma said.

"I have an apple and a fruit drink in the refrigerator for you." Dylan led the way out of the studio toward the kitchen.

"I have to get going," Lola said, grabbing her purse. "I'll see you tomorrow."

"I'll walk you out."

"No. You take care of Emma. I can find the front door." Lola grinned at him and left, skirting the pool and walking into the main house.

She entered through the patio doors and found Justin sitting on the stairs, fat tears streaking down his face.

"What's wrong, Justin?"

He brushed the tears away, stood and glared at her. "What do you care?"

"Maybe I can help."

"I don't want you here." He ran up the stairs. A few seconds later Lola heard a door slam.

She wondered if she should let Dylan know what had just happened. She opened the front door and went to her car. By the time she got there, she'd decided he needed to know if he was going to help the boy. She pulled her phone out of her purse and called Dylan.

"I just found Justin sitting on the stairs and crying."

"Did he tell you what was wrong?" Dylan asked.

"No. I just wanted you to know."

"Thanks. I'll check on him. I'll see you tomorrow." He disconnected.

When he hung up with her, she called her mother and asked a big favor. Why she felt the need to help Dylan was beyond her. But right now she could use some good karma.

Dylan was surprised to see Lola back at his house a little while later. With her mother, the energetic and still beautiful Grace Torres.

"I'll stay with the kids. Mom goes with you to school tonight," she said matter-of-factly, standing on his threshold as if they'd talked about the plan and just needed to work out the details. Then she brushed past him into the house, calling Emma and Justin's names, explaining to them when they appeared what she'd just told him.

Grace smiled at him and raised her eyebrows. "I'd go along if I were you," she said in a mellow voice.

He felt as if a weight were lifted off his shoulders.

He'd been dreading this evening, not knowing precisely what he should say to or ask the teachers, eager to get it right for Justin and Emma. He'd been worried, too, about how they'd do with a new babysitter he'd had to call when the regular one bailed. He quickly texted a cancelation to the sitter, and turned to Lola, who was in the hall promising the children she'd play whatever games they wanted as long as they did what their uncle said.

He was so grateful he almost hugged her. Well, mostly for that reason. He wanted to hug her just so he could touch her, too. Sexy Lola kinda flipped his switch. But he shouldn't be thinking of her in that way. Getting her in a clinch would blow the fragile relationship they were beginning to establish in the studio, something he wasn't willing to ruin for a hookup. For her sake.

He gave Lola last-minute instructions about the kids, urged them to obey Miss Lola and be good, then grabbed his keys. An evening he'd been dreading was turning into something wonderful.

Grace Torres was as beautiful as her daughter with a slim build and long dark hair tumbling over her shoulders and her large dark eyes. From the moment he opened his front door to the moment they entered the school grounds, Dylan could hardly take his eyes off her.

She smiled at him as she looped her arm around his. "Thanks for inviting me. I haven't been to a back-to-school night in years."

School had always made him uncomfortable, especially after the band started to gain in popularity. He'd been happy when he'd finally graduated high school because he never had to go back. Even then, he'd known college wasn't for him.

"Thank you for helping me. I have no idea what I'm doing." The common area of the school was crowded with kids and parents going every which way. Dylan was used to confusion, but this confusion seemed to have no purpose to his untrained eyes. But then he wasn't a real parent, just a pretend one, though he hoped Emma and Justin didn't realize he often felt he was just playing at the role.

Grace waved at people. Some waved back, but a few looked confused as though trying to place her. "Didn't your parents ever attend back-to-school night?"

"Never went. The only time they showed up was to bail me out of trouble at the principal's office."

She slanted a glance at him. "A troublemaker, were you?"

He just grinned. "I never got into bad trouble." Lots of little things, but as an adult he knew what he'd done was more to get his parents' attention than anything else.

"You mean there's good trouble?" Grace laughed at him. "And trust me, I've seen it all. Seven kids, remember."

"You're going to be fun, aren't you?"

She just grinned.

"To be honest, I never got into the inside-of-a-jail-cell type trouble." No, he'd spared his parents and himself that humiliation, thank goodness.

"What kind of trouble, then?"

"Little things. I put firecrackers in a toilet. I got into a fight with the school-yard bully because he was shaking down the younger kids for their lunch money. The kind of regular kid trouble that was allowable."

The school was arranged around a central courtyard containing a flag pole with classrooms radiating outward in a huge circle. To the north side was the playground with a running track and baseball diamonds.

They walked through the school yard and into Emma's classroom.

"You could have brought the children," Grace said.

Dylan had noticed other parents with children. "I know. I'm glad they don't have to see me uncomfortable." He was afraid of not measuring up to what a real parent should be.

"I can understand that, but you are their parent and they need to see you in their environment."

"I also wanted to talk to their teachers without being overheard. Especially Justin's teacher. Justin isn't doing his homework and I want a list of what he's supposed to be doing."

Grace waved at a couple more of the parents. One hesitantly waved back.

Emma's teacher, Mrs. Morgan, nodded at them in welcome. She was a small, round woman with a smiling face and cheerful eyes. Dylan nodded in return.

Grace nudged him. "See that woman over there?" She indicated a statuesque woman with a boy holding her hand. She had a brittle look with her carefully coiffed blond hair and expertly made-up face. She wore designer jeans and a red silk blouse with one too many buttons opened to show her cleavage.

"I see her."

"Don't make eye contact."

Confusion settled over him. He glanced at the woman again and could see her eyeing him curiously. "Why not?"

"Just trust me," Grace said quietly.

"Do you know her?"

"Yes," Grace replied. "Her name is Ella Brass. She's looking for husband number four and you just hit on her radar."

He felt the urge to flee. He was a fish out of water and needed Grace's guidance.

Large banners looped from corner to corner printed with the alphabet and numbers. Children's drawings were showcased on a cork bulletin board. Folders were fanned out across the large round table in the corner. One folder contained Emma's name and he picked it up to glance through it. The folder held a stack of papers, a list of assignments and grades along with Mrs. Morgan's comments. Apparently, Emma was doing very well. One of Mrs. Morgan's notes detailed Emma's interest in writing stories and that she was reading at a fifth-grade level. Pride swirled inside him.

The room was divided into several work stations that showed the projects the children were working on. The teacher handed him a packet of papers and he glanced through them.

"Thank you for coming, Mr. Ward."

Dylan introduced Grace and Mrs. Morgan simply smiled politely.

Mrs. Morgan indicated the packet of papers in his hand. "This is a list of projects we'll be doing throughout the year. I usually send the list home with the children, but I try to also give it out because most children never remember to give it to their parents. Also, we expect parents to volunteer their time, though we know it's not always practical. I do hope you'll make the effort anyway."

"He'll be happy to," Grace answered for him.

"What do you need?" Dylan asked.

"I understand you're a musician. Our music program has always been one of the best, but we don't have qualified volunteers."

Grace snickered. "He'll be happy to help out."

"Good," Mrs. Morgan said. "Every Friday from ten to noon we have music class. Can you be here?"

Dylan could only nod. He had no idea what was happening, but he knew he'd been manipulated. "I'll be here."

"You can take the folder home with you. Emma is an exceptional child. She does her work neatly and on time. But she tends to talk. A little too much."

"Yeah," Dylan said wryly. He already knew that. Too much silence in the house and Emma filled it with her chatter.

"I do understand that she lost her parents, but she seems to be moving forward. She's always happy and willing to help out other students when she's completed her own work."

"I'm glad she's doing well," he said. "I'm sorry, I'm new at this—parenting. If I think of questions to ask, can I contact you?"

"Anytime. But I don't think you need to worry about her. Despite her loss, she's coping well."

Dylan agreed. Justin was the one he was most concerned about.

Mrs. Morgan turned to the next parent to greet them.

Dylan walked around the classroom. Grace was talking to a man and woman with a little girl between them.

"Hello, Dylan Ward," came a throaty, sultry voice.

He looked up to find the blonde woman who'd eyed him earlier. Her perfume was overwhelming. She touched his arm and he forced himself not to step back.

"Hello."

"I'm Ella Brass. I'm delighted our children are in the same classroom." She ran her fingers through her shoulder-length hair, a flirty pout to her lips. "I've been a fan of Calamity since the beginning."

"Thank you." Dylan glanced around for Grace, but she was talking to another mother who laughed at something Grace said. How was he going to get away from Ella Brass? Because she was the mother of one of Emma's fellow students, he didn't think snubbing her was a good idea.

"I was delighted to hear you'd moved to Pacific Palisades. I'd love to welcome you to the neighborhood properly."

Ding, ding, ding. Danger, Dylan Ward. Danger. He'd met too many women like her in his entire career. They weren't just groupies, but predators who took a man for a ride and sucked them dry. Most groupies were just happy to hang around the band, but Ella was what he called a *huntress groupie*. She wanted to snag, bag and tag him.

She pushed her son at him. The little boy looked away bashfully. "This is my son, Charlie. Do you give private music lessons? He's quite talented."

Charlie stared down at the floor.

"I don't give lessons." He knelt down on one knee. "Hi, Charlie. Do you know Emma, my niece?"

Charlie nodded. "She helps me with my math."

"Do you like math?"

He shook his head. "I like to draw."

Ella pushed herself closer to Dylan. "We must set up a playdate."

"I'll have to ask Emma if she wants one."

Ella laughed. "They're children. They don't know what they want. They do what we tell them to do."

Dylan stood. He studied the woman. He didn't want to be that kind of parent. He understood that there were certain things children had no choice in, but he didn't want to be a dictator and tell Emma who she should play with. His sister-in-law, Yvonne, had once told him that playdates tended to be more for parents to socialize than for kids and Dylan did not want to socialize with this woman.

"Emma has a say in who she wants to play with," he said, softly enough that Charlie wouldn't hear. No point in hurting his feelings just because his mother was pushy.

Ella's eyes narrowed. "You're going to be one of those kinds of parents."

Perplexed, Dylan asked, "And what would that be?"

"Understanding, pretending kids are little adults capable of making their own decisions." She looked annoyed.

Offended, Dylan said, "My niece and nephew are not my minions."

She opened her purse and handed him a business card. "Here's my phone number if your niece is agreeable to a playdate."

He glanced at the card: Empire Real Estate, Ella Brass, Real Estate Agent. She took her son's hand and started walking toward the door.

Grace grinned as she came back over to him. "I told you not to make eye contact."

"You were supposed to save me."

"Where's the fun in that? Once the deed was done, you needed to play it out."

Dylan laughed. "I've got your number, lady. You wanted to see me flounder."

"No, I truly wanted to see what you were made of."

"Did I pass the test?"

"You retained your manners in the face of overwhelming forces. And you weren't rude to her boy, which, unfortunately, can happen when the parent is less than nice. You need to stay away from that one. The lust is strong in her."

"Thank you, Yoda."

"All right, let's check out Justin's teacher and classroom."

Justin's room was on the other end of the campus. His teacher with a stoop-shouldered man with a balding head, but a cheerful smile.

"Mr. Ward," Victor Travis said. "A pleasure to meet you."

"You, too, Mr. Travis."

"I know you're here about Justin and I think we need to have a longer discussion about him at another time."

"What's wrong?"

"He isn't turning in his homework. He's a pretty intelligent, but he's a loner. I suspect there are…issues with a boy…" Mr. Travis's gaze flickered to the corner of the room. Dylan turned to see a woman with a hard face scolding a boy who glared at her angrily and then pushed her before stalking away.

The teacher continued, "Justin isn't talking about it. He acts out in class and I've had to give him a time-out several times."

"Does this bully have a name?"

Mr. Travis hesitated. "The problem is that no one has ever caught this child in the act. What we have is more of a he said/he said situation."

"What about the parents?" Dylan had had his own share of bullying as a child and he would do anything to shield Justin.

"We've…spoken to them," Mr. Travis said, though he didn't sound as though the conversation had yielded anything positive.

"What do I do?" Dylan asked. "He and Emma both go to therapy, but with Justin, it doesn't seem to be working. He won't talk about his feelings." Though Justin did write his feelings down. The therapist had suggested that for both children, as well as music they could listen to and books to read.

"Do you?" Grace asked.

He glanced at her. "I'm trying to deal with their grief. I don't have time to deal with mine." For a moment, the loss filled him and he clenched his teeth and breathed fast to keep the strong feelings at bay. He simply didn't have time for them, especially not here as he was dealing with Justin's own issues.

Mr. Travis nodded sympathetically. "We have a psychologist on staff. You might want to consult with him. Sometimes something as simple as a personality conflict can inhibit a child's need to express himself. And Justin does need help. He needs a way to express his grief in a way that's comfortable for him."

Dylan knew Justin was doing exactly that. "Thank you for your concern. The therapist he goes to specializes in childhood grief." The therapist had told him the loss would never go away, but distance and time would ease it. The loss of his parents had changed Justin's life in a profound way. Sometimes Dylan felt at sea himself. He was helping as best he could and the first step had been to find professional guidance for the kids.

Mr. Travis went over Justin's work, and showed Dylan his progress. "He's well ahead of the other students in math and reading, but behind in language skills and science. He's not turning in his homework."

"He's doing his homework. I check it every night."

"That's good, at least. I would like it handed in."

"I'll work on that," Dylan said.

Mr. Travis turned to the next parent and Dylan found himself outside included in a group of parents with Grace at the center. She was a magnet of some sort, but Dylan couldn't quite figure it out. She'd only been in the classroom for ten minutes and she already knew everyone.

Grace introduced him. Most of the men and women were polite, but he sensed they didn't quite know how to take him. He felt out of place enough as it was and didn't know how to bridge the gap.

"What brought you to Pacific Palisades?" one of the women asked him. She was a small, matronly looking woman with a pleasant face and nice smile.

"The school district for one." He didn't elaborate further. Most of the people nodded in understanding as though that matched their own reason for living here.

"He has a lot of things going on in his life," Grace said.

Dylan's troubles had been prominently displayed on the cover of *People* magazine. He said goodbye to the group and he and Grace headed for the door. He heard a boy's angry voice and turned back.

"Zachary," the mother said, "stop that. I'll tell your father and you'll be in big trouble."

Zachary looked unconcerned. Dylan approached with a smile. "Hi, I'm Dylan. I understand your son and my nephew are classmates."

The woman simply glared at him. "I'm Amelia Jarvis. This is my son, Zachary. Zachary, be nice." Amelia was a small woman with a wavy brown haircut that framed a round face.

Zachary ignored Dylan. "I want to go home now."

"In a minute," Amelia said.

"I think Zachary and Justin may be having some issues," Dylan said, choosing his words carefully. He had a feeling about this kid, based on his own years in school. He could spot a bully.

Amelia's face tightened. "If they are, then it is your child who is at fault, not mine. Zachary is a good boy." Zachary was almost out the door. Amelia pushed past Dylan and ran after her son.

He turned to Grace who studied Amelia with a small frown on her face.

"That was interesting," she said.

"I think he's the school bully," Dylan said as they made their way out.

Back in his SUV, Dylan took a deep breath. He'd survived back-to-school night.

"You handled all that like a veteran father," Grace said, approval in her voice. "You didn't even need me there."

"Right. I was drowning. I don't know if these people look at me like I'm crazy or what."

She smiled at him. "I saw the article in *People* magazine and they practically said you were Gandhi for taking on your niece and nephew."

"They're family. What was I supposed to do?" Leave them to suffer alone? Anthony and Yvonne had entrusted their most precious children to him. The least he could do was handle the job right.

"What about your parents?"

"I love my parents," Dylan said, "but they're very

involved with each other and their careers. Don't get me wrong—my parents love their grandchildren." His own childhood had been okay, even though his mother had been distant entrusting Dylan and his brother to a series of nannies. Though they had been remote, his parents had always been kind when they remembered they had children. "My brother knew leaving the kids with my parents probably wasn't the best idea. I don't know if I'm that much better."

Grace patted his knee. "Don't worry, you are. I can tell already."

"How?"

"That fact that you're worried speaks volumes. How about treating me to Popi Miquel's for a margarita? They have the best in Southern California."

He raised his eyebrows, surprised. "Okay, but you'll have to direct me."

She laughed. "Just kidding. Let's head home. I know you want to check up on those little darlings." Then, more quietly, she added, "And my little darling, too."

Dylan happily steered them toward his house. Perceptive Grace was right. He wanted to see them all. Emma, Justin...and Lola.

Chapter 5

"I'm done. If I have to think of another note, my brain will burst," Dylan said. "The kids only have a half day of school and they'll be home in just a few minutes. Let's do something fun. You, me and the kids."

Lola sighed. "I think we need a break, too. What do rock stars consider fun?"

"What do traditional music composers consider fun?"

"My fun usually involves food that someone else cooked, like my mother and father."

"Let's do lunch and then something else. Emma and Justin are not going to think lunch is fun, so we need to reward them with another option."

"If they're lucky, my father might let them cook."

"I don't think they'll go for that." Dylan picked up his iPad and started scrolling through it.

"I know something they might really enjoy," Lola said.

He looked at her.

"The La Brea Tar Pits and Museum," she suggested. She half expected her idea to be ignored. She loved the tar pits. She and Sebastian used to go there on bright summer days and watch the paleontologists work.

"That sounds interesting. I've never been to the tar pits," Dylan said, surprise on his face.

"How long have you lived here?"

"I'm feeling a judgy vibe."

"You should," Lola retorted. "The museum is open until five. We can eat a quick lunch and be there with plenty of time to explore."

"We'll grab them the minute they arrive." He jumped to his feet.

Lola put away her notes. After ten days of working with Dylan, she had lots of notes she intended to bring up with him later. They'd been working well together, but she still felt awkward at times.

They headed for the main house, rounding the pool just as Emma opened the French doors leading outside. Her blond hair was wild about her head as though she'd run all the way from the bus stop. Justin followed a few moments later at a more sedate pace.

Emma almost jumped into Dylan's arms. "We're home."

"I can see that," Dylan said after giving her a kiss.

Justin hung back, suspicion in his eyes. Lola had been trying to figure out a way to help Dylan with the boy, but the only thoughts she had always spiraled back to her mother. After all, Grace had raised seven children; one unhappy little boy would be a snap for her. Maybe she needed to talk to her about Justin.

"Come on," Dylan said, grabbing Justin's hand. "We're going out to lunch and then we have a surprise for you."

"What kind of surprise?" Emma asked.

"You'll have to wait for it," Dylan said, trying to speak in a mysterious way.

"I don't want to go," Justin said in a sour tone.

Lola paused to look at him. All that underlying anger worried her.

"We're going anyway," Dylan said.

"I have homework."

"Mr. Travis told me you don't get homework on Friday." Justin scowled.

"We're going to visit my parents' restaurant and have lunch. You met my mother last week. She's a terrific cook," said Lola, breaking in before the tension escalated. "My brother Sebastian usually eats lunch there on Fridays. He's a magician and works at the Magic Castle."

A spark of interest flickered across Justin's face but quickly disappeared. "What kind of magician?"

"Mostly card tricks, but he has other things he does when he's in Las Vegas."

"Can he make buildings disappear like David Copperfield?"

Lola laughed. "If he could do that he'd have made me disappear years ago."

Justin snickered at her. Dylan's mouth worked as though he were trying not to laugh.

"Okay," Justin finally said. "I'll go."

Lola simply smiled. She had him.

A few minutes later, they piled into Dylan's SUV.

"This is not the car I would have thought you'd have," Lola said as she buckled her seat belt.

"How do you know what kind of car is the real me?" Dylan backed out of the driveway.

"I know boys and toys. I have a brother who is car mad, but now he has a wife and whole new focus in his life."

"For your information, I do have a Tesla, but it's not the most comfortable car for kids. And my choices were this or a minivan. And a minivan just doesn't work for me. What did you think I had?"

Lola thought for a moment. "Something sleek, fast and sexy."

"I thought about a Dodge Viper once."

"A muscle car. I can see you in that."

The drive to her parents' restaurant took a little longer than normal because of traffic. Friday in Los Angeles was a getaway day and people heading out of the city clogged the freeways. They finally arrived, parked in the lot next door and hurried to the eatery.

"Lola, darling," Grace Torres smiled. "What brings you here?"

"Food," she said.

"Dylan, I'm delighted you're here." Grace gazed at the two children, smiling. "Welcome to Luna el Sol."

"I wanted to thank you again for coming with me to back-to-school night."

"I was happy to help you."

Emma walked to Grace and hugged her. Justin simply scowled. He glanced around, his gaze settling on the parrot cages with their toy occupants.

"Let's get you all some lunch," Grace said, indicating the family section in the restaurant.

"We thought we'd eat here and then do something fun with the kids."

"And what is your idea of fun today?"

Lola leaned toward her mother's ear and whispered, "We're going to the tar pits, but keeping it a surprise for the kids."

"Excellent choice. Let me call my friend Deedee. She'll do that VIP thing."

"I was hoping you'd say that." Deedee Holmes had worked at the tar pits for twenty years and would be happy to give them all a behind-the-scenes tour.

Grace swept them into the private family section of the dining room.

"How come there's stuffed parrots in the cages?" Emma asked, pausing next to one.

"The real ones were too cranky and loud." Grace opened the cage door and pulled the parrot out. She handed it to Emma. "This is Pierre. He needs a new home. He's not happy here. Would you like to give him one?"

Emma gazed imploringly at Dylan. "May I?"

Grace laughed, taking charge of Dylan's decision. "Of course, you may. Your uncle would never say no."

"But what about Justin?" Emma said.

"I'm too old for stuffed animals," Justin growled.

"Of course, you are," Grace said. She looked around

the dining room until her gaze settled on Sebastian, at a table demonstrating his latest sleight-of-hand card trick to a waitress. Sebastian looked up, smiled at Lola and Grace, excused himself and made his way over.

"This is Sebastian," Grace said. "Sebastian, show them your magic tricks."

From the look on Justin's face, Lola knew her mother had figured out a way to capture his interest.

Sebastian smiled at the two children. He held out a deck of cards, fanned them facedown. "Pick a card. Pick any card as long as it's the two of hearts."

"How would I know that?" Justin said.

"Pick a card," Emma said, nudging her brother and getting into the spirit.

They both pulled cards from the deck and looked at them. Both cards were the two of hearts. Sebastian turned the deck over to show that all the cards were the two of hearts.

"Okay," Justin said, looking intrigued.

"Turn your card face down," Sebastian ordered.

He shuffled the deck and fanned the cards, again showing them to Emma and Justin. All the two of hearts had disappeared and the cards were back to their original values. Lola had seen this trick a hundred times and still didn't know how he did it.

"Okay," Sebastian ordered. "Look at your cards."

Emma turned hers over and found that the two of hearts was now the queen of clubs. Justin's was the ace of diamonds.

"How did you do that?" Justin demanded.

Sebastian simply grinned. "Want to see another trick?"

"I want to know how you did this one," Justin commanded.

"I am under penalty of death to never reveal my secrets," Sebastian replied.

Emma's eyes narrowed. She clutched her parrot and tilted her head at Lola's brother.

Grace burst out laughing.

Justin tried to grab the cards and they fell all over the floor. He knelt and gathered them up, examining each card carefully as if trying to figure out how Sebastian had done his trick. Lola had done the same thing when she'd been a child.

"Well, Lola," Grace said, "while Sebastian is entertaining Justin, you and Emma head for the kitchen. I'm sure your dad would love some help in there. I'm going to visit with Dylan."

Lola felt herself being pushed toward the kitchen. She took Emma's hand and led her to the back of the restaurant. At the door, she looked behind to find that her mother was talking animatedly to Dylan while Justin and Sebastian sat at the table, the deck of cards fanned out between them. Dylan glanced back over his shoulder at Lola and smiled. It warmed her heart to see him embraced by her family, to watch Justin become fascinated with Sebastian's tricks.

In the kitchen, after instructing them to wash their hands thoroughly, Manny Torres was tall and lean with salt and pepper hair, a square-jawed face. He set Justin to chopping vegetables and Emma to tearing lettuce apart for salad. He gave Emma a stool to stand on and tied a large apron around her.

"Do I get a hat like yours?" Emma asked.

"Show me how good you can shred the lettuce and I'll think about it." Manny turned back to the stove.

"My mom liked to cook," Emma confided to Lola. "She was teaching me how to make blueberry muffins."

"Sounds like fun," Lola replied.

"My mom died. My dad, too. Justin and I came to live with Uncle Dylan."

"I know, sweetie," Lola said, her heart aching.

"Uncle Dylan says it's okay to be sad, but I don't want to be sad anymore. I want to be happy. I like living with Uncle Dylan. I like our new house. I like my school. I like my best friend, Charlie."

"That's okay. You can be happy and sad at the same time."

"Justin is sad all the time." Emma shoved the lettuce she'd shredded into a bowl.

"Why do you think that?"

"Because he won't talk even to our therapist. Dr. Phyllis is not a doctor doctor." Emma pointed at her forehead. "She's a head doctor. She keeps trying to get Justin to talk about his feelings. Justin won't do that."

Lola finished chopping up the carrots, beets and cucumbers and tossed them into the salad. "Why do you think he won't do that?"

"Because he's a boy," Emma said with the finality of her seven years of wisdom. "Boys don't like to talk about what's going on. Though he does write it down in a notebook sometimes."

"I have five brothers and my brothers always tell me what's going on. Even things I don't want to know." She knew more about her brothers' love lives than any girl should know.

"I hear him crying in his bedroom at night, but he locks the door and won't let me in."

"Maybe if you told him that when he's sad, you're sad too, he'd let you in." Lola didn't know if that was the right thing to say, but she could hear her mother's voice in the back of her mind and knew it was something Grace would say.

"He doesn't want to know when I'm sad." Emma finished with the lettuce and stood back from the prep table.

"That's too bad. Being sad isn't a bad thing. Sometimes you need to be sad."

"Are you ever sad?" Emma asked.

"I have been." Lola had been sad when she'd been forced to work with Dylan, but Emma didn't need to know that. "But most of the time I'm happy. I'm happy because my sister had a baby. Two of my brothers are married. I'm happy for them. My mom and dad love me even though I can't boil water and both of them are world-renowned chefs."

"And she's not too good at chopping veggies, either," Manny put in, leaning over and winking at Emma. "Not as good as you."

Lola pushed her dad back toward his station. "But you still love me even if the cooking gene skipped me completely."

"The cooking gene skipped Matteus, too, so we don't feel so bad about you anymore."

Lola glared at her father. "Dad."

He gave her an innocent look. "Lunch is ready. Lola, toss dressing on the salad and take it out. Miss Emma, you take the bread basket."

Emma accepted the basket from Manny and followed Lola out into the dining room.

Lola found Justin totally absorbed in Sebastian's card tricks. He looked annoyed when Lola announced lunch was ready.

Grace and Dylan looked up from whatever they'd been discussing.

"I'm hungry," Dylan said.

Manny followed with a large platter piled with one of Lola's favorites, *coxinhas*, deep-fried chicken nuggets with cheese sauce inside a dough exterior.

Emma and Justin watched curiously as Manny described what they would be eating. Emma sat down with her parrot in her lap. Justin sat next to Sebastian. He held a deck of cards that he refused to give back. Sebastian laughed.

Grace sat next to Dylan.

Lola loved the way everything was coming together. Justin didn't look angry or sad. Emma was so happy she bounced in her chair. Dylan looked relaxed. She could tell he really liked her mother. Grace and Manny always seemed to know how to treat people. This was one of Lola's happy moments and she smiled at Emma.

Emma leaned toward her and Lola bent over to hear.

"I'm happy," Emma whispered.

Lola just nodded.

* * *

Dylan had to admit he'd been remiss. He'd lived in Los Angeles for nearly ten years and hadn't been to any of the cultural activities the city had to offer except for some concerts at the Hollywood Bowl. Museums had never been his thing, but the tar pits were different and unique.

Lunch had been a surprise. Emma was Emma, always looking at the bright side of life. Justin had been fascinated with Sebastian and his card tricks. Dylan felt a little envious because Justin used to be fascinated with his life as a rock star. He wanted to be Justin's hero.

Justin had not only been on his good behavior, but he'd left the sullen part of him at home. Dylan was grateful.

Emma pulled on Lola's hand as they walked the path around the tar pits. A brisk October wind pushed at them. Dylan never got used to the dry Santa Ana winds that roared over the desert and seemed to scour the Los Angeles basin of any moisture.

Justin hung back as they walked toward the museum, his face a stoic mask as though he was totally prepared to be disagreeable for no other reason than the fact that he could.

"This is so cool," Emma gushed. She held her hat on with one hand, her long blond hair swirling in the breeze.

The large tar pit had been given a sense of reality with several huge mammoth sculptures positioned both in the pit and on the shore. The path around the lake pit was filled with parents and their children, along with several school groups with teachers riding herd. The smell of tar permeated the air. Bubbles appeared sporadically on the surface of the water.

"I love it here," Lola said. "And wait until we go into the museum. My favorite exhibit is the fossil lab. Even though this is called a tar pit, the gooey stuff is actually asphalt."

Justin looked interested. "What kind of fossils?"

"From mastodons to saber-toothed cats to mice."

"Mice," Dylan said in surprise.

"Mice are pretty durable." Lola stopped to read a plaque. Emma joined her and asked how to pronounce some of the words. "Throw in coyotes and horses and you get an idea of how dangerous the pits could be for animals just wandering by. Especially those who think they're going to get a quick snack. One of the exhibits inside demonstrates how difficult the tar was to escape. There are plungers in a vat of tar. I used to try so hard to pull the plunger up, but never did."

"Who knew?" Dylan said, amazed. "I should have visited earlier."

"Why didn't you come?" Emma asked.

"Just being busy," Dylan admitted, though the real reason was that museums didn't interest him. Though he was ready to admit this one was different.

"Did you know there are only a handful of pits like this throughout the world, and three of them are right here in California?" Lola looked up from her iPhone.

"Where are they?" Dylan asked.

"Iraq, Venezuela, Trinidad and Azerbaijan," Lola

answered. "We're standing in one of the most unique spots in the whole world."

"What are those bubbles?'

"Methane," Lola replied after consulting her phone. Her phone rang and she stepped away from them to answer it. She spoke briefly and then disconnected. "Our tour guide is waiting for us in the museum."

"Tour guide?" Dylan asked.

"My mother has a friend who works here and Deedee arranged for us to have a private tour with one of the interns."

Dylan was impressed. Lola always seemed to have a handle on things. She was so organized he sometimes felt intimidated.

The private tour guide, Jennifer, was a woman in her early twenties who explained she was a student intern volunteering her time in the fossil lab. Her gaze slid over Dylan, eyes widening in recognition, but she gave no other sign she knew who he was. She turned instead to Emma and Justin, knowing the tour was really for them.

"Since 1906, when serious excavation started, over a million bones have been unearthed from the pits," Jennifer said as she led the way into the excavation pit observatory.

"What kind of bones?" Justin asked, leaning over the railing and looking down into the pit.

"The most common bones found were from the skeletons of dire wolves. The second most common animal was the saber-toothed cat and coyotes are third."

"Why couldn't they get out?" Emma asked.

"The tar is very, very sticky. The biggest mastodon couldn't get out." Jennifer pointed out several paleontologists and explained what they were doing. "They use specialized tools to extract the bones."

Dylan found his gaze drawn to Lola over and over again. She looked as excited as Emma as she asked questions. She hung over the railing looking down, her hair falling forward in spiral ringlets. Her dark brown eyes were alight with curiosity.

Emma held Lola's hand and Justin stood next to Lola, not quite touching but obviously happy to be with her. All three watched, fascinated, as Jennifer explained the paleontologists' work, though Dylan thought Lola had probably heard the talk a number of times already; yet she acted as though it was new information she'd never heard before.

Lola tapped with her free hand on the top of the railing, and he could almost see the melody forming in her mind. Music was such an integral part of her that he was awed. Her music was inseparable from her. Her whole body practically vibrated with her music. She was so in control of her talent while his verged on chaos.

With her education, she would always have a plan B to fall back on. She could teach music on all levels, from theory to creativity. For him, music was more luck. If he ever got stuck, he didn't have the background to get unstuck. Usually he just started over. He could learn a lot from her.

She was so different from the women he'd dated in the past. In the early years of the band, he'd indulged in the groupies. Everyone in the band had, how could they not, but after a while adoring groupies became boring. Music was too important to him to keep playing around.

His most recent relationship, with Lindsay, hadn't worked out. He'd thought she loved him, but his lifestyle turned out to be the main attraction, and she walked away as soon as the kids entered the scene, never looking back. She didn't want the burden of dealing with the children. Her departure revealed his own lack of feeling for her, though. He'd not been deeply hurt by her rejection. He realized that though he'd liked Lindsay a lot, he'd never loved her. It was best for both of them that it was over.

Seeing Lola with Emma and Justin was eye-opening. He liked her easy relationship with them. In fact, he liked a lot about her. And liking Lola too much could be an issue, he reminded himself. She was a working partner and he had a lot riding on this movie. Any romantic entanglement with her might seem feasible, but if it ended badly it would affect their music.

Jennifer began talking about the excavations currently going on in the different areas around the museum, Project 23 in particular. "The museum was planning a parking structure. During the excavation we discovered a completely new deposit of fossils, so we boxed up the fossils and moved them. In fact, there was so much that when we finally finish examining it we'll probably double the size of the collections we have now, and currently we have more than three million different pieces of bone, plants and even bacteria."

Emma asked questions as they walked. Dylan lagged behind, watching the children. Emma was always animated, while Justin was reserved and distant. Today, he'd left that part of himself behind and eagerly asked questions right along with Emma.

They toured the museum, enjoying the exhibits. A sign about the lone human female who had been found in the pit caught Dylan's interest. A whole wall of dire-wolf skulls entranced Justin.

By the end of the day, Emma was so tired she could hardly keep her eyes open.

"I want to go to the Magic Castle tonight," Justin announced when they were in the SUV and heading back to Pacific Palisades. "I want to see Sebastian working."

Lola turned in her seat. "We can go on a Sunday. That's the only day children are allowed at the Magic Castle."

"I want to go tonight."

"You can go to the castle, but they won't let you in." Lola's voice was gentle as she tried to make Justin understand.

Dylan could feel Justin gearing up for a tantrum.

"How about we call Sebastian," Lola said, "and ask him if we can come next Sunday or, even better, Halloween."

"But…" Justin objected.

Dylan almost interfered, but Lola put a hand on his thigh and pressed down, preventing him from joining the conversation.

"Justin," Lola said in a reasonable tone, "the Magic Castle has rules. We can't just show up, because we're not members. We need to be invited by a member and the only member we know is my brother. I'll call him and see about his schedule."

"All right," Justin said. He sat back, arms crossed over his chest, the sullen expression back on his face.

The crisis wasn't completely averted, Dylan knew, because Justin wasn't going to be happy with the terms. "I'm willing to take you and Emma to the Magic Castle," he said cautiously, "but—and this is a big but— you need to turn in all your homework for the next two weeks and this includes all the back homework you haven't turned in."

The surprise on Justin's face almost made Dylan laugh. "But—"

"You want something," Dylan continued, keeping his tone conversational. "I want something, too. This is one treat you're going to have to earn."

Justin gave him a fierce scowl. He opened his mouth to speak, but Dylan interrupted him.

"I know things are difficult for you, for all of us, and not having your mom and dad around makes things even tougher. But I want good things for you, things I know they'd want for you, too. So, can you help me with that? And I'll help you."

Justin didn't answer. He pretended to look out the window, his lips firmly clamped together.

"You've got a tough road ahead of you," Lola said after the children had gone to bed. She and Dylan sat out on the patio next to the pool, two glasses of wine on the round table. The night had turned cold and Dylan had lit the fire pit, which warmed the air around them.

"I know," Dylan said with a sigh.

"You made a good start, though," Lola continued.

Dylan had used her mother's techniques. Grace had always used leverage and compromise to get Lola and her siblings to behave.

"That was hard," Dylan admitted. "I wanted to be nice and say, 'Sure, let's do this.' And the man I was a year ago when I was just the happy-go-lucky uncle would have done exactly that."

"You channeled my mother really well," Lola said.

"I got the first lesson in parenting at the back-to-school night and a second lesson before lunch today. She told me to be gentle but firm with Justin. Your mom is pretty awesome."

"My mom raised seven kids and I do think we all turned out pretty well."

"I agree." He ran a hand over his face and rubbed one eye. "I still need help."

She reached over and touched his hand. An electric jolt vibrated through her. She shouldn't have touched him but couldn't pull her hand away. He grasped her fingers tightly as though she were a lifeline.

Dylan Ward was not dating material for her. She never dated men in the industry, a decision she made after ending an affair with a man, Lashawn, who tried to steal her music. He'd wanted to use her to position himself for a huge project at Universal Studios. If not for an eagle-eyed musician who recognized a pattern in the melody as something she played around with a lot, Lashawn would have succeeded. The last she heard he was waiting tables at a restaurant in Manhattan, still waiting for his big break.

"Thank you for today," Dylan said. "Emma had a

great time and Justin really enjoyed himself." That was true, even in spite of the sulking attitude he'd displayed on the drive home when he couldn't get his way. "I could see he was as excited as Emma."

"What boy doesn't like bones?" she asked.

Dylan just laughed. "I thought he was going to jump down into the pit and start helping. The whole idea of excavating bones really appealed to him."

"Maybe he'll grow up and decide on paleontology for a career."

"I just want him to be happy," Dylan said, sadness in his tone. "That is the hard part."

She finished her wine and stood. "I need to be going. Do you want to get some work done tomorrow?"

He thought about that. "Justin and Emma asked me last night if they could go to the pumpkin patch tomorrow. But first thing Monday morning…"

"Okay." She tucked her purse over her shoulder. "I'll see you Monday morning after the children have gone to school."

He followed her through the house to the front door. "I really did enjoy today." He seemed loath to let her go.

"I did, too."

He opened the door and she stepped out onto the porch. He touched her arm, and she couldn't stop herself from turning to him. She saw the longing and question in his eyes, and in the next second, she stood on tiptoes and kissed him.

Desire rose in her. She slid her arms around his neck as he deepened the kiss. She pressed tightly against him.

When the kiss ended she felt panic rise inside her.

She turned and ran down the stairs to the driveway. She jumped in her car, started it and backed out. As she passed the front of the house she saw him standing on the path, watching her.

Chapter 6

Lola spent the weekend working. Well, trying to work. All she could focus on was Dylan's kiss. She wasn't sure how to feel about it. The touch of his mouth on hers had sent her reeling. It was just a kiss, one she'd initiated. But one he'd returned with passion. She'd been kissed before. Not by a bona fide rock star. Why did this bother her so much? This couldn't even get started. She didn't have the time or the energy for anything other than a work relationship.

She went to her bedroom and picked up her song notebook. She tapped her pencil on the spiral binder. Closing her eyes, she tried to clear her mind and focus. She hadn't intended to write the whole song, but their trip to the tar pits inspired her primal sense of music. Her muse refused to leave her alone, so she wrote and rewrote and sang and played and wrote some more all weekend, throwing herself into the work whenever her thoughts strayed back to that fiery kiss.

She accomplished so much, in fact, that when she finally sat down at the keyboard in Dylan's studio and started to play for him on Monday morning after he'd taken the children to school, his eyes widened in surprise, then he closed them, nodding his head along to the steady rhythms.

The music was tense and heavy with beat and a fearful undertone. "I envisioned this as the music for the massacre of Little Wolf's pack." Her fingers flew over the keyboard.

"I'm impressed," Dylan said. He listened as she pushed through the piece. "I like this, but I think the beat should be even stronger here." He pointed at the sheet of music she'd written. "The tension isn't deep enough. His family is dying and he's hurt and the music needs to reflect that more deeply. After all, he's surviving a traumatic experience and his anger is going to be deeper despite his sadness."

For a second, she tensed. Having her baby criticized hurt a little, even though he was right.

He took over the keyboard for a second and added his own edgy beat, throwing in the occasional syncopation, adding notes to the underlying ostinato. She hastily jotted down what he played.

They worked for a while like this, with him enhancing what she'd written, with her playing a riff to demonstrate a theme she wanted woven through the music, until eventually they took a short break. It had been a tense session. Lola wasn't always happy with his changes, and she sensed him resisting her efforts to return to her original vision.

"The producers wanted edgy," Dylan said of what they'd accomplished. "This is edgy."

Lola tried to keep her anger in check. He'd taken her music and turned it upside down, shifted it to something no longer hers, and the emotional impact didn't have the same value for her.

"I'm not sure I like it better."

Dylan handed her a bottle of water. "Little Wolf is not going to react in a soft, feminine way to the massacre. From the moment he was born he was trained and told he was going to lead the pack."

"Are you telling me this music is too feminine?"

"I want to keep the emotional impact of the song, but change it a little to reflect how deep his anger and sadness will be. He needs to be angry first and sad second."

Lola listened as he added his own signature beat to the music. She felt as though she'd lost control.

"I can tell by the look on your face you're not happy." Dylan took a deep sip of his water.

"I'm not," Lola admitted. "I worked on this all weekend."

"I'm not telling you your song is soft. It's not crap. You wrote a piece of music that isn't reflecting the action on the screen. It's a great piece of music, just not workable as background for the action."

Lola took a deep breath to calm herself. She didn't want to argue with him. This was why she hated collaboration. She shouldn't have to defend her artistry.

"Let's get some lunch. There's a great Thai restaurant near the beach."

She wasn't certain she wanted to eat lunch with the man who just said her baby was ugly and smelled bad. "I don't think I want to go out. Why don't you get lunch? I'm going to sit here and gather my thoughts and maybe spend a little time pouting."

"You're sure?" he said.

"I am. I don't want to look at you."

He looked confused. "Why?"

"You just told me my baby was stupid, ugly and smelled bad. I need time to be hurt and to find my big-girl panties before I move on."

"Are you going to be able to find your big-girl panties?" His lips quirked and he looked like he wanted to laugh, which just made her anger stronger.

"Of course. This is how I roll."

"Don't pout. I don't think I can stand you pouting." He definitely looked amused.

"It's part of the process," she snapped. Then she sighed and said more calmly, "Go and get lunch. By the time you get back, I'll be fine."

He tilted his head slightly, studying her. "Are you…?"

She pointed at the door. "Just go."

He left and she eventually wandered outside. She paced the perimeter of the pool and realized that his gardener had been a bit lax in the weeding department. She found a kneepad, gloves and weeding tools in the garden shed behind the studio and went back to the pool area and started on the plants.

She yanked at the weeds and mulched around the

rosebushes. Some scattered lyrics ran around in her head as she pulled the unwanted plants and dropped them in a large bucket. She hadn't seen a compost pile anywhere and wondered if she should start one.

She trimmed pulled more weeds and snipped the heads of dead flowers off a bunch of mums circling a tree. She worked steadily, letting her anger recede. She was a professional and she could work with Dylan. They'd managed nearly two weeks without a spat.

A peaceful calm finally descended on her and she sat back on her heels, listening to a bird call answered by another with a little trill. She realized that Dylan hadn't changed her work; he'd just enhanced the emotional impact. He'd made the melody better, and she'd acted like a spoiled child. Her parents would be disappointed in how she'd behaved. She owed Dylan an apology. And she would apologize…eventually.

Dylan hadn't intended to hurt her feelings. He did like her music. And her reaction had surprised him. He'd worked with his bandmates in the past and they all added and subtracted from whatever musical project they were working on. He had to admit her temper tantrum was the most civilized one he'd ever seen. With his bandmates, the process included a lot of shouting, pouting and threats. Once Ben and Sam had gotten into a wrestling match that ended with a lot of grunts, sweat and floor thumping. Both claimed the win.

Or maybe it was the kiss. She had been twitchy from the moment she walked through his door this morning. That kiss had surprised him, and he'd thought it

was going to be a friendly peck, but it had turned into something more. He'd felt excited the second his lips touched hers. Lola was a beautiful woman. She did turn him on, but he'd figured she wasn't that into him. And since she didn't say anything about it today he'd thought she was cool with it. It had just been a spontaneous moment of…what? Sympathy? Affection? Damn, she confused him. He didn't like it when women confused him. It meant he was a little more invested than he wanted to be. And right now, at this point in his life, he couldn't afford to be.

He drove to the Thai restaurant. He'd been so anxious to get out of the studio he'd not only forgotten to ask her what she liked, but he'd also forgotten his phone. He hoped she liked what he ordered for her.

The heady aroma of the food in the car made him hungry. He pushed the limit to get back to the house. When he burst into the studio she wasn't anywhere to be seen. He looked around and even went up to the second-floor bedrooms but couldn't find her. Her car was still in the driveway. Where had she gone?

He left the food on the kitchen counter and went back out to the pool area. He paused to listen and realized he could hear her singing. He made his way to the side of the studio and found Lola kneeling on a thick kneepad, yanking at the weeds.

"What are you doing to my garden?" he asked.

She glanced over her shoulder at him. "Saving it."

"I have a gardening service."

"Is that what they call themselves?" She snipped another flower off the bush and tossed it in a bucket.

"That rose over there was so badly pruned I had to cut it back to the ground."

He looked at the rosebush and realized the branches were now nubs. "But it's just a rose."

"A badly pruned rose. And this hydrangea is getting the wrong plant food."

"How can you tell?"

"The heavy foliage and sparse flowers. Hydrangeas need a high-nitrogen fertilizer to bloom properly. I didn't find any in the garden shed so I'm pretty sure this poor bush is not getting the right kind."

"You like to garden?" Dylan sat down on a bench.

"It's relaxing and helps to focus my thoughts. In fact, I think I have some lyrics. No music, just lyrics." She pushed herself to her feet, grabbed the bucket and dropped her tools and gloves inside. "I'll finish this later. I'm hungry."

She put the tools away in the garden shed and followed Dylan into the guesthouse and sat at the kitchen table. Dylan set out the Thai food containers, adding plates and silverware, and found her smiling at him. "What?"

"I'm over my sulk. This is a collaboration and I realize you get to slap my baby. But I get to slap yours back."

"I don't know about that. When guys slap my baby, it ends in a wrestling match. And I think you could take me two out of three falls."

She grinned. "You're on. Though I don't do my own fighting. I call my brother Matteus. He was a wrestling champ in college."

"You're not tough enough to back your own stuff up?"

She shook her head. "I'm charismatic and smart enough to have someone else do it for me."

Dylan laughed. If nothing else, she was entertaining. "I'm sure your brother would go easy on me."

"No, he wouldn't. He may have chosen to be one of the good guys, but he fights to win."

They ate their food. Dylan noticed her fingers tapping the table again. He was beginning to recognize the signs that told him she was thinking in musical patterns once more.

After lunch, they worked until Emma and Justin came home from school.

"Did you talk to your brother yet?" Justin asked Lola the moment he entered the studio. Emma ran to Dylan for a quick hug.

"Did you turn your homework in yet?" Lola sat with her hands poised over the keyboard. A look of amusement crossed her face and was quickly hidden.

Dylan winced. He knew whatever thoughts she'd been having had been lost by Justin's interruption.

"I have a list," Justin said, his tone grudging. "Mr. Travis gave me till Friday."

"When you can show proof that you've turned everything in to him," Lola said, "then I'll talk to my brother."

"Hello, Emma," Dylan said. "How was your day?"

Emma squirmed in his arms. "Great. Abriella was mean. My ponytail hurt and I took it down. Abriella told me to stop trying to look pretty."

Dylan stared at her. "What?"

"I know," Emma said gravely. "Like I have to try to look pretty. You always tell me I'm pretty."

"Well, you are." What was going on here? Dylan glanced at Lola helplessly. She just smiled and shook her head.

"I told her she was mean and I wasn't going to play with her anymore."

Drama averted, Dylan thought. He remembered girls in high school being mean and cruel. He didn't realize the attitudes started in second grade.

"Your snack is in the refrigerator. Why don't you and Justin eat and then do your homework?"

Emma nodded and skipped to the kitchen with Justin following more slowly.

"I remember this kind of behavior in high school, but second grade?" Dylan watched his niece as she ran out of the studio.

"Try kindergarten," Lola said.

"Who cares if Emma's pretty or not?" Dylan said.

"Obviously Abriella does. Pretty girls get the perks."

Dylan tried to think if he'd met Abriella and her parents, but nothing came to mind. "But…"

"Listen, maybe Abriella's parents are raising her to be pretty because being smart and educated isn't a priority. Did you meet Abriella's parents?"

"I'm sure I did, but I don't really remember. Your mom steered me away from a few women she said were poison." He remembered Ella Brass's predatory look.

She patted his arm. "It's not that bad. As long as you put a priority on education and intelligence, Emma and Justin will turn out fine."

"Did your parents do that?"

"You better believe it," Lola said. "When my dad emigrated from Brazil he only had a ninth-grade education. He got his GED and worked a lot of odd jobs early on until he got his big break in the music industry. When Matteus was in high school, Dad decided to go to college and he worked on his business degree for almost ten years. He actually graduated the same year I did. If that didn't inspire all of us, what would? No one is going to let their old man be smarter than you."

"College wasn't for me. I didn't like being in school when I knew I was going to be a musician."

"You are a lot more courageous than me."

"Why would you say that?"

"You didn't have a plan B if plan A didn't work."

"Sure, I did," he said. "My plan B was flipping burgers at the local diner."

"I flipped my share of burgers, too," Lola said.

That surprised Dylan. "But your parents...?"

"My parents guaranteed tuition. I had to come up with my own living expenses." She shrugged. "The struggle builds character."

"That's a lie," Dylan said. "I had character long before I had to eat ramen five times a week."

She frowned. "You sound a little resentful."

"Not at all. Everyone in the band worked hard. The first year after we graduated high school, we were on the road three hundred days as the backup band for the backup band. We were happy to see anybody in the audience when playing our set."

"After graduation, I was happy to get a job," Lola

said. "In between times when I wasn't working as a studio musician, I worked tables in my parents' restaurant. I learned to budget and make every penny count."

"Do you think you've made it?"

"Not even close. If I had made it, I would be working on this score by myself. No offense."

"None taken," Dylan replied. "Is that your barometer for success?"

"I don't know anymore. I hate to say this, but if what we did this morning is any indication, my music is getting better."

He could see how difficult it was for her to admit they were stronger together than they were apart. He admired her for saying so. He'd worked with a lot of people in the past and he always felt that he'd come away with a new skill that made him better and more versatile. He'd been excited to work with her even though he knew she'd been less than happy.

The chime sounded.

"What's that?" Lola asked.

"Front door bell. I have it routed to sound here in the studio when I'm not in the house."

He left the studio and went into the house, Lola following him. He opened the door to find a tall, slim woman with bleached blond hair, wide-set blue eyes and a well-shaped mouth. She wore a black miniskirt and a low-cut, white crop top. She looked familiar. Dylan must have met her at back-to-school night and just not remembered.

"How can I help you?" Dylan asked politely.

"May I come in?" she asked with raised eyebrows.

Dylan stepped back a couple of feet but refused to let her further into the house, nor did he close the door behind her. Her gaze flickered over Lola and immediately dismissed her. For some reason this irritated Dylan and he stood in the foyer, barring her from trying to move further into his home.

"What's going on?" Dylan asked.

"I'm Gwyneth DeSoto. Abriella's mother." Gwyneth gave him a flirtatious smile. "Your niece insulted my daughter."

Dylan had no idea how to respond. "How?"

"Emma told Abriella she wouldn't play with her anymore."

"Because she was being mean to Emma," Lola said, stepping to Dylan's side.

Gwyneth's gaze returned to Lola. "And who are you?"

"Family friend," Dylan answered. "Emma told us what happened."

"She owes my daughter an apology."

"According to Emma," Dylan said, "your daughter told my niece to stop acting pretty because she took her ponytail out…" His voice trailed away and he wondered what she would say next.

"That's not what my daughter said and she doesn't lie." Gwyneth shrugged slightly.

"Neither does Emma," Dylan responded, irritated at the implication. Did other moms and dads feel this way about their children?

"Mr. Ward. Dylan. You're new to this neighborhood." She tilted her head at him coyly. "And I know you're struggling with your niece and nephew." She touched his arm. "I know that a one-parent family is a challenge, but we don't need to let this get out of hand. I would hate for Emma to lose what few friends she already has."

Dylan was too surprised to respond. Did all parents fight their children's battles? Bullies, even with velvet gloves, were still bullies. He felt Lola's hand on his arm.

"Are you saying," Lola interrupted, "that Emma's future depends on her apology to your daughter?"

Gwyneth gave a delicate shrug. "Emma was mean to her." Her voice was kind, but her eyes were not.

"Did Abriella tell you what she said to Emma?"

"According to my daughter, Emma said she told her to stop acting pretty." Gwyneth sniffed.

Emma ran down the hallway. "Did not. Abriella is lying."

"Why should she lie?" Gwyneth looked shocked at being spoken to so bluntly by Emma.

"Nothing is going to be resolved through threats," Lola said. "Emma has nothing to apologize for."

Emma stood in the center of the foyer, her hands on her hips, lips in a tight, mutinous line.

"I think this conversation is over." Dylan gestured toward the open door. "Have a nice day."

Gwyneth's eyes narrowed. "If I were you, I'd reconsider…"

Dylan tilted his head toward the door. "Goodbye, Mrs. DeSoto." He walked forward, easing her out the door. Even as she stepped outside, he closed the door. Then he turned to Emma. "Next time, ask permission before you interrupt an adult conversation."

"But Abriella was lying."

"I know," Dylan responded. "I'm glad you were able to catch Abriella in that lie, but my job is to teach you good manners. Interrupting us was not polite."

Lola hid a smile and Emma looked crestfallen. "I'm sorry, Uncle Dylan, but Mrs. DeSoto made me mad."

"She made me mad, too, but I was polite."

Emma looked down at the floor. "I'll remember to be polite next time," she said in a half whisper.

"Thank you," Dylan said. "I feel like I've done my job."

After Emma skipped away, Dylan turned to Lola. "Do you think Mrs. DeSoto can carry through on her threat?" Dylan barely remembered grade school, much less second grade.

"Highly unlikely," Lola said. "You're famous. Everyone believes famous people first."

Dylan laughed. "I will remember that. What do I do about the situation?"

"Ignore it. You've said everything you had to say. Anything else will escalate it."

Something he didn't want. He glanced at his watch. "Let's get back to work."

After saying goodbye to Lola later that day, Dylan was surprised by another visitor—bandmate Wally Carleton, who showed up tired and frustrated, looking for a friend to commiserate with.

Wally was a tall, slim man with thick-rimmed glasses and a plaid shirt open over a blue T-shirt. Of all the band members, he'd always looked like the odd man out, the complete antithesis of a rock band's drummer. Some magazine called him the hot nerd and since then Wally had cultivated that look.

Now he lounged on Dylan's sofa in the living room, a glass of iced tea in his hand. He gazed out the patio doors to the pool area, dark except for the lighting at the bottom of the pool.

Wally turned to Dylan. "I know your first priority is Emma and Justin, but I don't like it when things aren't about me, too." Wally sighed. "And I know I'm being unfair. But my life has completely changed. I don't think we've ever stayed in one place for so long before. I liked being on the road."

"Really," Dylan said in surprise. "Aren't you working on the album for that tween star?"

"I quit. I can only take so many tantrums and this kid is all about tantrums. I miss being on the road. I didn't have to think about things or worry about the next step in my life. I just showed up and did my job. Someone made me food, did my laundry and packed my suitcases."

Dylan wanted to commiserate with him. "There are moments when I miss being on the road, too, but I wouldn't change anything." He not only liked being with the kids, but Lola was becoming a permanent fixture in his life and he liked having her around, as prickly as she could be sometimes. "You're making me feeling guilty," he said.

"Then my job is done," Wally said. "You're doing grown-up stuff and I'm running in place," he continued as he slid down on the cushions and leaned his head against the back of the sofa. "I always thought my future was with Calamity. My whole life is wrapped up in our band and now we're on hiatus I'm feeling a little out of sorts."

"You could try working on your personal life," Dylan said.

"You mean like finding a steady girl!" Wally's eyebrows shot up in surprise.

"Sure, why not? You're a nice guy, in a nerdy kind of way."

Wally was acting like he was in kindergarten again. "Maybe I could help in some way," Dylan said.

"Nah," Wally said, "I'll figure it out. Thanks for the iced tea and letting me unload on you."

Emma walked into the family room wearing her Hello Kitty pajamas. She stood in front of Dylan, her hands on her hips and an accusatory look on her face. "You said you were coming to tuck me in and read me a story."

Dylan jumped up. "I did, didn't I?"

She nodded forcefully, her blond hair swinging back and forth. "We have to find out what happens to Harry Potter."

Wally jumped up. "I guess I'm done complaining for the night."

"It's not like I didn't catch you reading Harry Potter while on tour," Dylan said with a laugh.

Wally shrugged. "I've read the entire set three times." He looked at Emma. "I can give you some insight into Harry Potter if you need it. Voldemort did it."

"No spoilers. I don't want to know until it's the right

time." She frowned at Wally with so fierce a glare only a seven-year-old girl could master it.

Wally shrugged. "I guess I'd better get going."

"You can come back tomorrow night and finish complaining," Dylan said.

"I'm taking you up on that offer."

Dylan opened the front door and let Wally out. Emma followed closely on his heels, making sure he didn't escape.

Wally waved as he walked away. Dylan shut and locked the front door and followed his niece up the stairs for the next chapter of Harry Potter.

Chapter 7

Sebastian sat at the round table, his deck of cards splayed across the wooden top. Their parents had asked them to check out this new celebrity restaurant. To Lola, the restaurant was pretty to look at, but something was missing and she couldn't figure out what.

"Is this a new trick?" Lola asked.

He slid the cards together, shuffled them and then held the splayed deck out to her. "Pick a card. Any card."

Lola shook her head. "Where have I heard that before?" He'd been using her as his audience since they were kids. "I want to talk about Dylan, not do card tricks."

"This is part of my new routine and I'm having problems with it." He held the deck out to her again. "I think better when I have a deck of cards in my hands."

Her brother had such nimble fingers. No matter how many times he practiced on her, she almost never figured out how the trick worked. She finally picked a card and put it back as instructed. He spread the cards over the table's surface and ran his hand around, mixing them up. He reached in and pulled out a card and held it up.

"Nope," Lola said. "Two of diamonds."

Sebastian frowned and gathered up his deck.

"Maybe if you told me what you're trying to do, I could help solve the problem."

"I never reveal my tricks." Sebastian sounded frustrated.

"But—"

"Never," he added with emphasis.

Lola shrugged. The waitperson approached. He handed lunch menus to them and asked about drinks. Lola ordered iced tea and her brother asked for water.

"Phoebe's House of Crepes," Lola read. "Is this supposed to be a French restaurant?"

"You know how Dad likes to check out the competition, especially when it's a block away from his restaurant."

"Sometimes Dad is crazy," Lola said as she scanned the menu.

The restaurant had murals on all the walls. The French theme was a bit jarring, with gendarmes riding bicycles and a representation of Notre Dame on a wall across from one of Versailles. Another wall showed women pushing strollers with tiny dogs on leashes. The waitstaff was dressed in black pants and white shirts.

The bistro tables were cute enough, but the wrought-iron chairs were uncomfortable.

"Is this supposed to be a joke?" Lola asked as she scanned the dining room.

Sebastian shrugged. "The décor is cheesy, isn't it? The crepes look good on the outside." He sniffed as a waitperson walked past with two plates of crepes that looked delicious.

Their waitperson returned. Lola ordered the lunch sampler and her brother ordered the dessert sampler. They had always shared their food.

"Yeah, well, Phoebe isn't known for her class," Lola said, "but she is fun. This restaurant does fit her personality. It's entertaining and gaudy."

Phoebe Lassiter was the host of a long-running game show on cable television. Her signature was her audacious wardrobe and unfiltered language. Lola wasn't certain what qualified Phoebe to run a restaurant, but celebrity-owned restaurants were usually moneymakers, unless a bad reputation developed that not even a celebrity name on the door could overcome. Usually bad food was the culprit.

"I'll reserve judgment on the food," Sebastian said. He gathered up his cards and tucked them in his jacket pocket. "How are things working out with you and Dylan?"

Lola hesitated. "We're doing all right, but the kids are having school issues. One mother just came over yesterday to complain. And from what she was wearing I had the impression she was hoping for a special apology. She had to be at least ten years older than him."

Sebastian shook his head. "He is a rock star."

"Yes." Just the memory of Gwyneth eyeing Dylan like he was prey set Lola's teeth on edge.

"You're just working with him. Why does a cougar on the prowl upset you?"

"She interfered with our work and she was mean to Emma. I've never liked mean people. If a woman wants attention, you'd think she would have been nicer."

"Do you want his attention? Are you being nice to his kids?"

Lola looked at him, shocked. "Romantic advice from the only brother I have who isn't married!"

"I'm looking out for my kid sister. Though I suspect our sister would have better advice."

"Nina's busy. She has a daughter and a husband and a business. I'm happy when she has time to answer the phone when I call. I don't want to burden her with my problems. You're stuck with me."

The waitperson brought them their lunch. Lola moved the lunch crepes to the center of the table and cut each one in half. Sebastian dug in. One sampler contained vegetables with a white sauce. Another crepe contained thin slices of turkey with a light gravy-type sauce and the third was filled with three cheeses.

Lola took an experimental bite. The cheese practically melted in her mouth. "Oh, wow. This is good."

"I agree," Sebastian said. "And I think you're upset because you're attracted to him."

"Don't be silly. He's a nice person and respectful of my talent."

"He's good-looking and talented and respectful. How can you not be attracted to him?"

"Because that would be unprofessional," she said in a sharp tone, irritated with Sebastian. She was attracted to Dylan and she'd already kissed him. If things ended badly, she would be in a heap of trouble because she was still contracted to work with him. She couldn't afford to do that just when she was beginning to enjoy the collaboration. "And we're starting to find our groove."

Lola finished her half of the lunch sampler and started in on the dessert crepes after cutting them in half. All of them were filled with fruit. The first one was blueberry. Not bad, but the blueberries weren't quite ripe and had a slightly tart taste.

"What you're saying is that the work is more important than anything else."

"Of course I am," Lola said, her irritation with her brother growing.

He gave her a knowing look and smile. "Methinks you doth protest too much."

"You're crazy."

"I don't think so." Sebastian shifted to the fruity dessert crepes, too.

"I don't want to talk about Dylan anymore."

"Fine." He gobbled his share of the second plate. "These crepes are terrific."

"I want to marry them and take them home." Lola tried not to smack her lips. The lingering fruit tastes mingled pleasantly on her tongue despite the tart blueberries. "Mom and Dad are going to love this place."

"I don't think they need to worry, especially since

this restaurant only serves breakfast and lunch." Sebastian finished the last of his crepes. "Since you don't want to talk about your love life, what do you want to talk about?"

"How about your love life? Or lack thereof." She couldn't contain her grin.

"Ouch. I don't have time for a love life."

"You should make time." Lola loved turning the tables on her brother.

"My love life is not interfering with my job," he said.

She laughed. He looked so solemn and serious. "A little bird tweeted at me that your love life is the pits." As in big-time. Her sister, Nina, had told her Sebastian hadn't gone out on a date in months.

"Which one of our brothers has a big mouth?"

"All of them," Lola said. "But the tattletale wasn't one of our brothers."

"Nina has a big mouth." Sebastian pulled out his cell phone and started typing.

"What are you doing?" Lola tried to see what he was so furiously tapping.

"Just keeping track of everything we tell each other."

Her eyes narrowed. "You're keeping gossip on a spreadsheet!"

"Where else would I keep it? I may require this information for my own needs in the future."

"Somehow there is something wrong with that." Lola wondered what he had.

"Just you wait. This is all going to come in handy one day and I might write a book. Or share with all my future nieces and nephews."

Lola sat back, staring in amazement. "I don't believe this."

"Information is power."

She held up a hand. "You need to step back from *Game of Thrones*." Sebastian liked to gossip. The family gossip was all in-house. Mom and Dad had learned early on to keep secrets secret. Being in the music business gave them access to the idiosyncrasies of the celebrities. And to stay employed they never gossiped, no matter how other people tried to coax them into revealing salacious information. The payoff wasn't worth jeopardizing their jobs.

"Noted."

Lola ordered a fruit crepe to go. When Sebastian had paid for their meal, they strolled the block back to Luna el Sol, handed the crepe off to their mother, then Sebastian headed to the Magic Castle and Lola to Dylan's house.

You rule your destiny,
Master of your fate.
Lead the pack to safety.
It's never too late.

Dylan always knew when a song felt right. He glanced at Lola, bent over the keyboard, making notes on the sheet music on the table next to her. The late afternoon sun slanted across the table. They'd worked for hours on this one song that had been reluctant to come together.

"Wow." She sat up straight and smiled at Dylan.

"This is perfect. The words send chills up and down my spine."

"We're brilliant," Dylan said.

"We are, aren't we?"

He leaned toward her and planted a kiss right on her lips. Her mouth was soft and the light scent of perfume surrounded her.

"What are you doing?" She pulled back from him, her eyes wide with surprise.

"High five," he said.

"We kissed again. You can't kiss me." She stood up and left, walking swiftly through the recording studio and into the living room.

Dylan followed, not certain why she was so upset. "But… I—I—I'm sorry. I thought…when you kissed me the other day… I didn't mean…"

She turned on him. "What was that? You've made me uncomfortable."

"I didn't mean to do that."

"You ruined everything." She paused.

"What did I ruin?" He was too astonished to make sense of her objection to his kiss. "Tell me."

"I've been able to control my attraction to you. You should be grown-up enough to control your attraction to me," she scolded.

"You're attracted to me!"

"What woman in the free world isn't?" she replied. She stood with her hand on her hips. "Besides, that's not the point."

"What is the point?"

"You stepped across the line. Do you kiss your band-mates after a good session of music?"

"I'm at a loss here. I was just showing my appreciation for the terrific song we created." He ran his fingers through his hair, frustrated and confused. "I'm sorry I offended you."

He didn't know what she was trying to say. He'd been trying to hide from his attraction to her. He knew he'd stepped over the line, but couldn't help himself.

"This is a working relationship." She stomped toward the door. "I need a break. I'll be back when I calm down." She flung the door open and stepped out into the pool area.

Dylan thought she would leave, but she turned toward the garden shed. When she returned, she held gardening tools and a bucket. She marched around the studio to the garden.

He went into the kitchen for a bottle of water and saw her striding toward the back of the garden. She knelt down and started to attack a rosebush.

Women had been chasing him for years and had always been flattered he'd even noticed them.

He'd certainly messed up here. He thought he was merely following up on what she'd started the other day. Instead she was furious. He watched her for a few minutes and then sat down at the snack bar where he could keep an eye on her.

For the most part, he'd only had a couple of relationships. The constant travel was murder for a serious love connection. While he was gone on tour, the women had been worried about him sleeping with his groupies. And when he'd returned he'd been bombarded with accusations of disloyalty. And now with the kids, his future love life wasn't looking good either. Not every woman was interested in a premade family. Emma and Justin didn't need any more emotional upheaval in their lives. And neither did he. Maybe she was right. Maybe this was a bad idea, and he needed to cool it.

Lola plucked spent blooms off the rosebush. She attacked the soil around the bottom, loosening it to give the roots breathing room. Then she trimmed back the branches, resisting the urge to hack at it. She disturbed a rabbit that took one frightened look at her and scampered off. When her anger was spent, she sat cross-legged on the cool grass.

She'd tried hard to keep their relationship on an even keel. And she would have been fine not knowing the gentleness of his kiss, doing her job, writing her music.

Dylan had to ruin everything. Because now she knew how good, how wonderful his kisses were and wanted more. That wasn't going to work. This kind of crap ruined careers and her career would suffer a lot more than his.

She was so mad at herself for letting him kiss her. She should have punched him in the face. Men got away with this kind of behavior while she struggled to be measured as a professional. And yet…her conscience said…she had kissed him first. She had acted unprofessionally, too.

Overprivileged rock star. He could go back to his career and everything would be fine, but she had a reputation to protect. That old double standard reared its ugly head again. He probably kissed women all the time and didn't have a second thought about it. One slip for her and gossip would spread like a summer firestorm. People would think she only had this job because of her personal relationship with him. They'd attribute any good work to him. Who would hire her after that, take her seriously? She couldn't afford to be seen as anything less than a team player.

Lola was a Torres. Her family were team players. They didn't cry when things went wrong and they didn't blame other people for any reason, no matter who was at fault.

She moved to a second rosebush, clearing away weeds and leaves. She trimmed the bush, aerated the soil and surprised a small gopher snake. She smiled at the snake, gently picked it up and put it down the gopher hole she'd found the last time she'd worked in Dylan's garden.

When she was finally calm, she put the tools away, brushed the dirt off her jeans and went back into the studio.

"I owe you an apology," she said.

Dylan sat at the snack bar reading. He looked back at her.

"I shouldn't have yelled at you. That was unprofessional."

"I shouldn't have kissed you."

She accepted his half apology. "We're going to complete this score and then I'm going to go on with my life."

"Got it."

"And we will speak of this no more."

The guesthouse door slammed and Emma rushed into the kitchen waving an orange piece of paper. "Did you know Halloween is next week?"

"One of my favorite holidays," Lola said. She had wonderful memories of her Halloween candy treats and the handmade costumes her mother sewed.

Emma handed the piece of paper to Lola. "I have a coupon for a free pumpkin at the pumpkin farm and I want you to help me pick one out."

Justin walked into the kitchen. His clothes were dirty and he had a scratch on one cheek. "Halloween's for babies," he said with a snort.

"You don't have to go," Emma said.

"What happened to your face?" Dylan asked.

"Nothing," Justin said. He glared at Emma as though daring her to say something.

Trying to avert a crisis, Lola asked, "Emma, do you have your costume yet?"

"No."

"What do you want to be?"

Emma suddenly looked excited. "I want to be a saber-toothed cat like the one we saw at the La Brea museum."

"I think we should dump you in tar and you can go as a tar pit," Justin said in a nasty tone.

"Stop being mean," Emma retorted.

Justin shrugged.

Lola and Dylan exchanged looks. "I don't think we'll find a saber-toothed cat costume."

Emma lifted her head high. "I'm going to make my own."

Lola couldn't resist a smile. "I'm going to help you."

Emma threw her arms around Lola's waist. "Thank you. Can we go on Saturday to the pumpkin farm?"

Lola glanced at Dylan. "That okay with you?"

"I'm in," Dylan said. "I haven't been to the pumpkin farm in years. Always did like the petting zoo."

"I'm staying home," Justin snarled. He marched out the door and across the patio to the main house.

They watched him go. Lola turned to Emma. "What happened?"

Emma hesitated, with a guilty glance at Justin slamming the patio door after he entered the house.

"That nasty Zachary Jarvis tripped him on the playground," Emma announced. She went to the refrigerator and pulled out an apple and a juice box. "I don't like Zachary. He's mean to all the little kids. Justin tried to stop him from picking on Susie. Zachary thinks he can do what he wants because his daddy is Philip Jarvis."

Philip Jarvis was Hollywood's newest actor who'd starred in the biggest summer blockbuster of the last ten years.

"I need to talk with the principal," Dylan said.

Lola simply felt sad. Bullies existed at every school and she hated when little kids were picked on. On this she could easily sympathize with Dylan.

"Are you going to talk to Mrs. Collier?" Emma said the next morning as Dylan drove the children to school.

"We're going to chat." Dylan pulled into the parking lot.

"I can handle this myself," Justin said in a sullen tone.

"Oh, no. The fact is you shouldn't have to handle this at all."

He parked and got out of the car. Emma waved at some friends. Justin slammed the door angrily.

Dylan kissed Emma on the cheek and Justin just glared at him before stomping away. Emma skipped over to her classmates and, with one last wave, joined her friends and they all headed to their classroom.

Dylan walked into the school office, amused at the line of posters about how to stop bullying. An older woman stood behind a long counter, smiling at him as she sorted several piles of paper.

"I'd like a moment of Mrs. Collier's time, please." He smiled at the woman who beamed back.

"I'll let her know." She walked to the back of the office and knocked on a door labeled Principal. Shortly after that, a tall, angular-looking woman with a sharply defined face, brown hair going gray at the temples and a pleasant smile appeared in the doorway, holding out her hand.

Mrs. Collier, the principal. Dylan remembered meeting briefly with her one morning when he'd dropped off Emma and Justin for school.

"Mr. Ward, what can I do for you?" They shook hands, and she ushered him into her office where they both sat.

"My nephew is being bullied by a boy named Zachary Jarvis."

Mrs. Collier nodded, her smile dropping. "We're aware of the problem."

"That's good," Dylan said, "that you're aware of the problem. That you know the school is liable and you have the power to fix this. Because if you don't do something, I will. I'm not the least bit intimidated by Zachary's father."

"Zachary's parents are aware of the problem as well, but there are a few issues—"

Dylan held up his hand. "We all have issues. I care about my nephew's safety. Whatever Zachary's issues are, help fix them. But fix this problem first. No child should be bullied."

"I understand, Mr. Ward." She sounded sympathetic. "We are handling the situation."

"But I don't think you are," Dylan said softly. He hated making threats. "From what I understand, he's still bullying younger children who don't have the ability to stand up to him. For a school that has a no-bullying policy, I've yet to see how you put that policy into action."

"Mr. Ward, you don't understand."

"I understand that you can't say anything. The fact you aren't doing anything is what bothers me." Mrs. Collier opened her mouth to speak, but Dylan held up a hand again. "I can't have my child in an unsafe situation. If you don't fix this, I'll contact other parents, do my own investigation of what is going on. And depending on what I find and what you do—or don't do—I'll take action. It might be legal. It might be pulling my children from the school and letting parents know why."

Mrs. Collier's face tightened, her lips thinned. "Don't threaten me."

"I'm just telling you what I am planning to do to protect my child. Because it's not in line with what you want to do isn't my problem. I have thirty-three million followers across Snapchat, Instagram, Facebook and Twitter. I will be happy to share my story with them and add my voice to the antibullying campaign, using my family's experiences."

Mrs. Collier nodded stiffly. "Point taken, Mr. Ward. Is there anything else?"

"No. I'm good. Have a great day." He left, his mind churning.

He got into the SUV and turned on the motor. He was going to research how to handle bullies even though his instinct was to tell Justin to smack the crap out of the kid.

At lunchtime Lola sat at the snack bar, a ham sandwich in one hand. "You can't tell Justin to smack Zachary. That's assault."

"Justin needs to know that Zachary has to hit him first." Dylan looked up from his internet search.

"Hitting Zachary isn't going to solve anything. He's probably taking out his aggression on the other kids because he's vulnerable in his home for some reason and can't control what is happening to him."

"My first responsibility is to Justin." He sighed. "What I really need to do is talk to my lawyer and see what legal means I have to resolve the issue if the school can't."

"I think we should let the school do what it can first, then we'll talk to the Informer." She emphasized the last word.

He gave her a curious look. "The Informer?"

"That would be Emma," Lola said. "I can tell you she is the kind of child who knows about everything and everybody. She may have only been at this school for a couple of months, but she knows what's going on."

"This article I'm reading lists what I should be doing about the bullying."

"Get started. You need to document everything, starting with Justin's behavior, Emma's comments and your conversation this morning with the principal."

"Will do." He typed furiously for a few moments.

"Don't forget, though, we do have a meeting this afternoon with John Milles and Bobby Ramirez."

Dylan glanced at the clock. "I know. I'll be ready to go in a half hour."

John Milles was listening to the most recent song they'd written when Lola and Dylan arrived in the conference room.

"This song for the first dream sequence is brilliant," John said.

Lola relaxed a little. She'd worried all the way over.

"It does catch the essence of the story and the relationship between Little Wolf and the shaman but…" John paused. "You need to punch up the melodies linking the songs. They fade too much into the background when they should be underscoring the tension."

Dylan nodded, but his mouth had grown tight and his eyes filled with anger.

Lola simply smiled at them. "No problem. We can punch up the melodies."

Dylan opened his mouth to speak, but Lola put her hand on his and gave a tiny shake of her head.

"And I don't like this part, either." Bobby Ramirez punched a key on his laptop and the melody streamed out. "It's too harsh for the softness of this particular scene when Little Wolf first meets Alina, the female wolf."

Lola listened gravely, taking notes on her iPad while Dylan's shoulders grew stiff with repressed irritation. She knew he wasn't used to being criticized this way by non-musicians. That ego of his would have to take a back seat. Though he was kind of cute with his red-blond hair flopping in his eyes and his hands clutched into fists.

"We'll make the changes," Lola said. "And thank you for your input." Lola might not like to hear complaints about her babies, but she knew when to let the client at least think he was right.

Outside in the parking lot, Dylan puffed up with his irritation.

Lola held up a finger. "You keep your anger in check until we get in the car and are out of sight. I can guarantee you, they are watching us from the window."

She glanced up and saw Bobby Ramirez standing

at the window just as she'd expected. Dylan pressed his remote, unlocking the SUV. As they drove away, Dylan exploded.

"Do you think George Lucas stood over John Williams with even one critical statement?"

"Neither you nor I are in that elite league. In the rock-and-roll world, you are a god among men. In this world...not so much."

"Thank you," Dylan said, "I think. But that score is fabulous, and they don't know what the hell they're talking about."

"Listen," Lola said in a patient tone, "no matter how hard you try, how hard you work at it or how great you become, your ego will pale in size to that of a movie producer, and we haven't even dealt with the director yet. So you have to stop right now, take off your crybaby panties and put on your big-boy boxers. You are now in my world."

"But you had a pity party at my house over your song."

"I had a hard time handling a cowriter. I have no problem dealing with producers."

He looked so surprised, even a bit petulant, Lola almost laughed.

"And how do you know I wear boxers?"

"You're a rock star, and I'm pretty sure you go commando. It was just a phrase."

"So are we going to solve this?"

"These people are not musicians. They've given us direction, like a code. We break their code, figure out what they really want. We'll make a few changes, add some bass and soften what they want softened. I can guarantee they'll forget what they even said. This is about control. *Little Wolf's Journey* is their baby and they have a lot of money invested in it. These are the kinds of guys who tell the waiter there's too many poppy seeds on their bagel."

"That doesn't make sense."

Lola smiled at him. "No, it doesn't. But they are the bosses and we're going to follow their guidelines. Relax. This meeting tells me one thing. We're right on track."

"How do you know?"

"They didn't tell us to throw every song away and start over. I'm hungry. Do you feel like chili-cheese fries? I love chili-cheese fries."

"Really." He gave her a sidelong look.

"Carbs, meat and cheese is like a hug from grandma. And you need a hug."

"Where are we going?"

"To Grandma's."

"Excuse me?" he said, confusion on his face.

"You haven't been to Grandma's?" She couldn't believe he hadn't visited one of the most iconic fast-food places in Los Angeles. "Turn right on Wilshire and I'll introduce you to Grandma's."

Grandma's was several steps up from a hole-in-the-wall diner. A long counter of white Formica with matching stools spanned the rear of the eatery. A long bank of windows faced Wilshire Boulevard. Tiny tables with bistro chairs dotted the space beneath the windows.

A banner on one wall proclaimed Grandma's had the world's best chili-cheese fries.

The aroma of onion and garlic floated through the diner. Five customers sat at the counter. One glanced curiously at Dylan and Lola as they entered, bringing a gust of cool wind with them.

Lola raised a hand as she walked along the counter.

A petite woman with pale brown hair, hazel eyes and a round face looked up from the stove she stood in front of. "Hey, Lola. Rough day at the office?"

"Yeah," Lola said.

The woman scanned Dylan. "Is that who I think it is?

"Yeah. Dylan, meet Marcie Becket," Lola answered. Marcie stared at Dylan and Lola couldn't help but ask, "Are you going to have a fangirl moment?"

Marcie laughed. "Later, when I'm alone and can do something about it. The usual?"

"Times two." She gave Marcie a thumbs-up.

Lola led Dylan to a larger table at the back of the diner. She sat down and grinned at him.

He sat across from her. "Everything is so…white." Glaringly white.

Lola nodded. "That forces you to eat neat. One of the attractions of this place is the cleanliness. White allows you to see every speck of dirt. If you don't see it, you know this place is clean."

He felt on trial. The woman at the stove stole a glance at him. He frowned at her. "Marcie Becket. That sounds familiar."

"'*Marcie's Playground.*' Does that ring a bell?"

He stared at her. "That's Marcie Becket. The Killer Dukes wrote that song…"

"That would be her," Lola said.

He stared at the woman as she opened a large refrigerator and brought out a package of something he couldn't identify.

"She's a real person!" Dylan said in wonder. "I thought it was just a song."

"She's a real person."

"She works in a diner."

"She was married to the lead singer of Killer Dukes. He went crazy, the whole shebang—too many drugs, too many women, too many fights. The whole tragic heavy-metal issues some guys fall into. She divorced him, received a nice chunk of change and now she owns this diner and most of the block. She is not just a diner waitress."

"How do you know all this? I've been on the scene for years."

"The whole disaster happened almost twenty years ago. I think I was eight." Lola eyed him.

Marcie approached the table with two glasses. On closer inspection she was older than he thought, maybe her late forties with a faint sprinkling of crow's-feet at the outer corners of her eyes. She smiled at Dylan and even though she wasn't what some might call classically beautiful, something about her was deeply attractive.

"Two cherry cokes," she said, putting the glasses down in the center of the table. "Your order will be up in five minutes."

"Thank you, Marcie," Lola said.

After Marcie returned to the kitchen, Dylan leaned across the table. "How do you know her?"

"My mother sang backup for the Killer Dukes once."

"That sounds like a story."

"It is, but it's their story to tell. Mom struck up a friendship with Marcie and they've been thick as thieves since then. Dad taught her to cook and manage a restaurant."

Dylan was impressed and he was seldom impressed. "Wow, I've met a rock icon today and had a producer tell me how to do my job."

"We're going to talk about the meeting."

"Okay. Tell me how to deal with Bobby and John."

"You're making the meeting more complicated than necessary."

"I've never been told before that my music sucked." Dylan still felt residual anger.

"Not even on your first album?" Lola said.

"No. Calamity's first album generated a lot of approving buzz. Not enough to win a Grammy, but enough to put us on the map."

"John and Bobby didn't say the music sucked," Lola continued. "What they were really saying is that they pay the bills and have big egos, as well as a couple of Oscars that gives them their street cred. Just not in that many words. They can't have you thinking you are too fabulous. And besides, the film is their baby, like the music is ours."

"You go through this every time?"

"My first paying job was an indie film by this poor, little rich kid with more money than sense, *A Force of*

Habit. He tried to micromanage every part of the film and was so surprised when the film was entered into Sundance. The problem was everyone talked about the music and panned the film. And luckily I had parents who prepared me for dealing with the entertainment industry. And that was the beginning of Lola Torres. Trust me, the producers' comments didn't hurt at all."

She didn't add that she'd won an award for the music despite the bad press the film received. Dylan was so used to having his own creative freedom that adapting to someone else's vision was difficult, if not impossible.

"Maybe I should just drop out and let you have the project," Dylan said.

"Not on your life," Lola said. "You're no quitter."

"You weren't happy being forced to work with me in the beginning."

"I'm still not entirely thrilled, but our partnership is doing well. I have an ego, too, but I put mine aside. My babies have to eat."

She was one of the most confusing people he'd ever met. "You don't have kids."

"I will someday. And they're going to have to eat."

He shook his head. "You confuse me."

"In what way?"

"I haven't met anyone before who wasn't dazzled with me."

She shrugged.

Marcie returned with two baskets of fries. At the sight of the food, Dylan's mouth started watering. The aroma was so amazing he couldn't wait to get started.

Marcie set the baskets down, then pulled up a chair and sat.

"So what are you working on now?" Marcie asked Lola.

"We're working on the new Milles-Ramirez project."

"I read about the new animated feature. *Little Wolf's Journey.*"

"That's the one," Lola said. "You have the best information ever. You and my dad are the coolest insiders."

Marcie simply smiled. "And we always said if we could get a chunk of every bit of business done in our restaurants, we'd own LA." Marcie turned to Dylan. "How do you go from singing *'Annihilation Girlfriend'* to the *'Circle of Life'*?"

"I'm trying to stretch myself, be fearless and do something else."

"Please tell me Calamity isn't breaking up." She gave him such an earnest look, he was surprised.

"Calamity isn't breaking up. We're taking a break and doing some personal projects."

"Thank goodness. You are a talented musician and have something to say. And you're pretty to look at."

Lola chuckled. Dylan blushed. Then he smiled. "You are excellent to look at, as well. Lola, I like this one."

Marcie reddened, too. "Try your chili-cheese fries," she urged.

He dug in and after a couple of bites, he started to shovel the fries into his mouth. What had Lola said? *A hug from grandma!*

Lola smiled at Dylan after Marcie left the table. "I get that the producers are the money train. But, sometimes, I too feel like they have no trust in our creativity. I know we both want to do the best work possible. I do. I wish they'd let us be us and them be them. I'm done. I'm cleansed. Now I'm eating."

"I thought you thought I was overreacting. You couldn't say all this in the car?" Dylan asked.

"It doesn't count unless there is a basket of chili-cheese fries in front of me. Only then can I move on."

Lola was funny and a little outrageous. He admired her discipline and willingness to stick with him even though they'd had a rocky start. He really liked her. Wanted to know her better.

"Not much gets you down, does it?" Dylan asked.

"I have my moments, but then I remember the most important thing in my life, why I must go on."

"Your need to create music."

"No. My spite list. Which is a foot long."

"What is a spite list?"

"My list of people who said I would never succeed." She gave him a serene smile and dug into her food.

Chapter 8

Justin held out a paper to Dylan. Dylan needed a moment to come to the present. He was bent over his keyboard while Lola hummed a melody.

"That's good," she said, pushing back from the table.

"Uncle Dylan." Justin rustled the paper under Dylan's nose. "Look."

Dylan finally realized his nephew was trying to get his attention. He took the paper and read it, then glanced at Lola. "This is a note from his teacher saying he's turned in all his back homework."

"Can we go to the Magic Castle now?" Justin demanded. "Please," he added as an afterthought.

Dylan raised his eyebrows at Lola. "Are we ready to go?"

"Before I say yes, I want Justin to know I had every

confidence in him. Next Sunday is Halloween and I think the kids would enjoy the party," Lola answered.

"Not this Sunday?" Justin asked, looking disappointed.

Lola shook her head. "Sorry, Justin, I already set it up with Sebastian for the Halloween party."

Justin looked a little disgruntled but didn't complain.

"I'm proud of you, Justin," Dylan said, his hand on the boy's shoulder as he stared him in the eye. "Go change out of your school clothes."

Emma gave Dylan a kiss and followed Justin out of the studio to head for the main house.

"I really am proud of Justin," Dylan said, almost in wonder. "And I'm grateful to you. You helped get him to this point."

Lola smiled but shook her head. "Give yourself some credit. He knows you're in his corner now."

Dylan sighed. "I need some time away. You need to take me out on a date."

Lola looked startled. "I do? How did you arrive at that conclusion?"

"It just occurred to me."

"Where did you want to go?"

He studied her, wondering what would capture her interest. "I was thinking Paris."

"That's a couple of hours' drive. I'm sure I can find something closer."

"I'm not talking about Perris, California. I'm talking about the one in France."

She stared at him. "Paris, France. That's quite a hike. Let's do New York instead."

"Are you sure?" Had he heard her correctly? He'd never known a woman who didn't want a romantic dinner in Paris.

"We're talking a day there and a day back. I don't think you should be that far away from them. If something happened to one of the children you'd be half the world away. And we have a lot of work to do."

"We need to get out of our comfort zone a little."

"I'm not the type to just drop everything and leave for a long weekend."

Dylan smiled at her. "You need a little shaking up."

Her dark eyes narrowed. "Working with you is all the shaking I need. So I'm good on the shake-up front."

"We're going out to dinner in New York." He felt a flush of excitement. "Besides, there's a show we can see. Music is supposed to be phenomenal. We need to refresh ourselves, be inspired."

"What about the children?"

"I can get a babysitter."

She shook her head, frowning. "Why don't you call my mom instead? I think she'll be happy to babysit. When do you want to leave?"

He glanced at his watch. "How about now?"

"Now! How are we going to get a flight so quickly?"

"Taken care of." She didn't know he had his own private jet. By the time they got to the Burbank airport, the jet would be fueled and ready.

"First off, we need to make sure my mother can babysit on such short notice. Second, I have to go home and pack some clothes."

He reached into his pocket and pulled out his cell phone. "I'm calling her right now."

"And third—" she paused "—separate bedrooms." This might be a getaway weekend, but they were still professionals.

He saluted. "You got it."

Lola was out of her mind accepting the dinner invitation. She wasn't surprised that Dylan was throwing caution to the wind. She was surprised she agreed. Impulsiveness wasn't a part of her personality.

As appealing as a romantic dinner in Paris was, the logistics didn't work for her. They had too much work to do and time was running short.

She grabbed her purse. Depending on what her mother said, she'd need to rush home.

"Okay," Dylan called after her as she opened the door to step out into the pool area. "Your mom's good. She'll be here in twenty minutes."

"You need to tell Justin and Emma."

"Already done. I told them it was a special treat for them, and Justin gets to choose dinner because of his good work." He smiled at her, realizing how much she'd helped him understand how to motivate his nephew.

I'm nuts, Lola told herself as she entered the cabin of the Learjet, trying to contain her astonishment. Dylan had his own plane!

An attractive woman in her mid-thirties, wearing black pants and a white shirt, took Lola's and Dylan's suitcases and stored them in a closet at the back of the plane behind the tiny galley. She had dark brown hair and a pleasant smile.

Dylan gave Lola a quick tour. The cabin was long and narrow. The seats were white leather. A sofa hugged the right side of the plane and several pairs of chairs, one facing the other over a table, hugged the opposite side. The walls were polished wood with cup holders just under the windows and magazine holders beneath. The galley was at the back with a tiny corridor that lead to the toilet.

"This is your plane?"

He grinned at her. "It's really Calamity's plane. Wally got his pilot's license and a plane at the same time. I think he got some sort of deal."

"He bought a plane and it came with a license?"

"Something like that," Dylan said. "Just kidding. He did get his license first."

"So, he's the pilot?"

"Would you be worried if he was?" He smacked the side of the plane. "Clementine will get us where we need to go."

"You named your plane."

"Wally named her."

Lola took a deep breath. She sat down across from Dylan and fumbled with her seat belt. She was starting to regret allowing herself to be pulled along on this weird adventure and yet she couldn't help feeling a little thrill. She was going away with Dylan Ward.

"Welcome to Clementine Airlines. I am your pilot, Captain Wallace Horatio Carleton," a voice over the PA system announced. "You are required by FAA regulations, God and common sense to fasten your seat belt. Yeah, I know federal law and common sense normally do not belong in the same sentence, but we who are about to pilot this plane implore you to play by the rules. As this is my first solo flight…"

Lola gasped.

"…just kidding." He gave a snorting laugh.

Dylan leaned over to Lola. "Wally's the prankster in our group."

"That doesn't mean we're going to fly under bridges and buzz the Empire State Building?"

"No."

Wally's voice came back over the PA system. "Stop worrying back there, Ms. Torres. You'll be fine. Now, in the event that our plane crashes over water, your seat is a flotation device. If we should lose cabin pressure, masks will drop down in front of you. Put Dylan's mask on first because he's prone to panic, and then put on your mask. We have no emergency doors as this plane is too small. In the event of an emergency, once the plane is on the ground, don't get in my way. I'm the first one out."

Her faith in Dylan was being sorely tested. "Aren't you supposed to go down with your sinking ship?" she yelled at the pilot's cabin.

"This is not a boat," he yelled back.

"You said you were the captain."

Behind her the flight attendant twittered.

Wally chuckled. "I like your snark, Ms. Torres. Once the seat-belt sign is turned off, you may move around the cabin. Drinking is encouraged. That is all." After a slight pause, he added, "For the moment."

The engines started up and the plane eased itself backwards slowly. Five minutes later, they were on the runway taking off. The jet rose over Burbank and banked toward the east. Lola watched out the window as the buildings grew smaller and smaller. The plane leveled off and the flight attendant approached and asked if they wanted anything. Dylan asked for water and Lola requested a soda.

"I was thinking," Dylan said.

"No," Lola responded.

"What do you mean, no?"

"We're not talking about work. We're having a getaway and if you're going to do this grand gesture of dinner in New York, then we're using this time for recreation."

"Okay," he said with a sharp nod. "We'll catch a Broadway show after dinner. Maybe do something during the day tomorrow."

"I'd go to Bergdorf's if I was on my own."

"We can do that. I'm getting tickets to *Beautiful*. Hope you want to see it."

"*Beautiful?* I have been a Carole King fan as long I've been alive!" The idea of seeing the musical left her in shivers.

"Before that, dinner. Trenton's is one of my favorite places for dinner. It's just a few blocks from the theater. The food is excellent."

"Sounds good." She'd never been to Trenton's. In fact, she'd only been in New York a few times, but each visit had been memorable. She'd shopped and eaten her way through the city and loved every minute of it. "You're putting this weekend together pretty quick. Being a rock star is nice."

"Not me. I have the world's most awesome personal assistant."

"Who is that?" A personal assistant. They'd been working together for three weeks and she hadn't met this person.

"My manager."

She laughed. Her brother Daniel and her sister, Nina, had this kind of life. They wished for something and someone was there to make their wish come true. Lola wanted that kind of success. She wasn't jealous, but she wanted that type of achievement, too.

Wally sauntered out of the cockpit toward them and sat down. Lola straightened, suddenly alert. "Who's flying the plane? Tell me you don't have a blow-up guy in the copilot's seat."

"How did you know?" Wally had a huge smile on his face. He looked at Dylan. "You told her. That's supposed to be under wraps."

Dylan shook his head. Wally gazed at Lola. "I wanted to meet you. Every time I talk to Dylan, it's Lola this, Lola that. You're kinda short to be so impressive."

Lola sputtered. "I'm not that short."

"You're not that tall."

"My legs are just the right length to reach the ground."

Wally laughed and turned to Dylan. "When practical meets pretty, we get perfection."

Lola asked again, "Who's flying the plane?"

"Automatic pilot."

"Not good enough."

"Airplane fairies," Wally replied.

"Stop," Dylan said. "Both of you. Wally, go back to the cockpit and do your plane thing. You're intruding."

"I don't understand why I'm never wanted," Wally whined. He winked at Lola.

Dylan sighed.

"I'm going to take a nap," Lola said, "and when I wake up, I expect this plane to be safely on the ground in New York, or you will have to deal with me."

"Threats. Always threats," Wally said as he stood up and made his way back to the front of the plane.

Dylan loved New York. He loved the vibrancy, the electrical feel of it. Even at two a.m., the city was alive. Calamity had played Madison Square Garden a number of times, and each time he'd found himself staying a few extra days to look around.

Their taxi stopped in front of an apartment building. The doorman immediately jumped forward to open the doors.

"You keep an apartment here," Lola said. She stepped out of the taxi and stood beneath the canopy, hugging her jacket tight to her. The night had grown cold with a faint drizzle.

"Our management company does. We crash here when we need to." Dylan handed the taxi driver a tip and the man smiled back with a sincere thank-you.

After taking their luggage from the trunk of the taxi and pulling the suitcases to the entry, the doorman opened the door for them and ushered them inside.

"I'll bring your luggage upstairs for you, Mr. Ward." The man almost bowed.

"Thanks. We can manage our suitcases." He tipped the doorman, who tucked the money away inside his pocket.

"You tip well," Lola said once they were in the elevator.

"Stan is efficient and very discreet, for which I'm eternally grateful."

"Please don't tell me you've thrown furniture out the window."

"Never. Anything we break here comes out of our paycheck. So don't toss the Limoges."

"You know what a Limoges is?"

He shrugged. "I dated a socialite once." Beverly Moreland had been cute and cuddly, but had the personality of a viper. Their first date had been okay, but by the second she'd expected him to marry her and turned angry when he didn't pop the question.

The door opened, and a young man with dark blond hair and wearing a black suit stood looking stiff and solemn. "Welcome back, Mr. Ward. Welcome to New York, Ms. Torres." He adroitly took their suitcases. "Drinks and a light buffet are awaiting you in the dining room, in case you're hungry"

Dylan loved Matthew's British accent. And was even more amused since the man had been born in Sarasota. As a budding actor, Matthew was always trying new accents, attempting to make himself more versatile, more employable.

"You have a butler!" Lola whispered.

"Yes. Actually, Matthew's an aspiring actor."

In the living room, Dylan headed toward the buffet. Flying always made him thirsty, but before he could pour himself a glass of water, his phone rang.

"Uncle Dylan," Emma cried. "There is only one banana."

"How come you're not in bed?" A glance at his watch confirmed it was nine o'clock in Los Angeles. Her bedtime was eight, even on a Friday night.

"Miss Grace said I could stay up until nine thirty tonight because I helped her around the house and tomorrow is Saturday, so I don't have school."

"Okay," Dylan said. The therapist had suggested keeping the children to a schedule and he supposed an occasional deviation wasn't going to warp their personalities. "What's the problem?"

"I have to share the banana with Justin."

"You always share bananas with Justin."

"I don't want to share this time and I don't think I have to." Emma's voice held a whine in it. In the distance he heard Grace talking.

"Did you tell this to Miss Grace?"

"Of course not. That would be rude. I need you to tell Justin that I can have the whole banana for my peanut-butter sandwich."

Dylan closed his eyes. He'd had a tiny wave of guilt leaving the children with Grace. Wanting time away from them seemed selfish. He'd even called their grief counselor who'd told him his impulsive action wasn't going to damage them. This was the first time he'd been separated from the kids since their parents' deaths. "Then neither one of you can have any of the banana."

Emma groaned. "That is so unfair."

"Emma," came Grace's voice, more clearly than before. "Are you on the phone?"

"I'm saying hello to my uncle Dylan."

"You go in the family room so I can talk to your uncle."

Dylan heard the phone thump as it changed hands. "Mrs. Torres," he said.

"Everything is under control," Grace said quietly.

"Maybe I should just come home."

"This is your first time away since you became their guardian. We're going to handle this situation just fine. Trust me, they aren't arguing over a banana. This isn't my first time at the rodeo."

Dylan took a steadying breath. Grace had raised seven children and from what he could see they were just fine. "I guess you know what to do."

"Go back to having some grown-up fun." What was she telling him he could do? He didn't have the stones to ask her. Grace intimidated him on a grand scale.

"Stop worrying. They're just testing their boundaries with me and I would expect no less, but I know the most important rule of all—never show fear in front of the beasts."

Dylan grinned. "Then I'll say good-night."

Grace hung up and Dylan turned to Lola who still stood in the middle of the living room glancing around, amazement on her face. He loved looking at her. She was so pretty and so unimpressed with him.

She slowly turned around, gazing at the room. "This is quite the place."

Dylan tried to look at everything through her eyes. He saw the ultra-modern white leather sofas flanking the fireplace with black leather chairs in one corner and the black-and-white area rug covering the wood floor. The only color in the room was in the huge abstract yellow and teal painting over the fireplace. While the apartment looked luxurious, it was curiously sterile, probably because no one really lived in it.

"This place is not exactly my style," Dylan admitted. "The furniture is a little too stark for me and not terribly comfortable, but it is free." Always free and he'd been lucky that his manager, Max, said no one had asked to use it this weekend.

"Was that Emma on the phone?" Lola inquired. "What's going on?"

"According to your mother, she's testing her boundaries." He wondered what Justin was doing. If he really got into his testing Grace would probably never babysit them again, no matter how much experience she had with children.

Lola laughed. "She's in for a rude awakening, then."

"What do you mean?"

"You think Emma is manipulative. Grace Torres is a master. She will make Emma and Justin do things, be grateful and think the ideas came from them. I remember when I was around four, Mom was on the road with the Stones. I thought my life was over 'cause my dad had to do my hair and it was never right. I called my mother every night, telling her to come home and fix my hair, and she told me to get over myself."

Dylan sighed. "On one level I need a little downtime from the children and our work, but on another I feel like I've abandoned them." And the fact they'd wormed their way into his heart also made him feel even guiltier. They depended on him for everything.

"What's going to happen if you have to go back out on the road?" Lola stopped in front of a glass-fronted étagère and gazed at the artistic arrangement of china statues and elegant glassware.

Dylan shrugged. "I'm not going to go back on tour until they're older. Does parenting get any easier?"

"Like I would know! According to my mom, it does. I knew that having either my mom or dad gone was always a strain, but I understood that they were still taking care of us. I had nice things and I liked having them. I didn't understand that when I was four, but I understood it later. We all did fine and grew up without any hang-ups. Though life changed when Dad opened the restaurant and was home more."

Dylan thought of all the times he'd simply shown up in the past and turned their lives into an impulse. *Let's go to the zoo. How about a trip to Seattle to the Space Needle? Let's get ice cream!* "My coming into their lives permanently was a drastic change. I went from being Uncle Fun to Uncle Eat-Your-Peas and I know they're struggling."

"You make them eat their peas? You're heartless." Lola had wandered into the adjacent dining room. When Matthew said he'd set out a light buffet, he was issuing the grossest understatement. The buffet on the side-board covered every inch of space. The variety was enormous.

She took up a plate and started to fill it with a selection of the foods Matthew had provided them. "This looks delicious. Does he cook, too?"

"He has the number for every takeout within six blocks."

"They're going to be fine," Lola said. Her plate was crammed with bites of almost everything on the sideboard.

"I'm trying to make things as painless as possible."

"You're never going to take away all the pain. Just growing up is painful." She sat down at the table.

"But is being there for them enough?" Dylan filled his own plate, realizing he was hungry even though they'd had a light dinner on the plane.

Lola yawned. He could see that she was starting to fall asleep. He was used to staying up late. He finished his food, signaling Matthew. "I think Ms. Torres is ready for bed."

"Of course, sir." Matthew touched Lola's shoulder and she jerked upright and yawned again. "If you will come with me, Ms., I'll show you to your room."

"Thank you."

After she left, the room seemed empty. She had wormed her way into his life and he hadn't even realized how important she had become. Emma loved her and though Justin kept his feelings as hidden as he could, he was growing to love her, too.

Matthew returned and started to clear the sideboard. "Your room is also ready, Mr. Ward."

"My regular room?"

"Yes, sir."

Lola breathed in the scent of warm New York bagels as she sat at the dining-room table the next morning. Again, Matthew had provided a buffet and she'd helped herself to pretty much everything.

"You cannot get a bagel this good in Los Angeles," she said, spreading cream cheese on her bagel and scooping up some lox.

"It's the water," Dylan said.

"Water is water."

"No, not even." He scooped lox onto his bagel, as well. Like her, he took a moment to inhale the aroma.

"How do you know this?"

"I have a lot of downtime on the tour bus. I like to read."

"I should think you'd be writing songs or practicing or something."

He smiled. "I can only do so much practicing and composing. Even I need breaks from the pandemonium."

Despite having worked with him for several weeks now, she realized she didn't know anything about him. She knew about his loving relationship with the children, his musical talent, but she didn't know much about the Dylan Ward who went on tour, produced amazing music and fended off groupies.

"What are we doing today?"

He took a long sip of coffee before answering. "We have dinner reservations at Trenton's for six o'clock. The restaurant is only a couple of blocks from the theater. The show starts at eight. I thought we'd bum around New York until then." A twinkling look in his eyes told her he had something in mind.

"Well, I guess." She wasn't gung ho about that idea. They needed to get some work done in their off time.

"Sometimes, Lola, you have to drop the game plan and just live on the edge."

Being that impulsive just didn't work for her. "I don't know."

"When you got the job, what did you do to celebrate?"

"I did a little mental victory dance."

He shook his head. "You need a physical victory dance."

"I don't dance in public."

"That was a metaphor. Did you buy something to mark the occasion? Did you take a quick trip to your favorite clothing store?"

"I just couldn't work a trip to Nordstrom's into my schedule."

"Then you and I are doing your victory dance." He went to the buffet to pour himself another cup of coffee.

"I don't know." They really needed to be working.

"Every time Sam and Elise mark a milestone in their life, they hop a plane to somewhere and do something fabulous."

She frowned. "What do they do that would be considered fabulous?"

"For their first anniversary they went to China and walked the Great Wall."

"You got me to New York. I'm not going to China," Lola said, though the idea was intriguing.

"We could do something here. Why not Bergdorf's? You did mention you wanted to go. I think you should spend money on something you'd never buy."

She turned that thought around in her head. She always wondered what it would be like to spend two thousand dollars on a dress. Her sister, Nina, probably did something like that all the time. The thought sent a shiver of excitement through her. Why not? She had the money. She seldom spent anything on herself. Though she did spend a lot of money on her garden and house.

"Okay, then," he said. "Let's finish breakfast and go to Bergdorf's."

"You got it." She stood up and raced to her bedroom for her phone. She knew who to call for what she had in mind.

With a ball cap pulled low over his forehead and huge sunglasses, Dylan looked like any other tourist in Bergdorf's. Just gazing at the window displays made Lola hyperventilate.

Everything inside the store was glitzy and sophisticated in a way that took her breath away. They wandered through the first floor, their vision enticed by each new display they encountered. The colors were amazing. If she had to describe the store in one word, *lush* was the one that came to her.

"What do you have in mind?" Dylan said.

"Already taken care of." She started toward the elevators.

"How about I meet you back here for lunch in—" he looked at his watch "—two hours."

"If I'm going to be late, I'll text you." She punched the elevator button. "What are you planning to do?"

"There's a little shop a few blocks away that sells vinyl records," he replied. "My gift to myself is to add to my collection."

"I didn't know you had a record collection."

"Someday I'll show it to you." The elevator door opened and Dylan waved at her as she stepped inside.

A few minutes later, Lola walked into a lounge and a tall, slim woman approached. "Ms. Torres?"

Lola nodded.

"I'm Marina. Kenzie Russel called and asked me to take care of you." This was the plan Lola had made earlier.

Marina was almost six feet tall and in heels that made her even taller. She looked like a runway model with perfectly styled black hair, a couture pantsuit and makeup so expertly done Lola could hardly tell it was there.

"Kenzie is my sister's sister-in-law," Lola explained.

"She spoke very highly of you."

Lola had only met Kenzie a few times, but was impressed with the woman and her fashion sense. Having been a fashion buyer for years, Kenzie had made a complete career change when she headed to Reno to work for her grandmother.

Marina led her into a private room. "Let's get started."

The display of dresses, shoes, evening purses, undergarments and jewelry dazzled her. She wanted to impress Dylan. She'd looked him up on the internet to review the glamorous women he'd been seen with. She wasn't glamorous. She was just herself. She didn't want him to be disappointed with her.

"I hear you have a date tonight with Dylan Ward," Marina said.

"Not a date. We just work together and we're taking a weekend off."

"I didn't pick out any—" Marina did air quotes "—working-together dresses. Because Kenzie did say you were going to the theater tonight."

"We are. And to be honest," Lola said with a deep sigh, "I don't know what we are. I don't know why I'm telling you this." She'd lain awake for hours during restless nights, wondering about her relationship with Dylan. What had started as a working partnership had changed into something else.

Marina patted her shoulder. "Personal stylists are like bartenders. We hear everything."

Chapter 9

"You wanted unexpected," Lola said. "Let's do something unexpected." She hugged her coat to her. A cold, brisk wind swirled down the street.

Dylan held her hand as they stood at the curb waiting in line for a taxi. "What did you have in mind?"

She thought for a moment. What would her mother do? Grace was terrific at doing the unexpected with her family. "The zoo. Let's go to the zoo." In his ball cap and oversized sunglasses, he'd never be recognized. No fan would expect Dylan Ward to be at the zoo. It was just the right kind of anonymous place Dylan would enjoy. And besides she loved the zoo.

"Why not?" Dylan said as they stepped into the taxi. "Central Park Zoo," he told the driver who nodded and did a U-turn, generating a lot of shouts and loud horns at them. Dylan consulted his phone. He held it up for her to see the map. "We can grab a quick lunch at the café."

She nodded.

The ride didn't take long, and a little while later, the taxi dropped them off and Dylan purchased tickets.

The zoo had an oddly deserted look. The trees over-head were bare of foliage, leaving the bright blue sky, filled with white billowy clouds, easy to see.

"I thought the zoo would be more crowded," Lola said. "Isn't Saturday a big day for them?"

A few families wandered the paths. Groundskeep-ers swept up dead foliage. She could hear the roar of a lion or maybe a tiger. A glance at the map said the zoo contained bears and snow leopards. Maybe that was what she'd heard.

"I don't know that October is a prime visiting month," Dylan said. "Though I think I read that the animals are more active." He ushered her through the entry. "Why the zoo?"

"I didn't think you'd be recognized here."

"Do you think rock fans don't go to the zoo?"

She snickered at him. "I think rock fans don't think you'd go to the zoo. Do you?"

He hesitated, looking chagrined. "Took Emma and Justin to the San Diego Zoo this summer. The trip was one of the first things we were all comfortable doing once they'd sort of settled in and worked out their new life with me."

"You do a lot of things for your niece and nephew. What do you do for yourself?"

"I'm a grown-up."

"That doesn't mean you don't have to deal with your feelings." Lola turned down a path to the café, using the map in her hand as a guide.

"I'm a man," he said, his voice tired. "Which means I'm not comfortable dealing with my feelings."

Lola shook her head. "Consider this a judgment-free zone. You're safe with me. You can be open and honest and I won't judge you."

They went into the café, which had been decorated for Halloween with strings of pumpkin lights twinkling around the windows and decorations on the counters.

They grabbed sandwiches and bottles of water and sat at a table. "I don't know what my brother was thinking when he made me guardian."

"Maybe he thought you would be a good parent." Lola had no idea if that was true, but Dylan had been doing well with them and trying hard. He suddenly looked troubled and unsure of himself.

"But he could have made my parents their guardian."

"Do you think they'd have been a better choice?"

Dylan's face showed the intensity of his thoughts. "My parents have always been fixated on their jobs. They're both lawyers and my brother was a lawyer, too. They're not uncaring, just not always available."

"Maybe your brother and his wife didn't want that for their children. So they chose you instead."

"My life has always been travel, music and more travel. Not the most consistent conditions for a steady home life for children."

"But you made the decision to give that life up to create that consistency for them."

"Eventually I'm going back on the road, back to the studio."

"You're giving them time now," Lola said. "You're showing them how much you love them."

"I still don't think my brother and his wife made the right decision."

Lola touched the back of his hand consolingly. "I think they did. The fact that you're worried about everything tells me they did. If you weren't worried, you would have just parked the children with your parents and gone on with your life."

"I don't know what the next step is."

"Yes, you do. You're not in this all by yourself. You've created quite a support army—welcoming-committee Donna, your friend's wife, even my mother. She agreed to take the children in for the weekend so you could have some grown-up time."

"And I feel I've abandoned them."

"They're fine. I'm sure your brother and his wife had grown-up time, too. How often did your brother and his wife accompany you on your drop-in trips to do something special with the children?"

Dylan thought for a moment. "Only a few times."

Lola laughed. "I can guarantee you they were having grown-up time, then. You made that possible."

"I never thought of that. How grown-up do you want to be?"

"For this afternoon, let's just be kids and we'll be grown-up tonight." She finished her sandwich, tucked the half-empty bottle of water into her purse and stood up. "I want to see the big cats."

* * *

Dylan stood in the foyer, struck dumb by the sophisticated, elegant woman in front of him. "You look…incredible. Wow. Just wow." Heat spiraled through him. Who wouldn't want to escort this gorgeous woman for a night on the town?

Lola pirouetted. "You don't clean up so bad yourself."

Dylan wore a black suit and white shirt with a black tie. He'd swept his hair back into a ponytail and then tucked it into the back of his collar. But Lola looked like she was ready to seduce the world. She wore a black silk Zac Posen dress that hugged her figure to perfection, and she'd added silver shoes, jewelry and purse. She'd pulled her hair back from her face and turned it into a French twist that left her long neck bare. Silver earrings danced in her ears, the crystals in them catching the light and casting rainbow prisms across her cheeks.

"I'm speechless."

"That's a first." A sly smile curved her mouth. "If you're speechless, then who are you and what have you done with the real Dylan Ward?"

He threw back his head and laughed. He realized that he laughed a lot with Lola. She made life seem effortless. He laughed with his bandmates, but often it was at them rather than with them. He seldom laughed with his parents and too often felt laughter was the wrong message to send to Emma and Justin. Lola wasn't about making drama but getting the job done. She was a doer, putting in the work that was needed and sometimes more.

He held out her coat. "Shall we be on our way?"

He helped her into her covering, opened the door and escorted her to the elevator.

The doorman held the door to the street open and Dylan thanked him. He walked to the curb just as a camera was shoved in Dylan's face.

"Hey, Dylan," a man called, "what brings you to New York? When are you and Calamity going to do another album? Is it true you quit the band?"

Lola pressed close to him, a flash of irritation in her eyes.

The doorman pushed open the door and stood outside holding it open. Dylan and Lola followed. A taxi stood waiting, door open.

"Dylan," another voice called, "rumor has it your new girlfriend here broke up the band. Any comment?"

More questions were shouted at him, but Dylan smiled politely, not responding. He'd long ago figured out that even if he gave them what they wanted, they wouldn't leave him alone. So, he gave them nothing. No matter how he answered the tabloid reporters would print what they wanted, all too often with no bearing on the truth.

Lola slid into the cab. The doorman held the paparazzi at bay until Dylan scooted in beside her, then he closed the door. The taxi took off for the restaurant.

"Will they follow us?" Lola asked.

"I don't know," he answered with a look back over his shoulder. Traffic obscured his vision of the sidewalk. "Transportation is the one thing that can stop the paparazzi in New York. In LA everybody has a car, but not here."

"That was grueling," she said with a shudder. "Does it happen often?"

"Enough to make it interesting."

She twisted to look at him. "You sound so jaded."

"I have to be. The first couple of times it was exciting being the object of so much scrutiny, then it got old, boring and sometimes scary."

"What about those questions they kept shouting at you? I was a bit surprised to hear that I broke up the band."

"I didn't listen to them. Except for the new question about you, they're the same questions I've been hearing for the last six months. I want to say, 'Asked and answered,' but no one pays any attention to what I've already said, so why bother addressing the subject again? And don't believe anything. He probably made the question up the moment he saw you."

Dylan wanted to apologize for subjecting her to the paparazzi, but they were part and parcel of his life.

She patted his arm. "I'm no stranger to the media. You should have seen them swarming around my two brothers, Daniel and Nicholas. They're both in the public eye and I've seen firsthand what unethical tabloids can do. I'm neither frightened nor intimidated by them."

The taxi pulled up in front of the restaurant. The doorman walked briskly to the taxi and opened the door. The path to the door was free of photographers and Dylan breathed more easily.

Inside Trenton's, a hostess led them to their table in

a corner of the restaurant out of sight of the front windows. While in New York, Dylan preferred this restaurant over most others.

"I would never have thought Italian was your favorite."

He grinned at her. "Italian is the meat and potatoes of the world." He already knew what he wanted. Food played a big part in her life and he'd wanted to surprise her with the food he loved.

Lola studied the dining room from the red-and-white checked tablecloths to the wine bottles made into pendant lights hanging over each table. The down-home look was no indication of the amazing haute cuisine that came out of the kitchen. A wandering violinist threaded his way through the tables.

"What's good?"

A man approached the table wearing an apron, his black hair cut close to his scalp. "Everything," he said with a wide gesture of his hands.

"Lola, this is Chef Giovanni."

"Welcome to Trenton's." Chef Giovanni took Lola's hand and bent over to kiss it in the European style. He stood straight and winked at Lola. "Such a small world, Ms. Torres. When you return to your home, give my regards to your parents and tell them you had the best of Italy for dinner tonight."

Lola nodded graciously. "Thank you."

Chef Giovanni clapped his hands. "I surprise you." He rolled his Rs and grinned.

Two waitresses jumped toward the table with wineglasses and bottle in hand. "To start, this lovely Sangiovese from Tuscany…" He explained about the wine and its region of origin. "With the wine, a ciabatta flavored with olives and rosemary." He filled their wineglasses and snapped his fingers.

The waitresses placed on the table the basket of bread, so freshly baked the aroma rose in a full yeasty scent.

"This is overwhelming."

"Don't you like being fussed over?" Dylan asked.

"Not so much," Lola admitted. "It's uncomfortable. I don't feel like I've earned it."

"We've been working really hard. You can't force creativity and sometimes you have to step back and take a break." Dylan had once tried to force a new song and it had been a disaster.

"I don't know that I agree with you. You're the boss of your own creative destiny. For me, it never takes a break. I always have something percolating in the back of my head."

"What's percolating now?" Dylan leaned forward to watch her. She had a distant look in her eyes and her fingers tapped the table lightly.

"My agent is in talks with a video-game company and they need a musician to write supporting melodies for nine different instruments. Each one is different, yet still supporting the main beat."

Dylan frowned, trying to think how that would be. "Don't you want more?"

"What do you mean?"

"Why not play in your own group or sing or take a larger role in something?"

"Not really," she said, taking a bit of the ciabatta. "I'm happy being behind the scenes, in the background."

"I've heard you sing. You have a powerful voice."

"But not a huge range," she said. "I know my limitations. I can't imagine standing in front of a crowd of strangers belting out a song. Not happening."

"Sounds like a little stage fright to me."

"Not a little," she replied. "This bread is delicious."

"And the wine is excellent," he added. "You make it sound like you're happy to work in a box."

"I'm not the one working in a box."

He frowned at her. "Explain, please."

"Every job I've done so far is diverse and challenging. The anime movies, the TV shows, the commercial jingles and *Little Wolf's Journey* are all different. This children's game is going to be a huge test of my talent and if I get the job, I'm going to truly enjoy it. Until *Little Wolf's Journey*, all you've done is hardrock music. Good hard-rock music and innovative, but still rock music."

Dylan had never seen things that way. Hard rock had a reputation for being wild and rebellious. Rebellion had always been a part of his soul.

Giovanni returned with a waitress who held two small plates in her hands.

"For your appetizer—*insalata caprese*. Fresh mozzarella and tomatoes with basil leaves and a touch of extravirgin olive oil and glazed balsamic vinegar." Giovanni liked expansive gestures and with a flourish, he took each plate from the waitress and placed them in front of first Lola and then Dylan.

"This is amazing," Lola said, her eyes wide and lips curved in a happy smile.

The rest of the meal was just as wonderful. Prosciutto-wrapped chicken stuffed with provolone and accompanied by a wine sauce had always been Dylan's favorite. Giovanni did something to add a touch of spice to it. Dessert was a ricotta cheesecake with lemon zest.

Dylan enjoyed watching Lola eat. She took bites of everything and ate with gusto. She complimented Giovanni on each dish, discreetly took photos that she sent to her parents and gushed about the dessert.

Relaxation had never been a huge part of his life. His drive to succeed had him always working, always planning the band's next move. Being around Lola was restful.

"Found you," a voice said, interrupting Dylan's thoughts.

The paparazzi reporter from outside the apartment building grabbed an empty chair from a nearby table and dragged it over to Dylan's and sat down. He leaned his elbows on the table. He wore jeans and a white turtleneck sweater under an expensive leather jacket. Dylan knew a good photo could be worth hundreds of thousands of dollars and he had no intention of providing one.

Lola looked startled, her eyes going wide. Dylan scanned the room, looking for Giovanni. Giovanni never allowed his customers to be harassed.

"You never answered my question." The man gestured at Lola.

"I'm not going to answer anything," Dylan said. "I suggest you leave."

"If you call the cops, they won't be here for an hour. Answer my question and I'll leave quietly."

"Get out. Go. You're in my face," Dylan half snarled.

The man turned to Lola. "Tell me. You are…?"

"None of your business," Dylan said roughly. "I'm giving you a chance to back off."

The man shrugged. "I'm not intimidated by you."

"You're dumb," Lola said quietly.

Dylan noticed she had her phone angled at the man, taping him.

Giovanni walked into the dining room, carrying a tray for another table. He saw Dylan's look and nodded. He delivered the table's food and then pulled out his phone.

"Come on, Dylan, give me some of the secret buzz."

Dylan stood. Lola followed. He reached for his wallet and tossed a couple of hundred dollars on the table and grabbed Lola's hand. "We're leaving."

The man followed them. By the time they reached the host's station, two burly men appeared and took the man by the arms. The man struggled, his camera swaying back and forth.

"Mr. Ward, go." Giovanni gestured to the bouncers who continued to hold the harasser.

"Take your hands off me!"

"No shoes, no shirt, no sense—" Giovanni pointed at his head "—no service." He nodded at the two burly men who escorted the man through the bar to the back of the restaurant. Giovanni turned. "The cops are on their way and will be here in a couple of minutes. Don't worry, he won't be following you anymore tonight."

"I owe you, Giovanni," Dylan said with heartfelt gratitude.

"What's your phone number?" Lola asked.

"Why?"

"I videotaped the whole thing. You should have it for the cops." Lola entered Giovanni's phone number into her phone and Dylan watched as she sent him the movie. "Tell the cops we'll be in tomorrow to file a complaint against him."

Giovanni saluted them.

"Thank you for an excellent dinner," Lola said. Dylan held the door for her and they walked out into the cold night air.

Later that night, all the way home from the theater, Carole King melodies floated through her mind. The musical had been perfection, the music unforgettable, inspiring, and Dylan's arm around her shoulders as they sat in the audience had been priceless. More than a few women, who'd recognized Dylan, had studied her with envy. She'd never, in her whole life, been out with a man other women had salivated over the way they'd drooled over Dylan.

She couldn't stop the songs from looping through her thoughts. A few times she found herself singing out loud. Dylan joined her, his voice a lush baritone complemented by her richer contralto.

In the foyer of the apartment building, she danced

across the marble floor, the doorman grinning as he tipped his hat to her.

"Nice evening, Mr. Ward?" the doorman said.

"Perfect, Stan," Dylan replied.

The elevator was waiting for them. They stepped inside.

"Thank you. This night was amazing," Lola said as they ascended in the elevator.

"You're welcome. I had fun, too."

The door swung open as they approached. Matthew stood aside to let them into the apartment.

"It's late," Lola said, "why are you still here?"

"On my way out, now that you are safely home," Matthew assured them.

Lola stared at him for a moment. "What happened to your British accent?"

"Tonight, I'm practicing a new character." he said with a flare as he buttoned his jacket, "I'm a Romanoff."

She laughed as he walked out the door.

Dylan took her coat and hung it in the hall closet. Damn, why did he have to be so nice and neat? A lethal combo as far as she was concerned. She kept waiting for the arrogant rock god to appear. It would make it so much easier not to like him.

"Lola? Why do you have such a weird look on your face?"

She let out a long breath. "Tonight was, like, the best date I've been on in years. In fact, I've ever been on."

"Good. For a moment, I thought I might have lost my game."

Well, she knew what this was going to lead to. She'd

known it from that first kiss at his door. She'd been fighting it, and she was tired of the battle. He really rang her bells, even if this wasn't her best idea. But then again, they were grown-ups and he probably did this all the time. She could, too. In for a penny, in for a pound.

"Dylan." She reached over and grabbed his jacket lapels and kissed him, knowing she wasn't making the best move, but damn did she want him. To be honest he was everything she ever wanted in a man, but she didn't know it until this moment.

He slipped his jacket off and he reached up and let down his red-gold hair.

Lola caught her breath as his hair fell around his shoulders and she had to stop herself from reaching up and grabbing a handful of the silky locks.

He loosened his tie and slowly pulled it from his neck. Then he stared at her as if deciding what to do next. He walked into the living room and went behind the bar. "How about a nightcap?" He held up a bottle of white wine.

She nodded and sat down on the sofa, kicking off her shoes and drawing her legs up under her. He poured the wine into two goblets and then sat down next to her, handing her one.

She wondered if he knew how sexy he looked. He probably did. This guy could have any woman he wanted. And he wanted her. She wasn't sure if this would be one night or last until they were finished working together.

"To us," he said and clinked his goblet against hers.

"To a successful musical partnership and…" His voice trailed off as he looked at her.

She sipped her wine, suddenly nervous.

He set his glass aside and took hers and set it on the table, too. Then he pulled her into his arms.

Her breath caught in her throat as he ran a finger along the side of her jaw and down her neck. Heat flamed inside her. He slid his finger down toward her cleavage and she knew how badly she denied her attraction to him.

"I want to make love to you," he said in a throaty voice.

She swallowed. She tried to tell him she felt the same, but nothing came out. Instead, she nodded.

He kissed the side of her neck, his lips moving lower and lower.

She couldn't breathe. Her whole body felt constrained. Without thought, she reached behind her and pulled the long zipper down, letting the dress slide down to puddle around her waist. She fought the urge to cover her naked breasts.

"You are beautiful."

She let out a long breath.

He leaned over and kissed her.

Lola was aching for him. She moved against him and slid her hands around his back and grabbed his hair and kissed him harder.

He groaned against her mouth and pulled her closer. She kissed him again, their tongues darting back and forth, fanning the flames of passion growing inside her.

Lola felt as if he was going to consume her. And

she wanted him, too; she let go of his hair to unbutton his shirt.

Dylan pulled off his now-open shirt. He used his mouth and hands to explore her skin. He kissed a trail down her neck. He lifted her hips and slid her dress down her legs. It drifted to the floor like a black cloud.

He ran his hands up her legs and planted a wet kiss on her stomach. When he reached the tops of her breasts, he pressed his mouth to one nipple, teasing it to stiffness. Nothing had ever felt so fun, so sexy.

She wasn't sure how she got his pants undone, but he was naked and hard against her.

"Give me a sec," he breathed into her ear.

He reached behind him into his crumpled pants pocket, bringing out a packet he quickly ripped open. He slid the condom over his penis and turned back to her. His hands shook and she was thrilled that he was as excited as she was.

He kissed her hard. She arched her back and his hands moved to her spine. He moved down to her hips, sliding his fingers into the waist of her panties and tugging them off. He pulled back to look at her.

"Incredible." Then his kiss was harder and more demanding. He pushed her back against the sofa.

She cupped his butt. His hot naked skin burned her hands. He felt so good, so hot. Part of her couldn't believe she was really here with a rock star doing the dirty.

A moan escaped his lips.

He nudged her legs further apart and he slid a finger into her soft, molten core. He moved down and slid his tongue over the wet sensitive skin. He glided his tongue over her skin again and again. Sighing, she didn't think she could stand much more. Just when she thought she couldn't take any more she felt her orgasm building. Then he shifted and slid inside.

She wriggled, trying to get him in deeper, but he pressed her into the sofa.

"Don't move."

"But…"

"Lola, trust me."

She did. For a few seconds, they just stayed like that. Their skin touching, their breath mingling together. She fought the urge to pull him closer, letting this be his show. "Make love to me, Dylan."

He kissed her deeply and started to move inside her.

She ran her hands up his smooth back and leaned in to his kiss. He groaned and thrust inside slowly, deliberately. He started moving in unhurried strokes with her. She curled her legs around his hips. He began thrusting inside her harder and faster. He teased and pinched her hardened nipples with his lips. The seductive action set her off and her body exploded in orgasm. She moaned deep in her throat as the volcanic explosions went on and on until she went limp.

"Damn, that was hot," he said.

Her head fell back on the sofa, as sensations sparked through her body until she calmed, realizing what they'd just done. "We can never do this ever again."

"What?" He stared at her in disbelief.

She moved away from him, overcome with the inappropriateness of what just happened. "No, really we can't. I think I lost brain cells." She had never in her whole life had an orgasm as intense as this. And what had happened to the idea of keeping their relationship strictly professional?

She reached down and grabbed her dress, holding it to her breasts. She jumped to her feet.

"Lola," he cried.

She ran into her bedroom, closed and locked the door.

Chapter 10

Lola sat on the plane, listening to Wally's chatter from the cockpit. Lola wished Dylan would just sit up there with him instead of trying to talk loudly over the droning sound of the engines. The flight attendant served her iced tea and retreated to a seat at the back next to the galley.

Her thoughts whirled. How had last night happened? She'd been so careful to keep their relationship on a professional level. Waking up this morning left her feeling out of sorts, yet totally satisfied. She had never felt this good with any of her past lovers, as few as they had been. Sex had never been a huge drive for her. But last night had created its own kind of music.

She wanted to blame the wine and the great food and the fantastic show, but she did get on the plane knowing that the weekend with him would change things. Now she was entangled in a risky situation, when the only risks she ordinarily took were in her professional life, not her private life.

She liked him. She liked his niece and nephew, she liked the way they worked together despite the disagreements. At times, she didn't like their adversarial stands, but working with him was exciting and fun and that was reflected in their music. They could write great love songs. One had already started in her head, though she wasn't certain that was where she wanted to go.

Her fingers tapped the melody against the tabletop. Next to her hand was her notebook opened to a clean music sheet. She wanted to put the melody down but it hadn't quite gelled in her mind.

"You're thinking about music," Dylan said.

"Yes and no."

He studied her. "What's wrong?"

"Sleeping with you was a huge mistake."

"I don't think it was a mistake." He had a smug look on his face that irritated her.

"I fell right into it with you without a second thought. You didn't even have to try." She felt like a groupie.

"I'm not quite sure how to comment on that." He looked confused.

"Rock star, duh," Wally called from the cockpit.

Heat swept up her cheeks and she looked away from his piercing gray eyes.

"Wally," Dylan shouted. "Not now."

"The worst part of this," she continued, "is I have a love song running through my head."

"Why is that bad?" He leaned toward her, trying to take her hand that was still tapping notes on the arm of her chair.

"It's not a bad thing," she said. She had the feeling her subconscious was trying to tell her something and she didn't want to listen.

She grabbed her pencil and started adding the notes to the sheet music. Her fingers flew. A few minutes later, Dylan was talking out the lyrics. He grabbed his iPad and opened his music app and started working the music more, adding a harder edge that she didn't like.

"This is a love song," she said, annoyed. "That beat is too hard." She began to sing softly.

"Love is like stars across the night sky.
Love is like music in your heart.
Love is a circle that never ends."

"Listen, about last night," Dylan whispered.

"I don't want to talk about it anymore."

He could have any woman he wanted. He'd chosen her. But that didn't make her feel special. She felt like the next woman in line. She glanced at him. His face was intent as he studied her notes and played them softly on his iPad. He glanced up at her, but she looked away, unable to meet his gaze.

Getting through the last few songs was going to be very uncomfortable.

Grace sat on the sofa, her legs tucked up under her. Lola prowled her living room, too restless to sit still.

"Did you finally do it with him?" Grace asked, with a shrewd look at her daughter.

"Mom," Lola said, sitting down next to her mother, "does Nina discuss her sex life with you?"

"All the time," Grace said calmly, "as well as Sebastian, Nick, Daniel. Sometimes even Raphael, but never Matteus. He's very private."

Lola supposed that being the eldest put Matteus in a different position.

"Really, Mom. They don't talk to Dad?"

"Not in detail. It's more like a pep talk. And Dad's only answer is 'Wear a condom.'"

Nothing ever seemed to ruffle her mother's serenity. She took everything in stride with a composure that rivaled Buddha.

"Yes, I slept with him."

"Who can blame you, dear? He's a very attractive man."

"I feel like one more in a long line of women who've already passed through his bedroom door."

"Did he treat you like just another conquest?"

"I don't know." She cringed. "I don't think so."

"It's all in your head, isn't it, sweetie?" Grace slid an arm around her daughter.

"I'm confused," Lola finally admitted. "He took me to New York. I shopped at Bergdorf's. We had dinner at this terrific restaurant and went to a show. He doesn't have to date women. Usually, they throw themselves at him."

"You didn't. He still chose you." Grace hugged her

tight. "His life has changed dramatically. He's changing into a man he never thought he'd have to be."

"What kind of man is that?"

"A father," Grace said. "He never wanted to be a father. He didn't feel ready to take on two children."

"How do you know that?"

"Because he told me."

Lola closed her eyes. The image of Dylan with Emma and Justin flitted across her mind. Even in the few weeks since she'd started working with him, he'd changed. Each day he became more in tune with them, anticipating their needs and being more comfortable in dealing with them. His role of being a father was something he embraced more easily each day. And the children responded to him. Even Justin was acting out less. Though Emma was still manipulating him with ease, he was more aware of it and less susceptible as time went on.

"What else did he tell you?" Lola asked.

"Most of what he had were questions, but a few things were in confidence and I can't violate that trust."

"Oh," Lola said.

"You and Dylan need to talk. You do have a relationship with him."

"It's a working relationship," Lola stressed.

"For the moment," Grace said, kissing Lola's forehead.

Even though Grace had spent a lot of time in a business where sex was recreational, Lola wasn't comfortable talking to her about this. Grace had never been judgmental; she lived in the real world and understood urges. Lola tried not to shudder, considering this.

"You're making this more difficult than this needs to be," Grace said soothingly.

She was overthinking this again.

"Lola," Grace said gently, "sometimes life happens and it's not in your plan."

"You mean go with my gut."

"You spend so much time living in your head, you forget about your other…needs."

Lola sighed. "On the plane, we wrote a love song. I don't know if it's for us or the movie."

"Finally, we get to the crux of the problem. Are you in love with him?"

"I don't want to be." But she was.

"Sweetie, you have choices," Grace said. "You can finish off your contract, leave and never see him again."

Pain swept through her at that thought.

"Or you can explore your feelings with him," Grace continued, "and see where things go."

"Doesn't that take two of us?"

"You're not going to know until you talk to him."

"I'll have to think about that."

"You could be missing the chance of a lifetime," Grace said gently. "Your father was not my plan A, but he wore me down until I said yes and I've never regretted it. He was this man from Brazil who could barely speak English, but he had so much music."

"The music Dylan and I write feels life-altering. I feel like I'm losing myself."

"Do you really think you're losing yourself or are you finding someone you didn't think you would?"

Lola was so confused. She burrowed her head against her mother's shoulder.

"Of all my children," Grace said, stroking her head, "you are the most self-contained. Maybe you need to just let go and see where Dylan takes you."

Chapter 11

Emma chattered, telling him all about how wonderful Miss Grace was, that they'd baked cookies and gone shopping. Justin was less talkative. They sat on the bed in Dylan's bedroom, watching him unpack.

"How about your weekend?" Dylan asked, trying to draw his nephew out.

Justin shrugged. "Sebastian and his brother Matteus took me kickboxing at a gym. Matteus is a cop." Justin actually looked just as impressed with Matteus as he was already with Sebastian.

"Justin told me he had fun," Emma added. She stood up, her stuffed bear tucked tight in her arms. "Sebastian is teaching him card tricks."

Dylan bent over to kiss her forehead. "I want Justin to tell me."

Justin shrugged again. "I want to go back and do it again. I like kickboxing."

Dylan did see he was more relaxed, more open. "I'm sure we can arrange something."

"Did you know Lola has five brothers? I think that's too many," Emma said with wide-eyed amazement.

"Did you tell Miss Grace how you feel?"

"No, of course not. That would be rude. You told me to mind my manners."

"Miss Grace knew what she was doing," Dylan said.

"I guess. Mr. Torres says if I learned to cook, he might let me work in the restaurant."

"Do you want to be a chef?"

"Maybe," Emma said. "I think it would be fun to be a mermaid." She thought for a moment. "Or Elsa with magic to make ice cream."

"Those are really good goals."

"You can't be a mermaid. They aren't real and neither is magic, so you can't be Elsa," Justin said nastily.

"You keep practicing card tricks. That's magic. Sebastian said so."

Dylan could see they were gearing up for a huge argument. He held up a hand to forestall them. "Before we get to the yelling part, both of you get your showers and into your pajamas. It's almost past your bedtime."

Emma glared at her brother who glared right back. "Stop being mean to me."

Justin ran down the hall and Emma followed.

At times, Dylan wanted to tear out his hair. He couldn't remember if he and his brother had argued over stupid stuff like this.

He'd had some of the best times in his life with his brother. Even after they'd grown up and taken such radically different paths, they'd been close because they'd only had each other. And his sister-in-law had encouraged their closeness. How could Dylan help Emma and Justin develop the same thing? He didn't know. He needed to talk to the therapist, or maybe Grace would have a suggestion.

The front doorbell rang. Dylan ran down the stairs and opened the door to find Wally holding out a brown bag. "I brought the beer and pretzels."

"What are you doing here so late?"

"I had the sense you needed a little man time." Wally brushed past him.

From the second-floor landing, Emma called down. "Hi, Uncle Wally."

"Hey, kid," Wally said, walking down the hall to the family room.

"It's late," said Dylan.

"We used to stay up all night, jamming and talking, and the next morning drive two hundred miles to our next gig." Wally held out the beer enticingly.

"We were sixteen," Dylan said with a smile. He never could resist Wally, the practical joker of the group.

"That was only ten years ago."

"A lot has changed in ten years," Dylan led the way to the kitchen. He took the beer, removed two cans and put the rest in the refrigerator. He opened the package of pretzels and dumped them in a large bowl. "Let me get the kids to bed, and then I'll talk with you and we'll have a beer."

"We'll drink them all until one of us passes out," Wally said.

"That's going to be you, by yourself."

"I'm fine with that." Wally took a can from Dylan and hunkered down on the sofa. "I'll wait here for you."

After getting the kids to bed, Dylan settled down in his favorite chair. Wally was on his second can of beer and half the pretzels were gone. "What brings you here so late on a Sunday night?"

"Your love life."

"What's wrong with my love life?" Dylan asked with a sigh.

"It's shameful. That woman has you tied up in knots."

"Lola is…"

"You like Lola," Wally said. "What's the problem?"

"There's no problem." Even to himself, Dylan sounded defensive.

"I think there is," Wally replied. "I think you're falling in love with her and you have found the one."

"How do you know?"

"Sam had the same look on his face when he found Elise." Wally took a long sip of beer and shoved the pretzel bowl at Dylan. "These are good. Have some."

Dylan took a handful. He didn't want the beer or the pretzels; he definitely didn't want to be psychoanalyzed by Wally, whose idea of therapy was the perfect practical joke on some unsuspecting friend.

Lola had come to mean something to him. He liked her. He respected her talent. She was fun to be with and was good with Emma and Justin. The children liked

her. She'd made it clear, however, that she wanted a professional relationship, even after they'd made love. He had to respect that.

They needed to finish the music for the movie and then he'd think about where to go next. This experiment with Lola had him thinking about the direction Calamity could go in. He wanted to get back to writing music for them.

He hadn't said anything to his friends, but the lifestyle had been growing stale for him. Getting what he wanted when he wanted it wasn't attractive to him anymore. He wanted to be more than just a rock star, but he didn't really know what that was. With the children in his life, he had more going on outside the music business. He liked taking them to school in the mornings. He even enjoyed packing their lunches, helping with homework and talking to their teachers. He also enjoyed volunteering at the school.

Taking time off was allowing him to step back and figure out what he needed. What Calamity needed.

"You are really enjoying being a dad, aren't you?" Wally asked.

Dylan nodded. When Sam had embraced domesticity, Ben, Wally and Dylan had laughed at him.

Sam hadn't cared. He loved his wife, his children and his life, despite the occasional schizophrenic aspect of it. He kept his home life private and completely separate from his professional life. He still rocked as hard as they had when they were first starting out and, unless they were tour, he quit at five o'clock and went home to have dinner with his family.

"What are you feeling?" Wally asked. "I think you're considering a future with her."

"What's not to like? She's funny. She understands my life and doesn't seem intimidated by it." Or at least that was the impression he had. "She knows who she is and what she wants." Dylan admired that her focus on her professional life was so targeted. He understood she was building her career. He had been just as laser-focused, but now he felt he could relax enough to try something categorically different in his career.

Was he thinking about a future with her? Maybe. She was the first woman he'd ever pursued. "We've got a thing. I don't know where it's going."

"You have a thing!" Wally said after a long sip of his beer. "I can't think of any time you've had a 'thing' with a woman, so I'm putting this in the category of seriouser."

"That's not a word," Dylan said.

"It is today." Wally levered himself to his feet. "I've got to get home."

"No, you don't. You've had a couple of beers. Guest bedroom or Uber, your choice."

Wally grinned. "I love how you take care of me. I don't like strangers driving me around unless necessary. I'll take the guest bedroom. Will you tuck me in?"

"Sure. You want to hear a story, too? I have *Goodnight Moon*."

Wally laughed. "That was my favorite when I was five."

Dylan didn't doubt it. He'd met Wally's parents and if he would allow it, his mother would still be reading him stories and tucking him in at night. "I know. Your mom told me."

Wally gave him a pained look. "I'll tuck myself in." He headed to the stairs. "Good night, moon."

"Good night, Wally." Dylan watched his friend head upstairs to bed.

He sat for a while longer thinking about Lola. Sam was happy in his relationship. Dylan wanted that for himself, amazingly enough. Until he'd had to take care of the kids, until he'd met Lola, he hadn't thought much about settling down. He'd thought about his band, his music, having fun. Now he wanted more.

"I don't like this tune," Lola said, shaking her head. Dylan hadn't captured the point of the movie's critical moment. After their weekend, going back to work on a rainy Monday seemed anticlimactic.

"What about the tune don't you like?" Dylan asked.

"This is the dark moment in the movie when the hunters return and put the pack in jeopardy and right now everything isn't going to be okay. The tune needs more doubt, more anger, more fear. This is a big moment. Little Wolf is fighting for the future of his pack and his love." She hit the keyboard hard. "This is the edge the producers want. Dark and somber and filled with desperation." Kind of like how she felt at the moment. Not the desperation, though, just the dark and somber. She played the music again, adding a deeper bass to twist it into something almost malevolent.

Dylan paced back and forth across the studio. She watched him. He'd been acting mad all morning and she knew their weekend in New York still gnawed at him. She thought he'd understood her feelings.

"Are you angry with me?" she asked.

"Why would I be mad at you?" He stopped pacing to glare at her.

Because, she thought, *you're acting like a five-year-old who didn't get what he wanted and is taking his resentment out on me.*

"Do we have time for this? I thought we worked it out on the plane." She knew they'd make no progress on work until they addressed this.

"We didn't work anything out on the plane."

"You agreed to keep things on a professional level." She wanted to pound the keyboard in frustration. She felt the pull toward him, but she fought it. He should fight it, too. For both their sakes. There was too much riding on this job.

"I don't want to keep things on a professional level." His voice was now soft and serious, and he stared at her as if she'd wounded him.

She looked away and tried a different tack. "What do we have in common besides music?"

"We have this…" He came over to her and kissed her, his lips soft and moist on hers.

Dylan pulled Lola to him and then planted a kiss on the soft skin of her neck. "You have the most beautiful skin." He ran his fingers down her arm, soft as silk.

"You think I'm going to be swayed by compliments."

"You're not that easy." He ran his tongue up to her ear and gently bit the lobe.

Her body shivered in his arms. "Glad you think so."

"I do."

"Then why are you trying to seduce me after my big we-can't-do-this speech?"

His hand strayed to her small perky breast. "I like to test my limits."

She bit her bottom lip and he was a goner. Her brown eyes told him everything he needed to know. She wanted him. The desire rising in him should have frightened him, but it didn't. It felt right with her. She got him in a way no other woman had. He was a man not a rock god. With her he could just be Dylan. He hadn't thought normal could ever feel sexy. But it did with her. Hell, he was comfortable with her. Safe. She didn't want anything but him. He let out a breath.

"What?" she asked, drawing back slightly.

"You know what I like best about you?"

She grinned. "My sparkling personality and hot body."

"Well, yeah, but that's the frosting." He teased her with a series of light kisses along her jawline.

"What's the cake?"

"You are yourself with me. And I can be me with you."

"Not what I expected to hear."

His gut twisted. "Wrong thing?" In some ways, she was hard to read.

"Not at all." She pressed herself against him. "Perfect."

"I am, aren't I?"

She chuckled, her throat vibrating against his lips.

His body was so ready for her. The thought that this amazingly marvelous woman wanted him for who he was humbled him.

God, he wanted her. "Tell me you really don't want me."

Lola blew out a long breath. "I…don't…"

He palmed her cheek. "Ego taking a nosedive." He loved that she kept said ego in check. She was hot.

"You'll survive," she whispered.

"Only if you help me."

"Exactly what kind of help do you need?"

Dylan jiggled his eyebrows. "That kind." Shivers ran down his spine and a pleasant ache settled in his groin. He kissed her neck. He licked the hollow of her throat, inhaling her delicate scent.

Lola ran her hands through his hair, balling it in her fists.

God, he loved that. He nibbled the tender spot where her shoulder connected with her neck. A sigh escaped his lips. "Lola, you are magic."

She giggled, then pulled out of his embrace and pulled her shirt over her head and tossed it over her shoulder. "You win." She shimmied out of her jeans. She stood before him naked.

"Yay me." He quickly undressed. Before he dropped his pants, he dug a condom out of his wallet. She grabbed the packet from his fingers and pushed him down on the chair. She ripped it open and put it on him, each tiny gesture of her fingers sending him spiraling into intense desire.

Well, okay, he thought. "Are you in a hurry?"

She glanced at the clock over the fireplace mantel. "The kids will be home in about two hours. We have time."

He grabbed her around the waist and pulled her down on top of him. She straddled him in the chair and the heat of her skin burned him. Slowly he eased a finger inside her. She moaned. Taking his time he pumped inside, getting her ready for him. The velvet texture of her skin consumed him. He moved with a languid pace and her head lolled back.

Her whole body trembled as she leaned toward him, and he fondled her breast. Her nipples beaded to hard points and he leaned in and took one in his mouth. God, she tasted so delicious.

Her lips parted. "You are so good." She fit her body closer to him, molding against his.

"I aim to please." He leaned over and kissed her again. "You feel wonderful." He slid two fingers deeper inside her and her muscles contracted under his touch.

"Now." She adjusted her frame and his fingers slipped out of her and then she raised her body and lowered herself on him. For a second he thought he might explode. Slowly she moved over him taking him all the way inside her.

He could feel her orgasm building. Spurred by the intense sensation, he grabbed her hips and moved her over him.

A low moan escaped her mouth. She was almost there. Thrusting her hips up, she took him all the way inside her. His body rushed towards that peak. Her muscles clenched around him. He looked up and her back arched.

"Yeah!" she said, breathlessly.

He lifted his head and slammed her hips over him. He couldn't breathe. She was almost over the edge. He pushed his hips up and buried himself inside her, pumping hard.

She spasmed and he let go inside of her.

Chapter 12

The phone rang. Lola opened one eye, wondering who was calling. Dylan reached for the phone from his position on the sofa, her body draped over his. Sometime later, they moved to the comfort of the living room sofa.

"Dylan Ward," he said. As he listened he sat up straight, gently moving Lola out of the way, and the drowsy, sexy look in his eyes faded. "I'll be right there."

Lola straightened. "What?"

"Get dressed. That was the school. Justin was in a fight." They both pulled on their clothes in a rush.

"I'll drive," Lola said as they ran toward the door.

"I can drive."

"No, you're upset. You need to find your Zen, or I'm going to have to stop by the ATM and get bail money."

She unlocked her SUV and stood with her hands on her hips, daring him to challenge her.

He shrugged and got in her car. She turned on the engine and started driving.

It seemed to take forever, but they finally pulled into the school lot and headed for the office. There, several busy women worked while Justin sat on a bench with one arm around Emma. Emma was crying.

"Uncle Dylan," Justin yelled. He jumped to his feet. "He hit Emma. That bully hit Emma."

Emma looked up and Lola saw a bruise on her cheek. Dylan's mouth tightened and his eyes narrowed.

A man appeared from the office beyond the waiting area. "Mr. Ward, I'm Donald Moss, the assistant principal," he said. He gestured into his office. "Please, if you would? Mrs. Collier is at a conference today."

"I'll be right back," Dylan said to Justin and Emma.

"I'll stay with them," Lola said.

"I want you to come with me so I maintain my Zen."

"I'm fine, Uncle Dylan," Emma said.

"We're watching them," one of the clerks said.

Lola followed Dylan into the office.

Another man and woman already waited in the room. Amelia Jarvis stood next to a man Lola assumed was her husband. He glared at Dylan, a belligerent expression on his face.

Amelia jumped to her feet. "Zachary has a chipped tooth. Your nephew punched him and he fell."

Donald Moss held up his hands. "Mrs. Jarvis—"

The woman went on ignoring him. "I want your nephew kicked out of this school."

"Mr. Travis witnessed the whole thing and I have his statement, Mrs. Jarvis."

"I don't care what some teacher says. My son is a good kid," Philip said angrily.

"Mr. and Mrs. Jarvis, I have several witnesses to what happened. Two of the playground monitors also saw the altercation and I'm afraid Zachary was the instigator. He grabbed Emma Ward, shook her and slapped her in the face. Her brother rescued her."

"I don't believe it," Amelia snarled.

"Zachary is on suspension," Donald said firmly.

Philip Jarvis glared at Dylan. "I'm going to sue you."

"No, you're not," Dylan said calmly. "I know enough about bullies to know that experts believe this behavior tends to start at home. If you want to have your family under scrutiny, then I look forward to the depositions."

Philip growled, "I'll take this to the media."

"No, you won't. Think of the PR nightmare. Because bullying is a national epidemic. Do you really want the media to focus on this, considering the statement of several credible adults? How is it going to look that your son was bullying some poor little orphaned girl whose older brother had to come to her defense?"

Ouch! Ouch! Lola thought. Dylan was playing hardball and she was proud of him even though she knew he wanted to punch Philip Jarvis in the face. Her parents had always told her meeting violence with violence never solved anything.

Amelia Jarvis raised her chin, a cold look in her eye. "No need to go any further with this. I'll be home-schooling Zachary from now on."

What Zachary needed was therapy along with his parents, Lola thought sadly.

The Jarvises hustled out of the office and Donald turned back to Dylan. "I'm sorry, Mr. Ward, but I'm afraid Justin is going to be suspended as well, for fighting. Ordinarily it's a week's suspension, but I'm going to give him a day considering the circumstances."

Dylan nodded. "I agree. Fighting never solves anything. I'll be taking them both home, then."

The assistant principal nodded.

Dylan strode out of the office. Lola could see by the stiffness in his shoulders he was still angry but in control. "How am I going to handle this?" he whispered to Lola.

"What does your gut tell you?"

"He took care of business. Took care of his sister. I can't be angry about that."

"I understand, but you already said fighting doesn't solve anything."

"But it did," Dylan said. "Fighting got Zachary off his back and out of his life."

"Did it solve his problem? Yes. But it didn't solve the underlying problem. Justin is angry. He feels he has no control over his life."

"Then I need to have a long talk with him." Dylan nodded at the children still sitting on the bench. He gestured for them to come and he headed to the counter to sign them out of school.

"Uncle Dylan is angry, isn't he?" Justin said in a small voice to Lola.

"Not with you, sweetie," Lola reassured him. Emma slid her hand into Lola's. "Let's go home."

Justin tried to slink up the stairs, but Dylan stopped him. "We need to talk." He glanced at Lola, who nodded.

She smiled down at Emma. "Let's go to the studio. I want to play a song for you. I want you to tell me if you like it or not."

Emma grinned and, holding Lola's hand, went out the French doors with her to the studio.

Justin stood on the bottom stair glaring at Dylan.

Dylan studied his nephew. "Come on, let's get a snack." He went into the kitchen. He gestured for Justin to sit at the table. While he washed two apples, then cored and sliced them, he used the time to think about how to approach Justin. This talk had been a long time coming and he didn't want to make the situation worse. He poured a glass of milk and set it in front of Justin. Then he opened a jar of Nutella and set it on the table. He picked up a slice of apple and dipped it in the Nutella, then took a bite.

Dylan said, "We need to talk about what happened today with Zachary."

Justin's face went up, his eyes angry. "He hit Emma. Nobody hits Emma."

"I'm not mad because you defended your sister. I'm proud you stood up for your sister."

"But I'm still suspended." He crossed his arms, his lips tight.

"Mr. Moss could have suspended you for a week, but he still has to follow the rules."

"I want to go home, back to Portland," Justin said, his tone a touch defiant. "I can live with Grandma and Grandpa."

Dylan knew he couldn't tell Justin that his grandparents didn't want him, didn't want the responsibility of kids again at their age, especially when they were so close to retirement.

"I want you to stay with me."

"I hate it here. I hate school. I hate the other kids. I hate my teacher. I hate that stupid therapist you make me go to."

Dylan took a deep breath. "Do you hate me? Do you hate Emma?"

"No."

"Do you hate Miss Grace, Lola or Sebastian?"

"No," Justin said grudgingly.

"See, there are good things here." Dylan kept his voice soft and neutral. "There are a lot of people who love you. I love you. Emma loves you. Lola likes you a lot and Miss Grace is very fond of you. I don't think Sebastian would teach you card tricks if he didn't like you."

Justin scowled, unconvinced.

Dylan knew that deep down inside the real problem was that Justin missed his parents. Dylan wanted to pull Justin into his arms. "I miss my brother. A lot. I'm angry that he's dead. I'm angry and I'm sad and I don't know how to make it better for all of us."

"How come I don't get to say where I live?" Justin's hands clenched into fists.

"Your dad left me in charge and my job is here. I'm sorry I tore you away from Portland and your friends. I should have found a way to make the move smoother, but I was anxious to get you and Emma settled." At the time, Dylan had considered how the children would respond to the upheaval in their lives. "We're not going back to Portland to live."

Justin looked mutinous. He pushed away and stalked out. At the door he turned and glared at Dylan. "This place sucks." He stomped away, running up the stairs.

Dylan took a deep breath. He reached for a slice of apple, poked it in the Nutella and ate it quickly.

This parenting gig was hard. He felt as though everything he did or didn't do was going to leave a permanent stain on their spirits. He wouldn't know if he did all the right things until they were adults. Parenting had no instant payoff, no way of gauging what was the right or wrong thing to do.

He had to admire Grace Torres. She'd had seven children and all the ones Dylan had met had turned out great. Especially Lola. A part of him was proud. Lola thought he was handling the children well. And Grace seemed to think he was doing an okay job, too. So maybe he was.

Writing music was easy. If the song was good he might get an award or just a large royalty check. If it sucked, the song would die an inglorious death, and he would move on to something else. Parenting, not so much.

Lola returned with Emma.

"There's no milk out in the studio kitchen," Lola said.

"I had a banana," Emma said.

"Milk is good for your bones," Lola said.

Emma giggled. "That's what the cow on TV says."

Lola opened the refrigerator and took out the milk to pour Emma a glass. Emma sat down next to Dylan.

"How do you feel?" Dylan asked his niece.

"I'm okay," Emma said. She took an apple slice, dipped it and munched on it. "Lola gave me ice to put on my cheek."

Her cheek had a clear imprint of a hand.

"I thought you had a banana," Dylan said. He was always surprised at how much food she could put in her tiny body.

"I'm still hungry."

Lola handed her the glass of milk and sat across from Dylan.

"Why did Zachary hit you?" Dylan asked.

"He said he was going to beat up Justin and then me. He was being mean and I told him I was going to tell my teacher on him. He said he didn't like tattletales and I said I didn't like bullies. And then he hit me. He told me he wasn't a bully." Emma drank her milk. "And then Justin hit him."

Dylan rubbed his face. "I don't like fighting."

"Are you punishing Justin for hitting Zachary?" She finished her apple and sat at the table, watching Dylan with her huge blue eyes and bow-shaped mouth.

"No. A day's suspension from school is enough."

Emma glared at him. "That's not fair. Zachary hit me first."

Dylan stared at her. Emma was usually pretty co-operative.

"You're mean." She pushed back from the table, jumped down and walked away, her little body stiff with her sense of injustice. Like Justin she marched up the stairs, and after a moment, he heard her bedroom door slam. And then it slammed again. He rubbed his forehead.

He glanced at Lola. "That did not go well."

Lola shook her head. "No, it didn't. Emma and Justin are mad at you because they think they did the right thing even though they didn't do the wrong thing. I don't know. I don't have children. Not my call. I'm the youngest of seven children. Technically, I'm still the baby." She crunched on an apple slice.

"You are no help."

She smiled at him. "I know."

"What do I do now?"

"I'm pretty sure you're done being musician Dylan for the day. So maybe I should just head home."

He reached across the table and took her hand. "Don't go. You're the only person in this house who likes me right now."

She laughed. "That's because you haven't said anything I don't want to hear." She stood, leaned across the table and kissed him.

"That could still happen."

"Not a chance. You like my body too much."

He couldn't dispute that. He liked her body way too

much and he liked her even more. "Thanks for helping today."

"Thanks for the great sex today." She tickled his ear and started to rinse the dishes and put them in the dishwasher.

"You're welcome. Should I check on them?"

"Right now, they're mad at you, at me, at the world. Let them calm down." She leaned against the counter. "You need to think about what you're going to say to them."

"What should I say?"

"Be honest. While it looks like Zachary is never going to bother them again, the probability is he might."

"His mother is going to homeschool him." He wondered how that was going to work out.

"That's only going to last so long. He'll be back."

Dylan went to her, slid his arms around her and kissed her. She held him tightly. "Everything is going to be just fine."

"Why do I feel like I still have a few hurdles to conquer?" What was next?

"Because that's life. You still have puberty, dating and car insurance ahead of you."

Dylan groaned. "I can't wait."

She laughed, poking him in the chest. "And then there's college, marriage and grandbabies…"

"All I need to do is get through today with my sanity intact. I'll worry about the rest some other time."

She pulled his head forward and planted a kiss on his cheek. "You'll survive. Since you don't want me to leave, why don't we try to get some work done?"

He glanced worriedly at the stairs. "Okay."

* * *

"I need a break," Dylan said an hour later. "I want to check on the children." He stood and stretched. His muscles were cramped from sitting so long. He and Lola had one more song to write and then they could take some time to fine-tune the music.

"They've been pretty quiet." Lola put the keyboard aside and stretched, as well. "Why don't I order a pizza for dinner?" She reached for her phone and started to dial.

Dylan went into the main house and stood for a moment at the bottom of the stairs wondering what to say. He ran a few scenarios through his mind. He was sorry that Justin was so unhappy, but there would be no returning to Portland except for visits.

He knocked on Justin's door. Justin didn't answer. Dylan knocked again. "Justin." Maybe he was in Emma's room. He knocked on Emma's door. Again, no answer. He opened the door. The room was empty. Justin's room was empty, too. Where could they be?

Dylan searched the second floor. Including closets. Nothing.

"Pizza will be here in thirty. What's wrong?" Lola said when he descended the stairs.

"I can't find Justin or Emma."

Lola frowned. "They must be here somewhere. The house isn't that big. I'll check outside."

Fear began to build in him. He searched the rest of the house and the garage. No Justin or Emma. Where could they be? He fought the rising panic.

"They aren't outside," Lola said, closing the patio door behind her.

"They aren't in the house." He felt hollowness in his stomach. For a second he couldn't breathe.

"They wouldn't just leave without telling you, would they?"

"Justin was pretty upset when I told him he wasn't going to live in Portland."

"We need to call my brother Matteus. He'll know what to do, even though he's with Homicide." She pulled her phone out of her pocket.

Dylan's phone rang and he glanced at it. "Your mother is calling me."

Grace sounded calm when he answered. "Are you missing a couple of children?"

"Thank God," Dylan said. "I was just about to call the police." The relief was so great, he almost staggered. "Are they all right?"

"They're fine."

"I'm on my way," he said.

"No. I've had a few runaways in my day and know how to handle it. I'm going to feed them dinner and then we're going to talk. I will bring them home. Just relax."

"Thank you," Dylan said, his relief so profound he could hardly stand.

"Don't worry about it."

"How did they get to you?"

"Taxi. I already took your credit card away from Justin. But you'll have to cancel the plane tickets to Portland. I already confiscated the boarding passes." Dylan didn't even realize his credit card was missing.

How had Justin even gotten ahold of it? What taxi service would pick up unaccompanied children?

"I'm dumbfounded."

"Just be happy Emma insisted on saying goodbye to us. Give me another hour or so and then I'll bring them back."

"I didn't think a taxi would pick up children without an adult."

"A lot of parents use taxis to ferry their kids around here," Grace explained. "And Justin had a note, allegedly written by you, telling the driver it was fine to pick them up and take them to the airport. So he didn't think anything of it."

"Thank you again. How am I going to play this when you get here?"

"Calmly," Grace said. "I'll coach you." She disconnected.

He found Lola wiping her eyes. "They're safe," she said after a moment. Her voice was thick with emotion.

"Your mother has everything in hand." He sat down on a chair. "Do you think she'd take a job as my nanny?"

"Funny, but no."

"I had to give it a shot."

"Our pizza should be here soon. We should sit down, relax and give my mother the time she needs to help them."

"She said I needed to be calm."

"Yes, you do. We're going to work this out."

"Justin hates living here. And I think a tiny part of him hates me." Dylan ran his hand through his hair. He felt hollow and lonely inside.

"Justin is angry with you because it's safe." Lola pushed him down on a stool at the snack bar. The doorbell rang and she went to get the pizza, bringing it back and setting it before them.

"You need to eat something." She bustled about the kitchen, bringing him a plate and a soda. Then she sat next to him and reached for a piece of pizza.

"How do I prevent him from trying again?"

"Let's just wait until my mom gets here," Lola said in a soothing tone. "She has a way of working things out and she would just say you're borrowing trouble until you know more."

An hour later, Grace walked into the house with Sebastian holding Justin's hand and Matteus cradling a sleeping Emma. Lola directed Matteus to Emma's bedroom. After he settled her on the bed, Lola removed her shoes and covered her with a blanket. She didn't want to wake the child by insisting she sleep in pajamas. For tonight, her clothes were fine.

"I've got to be back," Matteus said, kissing his mother on the cheek. Lola gave him a hug. "I'll see myself out." Matteus left the room.

Justin sat on a chair in the living room, looking lost and tired. He held a deck of cards in one hand while he eyed his uncle warily.

Grace sat down on the sofa and Sebastian made his way to the kitchen. Lola showed him the pizza box in the refrigerator and he grinned as he took it out and sat down at the snack bar to eat.

Dylan stood hovering uncertainly.

"Sit down, Dylan," Grace said gently. "We're going to talk, quietly and calmly. Justin, tell your uncle what you told me. And the rules are, Dylan, you have to listen and not interrupt."

Dylan nodded. Lola wondered if she should join Sebastian in the kitchen. This was between Dylan and Justin. But Dylan grabbed her hand and held it tightly.

Justin raised his tired gaze. "You're not fun anymore. It's rules and more rules and less fun."

Grace held up a hand. "All right, Justin, now it's Dylan's turn."

"Seeing you every day instead of a couple of days a year is difficult. Your parents didn't leave me with an instruction book and I'm trying the best way I can. I'm trying to be the person your parents wanted me to be with you. They trusted me to do the right thing and I feel like I've let them and you down."

"Justin," Grace said.

"My mom had lots of rules, too." Justin bowed his head.

Dylan thought there was a compliment there.

"But we still had fun," Justin continued. "You're no fun anymore. I don't think you love us anymore and you don't listen."

Dylan was shaken by his statement. He wanted to object, but Grace held up her hand, giving him a moment to think. He wanted to jump to his own defense.

Grace finally said, "Your turn."

"I do love you. More than anything. You and Emma are all I have left of my brother. And yes, I could be a fun uncle, but I'm not anymore. Now I have to make sure you're safe, that you eat right and do your home-work." How did he make this situation work for them? "I'm sad that I can't be who you want me to be anymore. I miss my brother more than anything, but we can't go back in time and change what happened."

Justin nodded at that.

Grace smiled at Dylan. "Now, both of you need ways of coping. Justin's emotions are out of control. He feels overwhelmed and unloved. And I think your emotions are out of control, too, Dylan. You have them buried so deep inside I don't think you can find them. You take the children to a therapist, but do you go to one?"

Dylan didn't. He shook his head. "I'm a grown man."

"That doesn't mean you don't need help in recog-nizing your own needs." Grace shifted in the chair to address Dylan directly. "You both should find some activity you can do together that's just for the two of you. Something physical. Something that gives you an outlet for your emotions, especially when they over-whelm you."

Justin nodded. "I want to go camping. My dad took me camping."

Dylan smiled. "When I was a kid, he took me camp-ing, too." His parents had bought them the best camp-ing equipment and since Anthony could drive, just gave him the family van and told them to have a good time. And they had. He remembered their nights around the campfire, the sizzle of the burning wood and the taste of their food.

"When can we go camping?" Justin leaned forward looking eager.

"It's a bit cold now."

"Then go camping in Hawaii," Lola put in. "It's not cold there. My sister and I went to Hawaii once for a girls' week and we met people who were camping on the Big Island. They said it was fun. Not that I think camping isn't fun. I just prefer a hotel room with a minibar."

Dylan squeezed her hand, letting her know he wasn't going to subject her to camping. "You and Emma could have a girls' weekend with your mother," Dylan suggested.

"Dylan added thoughtfully after a moment. "How about we go back to Portland for Thanksgiving instead and put off camping until after Christmas. You can visit your school friends." Dylan felt a surge of guilt. He'd recognized when he and Lola needed a break from their routine and whisked her away for a fun weekend in New York, but he hadn't recognized when Justin needed a break. He wondered what kind of quality time he would have to create for Emma. He didn't get the feeling she liked camping.

Justin's face lit up. "Can I call my friends and let them know I'm coming?"

"You can." For the first time, Dylan felt things were looking up. He and Justin were finally coming to an understanding.

"I have some articles I brought with me," Grace said, "on coping skills and I want you both to read them and find a way to incorporate some of those skills into your lives." She stood.

"Thank you, Grace. Justin," Dylan said, "I'll call Grandma and Grandpa and tell them we're coming."

Justin jumped up, looking excited and happy for the first time in a long time. "I can do that."

Justin's mood change buoyed Dylan. This was what he wanted—kids who loved him and were happy. This was why he'd taken the movie project, to be closer to them. At that memory, he spoke again.

"I'll have a very special treat for you soon. You'll get to hear the music Miss Lola and I have been working on for a movie, a movie you'll like. We'll get to see it before anyone else does." He'd make sure of that.

Justin's eyes grew wide.

"Now," Dylan said, trying to keep his voice soft. "It's time for bed. You can get started tomorrow."

Justin ran over to him and hugged Dylan tightly. The boy's arms around his neck made Dylan so happy he felt ecstatic. Justin hadn't hugged him in so long, he hadn't even realized how much he missed it.

"I love you, Justin," Dylan said, patting him awkwardly.

"I love you, too," Justin replied, his voice muffled against Dylan's neck.

After Justin left, Grace handed Dylan a file with the coping articles in it. "Stop keeping your feelings bottled up inside."

"I guess I did turn in to a bit of a dictator."

"Overcompensation. You've been floundering in uncharted territory. And don't sell yourself short. You did a lot of right things, but Justin doesn't understand that. All he knows is that his world has been in upheaval for months and he hasn't been able to cope. And keeping his feelings bottled up didn't help. Most men in your position would have just dumped the children on their grandparents and continued to be the Disneyland uncle or hired nannies to take care of things and gone about their lives. But you didn't. You took on a responsibility that says you care. And that's half the battle." Suddenly, Grace yawned.

"You're exhausted dealing with my family problems."

"I am." Grace had called Sebastian earlier for a ride home and he texted he was waiting in the driveway.

"Thank you for everything." Dylan walked them out and stood at the front door with Grace.

Grace hugged him. "Good night, Dylan. Good night, Lola." Dylan opened the front door to let them out.

Her mother walked down the steps and climbed into Sebastian's car. Dylan wrapped an arm around Lola's shoulders. "This has been the most exhausting day."

"Who knew afternoon sex would lead to evening runaways?" Her voice was light and teasing, but the look in her eyes was solemn. She grabbed her jacket out of the hall closet and draped her purse over her shoulder. "You did good today. I'll see you next Monday."

"Are you sure you don't want to…" She had been his rock for weeks now. He'd come to rely on her and his heart swelled with the depth of his emotion for her.

She didn't let him finish. She held a finger to his lips. "Stop. You need quality alone time with those children."

He kissed her. "I think I love you." He didn't intend to blurt that out, but the words seemed right.

She looked startled, then confused. She drew back

and stared at him. "I—I—" She took several deep breaths, then turned and bolted toward her car.

He leaned against the doorframe. What had he done? He'd just lost some straight-up man cred. Telling her this way was as much a surprise to him as it had been to her. But in that moment, he knew he loved her. Really loved her. But he'd been afraid, so he'd prefaced it with *I think*. Now he'd scared her off.

How could he misplay something so badly?

No. No. No.

How could he do that to her? Just blurt out those words? What was he thinking?

She lay on her bed watching the digital readout on her clock tick away the night. She'd replayed the scene over and over in her mind, unable to sleep. And now at four in the morning she got up and wandered into the kitchen to fix some tea.

Her own feelings were a jumble. He said *I think* not *I do*. What did he mean? The evening had shown her how much she loved his children. And she had to admit, she loved him, too. How could she not? He cared so much for his niece and nephew, and seeing the panic in him when they'd gone missing had made her feelings deepen.

He could have taken the easy way out, but he hadn't. He could have just dropped Emma and Justin off at their grandparents and called it a day.

She turned on her electric kettle to heat water and leaned against the counter, waiting for it to boil. What was she going to do? Part of her wanted to run to her mom for advice, but she was a grown-up. She had to figure this out for herself. Her mother had already helped so much with Justin and Emma.

The water boiled and she poured it into a mug and dropped in a tea bag. While it steeped, she took an apple out of the refrigerator, cored and sliced it into wedges.

She went back into her bedroom and grabbed her phone. She dialed Dylan and he answered immediately. From the clarity in his voice he hadn't been asleep, either.

"How do you love me?" she asked without preamble.

"Is this a trick question?"

"Do you love me like a friend or like a lover or like a she's-good-with-my-kids love?"

He didn't answer right away. "I love you like a woman. I love you like the woman I want to have in my life."

"Okay. Now I know how to proceed. I'll talk to you later." She disconnected.

A second later her phone rang.

"Why did you hang up on me?" Dylan asked.

"I have things to think about."

"Can I help you think about them?"

"You're the reason I have to think about them."

"Is that bad?" He sounded uncertain.

"No."

"Do you love me?"

"Yes, I do. But I have to think about things." She disconnected again.

"Sorry, we're late," Bobby explained. "Traffic was a bear this morning."

"The 10 was a parking lot. Where do all those cars come from?" John said.

"I always want to know where they're going," Lola said, trying to ease the tension.

"We've listened to the whole soundtrack." John sat down and opened his briefcase, pulling out a notebook.

"It's brilliant," Bobby said. "Truly brilliant."

"Thank you," she said. In her head, her thoughts said, *But...* She clasped her hands together to keep them from trembling.

"We have an issue with this one area," John said, tapping his notebook. "We changed a few words here and there."

That is not good, Lola thought. She'd had a producer change some wording on a song she'd written for a commercial in order to give himself a songwriting credit. Fortunately, Lola's agent had objected strenuously enough the man had backed off. If these two thought they could do the same thing, they'd need to reread her contract. Her agent was a smart man and he'd had a provision inserted to prevent such things from happening.

"What were you thinking?" Dylan said, waves of tension coming off him.

Lola could see he didn't like these two men micromanaging him.

"We want you to bump up the tension in the chorus a little bit. Nothing two professionals like you can't

Chapter 13

A week later, Lola and Dylan sat in the producers' conference room. John and Bobby were running late.

"They're making us wait," Dylan complained. "Don't they know we still have work to do?"

"Calm down," Lola said. She'd never seen Dylan so nervous before. "You're freaking me out. We only have one more song to write. We're ahead of schedule."

She had spent the last week thinking about his declaration of love. When the producers asked for a meet this morning, she was happy to go if it meant she didn't have to confront her own feelings just yet, no matter how awkward things were between her and Dylan.

The door opened and Bobby entered, followed a few seconds later by John Milles. Both of them smiled.

handle." John added as he pushed his notebook toward Dylan.

Ego stroke, Lola thought. Dylan stiffened and she put a hand on his arm, trying to tell him to let it go. They signed the paycheck.

"Okay," Lola said, glancing at the notebook with John's notes. He'd written out the chorus and she simply smiled. "How about this instead?" She started to sing.

"Take the pack, fight for your life.
Fight for your life, fight for your life.
Fight for your life, fight for your life."

John grinned at her. "Perfect."

She smiled back. Dylan stared at her. She shook her head slightly. She'd answer his questions later.

"Take the notebook. We made a few more notes, but nothing major."

"Not a problem."

John gathered up his briefcase. "You two did well. I see an Oscar coming your way."

"I hope so," Lola said.

After the two men left, Dylan stood up. "I don't understand."

"What?"

"All you did was add two more fight-for-your-life lines to the chorus and they were happy."

"Yeah," she responded, picking up John's notebook and tucking it in her purse. "Sometimes they don't know what they want and I have to figure it out. I told you, they simply want to be in control. The movie is their project and they're writing me a check. And so far, they've spelled my name right and the checks have always cleared."

"They were satisfied with having one line repeated two more times." Dylan looked so incredulous, Lola had to laugh.

"That's all. Come on, we need to make the adjustment and finish the last song."

"About Monday night…"

She held up her finger. "No. We're not talking about it yet. We need to finish the project and then we'll talk."

"Then let's get this puppy done."

The Magic Castle had been built by a real-estate magnate in 1908 and looked very much like a castle, with turrets and secret passages and a brooding manner as it sat high on a hill overlooking the city.

As they stood in line to check in for Sunday brunch, Justin practically jumped up and down with excitement. For his Halloween costume, he'd chosen to go as Captain America. Emma was Scarlet Witch. Dylan chose to be Thor. Lola was Black Widow. Dylan had to admire her costume. She looked good in black leather. He loved the way her outfit cradled every curve of her body. He could hardly take his eyes off her as she walked into the Magic Castle, and she could feel the sensual heat in his gaze.

He looked good, too, as Thor. His long muscular legs drew a lot of attention from some of the women in line behind them. *Chris Hemsworth, eat your heart out.*

The foyer was small and cramped with a little gift

shop to the right and a row of bookcases to the left that slid aside to let patrons enter. A hostess took their names and noted they were Sebastian's guests, announcing that Sebastian would meet them inside.

Dylan kept giving her sideways looks. She'd refused to answer any of his questions, telling him he just had to wait. The longer she evaded the questioning look in his eyes, the tighter he gripped his hammer, the deeper his tension grew. What game was she playing?

After they checked in, Lola showed Justin where they would enter the club.

"How do we get in?" Justin asked at the closed door.

"Try *open sesame*," she whispered.

He did and the door slid open into the bar.

The Magic Castle was decorated for Halloween with spiderwebs dancing across the ceilings and pumpkins sitting on the bar.

"Where's Sebastian?"

"He'll meet us upstairs." To one side of the room, a man sat at a table demonstrating a card trick to the children gathered around him. He explained what he was doing.

"We completed the job," Dylan said, trying to coax her into talking to him as they walked up the stairs to the dining room.

"I know," she said.

She'd been evasive all morning, putting him off, and he was starting to worry.

"Your whole being-evasive thing is very sexy."

She gave him a saucy grin. "Thank you."

Another bar resided at the top of the stairs to the

right, and to the left were tables set up for dining. The room felt cramped, with families moving back and forth being seated at their tables by a hostess who explained how the buffet worked.

Their hostess led them to a table next to a window overlooking the grounds. A few minutes after they sat down, Sebastian joined them.

"Welcome to the Magic Castle," Sebastian told Justin and Emma.

Justin fidgeted as he sat. He looked at everything. Emma was less excited but still curious. She watched the other children and seemed to be comparing her costume to theirs.

"This is pretty exciting." Dylan had a feeling magic was going to be Justin's outlet. Since an associate membership was offered, Dylan planned to join for Justin's sake.

"I love it here," Lola said.

"It's certainly different," Dylan said.

"I want to learn magic," Justin announced. He'd already worn out the deck of cards Sebastian had given him.

"I can help with that," Sebastian said.

After brunch, they went into a theater for a show, which was thoroughly enjoyable with a number of tricks that were unexplainable. After the show they adjourned to a long hall where a number of magicians had set up tables to display their sleight-of-hand tricks. Photos lined the walls showcasing members. Children crowded around, their faces alight with laughter while adults stood at the back.

Justin was fascinated, but Dylan was on edge. Every

time Lola bumped into him he wondered what she was planning.

Sebastian sat at a table, grinning at Lola. She smiled back, a conspiratorial look on her face.

Sebastian held out his deck to Dylan. "Pick a card."

"But…" He gestured at Justin.

"This one's for you," Sebastian said, his voice mysterious.

Dylan reluctantly took a card. He showed the king of hearts to Justin and Emma.

"Put it back in the deck," Sebastian ordered.

Dylan did as instructed. Sebastian shuffled the deck. He cut the deck. He pulled a card out.

"Is this your card?" Sebastian held up the five of diamonds.

"No," Dylan said.

Sebastian looked surprised. "This has never happened to me before." He glared at the deck of cards and chose another card. "Is this your card?" He held up the seven of clubs.

"No," Dylan said, frowning.

Emma giggled.

Justin looked disappointed. "I thought you knew card tricks."

"I do," Sebastian said. He held up another card.

"No," Dylan said.

"There must be something wrong with this deck," Sebastian said.

"It's broken," Justin said.

Sebastian tapped the deck on the table and held it out to Justin. "Blow on it."

Justin blew. Then Sebastian offered it to Emma to blow on it. She did, a fierce frown on her face.

Sebastian spread the cards across the table facedown and then went back to the first one. Slowly he turned it over. One by one the cards flipped over like dominos. "Look, I see what's wrong."

Instead of cards with familiar suits, a letter on each card spread across the table.

Emma gasped. "Look," she said and started clapping her hands.

Lola loves Dylan. Lola loves Dylan. Over and over again.

Dylan was stunned as he stared at the cards.

"What do you know," Sebastian said in wonder. "I guess there's nothing wrong with this deck, after all." He grinned at Dylan.

Dylan stared at Sebastian and finally Lola.

Dylan grabbed Lola and planted a kiss on her lips. She responded, her body molding to his.

Emma jumped up and down, clapping. "Lola loves Uncle Dylan," she chanted.

"Are you two going to get married?" Justin asked, his eyes narrowing.

Dylan held Lola tightly. "I'm in."

Lola nodded. "Me, too."

"Do you know what this means?" Emma said to Justin. "Grace is going to be our grandma!"

* * * * *

She shoved the towels forward. "I…I…had my shower. The bathroom is free. I brought you extra towels. I didn't…" She stopped herself, distracted by the wide expanse of his chest. She let her gaze travel down his mocha-colored chest to his perfect six-pack abs. *Stop staring*, she ordered herself. But her eyes refused to obey. *Stop staring*, she tried again.

"Thank you." He reached out for the towels and his hand touched hers. She jumped at the electrical charge generated by his touch.

She couldn't seem to let go of the towels. "I… Matteus…"

She was really trying to get out some words that made sense. How could she be so tongue-tied with a man she'd known almost all her life?

Then she noticed he wasn't moving his hand either. Something broke in her, and she knew this was her chance. All the years of longing for him, of loving him, coalesced. She leaned forward and kissed him. Not like the tame kisses he'd offered before, but a woman's kiss filled with years of yearning.

Jackie and Miriam have been writing partners for twenty years, though some days it feels like forever. Jackie is a spontaneous writer and Miriam is the planner. Despite such diverse approaches to writing, they have managed to achieve a balance between their unique styles. Jackie is creative, passionate and dedicated. Miriam is focused, thoughtful and detail-oriented. Jackie loves dogs and thinks she doesn't have enough of them. Miriam loves cats, though currently, she is catless. Between the two of them, they work hard to bring their stories to life.

Books by J.M. Jeffries

Harlequin Kimani Romance

Virgin Seductress
My Only Christmas Wish
California Christmas Dreams
Love Takes All
Love's Wager
Bet on My Heart
Drawing Hearts
Blossoms of Love
Love Tango
Seductive Melody
Capture My Heart

CAPTURE MY HEART

J.M. Jeffries

Jackie:
To Miriam. It is an honor to play at your side.

Miriam:
To Jackie, who keeps me young at heart.

Dear Reader,

Some of our earliest memories are of our favorite toys, which fade away as we age. But every once in a while, you see a LEGO set or a Barbie, and for a moment, you recapture the sweet innocence of childhood. Knowing that the child still lives inside you makes you grateful.

Matteus Torres has forgotten the pleasure of toys and the wonder of love. In his grief for his late wife, he doesn't realize what he's lost. Lennox McCarthy has been designing toys all her life, and she brings that talent to her new toy store. When Matteus enters her life, she has to lead him back to the magic of play.

Best,

J.M. Jeffries

Chapter 1

Lennox McCarthy assembled the last banker's box and started putting her awards, photos and personal items inside. She felt a mixture of elation, excitement and terror. She looked around her office, the walls bare of all her personal mementoes. How did four years break down into a few boxes so easily? Or maybe not so easily.

Carrie Breen perched on the corner of Lennox's desk. "I'm going to miss you."

Lennox smiled at the other woman. Carrie was cute, petite and perky in her own blond-haired, blue-eyed way. She loved weird clothes like the color-splashed overalls she currently wore, and funky accessories like the green feathers in her hair. She'd been Lennox's assistant for the last two years. Lennox had come to rely on her.

"I'm going to miss you, too," Lennox said. "But every once in a while a person needs to shake things up." She added her favorite pen to the box and took another look around, careful to leave nothing behind. She'd spent a lot of happy years in this office. Well, happy until Nate Talbert, the founder of Talbert Toys, had retired. She still missed Nate but hoped he was enjoying his new life in Florida.

She ran a finger along the edge of her drafting table. At one point she had carved her initials into the surface, along with those of the one man she had longed for and loved since she'd been a child: LM loves MT. No one knew this little secret. Except her cousin, Naomi.

"Shaking up your life," Carrie said, "is getting a divorce or being forced to move to Patagonia."

"Patagonia isn't all bad, if you like sheep," Lennox said. She wasn't even certain where it was, but she did have a parka that said Made in Patagonia.

"Yeah," Carrie said with a grimace. "Nature and I don't get along."

"Besides, since Nate retired, it's not as much fun working for Ben and Bernice." In fact, ever since Nate left, leaving his son and daughter-in-law in charge, she'd been planning her own exit strategy. Nate had been a toy visionary. He'd started the company with a knack for knowing just what children wanted in their toys. Probably because, like Lennox, he was just a big kid at heart. He'd trained Lennox in how to develop creative, brain-challenging toys.

"Ben and Bernice," Lennox continued, "are all about the bottom line. They could be selling air fresheners, for all they care." Talbert Toys Company had been Lennox's first big job after graduating with a degree in toy design from Otis College of Art and Design. She'd tested toys for a local toy company as a child, getting to play with a lot of fun toys, and that amazing experience had brought her to this moment in her life. She was ready to strike out on her own.

"Ouch," Carrie replied, "but true."

"You need to start making your escape plans," Lennox said. "I knew when I was dreaming about my Real-Kidz toy line back when I was studying in Germany that the technology wasn't affordable then. But now that the price of 3-D printers has come down, I'm ready to get started." The ability to leave Talbert had been made possible by her grandmother, who had willed her massive Victorian mansion to her. Lennox would never be able to express her appreciation.

"I don't know about the practicality of your idea. It has too many limitations." Carrie studied Lennox, her blue eyes sparkling. The waves of her green feathers moved in sync with her head.

"I'll take that chance," Lennox said. "I'm young enough that failing isn't going to hurt me. I'll pick myself up and start over." She wasn't worried. She knew her RealKidz line would be a brilliant one, allowing children to learn creative play with dolls that reflected their own ethnic backgrounds. She didn't see what limitations Carrie was worried about.

Carrie jumped off the edge of the desk and enveloped Lennox in a tight hug. "Good luck, then."

Lennox took one last look around her office. Her

desk, looking bare and tidier than ever before, seemed forlorn. She would miss Talbert Toys, but she was ready for her own future. Ready for her own toys. Every moment here had been a part of this growth.

She lifted the box in her hands and started out the door, Carrie following her. She walked down the long hall and into the reception area. A crowd of Talbert employees waited for her in the foyer. Everyone murmured goodbye. After a final awkward hug from Ben and Bernice, Lennox was out the door and into the parking lot. She didn't look back.

Two years later

"I don't know, Mom," Lennox said, trying to tamp down the fear in her heart. She hadn't seen Matteus Torres since he'd married Camille. Not long after the wedding, Lennox had left for a year in Germany to study toy design, her heart breaking at losing the man she'd been half in love with almost all of her life.

"Everything will be fine," Dorothy McCarthy said. She checked her makeup in the car mirror on the rear of the sun visor. "Matteus isn't going to bite."

He already had a chunk of her heart. Not seeing him had covered over the hole, but she wasn't sure if seeing him again would rip it open and she'd be that same silly girl whom infatuation had engulfed.

Only her cousin knew how she felt about Matteus. She'd kept that secret tight inside herself. Though she suspected her mother knew, she'd never said anything. "I know that. But he's been practicing law for only six months." Before that, he'd been a homicide detective with the Los Angeles Police Department while taking online classes for his law degree. Once he passed the bar, he quit the department to set up his solo practice. Lennox didn't know why he'd decided on the career change, but she suspected his wife's death from cervical cancer had had some bearing on his decision.

"That doesn't make him a bad lawyer," her mother replied.

Lennox shrugged, not willing to comment. Her mother opened the passenger door. Intense July heat billowed inside the cool interior, along with gas fumes and smog. "But…"

"He's won every case he accepted. His business has grown enough for him to take on a partner. Besides, you need a lawyer. Why not Matteus? He's a family friend and he will fight for you." Dorothy leaned into the car to study Lennox, who sat frozen behind the wheel. "Come on, dear. This is just an informal meeting. The final decision is yours."

Lennox stepped out into the heat, closed the door and locked her Honda CR-V, wishing she could just forget about Ben and his wife and this threat of a lawsuit if she didn't comply with their demands.

Luna el Sol was cool inside. Lennox had so many happy memories of being here, and they all rushed in now. The hostess smiled at them. "It's great to see you again, Mrs. McCarthy, Ms. McCarthy." Lennox returned her smile as she followed her mother and the hostess.

She caught a glimpse of herself in the mirror on one

wall. She looked perfectly professional in her navy pant-suit. Her makeup was flawless and her short-cropped black hair made her neck look long and swanlike. Tiny pearl earrings contrasted with the medium brown of her earlobes, and the gold chain with a tiny teddy-bear pendant hung just above the hollow between her breasts.

Dorothy smiled at the woman. "Chloe, this is my daughter, Lennox."

The hostess gave a radiant smile that somehow still didn't make Lennox feel wanted.

"Hello, Ms. McCarthy. Welcome to Luna el Sol."

"I practically grew up here." Lennox knew she was being childish, but she couldn't help it.

"Oh!" The hostess looked startled. "Then come with me, please." With a toss of her shoulder-length brown hair, she turned and led them into the dining room, through the lunch crowd and into the private section at the back set aside for the Torres family and their friends.

Lennox skirted around a large parrot cage. At one time, Manny Torres had purchased live parrots for the restaurant thinking it would add to the exotic, tropical atmosphere. The parrots had been a disaster—too loud, too messy. One had even taken to using foul language that wasn't fit for children. Manny had given the parrots to the Los Angeles Zoo, along with a hefty donation, and replaced the live ones with stuffed, lifelike parrots he'd bought at the zoo's gift shop.

Lennox paused at the entrance to the private area set aside by a half wall filled with green plants.

Matteus Torres leaned against a sideboard chatting with his mother, who sat at a table with place settings for four. Lennox's breath caught in her throat. *Please let me be able to toss out a coherent sentence.*

He looked so handsome in a dark gray blazer, black-and-red tie and black trousers. He'd kept his hair cut short to his scalp, accentuating his high cheekbones and dark brown eyes. He was thinner than she remembered, and the look in his eyes held a touch of something she decided was sadness, even though Camille had been gone for nearly four years. Suddenly, her heart ached for him. She wanted to hug him tight, kiss away the shadows and make his life better. Lennox gripped her hands into fists and demanded she control herself. The last thing she needed was to make a fool out of herself.

She stumbled, caught herself and plastered what she hoped was a genuine smile on her face.

Grace Torres jumped to her feet at the sight of Dorothy. The two women embraced. In her youth, Lennox's mother had been a backup singer with Grace. Her end goal hadn't been music but money to go back to college and get her degree. Once she'd saved what she'd needed, she'd left the music business behind without ever looking back. Dorothy now taught economics at University of Redlands.

Matteus looked up and grinned at Lennox, his eyes lighting up. "Look at you," Matteus said, taking Lennox's hand. "You're all grown up."

Heat curled through her. After all these years, his touch still electrified her. Not that he'd ever touched her in anything but a friendly manner. He'd placed her in the friend zone a long time ago and she was going to stay there forever.

"And you got older." He frowned. She hit him on the arm. "I didn't say old. I said older."

Grace burst out laughing. "He was an old man when he was three."

Lennox laughed politely. Matteus had always been serious and responsible.

Like Dorothy, Grace Torres was an elegant woman with dark hair swept back from her face and secured with two ornate combs, one over each ear. While Dorothy was small and compact, Grace was tall and slim, despite six pregnancies and seven children. The twins, Daniel and Nicholas, a couple of years older than Lennox, had teased her mercilessly. Nina had been her best friend until Lennox's parents moved back to Redlands after her father had concluded his residency at Ronald Reagan UCLA Medical Center.

Grace embraced Lennox. "Hello, darling. You look fabulous."

Lennox returned Grace's hug. "Thank you. And you still look like you're thirty-five."

Grace, who was beautifully groomed in a cream-colored pantsuit with a purple blouse and a gold chain necklace, kissed Lennox on the cheek. She winked at Dorothy. "Your daughter always did know how to throw out a compliment and make it sound sincere."

"It's a gift," Lennox said, heat spreading across her cheeks, but she had meant it.

"Come." Grace spread her arms toward the table set for four. "Let's eat and then we'll talk."

Matteus held the chair for his mother and then Dorothy, then sat across from Lennox. Lennox couldn't remember a time when she hadn't been in love with him. Seeing him now after so many years left her feeling awkward. She remembered skinning her knee when she was seven and how Matteus had cleaned the scrape and bandaged it. She'd told him, with all the innocence of her childhood, *I'm going to marry you when I grow up.* She remembered that he'd laughed and she'd been angry, not understanding why he didn't know how much she adored him. After that, she found herself holding back from ever saying anything like that to him again, in an effort to protect herself.

Matteus had told her she'd always be too young for him to marry. She had pouted. He was only six years older. Lennox had promised herself she would show him that those six years wouldn't make a difference. Instead, he'd married Camille and broken her heart, and she'd run to Germany to hide and lick her wounds.

"I'm sorry about Camille," she said.

Pain filled his eyes. He nodded but didn't say anything, then looked away from her.

She forced herself not to reach out and touch his hand. She wanted to comfort him, but it would have been too painful for her. "I'm sorry I didn't make the funeral," she continued, "but my boss sent me to China for a month to do some research on their toy-manufacturing companies. Nate had this idea for a toy, but our US facilities didn't have the tech and China did."

"You must have enjoyed being in China." His voice was flat.

"I ate my way through Beijing. If not for all the walking I did, I probably would have come home twenty pounds heavier." Beijing had been a huge culture shock, though most of the people she'd dealt with had been friendly and informative.

"You've done a lot of traveling."

"When I worked for Talbert Toys, yes. Travel was one of the perks of the business. But since I left and opened my toy store, my longest trip has been to Sacramento for a toy convention." Nate had sent her everywhere, telling her how well-rounded she needed to be before she struck out on her own. And when she did finally leave, she had been ready for the change from employee to toy store owner.

A waitress came for their drink order. Grace and Dorothy ordered white wine, while Matteus ordered a Coke and Lennox asked for ice tea.

Food with Grace and her family was always a celebration. After they placed their orders and the meals arrived, Grace talked about what they were eating, telling them the history of each dish, while Dorothy tried a bite of everything. Lennox ate on autopilot while she studied Matteus. He was better looking now than when they'd been children. Though his face was gaunter and his demeanor more mature, he was still her childhood hero. That one dream had sustained her through her childhood—until he'd married Camille and burst her bubble.

He seemed to be studying her now. "I still can't get over you being paid for playing with toys when you were a kid."

"At the time," she responded, "I thought life wouldn't get any better. Until I got to college and started learning how to design my own toys." Knowing now what went into toy design made her admire even more the people behind the toys she'd tested.

"I have to admit I was just a teensy bit jealous."

She grimaced as she stared at him. "You were already an old man when I started. How could you be jealous?"

"I'm only six years older than you."

"That's like dog years for you," Lennox said, challenging his perception of her. Her quick wit was a defense mechanism she had honed around him. Laugh so he couldn't see how much she hurt over his lack of attention.

His eyebrows went up in surprise. "Dog years?"

Grace started to laugh. "Some things never change, Matteus. She still baits you every chance she gets, and you fall right into her trap."

Matteus assessed her for a moment longer and then he laughed, too. "I'm glad you've maintained that sharp, witty sense of humor."

It was her greatest weapon. "Sure you are, Grandpa."

The meal ended with apple pie for dessert. Lennox leaned back in her chair, stuffed and satiated. She'd forgotten how wonderful the food in the Torres family restaurant was. She enjoyed cooking and even pulled out some of Manny's recipes on occasion, but in reality she used her microwave more than her oven.

"So what's the problem?" Matteus finally asked when the plates had been cleared.

"Toys are considered intellectual property," Lennox said. "I left Talbert Toys to open my own toy store and start designing my own toy line. They're suing

me for theft of intellectual property and copyright in-
fringement."

"Explain in more detail," Matteus said. He placed his
elbows on the table and leaned toward her.

Lennox nodded. "My idea was to use photos of a
child and replicate them in a customized doll reflecting their own ethnicity and appearance. I worked out
the idea using 3-D-printer technology. At the time, the
technology wasn't quite there, but it is now. I filed my
patent, copyright and trademark papers, and a couple of
weeks later I received this." She opened her purse and
pulled out the envelope containing the complaint against
her and the summons detailing the lawsuit. "Talbert
Toys is suing me, claiming I worked out the idea during the time I worked for them and so they own it, not
me. They claim I stole the idea from their development
team and they want it back, or they're going to sue me."

"Did you work on it while you worked for them?"
He opened the envelope and read the complaint and
summons quickly. He returned the papers to the envelope, frowning.

She knew he had to ask that question, but it still
hurt. "No. I was studying toy design in Germany when
I started fleshing out the idea, but then the price of an
industrial 3-D printer was beyond anything I could afford. Only recently has the printer finally become ac-
cessible to the point I can afford one and put my line
of RealKidz dolls into production." She'd been in the
process of researching the 3-D printer she wanted when
the paperwork arrived.

"That's the kind of thing that ends up as a collector's item or a treasured family heirloom," Matteus said.

"I love this idea," Grace said. "Can you imagine how great it would be to get a replica doll for every year of your child's life? It would be like watching them grow up over and over again."

"And," Dorothy added, "it would help children develop positive body images instead of trying to look like Barbie or Ken." Dorothy smiled at Lennox. "I always knew my daughter was brilliant."

Lennox felt her face heat in a flush.

"Did you tell anybody?" Matteus asked, frowning.

"I talked to my cousin about my idea, but not in detail, and of course my parents." She wracked her brain. Had she told anyone else besides Naomi? She remembered a distant conversation with her assistant. "And I think I may have mentioned it to my assistant, Carrie, but only in vague terms, and it was my last day at work. I knew what I was contractually obligated to do for the company. I was very careful." Had Nate still run the company, she would have gladly shared the idea with him, but not with his son. Ben had never gotten her best. When she'd realized that, she knew it was time to go out on her own.

"Can you prove your idea predated your employment with Talbert Toys?"

She rubbed her temple. "I have all my old notebooks, graded tests and class papers somewhere, and can get authentication from some of my professors. Also, paper and ink deteriorate in specific ways that can be dated quite accurately. I just don't know where my stuff might be." She'd even written a second paper on her idea while she'd been in Germany. Professor Schröder had been impressed. They'd kept in touch through the years and had even talked from time to time after she'd left Berlin.

Dorothy patted her daughter's hand. "I've been thinking about that. I have a vague memory of your grandmother taking your boxes to store in her attic when I was redecorating the house. Your grandmother said there was lots of room."

"The attic?" She felt herself grimace. "That is where all things McCarthy go to die." She'd been in the attic recently and it had been stuffed to the rafters. It would take weeks to go through what was up there. And that was after her grandmother had already sold off in her antique store most of the relics stored there. "I guess I know what I'll be doing for the next several weeks."

"Or months. Naomi will help," Dorothy said.

"Thank you for volunteering her."

"And I will, too," Matteus said with a decisive nod. "These things move pretty slowly. We should have time to locate them."

"How much is this going to cost me?" She could see the money she'd saved for the 3-D printer flying out the window.

He smiled at her. "I'm prepared to give you the family discount."

She sighed, hoping that she didn't swoon. "And that is…?"

He reached out and took her hand, his fingers warm. "Pro bono."

She stared at him in astonishment, hoping she

wouldn't cry. Finally, a little ray of sunshine. "Really? Free?"

He nodded. "I'm doing okay despite being in practice for only a year. I can afford to work pro bono once in a while."

"I was so surprised when Mom said you'd quit the police force and opened your new law office. But now, I appreciate you hanging up your badge. I don't know what to say, other than thank you."

He smiled at her. "I'm going to need more info and time to do some research, but I have to get back to the office for an appointment now. How about I come out to Redlands on Saturday, and we'll go into more detail and I'll explain more on how a lawsuit works?"

Lennox found herself nodding. "That works for me. Or I could come to you if you need me to."

"No. I'm curious about your toy store. I want to see what you're playing with these days." Matteus leaned over, kissed his mother and gave a departing wave to the table as he stood up.

Lennox watched him stride out of the restaurant, starkly aware of how attractive he'd become. Her heart pounded so loud she thought her mother could hear it. She wiped her damp palm on her pants, still feeling the heat of his touch.

Later in the car, heading back to Redlands, her mother casually said, "I haven't seen Matteus in years. He's certainly turned into a very good-looking man."

"He's always been good-looking," Lennox said, her tone wistful as she merged onto the East 10 freeway toward Redlands. She'd thought she'd long gotten over her childhood crush, but seeing him again after so many years brought all her feelings back to the surface.

"You still have a crush on him, don't you?" Dorothy said.

She was so busted. And really embarrassed. "No! I was a child." She sounded a little too forceful, and the white lie lay heavy on her tongue.

Her mother didn't answer right away. Instead she studied the passing traffic, her fingers drumming on her thigh. "If you say so."

Yes, she did say so. She may have to spend time with him, but she was not going to revisit those old feelings. She was a grown woman now and in charge of her life—and her heart.

Matteus knelt on the ground in front of Camille's headstone, although it was more of a flat plaque flush with the earth to make grounds maintenance easier. The late afternoon heat was tempered by a faint breeze. Forest Lawn in Covina Hills was a peaceful place, with its rolling lawns and spreading trees. In the distance, the East 10 freeway was a parking lot with cars practically at a standstill. An accident had brought traffic to a stop as emergency vehicles used the shoulder to get to where they needed to be.

He enjoyed just sitting in this secluded spot. He brushed leaves away and placed the bouquet of tulips— her favorite flower—across the flat surface of the stone. Then he trimmed the grass away from the edges of the stone with the gardening shears he'd brought. He'd chosen this spot for her because of the magnificent view of the mountains. She'd loved mountain climbing and camping. When he'd first met the sophisticated, self-assured woman, he had no idea that she loved being outside. Once he'd discovered that part of her personality, he'd been even more enchanted with her.

She'd been his best friend and confidant. "Sorry I haven't been to visit in a while." Since his law practice had really started to take off, he'd cut down on his visits. At first, he'd visited her almost every week, but now it was once a month or so. The guilt ate at him, because he felt as if he was betraying her and their vows.

He'd met Camille when she'd first joined the LA County District Attorney's office right out of law school. He'd been a witness in a murder trial, and she'd guided him through the whole procedure with patience and humor. She'd been dedicated, smart and beautiful in a way that had taken his breath away. They'd dated for two years, were married for three and he'd been a widower for the last four. Those first five years had been the happiest he'd ever been. He didn't think he'd ever be able to capture that kind of emotion again. Lately he'd been going through the motions, trying to find his way.

"I met someone today," he said. "Or I guess not really met. More like reunited with someone. I know you don't remember Lennox McCarthy. She was at our wedding. She had a crush on me when she was a kid, and boy did she grow up into a beautiful woman."

He thought about Lennox and felt a little guilty at the attraction he felt for her, with her large amber brown eyes flecked with gold, attractive face and slender body. She was much taller than he remembered. Even though she'd attended his wedding, he had almost no memory of her from that day. His attention had been wholly on his bride. He remembered the way Camille had glowed with happiness and how proud he'd been to have found her.

"I used to be jealous of Lennox. She was a toy tester as a kid and always had these neat toys to play with that I wanted. And now she owns a toy store and is developing a line of dolls." He thought about Lennox's dolls and her plans. More than anything, he wanted to help her.

Camille's grave was on a small slope overlooking the grounds. A black hearse trailed by three limos and a half-dozen cars followed a lane that twisted and turned toward a huge white canopy covering an open grave. The line of cars stopped and mourners poured out toward the canopy. The rear of the hearse swung open, and pallbearers pulled a casket out and carried it to the grave.

"Lennox came to me for assistance," he said. "I'm going to help her."

A faint breeze touched his face. He imagined Camille sat next to him listening quietly, the wind blowing through her hair. He'd held on fiercely to his memories of her, but even as he sat here next to her grave, her image dimmed in his mind.

"I always thought of her as so self-sufficient and a lot of fun. Coming to me for help was really brave of her. And she doesn't seem to have lost her sense of fun, though she's turned out to be a really smart businesswoman."

After he'd gotten back to his office, he'd done some

research on her. And on the toy company she'd worked for. Her name had been linked to some very popular toys that had made a lot of money for the owners. She'd won a number of awards, and a profile on her in a trade publication had been very admiring.

"She's scared," he told Camille. "She hides it well, but I can tell." Years of being a cop had taught him to read people. Lennox was pretending to be composed, funny and grown-up, but underneath he'd caught a few glimpses of the frightened little girl inside. That being said, he could tell she was a fighter. And he would have her back.

He and Camille had dreamed of starting their family when the diagnosis of stage-four cervical cancer had come. Camille had faced her illness with strength and fortitude, even though he'd seen her fear beneath her bravado. His precious Camille. How had he made it this far without her? He had no idea.

Practically overnight, he'd gone from happiness to despair. Even though he'd tried to hide it from her, she'd known. She'd quietly made her own arrangements, planned her own funeral and made sure her will and life-insurance policy were up to date. And once she was gone, he'd pretended to be strong in public, but privately he'd cried in the shower. He still missed her, but distance made the ache less sharp. But somehow it magnified the guilt. He couldn't win.

He pushed himself back to his knees to finish tidying up the grave. "She's really pretty. I've barely even looked at a pretty woman since you left me. It feels strange." As if he were being unfaithful to her. That ate at the hole in his heart.

A mower sounded behind him. He pushed himself to his feet, brushing bits of grass off him. "I have to go. I'll be back. I promise."

He saw that the cars from the funeral had left and only a small clump of people were still gathered under the white canopy. He imagined that even at this distance, he could feel their grief.

Chapter 2

Naomi Martin, Lennox's cousin, used a box cutter
to open a shipping box. She stood in front of the cash/
wrap counter while Lennox stood behind it, her laptop
open while adding the action figures from the box to
inventory.

Naomi's mother and Lennox's mother had been sisters. Her parents had died in a car accident when she
was thirteen and she'd come to live with Lennox and her
family. They'd been inseparable from that time onward,
even though Lennox was three years older.

Naomi was small and petite like her mother. Her hair
was a mess of tight curls that framed a heart-shaped
face and dark brown eyes.

"This one is empty," Naomi said. She flattened the
box and went over to retrieve another one.

While Naomi opened the next container, Lennox checked her inbox. She'd sent Professor Schröder an email about the lawsuit, but he hadn't responded yet. Professor Schröder had encouraged her to open the toy store and be her own boss. He happily shopped for European toys for her that weren't for sale in the US and was always sending her little surprises in the mail.

Lennox found it hard to concentrate. Seeing Matteus after so long had shaken her. Her thoughts kept drifting to him when she should have been concentrating on her inventory.

"So how did it go? Seeing Matteus after all this time?" Naomi checked the contents against the packing slip, then handed the sheet of paper to Lennox.

"Awkward," she half sang, then added in a normal voice, "in the extreme."

"He is going to represent you, though, isn't he?" Naomi closed the box and set it aside before picking up another one. Once everything was logged in, they would arrange the displays.

"Yes. Though I still have to find those notebooks. Mom thinks they're in the attic here."

Naomi shuddered. "I've been in the attic. Be afraid. If your notebooks are there, you'll spend weeks trying to find them."

Lennox sighed. She loved her cousin, but if anyone could go to the bad place from zero to sixty, it was her. "Thanks for the moral support."

"I gotta be honest. Tie a string to yourself so I can find the body."

Lennox rolled her eyes. She was just going to ignore

her. "I thought I'd tackle the attic after we close today. Maybe I'll just see them stacked neatly in sight and all will be well again." Or maybe not.

Her grandmother had been a bit of a packrat, so Lennox had been avoiding the attic. Not because of the work involved, but because of the memories. Lennox had spent many happy hours puttering in the attic with her grandmother, looking for things to sell in the antique store. Her grandmother decided what she wanted and Lennox's job had been to clean the item, and if she could carry it, take it down to the storefront.

Naomi laughed. "Good luck with that. I'll keep my phone on."

"Mom volunteered you to help me." Lennox smiled.

"Thanks, Auntie," she muttered.

The attic took up the entire third floor of the old Victorian house that had been built by Lennox's great-grandfather. Her grandmother had operated an antique store on the first floor. The second floor had been divided into two apartments. When her grandmother had been alive, she'd lived in one and rented the other. Currently, Naomi lived in that one while she finished her PhD in business administration, and Lennox lived in her grandmother's apartment.

Instead of an antique store now, the first floor had been repurposed into a toy store. Toys were now neatly displayed on counters, displays and along the walls, replacing dusty antiques in the rooms. Overhead, a Lionel train chugged its way through holes in the walls on tracks attached to the ceiling with brackets. The track wound around and through all the rooms.

The first floor was separated into two parts, with a large hallway going from front to back. Two heavy wood doors with oval etched-glass cutouts opened into the store from a covered veranda that wrapped around the whole house. A large curving staircase, with a privacy rope stretched across it, sat behind the cash/wrap counter and split into two sections at a landing midway up—one section going to Naomi's apartment and the other to Lennox's. A large stained-glass window overlooked the landing. When the evening sun shone through it, all the colors of the glass sparkled on the wood floor.

Lennox had positioned the cash/wrap counter a dozen feet in front of the staircase facing the front doors. Arched doorways led to the various downstairs rooms. Each room had a different theme. One showcased dolls; another was action figures tied to popular movies or TV shows. A third room was the book room, where every Saturday Lennox held story hour and invited mothers with their small children to attend.

On the other side of the hall arched doorways led to the train room, the science room and the plushy room, filled floor to ceiling with stuffed animals. Small alcoves throughout the rooms carried their own theme. Lennox was especially proud of the European toy room designed to provide a very different type of toy for children to enjoy, and which her old professor in Germany helped stock for her. Professor Schröder had retired several years ago, and searching for unique toys for her European alcove gave him something to do with his time.

"If you don't see me in three days," Lennox said with a wry smile, "avenge my death and sell my things."

Naomi saluted with a turtle figurine in one hand. "Aye, aye, Monty Python," she laughed.

Lennox joined in while she entered items into her inventory. They went through two more boxes.

"I can't believe after all the years you worked for them, Ben and Bernice would do this to you."

"For Nate, toys were a passion." Nate Talbert had started the toy business as a young man. When he decided to retire, he sold the business to his son and daughter-in-law. "For Ben and his wife, the business is nothing more than a paycheck. Once Nate retired, I didn't care much for working for Ben and Bernice, which made it easy to move on." And take all her future toy ideas, when she had them, with her. "I never regretted making money for Nate. About a month after Ben took over he shared his vision of what he thought the company should be. I didn't agree. He wanted cheap toys made in China that wouldn't last and I knew I couldn't stay anymore." Nate had always used American companies because he believed in quality.

Nate Talbert had been the heart and soul of Talbert Toys. Nate understood the way toys should work in promoting creative play. Ben was just interested in the bottom line. The first thing they'd done, once Nate retired, was stop all the charity work the company had sponsored. No more Christmas toy drives, no more toys for hospitals and no more giveaways to disaster victims or homeless children. Lennox had thought to object but kept her feelings to herself.

Lennox had been the first toy designer to leave, followed by two more. In the last two years, Ben and Bernice hadn't been able to keep a decent designer on staff for longer than five or six months. A half a dozen times, Lennox had been tempted to pick up a phone and call Nate, who'd moved to Florida with his wife, and let him know what was happening to his beloved toy company. Yet she didn't want to go there, so she let it drop and worked on her own toy dreams.

Lennox was grateful to Nate for giving her a job and taking the time to help her understand the function toys had in today's society. She'd thrived under his tutelage. But once he'd left, she'd been anxious to get started on the next chapter of her own life. One that didn't include Ben and Bernice and their greed.

The front door opened and Virginia Anderson, known as Virgie, bustled into the store. Virgie, who owned a combination bakery and cafe next door, had been Lennox's grandmother's best friend.

Small and wizened with pale, white skin, fading blue eyes and wispy gray hair framing a round face, Virgie was all alone in the world. Her husband was dead and they'd had no children. Lennox's grandmother had specifically asked Lennox to keep an eye on her old friend, and Lennox took her task seriously.

"I brought fried chicken," Virgie said. She perched a large plastic sack, filled with several Styrofoam containers, on the counter.

Virgie was an old-fashioned cook. Like Lennox, Virgie lived over her store, even though she probably spent more time with Lennox or Naomi than on her own.

"My stomach is doing the happy dance," Naomi cried. She reached for a container, but Virgie slapped her hand.

"I'll lock up, Naomi," Lennox said. "You and Virgie go on up and get dinner ready."

Lennox waited until they were upstairs before she went to the front doors and securely locked them. Other businesses were closing up for the night, as well. The angled parking spaces in front of the stores were mostly empty. The street was treelined and anchored with a church on one corner and a jewelry store on the other. Across the street was another church and a couple more storefronts, with an art gallery in between a pizzeria and an apparel store.

She set the alarm, put the day's money in the floor safe, turned off the lights and headed up to her apartment.

Naomi was setting the table while Virgie ladled gravy over the mashed potatoes and put the bowl on the table.

"Everything smells delicious," Lennox said to Virgie.

They sat at the table and started to eat.

"Tell me what's happening," Virgie said.

"So far, I've hired a lawyer. You might remember him. Matteus Torres. He came to my parents' twenty-fifth anniversary party."

Virgie closed her eyes. "I don't remember him specifically, but I do remember Grace and Manny Torres. The show-business people. They were nice, for show-business people."

Lennox had to stop herself from rolling her eyes.

Virgie made show-business people out to be like they carried the plague or something equally distasteful.

"How many show-business people do you know?" Naomi asked.

"I've been around, child. I've met my share."

Of that Lennox was sure, she thought as she interrupted. "Matteus is their oldest son and he's now a lawyer, and hopefully he and I will get this lawsuit straightened out." She took a bite of her chicken. The taste was divine. Virgie knew her way around a kitchen, that was for sure. "My mother thinks my old school notebooks are in the attic."

"Goodness," Virgie said, "you'll be searching for years in there. I loved your grandmother like she was my own sister, but she had a tiny bit of a hoarding problem."

"Maybe," Naomi said. "I do know a person could get lost up there and never be found again."

"I'm not sure where to begin," Lennox said. She took another bite of her chicken and her eyes nearly rolled back in her head. Virgie's bakery and café was the most popular eatery in town for a reason.

Virgie took a deep breath. "I have a friend whose son works for the US Geological Survey team. He could map it for you."

Naomi laughed. "You're funny, Virgie."

But seriously, that might not be a bad idea. "After dinner, I'm going to go up and take a peek." Lennox had to start somewhere. "When I was six, Grandma let me play in the attic and I found a cheval glass and thought it was the magic mirror from *Snow White*." The mirror now stood in her bedroom, and every time she looked at it, she was reminded of her grandmother.

"You'll find what you need," Virgie said firmly. "And you will be vindicated."

"I sincerely hope so," Lennox said.

"Take up plenty of cleaning supplies," Virgie added. "I don't think the attic has been thoroughly cleaned in years. The dust bunnies are probably breeding."

Lennox shuddered. It wouldn't be just dust bunnies up there. She'd have to take bug spray with her, too.

After Virgie left and the kitchen was clean, Lennox and Naomi stood in the hall outside Lennox's apartment. A door at the end of the hall opened to the staircase leading to the attic. She turned on the light in the narrow staircase. As they climbed, their footsteps thudded on the bare wood treads.

"It's dusty up here," Naomi said with a sneeze. She flipped on an overhead light and turned around in a circle. "Virgie is right. We're going to have to clean before we can really do anything."

The attic was packed with boxes, sheet-covered furniture and more boxes. Lennox looked around, feeling helpless in the face of her enormous task. She opened a box to find photo albums inside. Most of the photos were of her father when he'd been a child. He'd been a darn cute kid. She paged through the album, finding a photo of her grandfather in his army uniform standing with her grandmother. Her grandmother carried a bouquet of flowers. The caption said Wedding Day, 1944.

"Look what I found," Naomi said, excitement in her voice. She carried a huge box over and set it on a vanity table covered in a flowered sheet. She opened it and pulled out a doll wrapped in tissue paper. She unwrapped the doll and held it up for Lennox's perusal. "Madame Alexander dolls. I wonder where Grandma got these."

"You know we're going to get lost in every box we open," Lennox said, taking the doll and smoothing out her lavender velvet dress. The doll was a little dirty but in excellent shape. "We'll take this box downstairs. Someone might be interested in them."

"There are no labels on any of these boxes," Naomi said with a sweeping gesture of her hand.

"Grandma always knew where everything was." Their grandmother had had a terrific memory and her own way of organizing that Lennox had never figured out.

"Maybe we should hold a séance and ask her. Invite Lady Rowena from down the street. She's a mystic. She told me once that her people were Gypsies from Romania."

Lennox said with a chuckle, "Yeah, via Houston."

Naomi and Virgie giggled.

"It's good you can laugh in the face of your Waterloo," Naomi said.

Lennox sighed as she looked around. Waterloo would have been cake compared to this. "We've been here for five minutes and I'm overwhelmed."

Naomi waved her hands in the air. "I'm giving you permission to be overwhelmed, but once the five minutes are up, then you do what you have to do."

Lennox punched her cousin's arm. "Let me have my moment of self-pity. I've earned it."

Naomi laughed. "If we're going to search this attic, we're going to have to be more organized, along with a couple of bottles of wine."

"I like how you think." Tears gathered in her eyes. "This is going to be very emotional."

"Grams was a grand old girl, and I still miss her." Naomi closed the box of Madame Alexander dolls and set it by the door to the stairs. "Come on. We can't do anything tonight. Let's go have that glass of wine and figure out how we're going to attack this."

"Like we're the angry, barbarian horde." Lennox turned off the light, a mental list of supplies growing in her head.

"I'll get out my *Game of Thrones* cosplay outfit."

She loved Naomi. Her cousin had a sense of fun similar to her own.

Matteus parked his car in front of Lennox's store the next morning. He had a contract for her to sign and a few questions to ask.

The old Victorian home was beautiful. It had been lovingly cared for. He remembered coming once with his mother—he couldn't remember what she'd purchased from Lennox's grandmother, but he had enjoyed exploring the store, which took up the whole of the first floor.

A sign on the door said Open. Underneath were the daily hours. He noted the store was closed on Sundays. Another sign announced the current day's events. Saturday was story hour. He pulled open the heavy wood door and walked inside.

The store was packed with children and adults. The children laughed and yelled while tired-looking mothers tried to keep them in line. A harried Lennox stood behind the cash/wrap counter ringing up a sale.

He stood to the side, observing her. She dealt with each customer in an efficient yet friendly manner. The children were allowed to choose a piece of candy from a large fishbowl she had on the counter, and the mothers were given a smile. She glanced up at him, gave him a quick smile, as well, and then motioned to the next person in line.

While he waited, he explored the store, wandering from room to room. The Lionel train roaring on its track just above his head was a nice touch. The track wound through and around each room. One room even had a miniature village on the platform with the train.

Lennox had the store organized into themes. One room contained dolls and stuffed animals. Various alcoves, packed with toys, were especially enticing. He loved the small room devoted to European toys.

"I like your place," he said when the store finally emptied out except for a few adults wandering through the rooms.

"Thank you. Sorry it was so busy when you arrived. We have story hour on Saturday and more children came today than usual," Lennox explained.

He grinned at her. "I've always sort of imagined you surrounded by toys."

"A toy store isn't a stretch of the imagination, is it?

I'm never going to be the mysterious woman in the shadows."

"Not being mysterious isn't a bad thing," he said.

"Good, I don't want to be mysterious. Can I be known for my sense of fun?" she asked.

He chuckled. "I have a contract for you to sign and a few questions to ask."

"Let's go upstairs to my apartment." She picked up her phone and sent a text. A few moments later, a young woman came to the front of the store. "This is my cousin, Naomi Martin. Naomi, can you watch the store for a while?"

"Sure." Naomi took up Lennox's position behind the register.

Lennox led the way to a sweeping staircase with a red cord blocking it off. A printed Private sign dangled from the cord. Matteus followed her up the stairs to the second floor. She opened the door to an apartment and ushered him in.

Her apartment was larger than he thought it would be. The living-room-kitchen combo was neat and tidy. Dark brown leather furniture lined the walls in the living room, along with a bookcase that separated it from the kitchen and dining table. The kitchen was a long counter against the back wall. A small corridor led to an open door showing a bathroom wedged in between two closed doors he figured were bedrooms.

She'd decorated in muted sand tones, except for a large piece of abstract art on the wall behind the sofa, which was an explosion of color.

In the kitchen, she added water to an electric kettle and switched it on. "Tea? Coffee?"

"Tea would be great," Matteus answered. He sat down at the kitchen table and opened his briefcase. He removed a file folder and withdrew the contract he'd drawn up. He pretended to study the contract while watching her out of the corner of his eye. Yes, she had definitely grown up and was more beautiful now than he remembered. An unexpected rush of desire filled him.

The water boiled. She set a mug with a tea bag in front of him and then added a plate of cookies.

"What's the contract?"

"It's basically a contract for hire." He handed a stack of papers to her with little adhesive arrows showing her where to sign.

"Full disclosure?" she asked, pointing at a clause. "Of what? Do you really want to know what's in my refrigerator?"

"Only if I'm going to be using your home as my office."

She laughed. He loved the sound of her laughter, full and deep. "*Mi* casa, *su* office."

"*Oficina*," he said.

"What?"

"*Oficina* is Spanish for *office*."

"You're bilingual. I'm impressed."

"I speak Portuguese, Spanish and American English. Though I'm not fluent in Portuguese and Spanish. But I know enough to get around." His parents had given him a trip to Brazil as a college-graduation present.

He'd discovered that no matter how much he thought he knew, he didn't know enough.

"I speak American English, British English and German."

"German?" That wasn't really much of a surprise. He knew she'd gone to Germany for another year of study in toy engineering.

"German is the language of toys. Germans are great toy makers."

"Yep, you already told me."

She bit her bottom lip. "I'm nervous. I feel my whole life, my reputation, is at stake here." She took a cookie and bit into it. "Full disclosure of what, exactly?"

Did she have any idea how sexy she looked right now? He doubted it. The Lennox he knew wasn't a seductress. What you saw was what you got. "I'm going to need to know everything about your toy design, and this stipulation is for my own protection. If a client keeps a piece of information secret and it comes out later and influences their case in a negative way, I'm held harmless from future retaliation from a client because I didn't have all the tools I needed to work the case properly."

"I can understand that," Lennox said thoughtfully.

He tried to reassure her. "You're going to win this. You'll be vindicated and move on with your life."

She sighed. "Am I dumb to ask why me? Why Ben and Bernice would do this to me?"

"No, you're not dumb. I will say, though, that people will do heinous things in their pursuit of money. They lie, cheat, steal and murder because for some people, enough is never enough." As if he didn't know. As a cop, he'd seen a lot of humanity's cruelty to one another. He saw it as a lawyer, too, but not the brutal parts.

"Toys are supposed to make people happy." She read the contract. "Can I keep this for a couple of days to study? I don't like just signing something without understanding it. I'll drop it off at your office. I have to be in LA on Monday."

"Go right ahead," Matteus said. "Take as much time as you want. If your parents have a lawyer, you should have him take a look at it."

"Her."

"Excuse me?" he said, a little confused.

"My parents' lawyer is a her."

He grinned. "Why didn't you go to her?"

"She's recovering from surgery. I wanted to get my ducks in a row right away." She shrugged.

She hadn't hurt his feelings. "I'm okay with that."

She smiled, looking relieved. "Do you enjoy being a lawyer?" she asked.

"I do. It's interesting and I don't have to view dead bodies."

She laughed. "What kind of interesting cases do you take on?"

"I don't take every one. I just turned down a case where a man wanted to sue a paint company because after he painted his house, he didn't dispose of his supplies properly. Some rags that he tossed in a pile combusted and burned down half his house."

"That doesn't sound good. What happened?"

"A friend of mine accepted it, but he lost. He claimed the paint company was responsible for the rags bursting into flames and blazing down half the house, even though the paint can had a clearly printed warning that some chemicals were combustible and complete instructions on how to dispose of paint tools properly. And, ironically, one of the things that survived the fire was the paint can, with the warning and instructions still clearly visible."

"Our society is unusually litigious," she said.

"That's for sure," he replied. "People sue over the stupidest things rather than admit their own culpability. So one of my first questions is, do you want to countersue?"

She paused as though thinking about her answer. "I'm mad that they've attacked my integrity when I was nothing but loyal to them all the years I worked there. Nate Talbert started the company and he was fun to work for. If he hadn't retired, I might still be working at Talbert Toys. I might have even given him the RealKidz idea. He was a visionary and understood the power of creative play. He treated his employees fairly. A bestselling toy earned the designer a bonus. And he always gave us Christmas bonuses, too. Ben and Bernice are the Man. I didn't want to work for the Man."

He understood that and he liked her nonconformist spirit. Matteus made notes while she talked. "Do you keep in contact with everyone you worked with?"

"Not really. An occasional lunch date, a wedding or a girls' night once in a while, but not regularly. We've all gone on to our own things."

"Do you know a Roger Baker or an Annette Conklin?"

She tilted her head. "I don't know Roger Baker, but

Annette was the person Ben hired as my replacement. But she lasted only about four or five months. Why are you asking about them?"

"Because Talbert Toys sued them for theft of intellectual property, as well. Like you, Talbert claimed that designs the two of them developed after they left were stolen from Talbert Toys. Roger Baker lost and had to turn over his product. Annette's case was settled out of court." He glanced at his list. "Do you know a Delbert Reed?"

"No," she said with a shake of her head. "Is he being sued, as well?"

"Yes. Along with a Gillian Smith."

"I know Gillian. She worked there the same time I did but left right after Nate retired. She was really smart and innovative. That's a lot of lawsuits over the same issue."

Too many, he thought. "I agree."

Lennox frowned, marring her beautiful face. "What are you saying?"

"Talbert Toys seems to be developing a reputation for claiming other designers' ideas."

"Not Nate," she said firmly.

She defended the old man. That was interesting. He filed that away for later. Matteus checked his notes. "It appears to be after Nate Talbert retired."

"I didn't know Ben was stealing designs."

With her head bent over the table, a pen clutched in one hand, he couldn't stop a stab of desire coursing through him. How had she gotten so beautiful? He remembered her as knobby knees, skinned elbows and the awkward grace of a newborn foal.

"I want to talk to Nate," Matteus said. "Do you have contact information for him?"

"Of course. I'm not sure what the etiquette is when a friend's son is suing you."

"The next step is for me to file an answer to the lawsuit. And then we go into the discovery phase. I'll interview him as part of that."

She glanced at the clock on the wall. "Florida is three hours ahead, so it's midafternoon there. If I remember correctly, Nate and his wife go to some sort of senior meeting at their church on Saturdays."

"I don't need to talk to him today. I'd like to get a feel for him first. Tell me about him."

She gave a soft smile. "He was a tough boss, but he had your back and understood the importance of toys and the need to play. He was farsighted and was always thinking about better toys. He came up with the idea for Magnoblox, and for years it was Talbert's bestselling toy." She stood up, went to the closet and pulled out a container, then opened it. "When I need to think something through I play with them, too." She dumped the brightly colored blocks on the table and started fitting them together. "You can build almost anything with these blocks. They have magnets inside to keep the blocks bonded together."

The blocks were different sizes, shapes and colors, and on the outside looked like the blocks Matteus had played with as a kid.

Within a few minutes, Lennox had built a house

with doors and windows. From another container she pulled out small embellishments. She attached a Christmas wreath to the front door and set an owl on the roof.

"I'm impressed." Matteus's fingers itched to build something himself. She shoved some blocks at him and he found himself putting them together and grinning. In a few minutes, he had a car. "That was fun."

"I thought you would enjoy some time playing."

He always had, but recently he seemed to have forgotten how to play. For a second, he envied her ability to still have innocent fun. "My parents love word games."

Lennox giggled. "I remember that. Scrabble was a contact sport in your home."

Her entire face had lit up, and she looked so young and pretty. He took a moment to catch his breath. "Still is," he said wryly. "And now they have Dirty Scrabble, for date nights."

Lennox laughed. "My parents played Twister after I was sent to bed. That was a different kind of contact sport. As a child, I didn't understand the implications of what they were up to, but I do now. When I finally realized what they were really doing, I was appalled. No child wants to know that their parents had sex, and my parents used Twister as foreplay."

Matteus joined in her laughter, amazed at how comfortable he was with her. "I'm getting hungry. How about we get some lunch?"

"Okay, that sounds wonderful. Let me check with Naomi first to be sure she doesn't have something planned. After story hour, she tends to head to the library. She's working on her PhD in business. If she can stay, there's a terrific family-owned restaurant down the street. Naomi and I eat there a lot."

Matteus stood. "Sounds good."

They walked back down to the first floor. "We're thinking about getting some lunch. Can you stay a bit longer?"

"Sure, no problem," Naomi said with a wave of her hand.

"Do you want me to bring something back for you from Nellie's?"

Naomi finished ringing up a customer and paused to think. "Chicken-salad sandwich."

"Got it," Lennox said.

Matteus pushed open the front door and they stepped out into the stiflingly hot July afternoon heat.

Nellie's Restaurant was a pleasantly casual restaurant. The front area was the bakery, with a long narrow case to show the baked goods. As good as Nellie's pies, doughnuts and other confections were, Lennox believed Virgie's were better. A long, narrow hallway with chairs lined against the wall for waiting customers led to the dining room in the back, with doors that opened to a small courtyard behind that. The doors were closed against the heat, but once evening arrived and the air cooled, dinner would be served outside.

Lennox loved Nellie's. Nellie's was a fixture in Redlands, even though Nellie had long since retired and gone to San Diego. Her daughter and granddaughter now ran the restaurant.

"Hey, Lennox," Susan Williams said as she led them to a booth. "I wasn't expecting you today."

"It was a spur-of-the-moment thing," Lennox said.

The dining tables were covered in red-and-white-checked vinyl tablecloths. The decor was all homey little touches of silk plants, flowers and local artists' paintings on the walls.

"What's the special today?" Matteus asked as he slid into the booth.

"Minestrone soup, chicken salad and Cobb salad."

"Thanks."

"Enjoy your meal. Your waitress will be here in a moment."

"So now you're a lawyer," Lennox said when Susan had returned to the front of the restaurant. "I always thought you were suited to be a cop. After all, you always gave Nina and me the third degree." Especially when they were trying to hide what little trouble they got into.

"The third degree comes in handy in law, too. And that's because the two of you together were trouble. And I know my sister was the big plotter."

"We weren't trouble," Lennox objected, "just rambunctious and adventurous. Nina was my best partner in crime. Not that we committed any actual crime— just thought about it." Lennox and Nina were the same age and had been best friends as children. Lennox had even shared some of her toys. Actually, she'd always shared her toys because she knew all her friends wanted to play with them.

"I'm not surprised you invent toys," Matteus said. "You always had a vivid imagination."

Matteus had been a large part of that imagination. She remembered designing her wedding gown when she was eleven. Now, at the grand old age of twenty-nine, she realized that gown would make her look like a snowball. But she still remembered her vivid fantasy of walking down the aisle and seeing Matteus waiting for her at the front of the church. Funny, she hadn't thought about that in years. And there was a twinge of pain to accompany her vision.

A waitress came over and took their order. Lennox asked for the Cobb salad with ice tea and a chicken-salad sandwich to go for her cousin, and Matteus went with the chicken-salad sandwich and coffee.

"Are you dating anyone?" Matteus asked.

"Not anymore," Lennox replied. None of the men she had dated ever measured up to Matteus. She didn't even realize she was comparing them to him until Naomi said something once that made her reevaluate her dating criteria. "I dated one of the cops here in town, but he joined the FBI and was transferred. Before that, I dated a few guys here and there, nothing serious. I haven't really had time for dating since I opened the store and went back to work on my dolls. Getting my store up and running was more important than my love life. What about you?" There. That sounded so much better than "No one could measure up to you."

He shook his head. "No one since Camille passed." A shadow took over his face and Lennox looked away, not wanting to see his private pain. "Tell me about Germany. You must have had a great time there."

"I loved it. The food, the beer and the people were a hoot. I lived with a family that had small children. In return for part-time nanny duties, I didn't have to pay rent. I loved the university. It was a great time." For a while, the pain of losing Matteus to Camille had been dulled. And by the time she returned home, she had so many other interests she'd figured out a way to be happy for Matteus and Camille rather than focusing on her loss.

He frowned. "Germans have a reputation for being stoic."

"That's why they were funny. I spent most of my time studying toy design. I almost didn't come home. One of the toy companies there offered me a position, but I was homesick and missed my parents and Naomi. So I came home and accepted the position with Talbert Toys. But I do miss schnitzel and the pretzels. And the beer."

They sat in companionable silence for a few minutes. The waitress brought their lunch.

"Why a lawyer?" she asked after their waitress left again.

"I get to spend a lot of time in a very comfortable chair."

She stared at him. "Did you just tell a joke, Matteus Torres?"

"It's been known to happen," he responded. "I just saw how the legal system screws with people, and I wanted to help them. And I needed a job after I was medically retired."

"You look healthy enough." She eyed him critically.

"Automobile accident. My partner and I were following a suspect. He decided crashing into our car would halt the chase. The car rolled over and my leg was crushed. I still have pins in the ankle. When the department offered me a medical discharge, I decided to take it. Even after three surgeries and a year of physical therapy, I was never going to get the strength back in my leg."

Lennox had heard about the accident but hadn't realized it was so serious. She'd spent so many years trying not to think about him that the habit of shying away from her memories of him became second nature.

"But why a lawyer?" she pressed.

He seemed to be considering her question thoughtfully. "I admired Camille very much. She was dedicated to her job and loved it. At first, I just wanted to honor her memory, but the more I studied and got into it, the more I wanted to show that justice is for everyone, even the underdog—the one person who thinks they'll never win because going up against big corporations is already an intimidating process. That's when I knew civil litigation is where I wanted to be."

She thought about his words, her own admiration for him soaring.

Silence fell between them as they finished their food. The waitress brought their check and set it on the table.

"Even though you invited me," Lennox said, "and I insist on paying my half, is this time considered billable hours?"

Matteus laughed. "No, you're not paying. Lunch is

on me. As for billable hours, it's how you spin it. Office visit, date…"

"Is this a date?"

He looked at her strangely. "Maybe." He shrugged.

For the rest of the afternoon, she found herself wondering how to interpret his statement.

Chapter 3

Lennox spent the rest of the day working, and after the store closed she decided she would spend some time in the attic. Naomi climbed up after her. They'd brought extra flashlights, which they turned on and set on several side tables they'd found beneath dusty clothes. Lennox also brought a vacuum cleaner along with cleaning supplies.

The attic still smelled musty so Naomi opened the windows. Cool evening air slid through the attic while Lennox used a hand vacuum. They worked for a solid hour before Naomi decided she'd had enough cleaning. The attic smelled of pine cleaner. The surfaces they could reach were relatively clean.

"What's this?" Naomi pulled open the doors of a huge armoire and gasped. "Lennox." She sounded excited.

Lennox finished folding a dustcloth and turned. The armoire stood eight feet high and probably six feet wide. Lennox wondered how her grandmother had even gotten it up the narrow stairs. The double doors open wide revealed a line of shoes in clear plastic shoeboxes in a plethora of colors stacked beneath long white boxes. "I doubt my notebooks are in there."

"But there are shoes," Naomi said.

Lennox wasn't surprised. Naomi had never passed by a pair of shoes she didn't lust after.

She joined her cousin at the open doors of the wardrobe. Naomi reached in and pulled out a white box, which she set on a small table. She opened the box to find tissue paper folded over a sheath dress of vibrant purple silk with matching silk fringe and spaghetti straps. "How old do you think this is?"

Lennox eyed the dress critically. Her sense of fashion history was vague, but the dress looked like the height of 1920s style. "I think it's a flapper dress. So the twenties?"

Naomi pulled out a plastic box containing matching suede shoes with little kitten heels. Another box yielded a feather boa and matching hair clip. "I have to try this on." Naomi pulled off her T-shirt and jeans, and seconds later she stood in front of Lennox, posing in the purple dress. It was a bit tight across the bosom but otherwise fit perfectly.

"Wow," Lennox said. She peered into the wardrobe and spied what looked like a photo album. She pulled it out. The velvet cover was a little faded, but the photos inside were of her great-grandmother Ada Lennox

McCarthy. The first photo showed her on the steps of
a church wearing a white sheath dress and lacy veil
and carrying a bouquet of flowers. A beaming man
stood next to her. Lennox's great-grandfather Alexander Baron McCarthy.

Naomi leaned over her shoulder to peer at the book.
"Great-grandma Ada was a beautiful woman."

"Wasn't she?"

Naomi searched through other boxes, pulling one out
and setting it on another table. She opened the lid and
pushed aside the tissue paper to reveal a white dress.
"Here's her wedding dress. You have to try it on."

"No, I don't want to get it dirty. Besides, I think I'm
a lot taller than Ada."

"Don't be silly. We just spent an hour cleaning everything in sight. You'll be fine." Naomi tugged on Lennox's T-shirt. "Did you see the label? This is a Lanvin.
And here are matching shoes and these are... Ferraga-
mos. Who knew?"

Reluctantly, Lennox slipped off her clothes and
Naomi slipped the gown on over her head. The silk
dress slithered down her body, and while the dress was
several inches too short, it looked amazing, with intri-
cate lace insets and a skirt that flared over her hips, the
hem ending just below her calves.

Naomi shoved several boxes away and found a large
mirror leaning against the wall.

"Be careful," Lennox said. "The fabric is fragile."

"You have to see yourself." Naomi pushed Lennox
toward the mirror.

In another box she found a lace veil decorated with

tiny pearls and crystals. She twirled it over Lennox's head and said, "Remember when we wanted to play dress up and Grandma would never let us?"

"At five and eight, we would never have had any respect for these clothes." Lennox fingered the silk. "How Grandmother managed to keep them in such good shape is amazing."

"A skirt belonging to Queen Elizabeth the First is on display at Hampton Court in London and it's in good shape." Naomi stood back and clapped her hands. "When you marry, you have to wear this dress."

"Maybe I should find a man first," Lennox said with a laugh.

"Matteus is back in your life. I don't think he's as unaffected by you as you think," Naomi said. She made a few adjustments to the dress and Lennox couldn't help but see how perfectly the silk hugged her body despite being short.

"No," Lennox said sadly. "I think he's still mourning his wife."

"But it's not like she died yesterday."

"Four years isn't that long. You're projecting, anyway. I don't know if I want to get married. I have a lot on my plate. How can I think about dating when I might lose my business and be in the poorhouse?" Finding love was not at the top of her current bucket list. Surviving the lawsuit was. And Matteus probably thought she was still too young for him. To prove his point, now she was coming to him for help like she was little more than a damsel in distress who needed rescuing. This left her feeling angry.

Naomi shook her head. "Now who's projecting?" Naomi twirled, the purple fringe flying. "I've never known you to be so pessimistic."

"If justice had any say, Talbert wouldn't be suing me."

"We'll find those notebooks," Naomi said. "Just not tonight. Tonight we're playing dress up, and we're leaving the world outside. You've never turned down a play-date…ever."

"You are the best cousin slash best friend a girl could ever have."

"I know," Naomi said, blowing her a kiss. "I'm a multitasker."

Reluctantly, Lennox removed the wedding dress and carefully folded it, replacing it in the box and tucking the tissue paper carefully over it. While Naomi looked through all the boxes and tried on a couple more flapper dresses, Lennox sat cross-legged on the floor looking through the photo album and cataloguing what was in the wardrobe. Knowing what was there might be useful one day.

Even though they were enjoying themselves and Naomi was definitely loving her fashion show, Lennox couldn't help but feel a bit of sadness. She'd let Matteus go when he married Camille. Matteus was all about serious things. He was a serious man. What would he ever see in her, Little Miss Toy Maker? Camille had made the world a better place; Lennox just made it a little more fun.

After looking at a number of locations around the Los Angeles area, Matteus had chosen Pasadena to set up his practice. He already had ties to the area through his brother, Daniel, and his wife, Greer, who designed floats for the annual Rose Parade. And Greer knew pretty much everybody.

After a few months he'd realized he would need a partner and hired Sam Darven. Sam was an ex-cop like Matteus, which was one of Matteus's reasons for hiring him. He also added a dimension to his practice that Matteus liked. Sam specialized in contract law while Matteus was more involved in civil litigation. Like Matteus, he'd been injured on the job and medically retired.

The office was small and on the ground floor in a building that shared space with a bank. The front door opened to a tidy reception area. Behind the front desk, a short hall led to a modest conference room and two offices. Matteus liked the office. He'd even sold his condo in LA and moved to Pasadena to be nearby. After years as a patrol cop and a detective, he was tired of driving.

Sam rapped on the door to his office and then opened it. "You have a visitor."

Matteus looked up from his laptop. "Not a client?"

"Nina," Sam said.

Nina shoved Sam aside and entered. As always, she was dressed like a fashion plate in a silk dress in a subtle rose color.

Matteus stood in surprise. "What brings you here?"

"Just visiting. I needed to get away from Reno for a few days. I'm meeting Lennox for lunch and we decided to meet here since she's dropping off your contract." Nina sat down in a chair, crossing her legs at the knees.

"Where's the baby?" he asked.

"Sometimes the baby needs a break from me. Mom is watching Eleanor Grace."

"As though you'd leave her with anybody else." Matteus opened a small fridge behind his desk and offered her a bottle of water.

"Sometimes I let Scott watch her. Every little girl needs her daddy."

"And where is the baby daddy?" Whenever he saw his niece, he felt an overwhelming emptiness. Camille had wanted children. He wished they'd had at least one so he would still have some part of her.

"He's at a conference making the world a safer place for gambling." Scott Russell's grandmother owned a casino in Reno, and he was head of security.

"That's always a good thing. I wouldn't want to lose my money to just any casino."

"Family never loses in our casino," Nina said haughtily.

Matteus just laughed. "I'll remember that the next time I lose all my pennies on the penny slots."

"Let me write you a check now."

"For five dollars and seventeen cents."

"Oh my goodness, you're such a high roller—and such a cheapskate."

Matteus shrugged. "Like I'm supposed to be ashamed." He didn't find any entertainment value in gambling.

"Considering that you're taking bread out of my baby's mouth, you should be ashamed."

Matteus laughed.

Nina steepled her fingers. "So what can you tell me about this lawsuit that has Lennox tied up in knots?"

"I'm surprised she hasn't told you already. You've known each other since you were children."

"We sort of drifted apart when she left for Germany, and afterward our lives went in very different directions. We kind of stayed in touch but not regularly."

"It's not surprising that your lives became so different."

"I think it had more to do with you than anything else," Nina said.

"What do you mean?" He was going to play dumb on this one. It would be safer.

"You know she's always had a little crush on you."

He knew; he just didn't want to know. "She was a child. I'm six years older than she is." He'd assumed she'd grow out of her crush.

Nina shook her head. "No, you treated her as a child, and she isn't one anymore."

Yeah, that was the problem. And try as he might, he couldn't make himself think of her that way. "She's still too young."

"She's twenty-nine years old, Matteus, and she knows who she is and what she wants. And I wouldn't be surprised if her little crush hasn't gone away."

He didn't need to hear that. He didn't want to hear that. What was he supposed to do with that? "What are you saying?"

"Tread carefully, big brother. Tread very carefully." Nina had a fierce look on her face that reminded him of their mother. The kind of fierce look that seemed to say, "Don't screw up."

He studied his sister, surprised. The fact that she

was warning him gave him pause. "I'll take that under consideration, but I'm not ready to fall into another relationship. I don't think I can." Even though he felt an attraction to Lennox, he knew he would never act on it because that would be disloyal to Camille.

"I think you should leave your options open. Would Camille really expect you to give up your life just because she's not here with you? You can't mourn her forever. At some point you must come back to the land of the living."

Matteus didn't disagree with her. "I simply said I'm not ready. Now drop the subject." He couldn't keep the anger out of his voice.

Nina's eyes narrowed. "I see the intimidator hasn't lost his skills. Just so you know, I'm not intimidated."

He took a breath. "You rarely were," Matteus said with a grin. "You always knew how to fight back with words, which is why I always thought of you as the silver tongue."

She gave him a sly grin. "What a compliment."

"I feel sorry for your daughter and any other children who show up. No one is going to be able to get away with a thing."

"That's because my big ex-Special Forces husband is going to be the softy."

A knock sounded on the door. Matteus called out to enter, and Lennox opened it and walked in. She glanced at Nina and Matteus. "Oh, I'm sensing some tension here."

"Just setting some parameters," Nina replied.

"I don't want to know." Lennox set a large manila envelope on the desk in front of Matteus. "Here's your contract." She turned to Nina. "Are you ready for lunch?"

Nina smiled at her brother. "Do you care to join us?"

"No," he said. He didn't think he'd get out of there alive. "I have another appointment." He stood and walked Nina and Lennox to the reception area.

"That's good, 'cause now we can talk about you," Nina said in her snarky tone.

Matteus poked her arm. "You always were a brat." Nina just laughed. Matteus found himself grinning at Lennox. "You and I are going to need to talk later on this week. Have you started searching for the notebooks?"

"Yes." Her soft, pretty mouth turned down into a frown.

"That doesn't sound encouraging."

"We'd probably have more success finding the Holy Grail." Lennox shook her head. "My grandmother was a hoarder. A neat hoarder but, still, I don't think she threw anything away. When Naomi and I went up to clean, we found my great-grandmother Ada's wedding dress."

"Oh my God, did you try it on?" Nina said with a little clap of her hands and an excited look in her eyes. Nina was all about fashion.

"I did," Lennox said. "Unfortunately, I'm taller than my grandmother, but it still fit beautifully."

"We can fix that," Nina said. "My sister-in-law, Kenzie, knows every fashion designer in the world. Someone will know how to fix the dress."

"Unfortunately, I'm missing an important accessory."

"What? A veil?"

"No," Lennox said, "a groom."

Nina's gaze slid to her brother. "Well, we'll have to work on that."

Matteus was going to kill his sister. Now that she was married, she was in matchmaking mode. He could feel his testosterone ebbing away. When Nina plotted, stuff happened.

She gave him a raised eyebrow and a little finger wave and left Lennox following after her. Lennox glanced back and gave him a small wave, too, and then the door closed.

Matteus sat down A moment later Sam pushed open the door and peered in.

"Pretty lady there, Matteus," he said.

"Nina's married."

"I know that," Sam said with a laugh. "I meant the other one. The toy lady."

"She's just my client," Matteus retorted, annoyed.

Sam grinned at him. "Feeling a bit touchy, aren't we?"

Sam could still get a confession out of a rock. "I'm not being touchy."

"You like her," Sam pressed.

"She's a nice lady in a jam." And that was all he would say. Matteus strolled back to his office.

"I feel like I just want a hot-fudge sundae for lunch," Nina said as she expertly pulled out into traffic.

"Ice cream does have calcium in it," Lennox said. "And dark chocolate is good for your heart."

"Ahh, chocolate. Chocolate is a food group all by itself, and it is good for my heart." Nina tapped her finger on her chin.

She drove a couple of blocks and turned into a parking lot. The restaurant had a faded brick façade, and Dirk's Homestyle Cooking was lettered across the windows. Inside, the dining room was red vinyl, with shiny white floors and heavy brass lamps over the tables.

The waitress seated them and handed them menus.

"I already know what I'm ordering," Nina said, handing the menu back.

"I still need to look," Lennox said.

The waitress took their drink order and said she'd be back in a few minutes.

"I have to admit I'm a little disappointed you didn't bring the baby," Lennox said.

"As if I could pry that baby from her grandmother's arms," Nina said. "My mother is so overjoyed at the prospect of more babies, she's redecorating my old bedroom into a nursery. She's expecting more now that Daniel and Greer and Nicholas and Roxanne are married. And Lola is halfway down the aisle. She wants a Christmas wedding. Our family is going to explode."

"Your mother always wanted lots of family within arm's reach," Lennox said. "Some of my happiest memories from my childhood are when I was with you and your siblings."

Nina nodded. The waitress brought their drinks. They both ordered salads.

"I would think your happiest memories were from your toy-testing days."

Lennox shrugged. "Those testing days were with a

lot of other kids I didn't always know. We didn't interact all the time."

"My brothers were always jealous of some of the toys you got to play with. On Saturday mornings when we watched cartoons, sometimes you'd point at a commercial and tell them all about the toy and how much fun you had or how boring it was actually. If nothing else, you really taught them humility."

Lennox laughed, but then Nina's face turned serious. "So what can you tell me about this lawsuit?"

Lennox took a deep breath. "Talbert Toys is claiming they own the rights to a line of toys I'm just putting into production because I worked on the idea on their time, while I worked for them."

"You didn't, did you?"

"Of course not," Lennox said. "I started working on it when I was an exchange student in Germany. I have the notebooks somewhere, as well as two papers I wrote. I just have to find them. My mother thinks the notebooks are somewhere in my attic."

Nina shuddered. "I remember your grandmother's attic. It's a box jungle."

"A lot less dusty box jungle now. Naomi and I have pretty much cleaned it up. It was almost impossible to be in the attic before without sneezing at all the dust. Now I could spend hours in there just looking through all the stuff and finding treasures."

"I could help," Nina offered.

"Just a moment, but your dress is gorgeous—what designer is it?"

"My favorite—Zac Posen."

"I rest my case. I can't see you cleaning my grandmother's attic in anything without a label." In fact, Lennox couldn't even imagine Nina with a broom in her hands.

"I think I have a pair of jeans from Sears…somewhere in my closet."

Laughter burst from Lennox. "Right. I'll believe you when I see you in them."

"When you get this toy line moving, you're going to need a media specialist."

Lennox tilted her head. "Can you recommend somebody?"

Nina reached across the table and grabbed Lennox's hand. "Don't you dare hire anyone but me."

"I don't know that I can afford you."

"We can talk about rates later."

The waitress brought their salads, and Lennox dug in. The salad greens were crisp and fresh, and the homemade blue-cheese buttermilk dressing had just the right amount of tang to it.

"I'm kind of curious why you hired Matteus to represent you," Nina said.

Lennox played with her lettuce while she framed her answer. "I trust him."

"Are you still in love with him?"

"What!" Lennox dropped her fork. "No. Of course not. I outgrew my crush a long time ago." Even if her feelings had resurfaced now that she was around him again. "Besides, he's still mourning his wife."

"We all miss Camille."

Her friend sounded so sincere and so nice. But Lennox had always thought…

"Really? I never thought you were that fond of Camille."

"I never disliked Camille, but she was so serious. I always felt that Matteus needed someone a little more lively in his life."

"That's not what he wanted," Lennox said. She felt a need to defend him.

Nina studied her. "Carl and I were a lot alike. Being married to him was like being married to me. There are a lot of reasons why our marriage would never have worked, the main one being I was better at being Hollywood than he was. And that caused a lot of friction between us. I guess somewhere down the road I didn't see Matteus and Camille working out. There was no balance in their marriage."

Lennox wondered how it was with her second husband. "Do you have balance with Scott?" Scott Russell seemed to Lennox the perfect match for Nina after the disaster of her first marriage to Carl.

"Oh yes. Scott is perfectly fine with me being the pretty one, even if I am still carrying around a few extra pregnancy pounds."

"But being pretty has nothing to do with weight. You're in the spotlight. People recognize you. Scott may have the ability to save the world, but you're the person people call to smooth over all the bumps."

"Carl never understood that. He was always in competition with me."

"And he didn't like coming in second place," Lennox said.

Nina stared at her wedding ring. "I'm so sorry you missed the wedding. It was great."

Lennox simply laughed. "I'm sorry I had to have my appendix removed at the same time. Want to see my surgical scar?"

"Not a chance," Nina said, holding up her hand. "I've missed you."

"Back at you," Lennox said. "Our lives have gone in such different directions." And those directions were so far apart, Lennox didn't even know if they could find a way back to their old friendship. But she wanted to try.

Nina sighed. "I always thought being around Matteus was painful for you."

She blew out a long breath. She could be honest with her friend. "I didn't mean to let my feelings get in the way of our friendship."

Nina smiled. "Nothing to apologize for. We're reconnecting now."

Lennox took her friend's hand. "And that's what's important."

Chapter 4

"Wow," Sam said as he stepped out of Matteus's car and stared up at the old Victorian house. "What a great place for a toy store. I love houses that have all those nooks and crannies like Victorians do."

"I don't know about nooks and crannies, but there are a lot of alcoves that contain a lot of toys." Lennox's toy store was a wonderland.

Matteus pushed open the door and entered. Naomi puttered around a display while Lennox rang up a customer and bagged a couple of stuffed animals. The customer, a woman with steel-gray hair and pale blue eyes, thanked her, then took the bag and skirted around Matteus to the front door.

"Matteus," Lennox said. "What are you doing here?" She eyed Sam curiously.

He leaned toward her and in a low voice said, "Sam has a secret toy addiction he doesn't want anyone to know about, so we're pretending to visit a client."

Lennox grinned. "Hey, Sam, what are you most interested in? Let me guess." She pressed a finger against her cheek. "*Star Wars.*"

He looked surprised. "No, that's not my thing."

She studied him a moment more. "I know. And I have just the thing for you. Come with me." She took him by the hand and led him toward the back of the store.

Matteus followed, curious to see where Lennox would lead his partner. She pushed through the doll room and into a small alcove then stood back.

"Ta-da." She spread her hands wide. "*Lord of the Rings.*"

Sam just stared.

Lennox put a hand on Matteus's arm and drew him away. "We'll just leave him alone."

Matteus followed her back to the main area. "I have this image of Sam in his office playing with his Gandalf and whispering, 'You shall not pass!'"

Lennox shrugged. "Everyone is allowed their little personal addiction." She stopped to pick a stuffed animal up from the floor and place it back on a display. "So what brings you all the way out here?"

"I wanted to take a look at the attic," he said.

"Goodness," she said. "You don't want to look in there. It's the rabbit warren of death."

"I just want to gauge for myself how long it's going to take you to find these notebooks," he said. "Besides, I spent a lot of time looking for clues in a former life."

She led the way to the stairs up to the second floor, and from there up to the attic. She turned on the lights and stood to the side.

Matteus could see where she had cleaned. The area closest to the door was free of dust. He could also see trails wandering through piles of boxes, furniture covered in dust sheets and more boxes.

"Now you see why it's going to take a bit of time to unearth those notebooks."

"This is a whole lot of chaos." He took a few steps down a small aisle and found a couple of steamer trunks that looked like they went back to the 1930s, with labels of someone's travels on the lids.

"I thought that maybe the notebooks would be in front, but they aren't. My grandmother had her own method of keeping track of things, and I have not been able to figure it out."

He opened a box and found several feather boas nestled in tissue paper. Another box contained a hat with colorful ribbons around the brim. "I know this is really important, but a little part of me feels like I'm going on a treasure hunt without a map."

"Me, too. Though I have to admit, I'm having fun. If time weren't an issue, I'd really enjoy looking through all of this. One of the antique stores in town called me this morning about taking some of the furniture on consignment. At least I'll be able to pare things down up here."

He opened a steamer trunk and found a stack of photo albums. "Wonder what these are." He lifted one out and opened it.

The first photo showed an open field. A second showed a foundation being laid, with workers standing around looking down.

"Look what you found," Lennox said, taking a second album and opening it.

"What am I looking at?" he asked.

"The building of our church. The First Baptist Church of Redlands. Pastor John is going to want to see these." She paged through the albums. "This appears to be a complete history of the building of the church."

"Another treasure unearthed."

She looked around. "We could be lost up here for months, looking at everything and searching for the notebooks."

"I think you're going to need help." He couldn't see how she could find anything up here on her own.

"Are you offering?"

He nodded. "I think my mother might want to help, too. Since my brother, Nick, did a family-genealogy project, she's been very interested in the past."

"How about Sunday?"

"I think it can be arranged. I'll let you know."

Lennox opened another steamer trunk, only to find it empty. "My mother will probably want to help, too." She closed the trunk, turned and stumbled.

Matteus automatically reached out to grab and steady her. She stood in his arms for a moment staring up at him—and before he knew what he was doing, he leaned down and kissed her.

For a second, she stood absolutely still, then her lips

responded to his and she leaned forward, her hands on his shoulders.

She smelled faintly of vanilla and spice. Her lips were soft and yielding. One hand slid around her back. He started to puller her closer when she put a hand on his chest and pushed him away.

"Whoa, whoa, whoa," she said. "What are you doing?"

He stared at her. He had no idea why he had kissed her. "I'm—I'm…sorry." He turned abruptly and raced down the stairs.

Once he reached the ground floor, he found Sam at the counter picking up a bag.

"We have to go," Matteus said.

"Why?"

Matteus grabbed his arm and pulled him toward the door. "We have to go." He opened the door and shoved Sam out into the afternoon sun.

He unlocked his car and ordered Sam in. Once he started the motor, he hesitated. He glanced up at the attic.

Lennox's face was framed in one of the windows, staring down at him, her fingers covering her lips, a dazed look on her face.

"I kissed her," Matteus said. He put the car in gear and backed up.

"So what?" Sam said.

"I liked kissing her, and I'm not sorry," he confessed. And he realized he wasn't, even though he'd apologized to her.

Still, Matteus needed to get away as quickly as he

could. He dropped Sam off at the office and drove back to Forest Lawn. He found himself pacing back and forth across Camille's grave. The hot sun bore down on him. A faint breeze carried the smell of fresh mown grass and the sigh of trees.

Finally, he threw himself down on the ground. "I messed up, Camille. I didn't intend to kiss her. I don't know what happened. I swore I would never cheat on you."

The image of Camille laughing at him came to mind. At the end of her life she'd had so little time left, and he'd tried to make that time meaningful despite her weakening condition. He'd taken her to Griffith Park and they'd parked at a picnic area. Using his brother Daniel's telescope, they'd spent time looking at the night sky and just being with each other. The moment had been peaceful and tender. She'd taken his hand and held it to her heart.

Don't grieve too long for me, Matteus. You still have all your life ahead. There are going to be wonderful moments and you should take advantage of every one of them.

Lennox's kiss had been a wonderful moment, and for the first time since Camille passed, he felt alive again. Every nerve ending tingled with the memory of Lennox in his arms, the scent of her skin, the feel of her lips. How could such a wonderful moment make him feel so guilty?

He already knew the answer to that. Because he allowed the guilt in.

He sat for a long time just looking at the trees and

thinking. He knew deep in his heart he was ready to say goodbye to Camille, and the idea brought such sadness to him he didn't know what to do. So he sat and continued thinking, brushing leaves away from the tombstone with her name engraved on it.

Moving forward was so difficult.

Lennox sat on a stool in front of the snack bar in her apartment while Naomi sifted through food in the refrigerator, bringing out the two steaks she'd brought earlier. She placed two sweet potatoes in the microwave, turned it on and then pulled out a skillet for the steaks.

"Are you going to tell me what's bothering you? You seem a little off." Naomi pulled plates out of a cabinet, along with two wine glasses, and searched for the corkscrew. After finding it and opening the bottle, she poured a glass of wine and set it in front of Lennox.

"I'm fine," Lennox snapped.

"If this is fine, I'd hate to see what bad is." Naomi slapped the skillet on the stove, plopped butter into it, along with a splash of chardonnay, and dropped mushrooms and onions in to sauté.

"He kissed me," she said, her voice faint with the surprise she still felt.

"Not unexpected," Naomi said.

"What do you mean?"

"The two of you have been on eggshells with each other since you first hired him."

Lennox stared at her hands, remembering the feel of his muscles beneath her fingers. "I thought it was just me."

"Aw, cuz, you've got no game. You are easier to read than a picture book."

"I have skills."

"When it comes to making toys." Naomi stirred the sizzling onions and mushrooms for a few moments. The microwave dinged and she checked the sweet potatoes. Satisfied they were done, she placed them on the plate, covering them with foil to keep warm.

Lennox sighed. "You're right."

"How did the kiss feel?"

"Angels sang, the heavens parted and all the calories fell out of my Snickers bar."

"Awesome. Guilt-free chocolate."

Lennox sipped her wine. She was still reeling from the kiss. From the surprise of the kiss. She touched her mouth. It had felt so right. And he didn't once make a comment about the six-year difference in their ages.

"I wasn't expecting a kiss," Lennox mused, more to herself than her cousin.

"Matteus is certainly full of surprises." Naomi spooned the onions and mushrooms onto a plate then added the steaks.

Lennox felt punched in the gut. She'd wanted more than what seemed like a wayward kiss. "Do you think he's getting over his wife's death? Does the kiss signify something?"

"I don't know," Naomi said with a laugh. "I'm not in his head."

"What help are you?"

"I'm here to listen," Naomi replied. She flipped the steaks.

"What am I going to do?"

"What do you want to do?"

"I can't get my hopes up, thinking he's finally seen the adult me and not some brat who used to follow him around."

"I'm pretty sure he not only saw but felt the adult you." She cut into a steak to see how done it was. "Just another couple of minutes." She handed Lennox utensils and then refilled her wineglass. She poured a glass for herself and leaned against the counter, sipping it. "What are you going to do?"

Lennox thought about that. "I don't know. Do I ignore the kiss? Do I acknowledge it? Do I pretend everything is just fine between us?" She didn't know what to think, how to act, how to go forward.

"Maybe you need to consult a relationship therapist."

"Not on your life."

Naomi checked the steaks again, decided they were done, forked them on to plates and smothered them with the onion-mushroom mixture. She added the sweet potato to Lennox's plate and set it in front of her.

Lennox sliced open the potato and added a generous helping of butter and a sprinkle of brown sugar. Realizing she was hungry, she attacked her steak.

"I think you should just go with the flow," Naomi said, sitting down next to Lennox. She leaned her elbows on the snack bar and studied Lennox. "See where this kiss leads. What's the worst that could happen?"

"For me, it was when he married Camille. What happens if he decides I'm still too young for him and finds someone else?" That was her most real, deep-down fear.

Naomi cut into her steak, took a bite and chewed, her face thoughtful. "I don't think that's going to happen. Yeah, life is unpredictable, but I think that kiss meant as much to him as it did to you."

"Then I'm just going to have to wait and see what happens."

"If that's the way you want to play it."

Mired so deeply in her thoughts, she couldn't think of anything else to say.

Every morning when Lennox opened her store the next morning, her first chore was to make a pot of coffee. As the coffee brewed, she unlocked the door and found Nate Talbert sitting on the porch swing.

"Nate!" she said in surprise.

Nate Talbert was a slim, dapper-looking man with white hair framing a tanned face. She knew he was nearing eighty but he looked twenty years younger. His pale blue eyes twinkled at her. He held out his arms and she went to give him a hug.

"Come in," she said, opening the door and gesturing him inside the store.

"What a nice toy store," Nate said. He walked around the entry, taking in every display.

"Thank you," Lennox said. "You didn't come all the way from Florida just to compliment me on my store."

He laughed. "I'm an old man with a lot of time on my hands. I can do what I want. Do I smell coffee?"

Lennox went back to the cash/wrap desk. The coffee was ready. She poured him a mug. She couldn't start her day without at least a whole pot, an addiction she shared with Nate. She handed him the mug and watched as he added cream and sugar. She preferred hers hot and straight.

"Why are you here?" she asked again, more directly this time.

"To apologize for my son's behavior."

Lennox leaned against the counter. She rubbed her forehead. "That has nothing to do with you." The lawsuit had been keeping her awake at night as she fretted over finding her notebooks and proving Talbert Toys didn't own her idea.

"Yeah, it does." Nate sipped his coffee as he walked around the foyer looking at the different displays. Occasionally his hand snaked out to pat a box fondly. "I thought I taught him better."

"I don't blame you. You taught him how to do business, and he chose not to do it that way." She wondered if he knew about the other lawsuits.

Nate frowned. "I still feel responsible."

She could see the conflict on his face. "You shouldn't." She knew he loved his son and didn't envy the position he was stuck in.

"I thought he understood my life's work." Nate picked up a stuffed bear and studied the workmanship before putting it back. "I know he wanted to be a surfer, but I didn't see a future in it. Maybe I'm the one who was wrong and should have just let him do what he wanted."

Lennox shrugged. "He could have been a grown-up and said no. Sometimes, a person has to put on their grown-up pants and make their own decisions."

Nate simply sat down on a stool behind the register and studied Lennox. "I'll talk to him about this silly lawsuit."

Lennox wasn't certain that his son would listen. She had a good idea for her toy line, and Ben wasn't going to let it go anytime soon. He saw dollar signs, and that was one reason she knew her dolls would work. Ben was a businessman first and foremost.

"As soon as I find my notebooks, I can prove I didn't develop the idea while working at Talbert Toys." The idea of digging through the attic again left her feeling breathless. So much work and so little time.

"What can I do to help?"

"Thank you for the offer, but I have a lawyer and I'm going to let him handle this." She felt a moment's suspicion before dismissing it. This was Nate, and she had always trusted him.

"I feel like I owe you something."

"You don't owe me anything. You gave me a job and took a chance on me, and that's all you ever needed to do. This is Big Business 101. I get it." What she really understood was that Ben was trying to intimidate her. Did he think she wouldn't fight for her idea? Did he think she'd just turn everything over to him just to avoid a battle? She may have worked for him, but he never did understand her. "I think you should just go back to Florida and enjoy your retirement. Better yet, go visit Cuba and live your Ernest Hemingway dream."

Nate brightened at that. "You remembered."

"Of course, I remember. Go write a book. Catch a marlin, but stay away from the rum and the cigars."

Nate laughed. "I'm going to do that, but, first, I'm going to stick around here for a while just to see what's going to happen."

"In that case, I think you should talk to my lawyer."

"Matteus Torres," he said. "Didn't I already talk to him?"

She handed him Matteus's business card. "Yes, but he has some follow-up questions."

"I can do that." He pocketed Matteus's card, then reached out and hugged her. "You were always my favorite."

She hugged him back. "How do I use that?"

Nate laughed. "I'll think of something. So—show me around your store. Love that." He pointed at the train currently chugging past. "You know I adore trains."

"I'm delighted to do that," she said. "You can be the engineer."

He grinned and gave a little hoot. She started with the main room and stopped to touch toys and in one instance rearrange a doll display. He stood back after pairing boy doll with a girl doll and tilted the heads together.

"What's going on with your love life?" Nate asked, a sly grin on his face."

"I'm sort of dating this guy named Troy. But, it's serious."

"Sort of dating?" Nate grinned at her. "I've never known you to sort of do anything."

"What are you saying?"

"You know what I'm saying. I've never met anyone as determined as you."

She liked Troy, but compared to Matteus he was

bland. Matteus was exciting and interesting and when she wasn't with him, she wished she was. He made her think about what scared her as well as excited her. She'd always had a crush on him.

She threaded her arm through Nate's and led him through the rest of the store.

Chapter 5

Annette Conklin was a short, curvy brunette with alabaster skin, amber-colored eyes and a heart-shaped face.

"Thank you for coming," Matteus said. He stood and gestured her into his office.

She watched him warily as she sat down. He offered her a bottle of water, but she shook her head. "I don't know why you want to talk to me."

"Talbert Toys sued you, claiming that they owned the rights to a toy because you developed the idea while working for them."

Annette nodded, a bitter look on her face. "I didn't, but I couldn't prove otherwise. They took my idea and I believe have made millions on it."

"Tell me about the idea," Matteus coaxed.

"My little sister was in the hospital and she was

afraid. She was only seven, extremely ill, and I wanted to help. I had the idea of a line of stuffed animals—kittens that purred, puppies that wagged their tails and teddy bears that crooned. I just wanted something that looked happy to help soothe a frightened child. The electronics were easy enough to develop and adjust for different animals. I sat down one day and put my idea on paper. But once I applied for the patent, Ben Talbert was knocking on my door claiming ownership."

"How long did you work for Talbert Toys?"

"Not long. Eight months. I left because my mom needed me to help care for my sister. He seemed to know I had no resources. I didn't know how to fight him."

"Did he intimidate you?"

"Actually, he was very polite to me but also intimidating in a nonthreatening manner. He knew exactly where the line was and how not to cross it. I didn't know what to do. I had a lawyer, but…" her voice trailed away. She sighed. "My sister is seriously ill and since I'm helping with her care." She bowed her head, hiding the sheen of tears in her eyes. "I ended up caving and let Ben have the idea. I figured I could come up with something else. I didn't think I could turn down the five thousand dollars he offered me."

"Ben Talbert offered you five thousand dollars?"

"Yes, but it was contingent on sales and recouping his losses from the research, development, marketing and distribution. According to him, those losses haven't been paid back yet."

Matteus frowned. This woman had gotten hosed. He

wasn't going to make her feel even worse by telling her she should have consulted a lawyer immediately. She could have gone to Legal Aid and had them look over the contract. If nothing else, they could have directed her to someone who did pro bono work.

"And how did he market the toys?"

"First, he put them in hospital gift shops and they were so popular, people were going to hospitals just to buy them. Finally, last month he expanded the line to the big-box toy stores, and they had lines of people waiting to snag one. I felt cheated." Tears gathered in her eyes. She swiped at them with a tissue which she kept balled in hand. "I felt forced to give in, which I did at my sister's expense, and I'm pretty sure I have no recourse. I'll admit, I wasn't thinking clearly. He can delay paying me as long as he wants and my sister is the one who will suffer."

Matteus was angry for this woman. Ben knew how to kick a person when they were down, and he covered his butt by offering the money but tying it up so he could delay as long as he wanted.

"Thank you for coming in. I want to do some more research. Can I call if I have additional questions?"

She didn't look relieved. She gathered up her purse and stood with him. "Are you going after Ben?"

"I am," he replied.

"Then I'll help in any way I can."

He held out his hand and shook hers before escorting her to the door. After Annette left, his receptionist waved at him, letting him know his next appointment had arrived.

Gillian Smith was a long-legged blonde with the looks that Hollywood adored. She was model beautiful, with green eyes and short-cropped hair in a Charlize Theron sort of style. She wore a dark lavender pantsuit that carefully hid the twenty or so extra pounds she carried. He recognized designer-quality clothing, thanks to Nina.

"Hello."

"Mr. Torres," she replied in a low voice tinged with a Southern accent. "Thank you for seeing me."

"I'm pleased you could meet with me." He held out his hand. Her handshake was firm, her palm dry. She gave him a small half smile, not quite revealing a slightly crooked tooth that added to her charm.

"From what I understand," she said as she sat down, "you're looking into improprieties with Talbert Toys."

"You're well-informed."

"Delbert Reed and I worked at Talbert at the same time. We used to talk regularly."

Delbert Reed was another name on his list. "I've been trying to find him." In fact, he'd called every D. Reed he could find in the LA area, and none had been a Delbert. Even the information-gathering sites that claimed to know everything about everyone didn't have any information on him that had been updated within a year.

She sat down and crossed her legs. "I haven't seen him in over a year. One day, he just disappeared. I don't know where he went. He never contacted me again. I assume you're interested in my tenure with Talbert Toys.

I designed educational toys for toddlers while I was there. But I left to strike out on my own."

"And they sued you for…"

"Ben claims I stole an idea that was in development. Which I didn't. My idea for education apps wasn't even on their horizon when I started my own development company. In fact, Ben said there was no money in apps for tablets."

"And you proved them wrong."

She nodded. "The lawyer said Ben had dated reports proving that my most lucrative app was in development before I left. Before even I knew I was going in that direction."

"And…," he coaxed.

"I believe the reports were falsified somehow. I just don't know how." She stared at her hands, mouth twisted with bitterness.

"Then what did you do?"

"I knew I hadn't done anything wrong. I hired a lawyer—I have his name with me—and the next thing I know the lawyer is telling me that Talbert will drop the lawsuit if I turn everything over to them." She paused, looking angry. "I had lost all legal rights to my educational apps. Effectively, they kicked me out of the business and I had to do something new."

"I'm sorry," he said.

"I might have fought harder, but I was going through a pretty nasty divorce." She stopped, her eyes watering. She wiped at her tears. "I just didn't have the energy to fight two different battles."

Anger was etched deeply in her face, but the blow

to her integrity had also caused wary shadows to form over her eyes, and the emotional stress suddenly added a haggard look to her face.

"What do you do now?" Matteus asked.

"I develop video games as an independent contractor."

"You landed on your feet," he said with another scan of her clothes.

"It took me a while, but I'm doing okay now, though I really liked working on apps." She sounded wistful.

Matteus made notes. In the back of his mind, he knew something was off, but he didn't know what. He needed more information. He was going to figure it out.

The banquet room at the Kimberly Crest mansion was large and already half-filled with tables and chairs. A work crew moved noisily about while Lennox stood at one end of the room in front of the long table lined with various baskets, trinkets, boxes and other things. Charity work had long been a family tradition, and this particular charity event was her father's baby. Lennox's job was to put together the baskets for the silent auction that would benefit the children's hospital's new oncology-research wing.

"Can I help?" Matteus asked.

Lennox whirled around. "What are you doing here?"

"I needed to talk to you. Naomi said you were here."

She felt a little lurch in her heart. He looked so handsome that her mouth went dry and her heart thudded so loudly she wondered if he could hear it.

"What do you know about gift baskets?" she asked as she opened a box of hand creams.

"Not much," he said, eyeing the table. "You put stuff in them and raffle them off."

"In California it's called an opportunity drawing," she said with a laugh.

"I know," he replied with a wry grin.

"In this case, the baskets are for a silent auction." Ribbons, bows, tape dispensers and sheets of cellophane littered the table.

"Naomi gave me all the info about the event."

She chuckled. "If you want to help, then start opening those boxes." She pointed at the rows of boxes under the table, then straightened the line of baskets. Even though some big-budget prizes were available, Lennox always added more. She wanted people to feel like they were really getting something, even if that something was only a line of skin lotions from a local store.

"My pleasure."

"Your family has always been very generous," she said, indicating a pile of envelopes. "Your dad threw in dinner at Luna el Sol. I'm planning to bid on that."

"You can eat at the restaurant any time you want," Matteus said.

"But your dad threw in a cooking lesson, too. I've been trying to get his recipe for lamb stew for years."

Matteus smiled. "My dad doesn't generally share his recipes."

"He gave me a couple when I was a kid. The simple ones an eight-year-old could manage."

Matteus laughed. "What else do you have?"

"Nina threw in a weekend at the Mariposa Casino in Reno. Your brother Daniel donated backstage passes to his talk show. Lola and Dylan gave me VIP passes to the red-carpet premiere of *Little Wolf's Journey.*"

"Lola and Dylan worked hard on the musical score for that movie last year."

Lennox was anxious to see it, too.

"You got some good loot," Matteus said.

"I know."

They started filling the baskets, making lists of what was in each.

"I spoke to Annette Conklin and Gillian Smith," Matteus said while they worked.

"What did they have to say?"

"That Ben and his attorney intimidated the hell out of them," Matteus replied.

"That's not surprising. He held it together in front of his staff, but I could always see the cheap, petty tyrant ready to break out."

"I'm not quite sure how to phrase this, so bear with me."

"Just say what you have to say."

"Did you ever have any kind of big emotional drama going on with you?"

"Other than leaving my job and opening my store, not really. Why do you ask?"

He paused and glanced at her. "Maybe this is just a shot in the dark, but Ben seems to be using people's misfortunes against them. Annette Conklin's sister is ill and has been in and out of the hospital for quite a while. Gillian Smith was going through a nasty divorce. They were both emotionally vulnerable."

She studied him. "The moment Nate said he was retiring, I started thinking about my own escape plan. I knew I didn't want to work for Ben."

"Sounds like nobody wanted to."

They went back to filling the baskets. Matteus opened boxes and distributed the various items while Lennox started lists of what was in each basket so buyers knew what they were bidding on.

"I think the only reason the company is still staying afloat is because Ben stole some good ideas," Lennox said.

"He didn't steal anything," Matteus said, "according to the law…"

"Semantics," Lennox said with a wave of her hand. "He stole people's dreams and their genius because he doesn't have any of his own."

Matteus put a hand over hers. "I'm going to fight for you."

She smiled at him, feeling protected. "I'm going to fight for me, too."

"Good," Matteus said. "Because if you don't fight, too, things won't be much fun."

"That man is not taking my work." She thumped the table with her fist.

Her phone rang and she pulled it out of her pocket. "Hey, Troy, what's up?"

Troy Webster was her date for the banquet. They'd been seeing each other off and on for six months. Though lately they were mostly off since he traveled a lot for his job in information technology. "Sorry, Lennox, just letting you know I won't be able to make it tonight. I have to fly back to New York to handle an emergency. I'm on my way to the Ontario airport now."

Lennox sighed, irritated at the cancellation. Now she'd have to either go alone or rustle up a last-minute date. "I'm sorry." Troy was on the banquet committee with her father. She liked him, but nothing had really sparked between them, even though he was a nice man. "Take care, Troy." She had the feeling she wasn't going to hear from him ever again.

She put her phone away and turned to find Matteus watching her.

"Bad news?"

"My plus-one for the banquet just canceled on me."

"A romantic interest?"

She shook her head. "Not really. Just someone who owns a tuxedo and knows how to navigate formal tableware."

"I own a tuxedo."

She studied him. "Are you and your tuxedo free tomorrow night for surf and turf?"

"My tuxedo and I are free tomorrow night."

"Excellent. There will be no smooching and no billable hours."

Matteus burst out laughing. "Deal."

She grinned, held out her hand and he shook it. "Deal."

"Wow," Naomi said with a critical up-and-down look. "You look totally and absolutely fabulous."

Lennox twirled around. Her strapless, floor-length gown was midnight blue lace over a cream silk lining. The gown was fitted to her hips and then flared out to billow about her ankles. She wore a diamond choker with matching earrings, black elbow-length gloves and a sparkly purse shaped like a train engine.

"You're not really going to take that purse, are you?"

"It's a Judith Leiber. Mom gave it to me for my birthday. I've been waiting for the right night to use it." And the charity event was perfect.

"It is just the right amount of playful." Naomi had chosen a dark red, floor-length gown of chiffon and silk. She'd pulled her hair up into a high ponytail that bounced seductively as she walked.

"Mom would never have given me this purse unless she expected me to use it." Sometimes her serious-minded mother surprised her.

"I thought you were planning to avoid Matteus in any situation except business. And then you invite him to be your plus-one!"

"I finally thought with Troy I'd broken the no-date banquet curse and then he called and canceled. So there I was, alone again, for the third year in a row. I could just hear the gossip. 'She's alone again. Can't she find a man?' What can I say? I caved."

She'd caved spectacularly. The words had come out of her mouth before she'd really thought about what she was saying. Yet she was glad she'd asked Matteus. She wanted him to see her grown-up and mature. She wanted to show him that those six years he worried about didn't mean anything anymore.

They'd already shared a kiss. Just the memory made her pulse pound and her breath catch in her throat.

"I'm kind of worried about you," Naomi said.

"I'm showing up at this banquet with a hot guy. I'll play it cool. We'll dance, I may even flirt a little, but I already established the no-touching rule with him."

"After one look at you, he's going to break that rule."

"He's going to have to work really hard, then." She whirled, the skirt flaring out around her.

The front doorbell rang. Naomi flew out of Lennox's apartment. Lennox followed her more sedately down the stairs and through the store. The problem with living on the second floor was that there was no direct access to the apartments.

By the time she walked through the foyer, Naomi was chatting with Matteus and her own date, Craig Hanson, who was a doctor at the children's hospital with Lennox's father.

Matteus stared at Lennox, a startled look in his eyes. He mouthed the word *wow*. Heat flooded through her.

"Thank you," she said with a flirty tilt of her head.

"We'll meet you there," Naomi said, half shoving her date out the door. After one last look at Lennox, she was gone.

"You look spectacular," Matteus said, admiration in his gaze.

"I was going for all grown up."

He nodded. "Mission accomplished." He held out his arm and she tucked her fingers in the curve of his elbow. "Are you ready to go?"

"Give me a moment. I'm channeling my inner princess."

"You look like a queen."

An electric thrill ran through her. "Even better."

With that, he opened the door and escorted her out into the warm night.

Chapter 6

With Lennox on his arm and his heart in his throat, Matteus opened the door to the mansion and led Lennox into the banquet room. A band played on a stage set up at the end of the room, flanked by their electronic equipment and several huge floral arrangements. A dozen couples danced, the men somber in their black tuxes and the women as colorful as exotic birds.

The room, filled with laughter and music, was decorated with white lights along the ceiling and bouquets of flowers on the tables, which had black tablecloths with white plates. People milled around the bars set up in the corners of the room. Half the tables were already occupied, and the baskets of goodies for the silent auction were arranged on a table at the back of the room. A number of people congregated there looking over the offerings.

Matteus tried not to stare at Lennox as she threaded her way through the tables, each one with a number held in place by a silver stand.

She was so beautiful, so graceful and so amazing. She sparkled as she introduced him to people. When they reached their table, he found Naomi already there with her date. He offered to get Lennox a drink and she asked for merlot.

As he waited in line, he felt a touch on his arm. He turned to find Richard McCarthy, Lennox's father, standing behind him. Richard McCarthy was a tall man with graying hair cut close to his skull. His dark brown eyes were set deep and held a slight twinkle. He looked fit despite a softness around his waist.

"Thank you for escorting my daughter," Richard McCarthy said to Matteus.

"You make it sound like a curse."

Richard grinned. "It sort of is. She's always had a date for this, but at the last minute something tends to happen."

"Like what?"

"Last year, her date was quarantined for bird flu. The year before, he was coming in from Fresno and was stopped at the airport because his name was on the no-fly list." Richard wrinkled his brow. "And the year before that, her date came down with the chicken pox."

"That must have hurt. Hopefully the curse isn't retroactive. I do believe I've had all my vaccinations."

Richard chuckled. "How is the lawsuit coming along?"

"Doesn't Lennox keep you in the loop?"

"Lennox doesn't want us to worry, and she is always telling us things are being handled."

"I don't have much to report, but this case has a lot more depth than I thought it would have."

"Is that good or bad?"

"*Interesting* is the word I'd use," Matteus said. *And challenging*, he added silently.

The line moved forward. "What do you think her chances are of winning?"

"It's a crapshoot. If it goes to trial, nine times out of ten the win is awarded to the person with the most likeable lawyer."

"That's ridiculous," Richard said with a frown.

"I'm going to take a moment and guess you've never been sued."

"I don't think there's a doctor in the world who hasn't been sued at least once."

"Except maybe Dr. Seuss."

"A sense of humor," Richard chuckled. "I like it."

"I can't imagine that someone would sue you."

"It's harder with children. Nothing is supposed to go wrong with kids. When I started in pediatric oncology, I was part of a team that discussed each child's treatment very carefully. Most parents understand the nature of cancer and that there's no one way to treat it. And they all hope for the best but prepare for the worst."

"That's got to be hard."

Richard nodded. "Every loss hurts. But every victory gives me the will to go on."

Matteus simply nodded, his thoughts going to Camille and her fight with cancer. He still missed her, but lately those moments were less intense. His gaze flickered to Lennox. She was laughing at something, her head thrown back, her eyes bright with amusement. He remembered when she'd so innocently told him she wanted to marry him and he'd been amused at her seven-year-old naivete. But now, all grown-up, she was so effervescent, so full of life.

Something stirred within him. The child Lennox disappeared, fading into the past, and the current Lennox made him want to come back to life after so many years of just existing.

He came back to himself to find Richard studying him intently, an amused look on his face. "She's beautiful, isn't she?"

"I don't think I realized until this moment how stunning she is."

"I'm her father, so I'm already biased."

He remembered his impulsive kiss and the way she had clung to him. Her mouth had been sweet and soft, her skin like silk.

Richard touched his shoulder. "You're next."

Matteus turned back to the bartender, gave his order and pushed all thoughts of Lennox from his mind.

Lennox perused the baskets she'd put together for the silent auction. People were being generous. She put her name down on a couple, along with her bid.

"Want to dance?" Matteus asked.

She realized her foot was tapping to the beat of the music. "Let's."

He led her to the dance floor. The music was a sedate waltz.

"You dance very well," she said after a few times around the dance floor.

"My mother believed in children being well-rounded and trained for every social contingency." He twirled her, then caught her and dipped her back. She grinned at him.

"Your mother knows best."

Happiness flooded her. This must be how Cinderella felt at Prince Charming's ball. Thankfully, her dress wasn't made out of magic or her shoes made of glass.

"My mother is pretty amazing." He twirled her again.

The music came to an end and they walked back to their table. The feel of his hand at the small of her back gave her an electric thrill. Finally, after so many years, she had Matteus to herself. All her childhood dreams resurfaced. She wanted him to come into her life and to be a part of her future.

Her father stood at the microphone. "If everyone will please take their seats. Dinner is being served."

People flooded back to their tables. Matteus pulled out her chair and helped her get seated. She caught Naomi looking at her curiously. She raised an eyebrow and shrugged.

The wait staff pushed out their carts, and the savory aromas of food filled the air.

"There are a lot of thoughts rolling around in your head," Matteus said in a low voice.

"I always have lots of thoughts in my head. It's a problem."

He grinned at her. "Me, too, sometimes. What are you thinking?"

No way was she about to tell him her real thoughts. "About the dancing, how pretty the room looks, how the silent auction is progressing. Those kinds of things. And the fact that I actually had a date who didn't have to cancel at the last moment."

"Actually, I was your plan B."

"I'm pretty good with my planning." She didn't add how annoyed she'd been at Troy for the last-minute cancellation, but the alternative had worked out just perfectly. She had Matteus. Having a part of her childhood dream come true gave her a lot of satisfaction. When she was younger, she'd used her imagination to go on fantasy dates with Matteus—mostly to the prom.

Not that tonight was a real date. This was a favor. *Funny,* she thought, *your prayers do get answered sometimes.* The jury was still out as to whether it was a good or bad thing.

"I think your planning needs some fine-tuning," Matteus said.

She smiled at him, hoping it didn't look sad. "You might be right, but this broke the curse. I'm going to be grateful."

He laughed.

The sweet sound reached all the way down her spine, thrilling her. *There,* she thought, *let me cover the pain with a little joke.* At least she could make him laugh. That was something.

A waitress set a plate in front of her. Lobster tail, a small filet, buttery green beans and baby carrots decorated the center. The spicy aroma roused her taste buds. Everything looked positively scrumptious.

Chatter in the banquet room stilled as people dug into their food. The band was on a break, so only the sound of silverware against porcelain plates filled the room, along with a few low murmurs.

"This is good," Matteus said, his voice ripe with approval.

"My dad knows how to throw a shindig." Her parents were seated at the head table with the top hospital administrators. This charity event was very important to them, not only for the construction of the new wing but for the new research facilities that were a part of it. It was going to be her father's legacy. She was so proud of him.

After the meal, the speeches began. When they ended, the music started up again. Lennox loved to dance and Matteus was such a good partner she hated for the event to end. At midnight, the winners of the silent auction were announced. She sighed. She hadn't won anything—again. But she did break the date curse, and she was grateful for that.

"Thank you," she said when she stood on her wrap-around veranda fishing for her keys. The road was dark and a streetlight flickered erratically. "I had a wonderful time tonight with you."

He leaned against the railing. "I'm glad I could fill in, although all the jokes about your previous dateless banquets were pretty funny."

"People are probably preparing for the apocalypse," she laughed.

"I'm happy I could be so accommodating."

She leaned against the railing next to him. "I really don't want the night to end."

He was silent for a few moments. "I don't either."

"Would you like to come in for a cup of coffee before your drive back to Pasadena?"

He shook his head. "I don't think that would be a good idea. Besides, I'll be back tomorrow. We're still tackling the attic, aren't we?"

"Yes," she said with a mournful sigh. The idea of rooting through the attic again made her skin itch. "I do have to find those notebooks."

"I need you to find those notebooks, too."

"If I don't find them, what are my chances?"

He thought for a moment. "I think Ben has this down to a science. He knows exactly how to apply emotional pressure, and you're financially vulnerable."

She gripped the railing. "Do you think he's going to try to bribe me?"

"I don't know what his strategy is. I'm meeting with his lawyer next week. But remember, you have me. I'm on your side. I'll protect you."

That gave her a thrill. She had always wanted a white knight. And he was the perfect man to fill out the armor. "And I appreciate your support." She didn't want to fight Ben. She wanted him to go away and leave her alone, let her get on with her life.

They fell silent. A night breeze ruffled the trees around them. A car drove by, twin headlights cutting through the darkness.

She found herself leaning against him. "I thought I

would just go on my way and be happy with my store and my toy line. The thought of losing everything scares me so much, I want to scream."

He slid his arm around her. "Everything is going to turn out fine."

She felt warm, protected. If only she could throw *loved* in there. It would be perfect. "I don't feel like I believe that."

He pulled her to him, his arms sliding around her. "It will." He kissed her. His lips were soft against hers.

Heat flared inside her. She pressed tight against him, her own arms around his neck. All her life she'd dreamed of kissing Matteus, and now it was happening—again. For the second time.

He broke away from her. "I think you better go inside."

"Do you want to come with me?" God, she sounded so needy. All those years of forging her own path and it was lost the second he came back into her life.

He smiled at her. "I don't think so. Though I appreciate the offer. But you are my client…"

Without another word, she turned away from him, crushed. Stalking to the door, she opened it, went inside, then closed and locked it. She leaned against the wall until she heard his footsteps descend the stairs. She slid down the wall to sit on the floor, her gown pooling around her, then covered her face with her hands, trying not to give in to the tears that threatened.

"What's going on?" Naomi skipped down the staircase and across the wood floor to sit next to Lennox.

She wore a skimpy top and boy shorts. The elegant woman of the evening was back to her sensible self.

"This did not go well," Lennox said.

"What didn't go well? You made it to the banquet with a date. The world didn't end."

"I'm talking about afterward," Lennox said, her voice muffled by her hands, which covered her face.

"Did you try to invite him in?"

"I didn't want the moment to end. I had a good time with Matteus. We danced, and I flirted with him. He kissed me, and when I asked him in, he turned me down."

Naomi put an arm around Lennox. "He's your lawyer. I don't think inviting him in was a good idea."

"Why must you be the voice of reason?"

"I drew the short straw this week. Your turn is next month sometime."

Lennox didn't want to laugh, but Naomi always knew how to make her be sensible. She pushed herself to her feet and with Naomi trailing her, she climbed the staircase to her apartment.

"I'm going to fix some hot chocolate." Once they were inside, Naomi went into the kitchen, where she opened cabinet doors and placed two mugs on the counter. "Why don't you get into your jammies? We have a lot to do tomorrow."

Lennox kissed her cousin's cheek. She fought a yawn as she headed into her bedroom and tugged at the zipper of her dress. She didn't know how she was going to survive a whole day in such close quarters with Matteus.

"I'm a grown-up," Lennox said once she rejoined her

cousin in the kitchen, wearing her pajamas. "I should be over him."

Naomi handed her a steaming mug of hot chocolate with little marshmallows floating on the top. "You are more in control of your feelings than you think."

Lennox shook her head. "I don't feel like I am."

"There are a gazillion lawyers you could have called, but you ran to Matteus for help."

"He's a friend," Lennox said.

"You wanted someone to fight for you and you chose Matteus," Naomi said patiently. "Why do you think that is?"

"Are you going to logic me?"

"You're my cousin. I can be honest with you without you being resentful. Can't I?"

Lennox sipped her hot chocolate. "No. I'm resentful that you're forcing me to be honest. I'm resentful that you're right. I'm still going to love you, but I'm still resentful too. At least for an hour."

"I can handle that," Naomi said. "Not much has changed. You've always loved Matteus."

"You don't need to throw out the *L* word," Lennox said.

Naomi shrugged. "I speak it as I see it."

Yeah, she always did. Which was something she usually loved about her cousin. Not tonight, though. Lennox was very uncomfortable and a little annoyed with Naomi being right more often than she liked. She had enough love for Matteus to equal five people. "I think he's afraid of me."

Naomi nodded. "You are the kind of person who demands everything. You give everything. That's frightening to some people and hard to live up to. You grab life with double fists and you hang on. I remember when you told everyone you were going to grow up and make toys. People looked at you like you were nuts. Yet you never wavered. You knew exactly who you were and who you were going to be. Most people don't even figure out who they are when they're thirty."

Lennox finished her hot chocolate. Waves of exhaustion pounded at her. "I have to think about what you said. When did my life become so complicated?"

Naomi stared at her. "Life has always been complicated. No one has ever stepped on your dreams before. They just got out of your way."

Lennox rubbed her tired eyes. "That's because everyone thought my dreams were crazy."

"Crazy cool," Naomi said. She hugged Lennox. "You'll get through this, and you will have the last laugh." She gave Lennox one more hug. "Now get to bed. Tomorrow is going to be one long day."

Chapter 7

When Matteus was in high school, he had been in charge of babysitting his younger brothers and sisters when both parents had to be away for some reason. He'd spend hours preparing various activities for everyone. One of his favorite was playing what he called Pirate. He'd bury small treasures in his mother's flower beds and make up a map with clues for his younger siblings, then let them loose to search. Looking around at Lennox's attic gave him the same thrill. He was on a treasure hunt for himself this time—and the treasure was the notebooks and a possible countersuit.

"We did some cleaning," Lennox said, "but it's hard to get at anything when there's so much."

"It's certainly a jungle," Matteus said.

"Yes, but it's a well-organized jungle," Lennox replied.

Like his mom and her mom, Lennox was dressed in jeans and a T-shirt. Naomi held a vacuum cleaner and a pail of cleaning supplies.

"What are you doing with all this?" Dorothy asked, indicating the furniture pushed into a corner.

"I called the antique store on Main and they're taking the tables and chairs on consignment."

Matteus opened the door of a wardrobe to find a row of clear boxes with shoes in them.

"My great-grandmother's wedding dress is in one of those boxes."

"Did you try it on?" Grace asked.

"We had a fashion show like you wouldn't believe," Naomi said. "We found tons of photo albums, too."

Strangely, he would have loved to see Lennox parading around in the old fashioned clothes. No, not *old*, but *vintage*—that's what they were called.

"I'd like to look at those." Dorothy reached into the wardrobe and pulled out a hatbox. She opened it to a feathered confection of blue and green. "I remember my grandmother wearing a hat like this. She had a matching parasol."

Matteus groaned. Okay, he didn't want to see the fashion show. Not when they had so much to do. They were never going to make any progress if everyone was constantly trying on hats and shoes and whatnot. It was a good thing Nina had gone back to Reno, or she'd be organizing another fashion show.

He took the hatbox from Dorothy, returned it to the wardrobe and closed the door decisively. "Notebooks," he said in a firm tone.

Dorothy growled at him and held up a finger. "Don't judge me. If you found a box of old baseball cards in here, I can assure you, you'd be going through them talking to all your old baseball-card buddies."

Matteus shook his head. "And I assure you I can resist the temptation."

"Right," Grace said with a snort as she picked her way toward the back of the attic with Naomi following.

"All right," Dorothy said. "We're going to be organized about this. We'll split the attic into sections." She gave everyone a section, and they all went to work. Matteus found himself in charge of moving large items so the women could get into the areas behind them. The farther back they went, the older the items seemed to be.

"Look what I found," Lennox said as she held open a box. Inside were framed display boxes filled with coins. "I wonder if they have any value."

"I know a coin collector who can take a look at them," Matteus said. She handed him the box and he set it near the door to the stairs.

By the end of the day, the elusive notebooks remained undiscovered. Matteus was disappointed, but the attic was mostly cleaned and they'd even managed to dispose of a few items. Dorothy claimed the photo albums, while Grace had found some beautiful hatpins from the nineteenth century that Lennox told her to keep. Naomi discovered a box of Steiff bears. Lennox, however, found nothing but disappointment.

"I had such high hopes today," Lennox said. Dorothy and Grace were in the bathrooms cleaning up, and Naomi was running water in the sink preparing to wash dishes. Matteus had ordered a late lunch, and the remains of the Subway sandwiches were scattered about the kitchen counter ready to be tossed into the trash bin.

"We didn't even get through a third of the attic," Matteus said.

They sat at her kitchen table drinking ice tea. Naomi collected the remaining plates and stood at the sink washing them.

"You found things you can turn into cash." Matteus finished his tea.

She still felt dispirited. "I can pay you now."

"We've already agreed on a no-fee arrangement." Matteus took a cookie from a plate piled high with his mother's best chocolate-chip creations.

"You're putting in a lot of billable hours," Lennox said. She took a cookie and nibbled at it.

He laughed. "I also stubbed my toe, scratched my hand and bumped into a hanging lamp." He rubbed his forehead. And almost lost his manhood, he wanted to add, when he found a spider nearly the size of a tabby cat. But he sucked it up, silently squashed it and soldiered on.

"I broke three fingernails and there is so much dust in my hair, I'm never going to get it out. I have enough antihistamine in my system to alleviate the sneezes in forty-seven countries."

Naomi shook her head. "I've got you both beat." She held up her arm where blood seeped through a large bandage. "I think I need stitches and a cocktail, in no particular order."

Lennox laughed. "We're the walking wounded."

"We're refugees from *Mortal Kombat*," Naomi replied.

"I have bruises on my bruises, too." Lennox drained her glass of ice tea.

"We still got a lot done," Naomi said.

"All we know is where my notebooks aren't."

Matteus shrugged. "That's more information than we had this morning, and we're narrowing down the location."

"Tomorrow," Naomi said cheerfully, "the antique store will haul away the furniture we were able to free. Once that furniture is gone, we'll have more space to organize what we do find."

"I'll return next Sunday and help out again," Matteus said.

"What happens if I don't find the notebooks?" she asked, trying not to let her discouragement show.

"You can't afford to think like that." Matteus took another cookie.

"And I can't afford not to prepare for the worst."

"What is the worst?" Matteus asked. "You lose the rights to your toy. You're a smart woman. You'll come up with something else. Do you think you're the first inventor who was cheated out of an idea? You pick yourself up, dust yourself off and get back up on the horse. For all I know, this is some sort of cosmic test to see what you're made of."

"Right now, I'm made up of dust and sweat," she said.

Matteus grinned. "Dust and sweat means you're moving forward. I'll be damned if I let that man win without a fight."

"You sound like this is personal for you."

"It is personal. That man is messing with your life and I intend to stop him."

Lennox sat a little straighter, feeling empowered by his words. "I'm fighting the good fight."

Matteus took her hand. "Excellent. Next time, I'll bring pizza and antihistamines."

"You were eating them like candy," Lennox said.

Dorothy and Grace returned just then.

"I have to get home," Dorothy said with a glance at her watch. "Your dad and I are having dinner with Dr. Solomon and his wife," she told Lennox.

"I have to get home, too," Grace said.

Lennox walked everyone downstairs, through the store and out onto the veranda. Grace, Dorothy and Naomi walked ahead said their good-byes and left in their respective cars. Naomi returned door and went back into the store, leaving Matteus and Lennox alone.

Matteus stood, brushed Lennox's cheek. "I'll be in touch," he said.

Lennox closed her eyes, the warmth of his touch making her knees weak. Finally, she nodded. She wanted him to hug her, maybe even kiss her again. She wanted to feel his arms around her, making her feel better, even though he would never do that with their mothers standing on the sidewalk watching them out of the sides of their eyes.

"Thanks for your help today," she said when she could finally trust her voice to be even and unemotional.

"My pleasure. I enjoyed my peek into the past."

"I knew my grandmother was a packrat. She did

have a vital excuse because she felt she was protecting history, but there's so much."

"We'll tackle it all one foot at a time."

"More like one inch at a time."

"Matteus," Grace called. "Are you coming?"

"Be right there, Mom," he said. "I'll call you later this week and let you know how the meeting with Ben's lawyer goes."

Then he turned and skipped down the stairs.

Lennox returned to the store and found Naomi leaning against the cash wrap counter.

"My hero," Naomi said with a breathless sigh.

"Are you teasing me?"

"I am," Naomi said with a chuckle.

"Are you enjoying yourself?"

"That, too."

She ushered Naomi into the store, then closed and locked the door.

"Someday my prince will come and fight off dust motes for me," Naomi said as she headed toward the stairs.

Lennox followed more slowly.

"I think he's beginning to give in to your allure," Naomi said as they walked up the stairs.

"What are you talking about?" Lennox stopped, frowning.

"Not a lot of men would spend an afternoon cleaning out an attic with a bunch of women."

"You make it sound like I'm using my womanly wiles to keep him ensnared."

"Aren't you?" Naomi grinned.

"I don't think I have womanly wiles."

Naomi burst out laughing. "Sure you do. You just haven't brought them out in a while."

"No one has been worth taking them out for."

"I think he's worth your time. I think you're an idiot for not pursuing him harder. The man is definitely receptive, even if he doesn't know it yet. I saw the way he touched you."

"He's still mourning his wife."

Naomi shook her head. "No. He's ready to move forward. The only trick is to let him know you are right in his path."

"I have to think about this." Lennox wanted the conversation to end. Matteus wasn't a prize to be won at the county fair.

"What's our next move?" Naomi asked.

"We keep working on the attic." Lennox was trying to be organized, but maybe she should just go up there and crawl around. She might spot something that would jog her memory and put her on the right path. But not now. She was tired, hungry and in desperate need of a shower.

Felix Lawson's law firm was situated on the fifth floor, over a bank in a tony area on Wilshire Boulevard a few blocks from Rodeo Drive. He had a dozen lawyers working for him, and his firm populated the entire floor.

Matteus stood at the entrance to his slick, modern-looking office.

Felix was a thin man, pale skinned and going bald. He made no effort to disguise his thinning hair. He wore a two-thousand-dollar suit and Italian loafers, showing off that he was good at what he did. His intent was to intimidate, which amused Matteus. The cop in Matteus came to the surface and he gave the man a blank look that betrayed nothing of what he was thinking.

"Haven't been in practice long, have you?" Felix said. His voice was deep and authoritative. The kind of voice that could easily sway a jury. "Are you here to settle?"

"No," Matteus said. Instead of sitting in one of the chairs placed in front of Felix's desk, he chose an over-stuffed chair flanking a long sofa at one end of the room, forcing Felix to come to him. Annoyance showed on the other man's face as he sat down on the sofa. "I thought we'd have a little talk before I file my answer."

Felix looked surprised. "Your client doesn't have a snowball's chance in hell."

Matteus didn't answer right away while he studied the other lawyer. "My client has no intention of set-tling."

"Miss McCarthy is a fool."

"But she has me on her side."

Felix nodded. "I look forward to facing you in your court. You're young and unseasoned, but you're build-ing quite a record of accomplishments. I'm going to enjoy schooling you."

Matteus laughed. This guy was good. He fought dirty, was a bully and was as tenacious as can be. He had made a reputation for taking on high-value clients and winning. "I remember when you got Liam Gains-borough out of his contract when he wanted to turn free agent. You had quite a reputation for fighting for the underdog and winning, but you sold out."

"Money's money. In every case I take on, my client is assured justice. Isn't that what the law is all about? Justice?"

"I'm not planning on getting rich or having an office like this." Matteus waved his hand at the sleek furnishings and the picture window overlooking Wilshire Boulevard. "And justice for the rich isn't always justice—just people with more money who can rewrite the rules in their favor."

Felix frowned. "Then why are you here?"

"I wanted to scope you out. You used to be a legend."

"I still am," Felix said with his shark smile. "You don't want to go up against me in court."

Matteus thought for a moment. "Actually, I do."

"You know something," Felix said. "What do you know that I don't?"

"Nothing that I have to tell you at this time."

Felix's eyes narrowed.

"I know what your client has been doing. You've been intimidating other toy designers into giving up their designs without a fight."

"Sore losers," Felix said in a dismissive tone.

"Or hapless victims," Matteus amended.

"It's all about spin," Felix replied.

Matteus stood. "In that case, we'll see who can spin the best. Nice meeting you, Felix."

"See you in court," Felix said.

Matteus simply shrugged. Felix may have had a huge staff, but Matteus had been a cop and he knew how to conduct an investigation and uncover the truth. He preferred it that way. He also knew Felix was not to be underestimated. He may have sold out for money, but he was still a good lawyer, a lion in his prime. Matteus had his work cut out for him, though he was confident in Lennox.

But they needed a smoking gun. Now it was time for him to find one.

Chapter 8

"Who was that?" Naomi asked. The box of Steiff teddy bears had been more than just bears. While the bears were the most famous of their toy lines, they also had other animals, one of which was a tyrannosaurus rex, in excellent shape at the bottom of the box, from the 1950s.

Lennox shoved her phone back in her pocket. "Matteus wants to have dinner with me tonight and discuss strategy."

"Is that what the kids are calling it these days?"

Lennox snorted. "Get your mind out of the gutter."

"But I'm having so much fun there," Naomi said with a giggle.

Lennox shot her a stern look. "Just business with food thrown in."

"If you believe that—" she threw out her arms and struck a pose "—boom! Look! I'm Rihanna."

Lennox closed her eyes and rubbed her forehead. "Don't you have a class? Some shopping to do? A manicure to get?"

"Not until I finish teasing you." Naomi rearranged the bears on the shelf. She handed her cousin a stuffed lion. Lennox went back to the internet to find a price for it. Two turtles and an owl later, Naomi held up the prize in the box—a Steiff bear from 1932.

"My word," Lennox said when she matched the bear's trademark ear button to its value. "This bear is worth fifteen thousand dollars."

"Really!" Naomi peered at the monitor.

"I don't believe it," Lennox said with a shake of her head. "I could pay Matteus's legal fees."

"But first you have to find someone to buy it," Naomi said, always the practical one.

"I think I know somebody who'd be interested." Lennox examined the bear, rechecking its ear button with the database. Same bear, same everything. The button was the Steiff brand. Excitement burst through her. "If we can find more treasures like this, I would have enough worst-case-scenario money."

"Are you thinking you might lose?"

"I'm thinking about survival mode and weighing all my options." How greedy was Ben? Did he want to destroy her? And if so, why? What would he gain? If he won, was he going to want more than just the rights to her toy line?

Brooding wasn't going to help her. She needed to ask Matteus these questions.

Matteus appeared at the toy store ten minutes before closing. Lennox had dressed in a simple cream-colored wrap dress with brown shoes.

He waited patiently while she finished up with the last two customers, then locked the front door and turned the Open sign to Closed. She did a quick money count and put the money in her floor safe.

"I'm ready," she said.

"I really like your store. I see you've put the teddy bears in a place of honor."

"They're not in a place of honor but a place that says Buy Me, Please." She pointed at the middle bear. "That one is worth fifteen grand."

He whistled and leaned close to study the bear. "For a teddy bear?"

"The Germans know how to make teddy bears."

She turned off the lights and walked to the front door. "Are you going to be able to part with that bear?" he asked.

"If I lose this suit, who knows how long it's going to take for me to bounce back? The store is doing well, but I'm really just making enough to pay my bills and Naomi with enough left over for taxes."

"I understand. I don't intend to lose."

"I researched Ben's lawyer and he's a barracuda," she said as they stepped out into the humid evening.

"I met him this morning, and we have our work cut

out for us." He opened the passenger door of his car and she got in.

"I can't decide if you're being evasive or confident."

"Will I beat him? I don't know. Can I beat him? Yes, I can." He walked around the car and opened the driver's door, then settled himself behind the wheel.

"I'm not quite sure what to make of that," she said.

"Until you can find a smoking gun, justice is a crap-shoot."

She let out a long breath. "I didn't think I'd ever get to this point."

"What point is that?"

"I think I'm irritated with my grandmother for being such a hoarder." Why couldn't her grandmother put the notebooks in a box clearly labeled Lennox's Notebooks? And make the box easy to find?

Matteus laughed. "Grandmothers were put on this earth for a reason. Yours was to mess up your lawsuit."

She sighed. "I guess so. Where are we going to dinner?"

"Have you ever been to Duane's Prime Steaks and Seafood at the Mission Inn in Riverside?"

"No, I haven't." She'd heard of it, though. Duane's was a landmark restaurant with terrific food. Her parents ate there every year on their anniversary and then spent the night in the hotel.

"The food is excellent," Matteus said. "Guarantee you'll enjoy it."

"Are you putting the tab on my billable hours?" Though she wondered why he was treating her to such an expensive dinner when they were just going to talk about strategy.

"I'm not the one with the fifteen-thousand-dollar teddy bear." He slanted a glance at her, amusement in his eyes.

"Unless I sell that bear, it isn't doing me any good. It's a very expensive knickknack."

"Do you think you'll sell it?"

"I know I will, and if I play it right, I could get a bidding war going. I've contacted several people who I know collect Steiff teddy bears. And I've had a few nibbles. The trick is to get them where you need them."

"Look at you, Miss Entrepreneur. What do you collect?"

She hadn't collected anything for a long time. "I used to collect comic books, but I sold them to help finance my store."

"Wow, you are single-minded."

"What would you have done to finance your legal career?"

"I sold the house Camille and I bought."

That surprised her. "Was that difficult?"

He shook his head. "I didn't want to live in it after Camille passed. And selling wasn't as hard as I thought it would be."

She glanced at him. He had an odd look on his face, making her think the decision wasn't as easy as he led her to believe. "I'm sorry."

He shook his head. "Don't be. I couldn't handle the memories."

Lennox touched his arm. "Tell me about Camille."

He stared straight ahead at the traffic before he finally began to speak. "She was brilliant, tough and beautiful. The first time I saw her, I knew she was going to be my wife."

Immediately, she really couldn't believe she had asked him to tell her about his poor dead saint of a wife. "That's very sweet." She tried to keep the pain from her voice. Why didn't he see her the same way?

"Took me a couple of years to convince her, though," he said in a wistful tone. "Her career was very important to her, and she didn't see marriage as something she could have at the same time."

"You must have had a hard time convincing her."

He grinned. "It took a lot of work to sway Camille that she could have marriage and a career."

"I can see you loved her very much," Lennox said, feeling glad she'd never let him know how she felt about him. She should have been happy for him, and she hadn't been. A stab of guilt made her realize her jealousy had blinded her when she should have been a supportive friend to him.

"I did love her, and a part of me will always love her, but I'm ready to move on." He glanced at her with something in his eyes she couldn't interpret.

Her breath fluttered and her heart pounded. What was he trying to tell her? Was he ready to move on with her? Though that wasn't what he had said. Yet, he'd already kissed her twice, and the memory left her reeling. She'd dreamed of him falling in love with her, but was now the right time? She had a lot on her plate, and she had little to offer.

He turned into the driveway of the Mission Inn, stopping at the valet hut, saving her from having to say anything.

The Mission Inn was a historical monument. As they walked up the long sidewalk leading to the reception area, Lennox knew she was the one who needed to keep their friendship on a professional level.

Duane's Prime Steaks and Seafood had a Spanish look to it, with stucco walls, heavy wooden beams and wood support columns. White tablecloths covered the tables, which held elegant plates and fluted wine glasses, and were flanked by brown leather chairs.

The hostess showed them to their table in a quiet corner.

"What do you suggest?" She glanced down at the menu, trying not to look at the prices.

"Everything. I like the rib eye with asparagus, but the filet mignon with garlic whipped potatoes is good, too," Matteus said.

"You come here a lot?"

"I have a couple of clients in this area. And I appreciate good food."

"Don't you consider it a betrayal to your dad?"

"My dad doesn't cook American food. I've brought him here. He loves it, too. Besides, when I want Brazilian food, Luna el Sol is the only place I go."

Their waiter came to take their drink order. Lennox continued to study the menu, trying to make up her mind. Finally, she set the menu aside and looked up to find Matteus watching her intently.

"So let's talk strategy," she said.

He nodded. "So much of our strategy depends on

finding those notebooks. Assuming we don't, how are we going to win this?"

Lennox's stomach felt like it was in free fall. She knew there was a real possibility those notebooks would never be found, but her mind kept shying away from that. "Plan B is what?"

Matteus regarded her solemnly. "I think plan B is finding everyone Ben has already sued and having them testify about what he did to them."

"You mean like character witnesses?"

"Exactly. It's not a perfect plan, but it does prove a pattern of behavior, and there is a possibility of fraudulent intent." Matteus frowned.

"But couldn't Ben's actions be interpreted as nothing more than protecting his interests?"

Matteus nodded. "Gillian said something—I can't remember exactly how she put it, but something in her story set off my alert button. I'll have to go back and read my notes. But we should also show that Ben targets people at their most vulnerable, as far as Gillian Smith and Annette Conklin are concerned…" His voice trailed off.

"And what?"

He didn't answer right away. "And I need to talk to the other two people Talbert Toys sued. I feel like I don't have all the information I need yet, and something about this whole thing doesn't feel right."

"What do you mean?"

"Something seems off. I spent enough years as a cop, and I could smell lies and guilt. Doesn't mean I can prove anything, but I just know something was off."

She pondered his comments. "Does that mean our strategy may change?"

"Yep. It means our strategy is fluid. If you can't find those notebooks…"

So much depended on those notebooks. She needed to get back to scouring the attic. They had to be there. She believed with all her heart those notebooks were there, somewhere.

The waiter came back for their order. Lennox settled on the center-cut filet mignon while Matteus ordered the rib eye. He refilled their water glasses and retreated again.

"What happens next as far as the suit is concerned?"

"I filed your official answer with the court in Riverside, and once that is accepted, we move into the discovery phrase where we start preparing for the fight. Now enough shoptalk. Tell me about your day."

"Other than displaying expensive Steiff bears and other assorted animals, my day was pretty tame. The antique store removed as much of the furniture from the attic that could fit in the truck. The way the owner gushed over everything, I have a feeling some of the pieces are going to end up in her house." Lennox remembered her own days of hunting at vintage-toy conventions and picking up a few antiques here and there. Sometimes the toy would spend time in her apartment, and sometimes she'd sell it immediately. She loved the joy of finding just the right toy for some of her customers who loved collecting.

"You're a collector yourself. Do you look for toys for any of your customers?"

"I do. I have several clients who collect certain toys like Barbie dolls, Hot Wheels and of course anything Star Wars. I know what's in their collection, and if I see something they might want, I shoot them a text and attach a photo and either get a yes or no. And for some clients I'll just purchase the item, knowing they'll buy it."

"Where do you find these toys?"

"On the internet. I have people who come into the shop wondering at the value of some toy. I go to vintage toy conferences, too. In fact, there's a conference this weekend at Staples Center."

"What happens at these toy conferences?"

"You should come along and see. Naomi is going to watch the store on Saturday so I can go."

He pressed his fingers to his temple. "I'm picturing a lot of nerds."

Lennox laughed. "I can't tell you his name because I signed a nondisclosure agreement, but one of my top clients is a well-known personality, and no one would ever call him a nerd. He's just crazy for Legos."

"You've caught my interest."

"That's all I can say. Do you want to come with me? You'll have a good time even if you don't collect vintage toys. Toy people know how to party."

He laughed. She loved the way he laughed.

The waiter brought their food, and they paused while he set it before them.

After the waiter left, Matteus said, "You make me feel like I'm too serious."

"Toys are serious business. If they weren't, I wouldn't be in this pickle."

"I'm starting to understand how competitive the toy business is."

"*Competitive* is the Olympics. *Cutthroat* is the toy business. How often have you seen a toy go viral, and in a week a dozen imitations crop up?" She cut into her steak and took a bite. Wow, it was good. Lennox hadn't had a steak this good in years.

"I've listened to my mother talk about the music industry all my life, and anytime money is involved people go off the deep end."

"Toys are the same way. I've watched mothers come to blows over a popular toy. Does anyone fight over a car?"

Matteus tilted his head. "I don't know about hot cars, but I've seen the same behavior over the newest electronics or video games. And concert tickets."

"Now you understand why people take their leisure time more seriously than their work. Toys are a passion. I think people want to experience the innocence of childhood for as long as possible."

"Is it that way for you?"

"No," Lennox said. "I'm good at recognizing the right toy at the right time. Which is why I know my toy line is going to take off." And Ben knew it, too. He may have wanted to live his life as a surfer, but Ben could smell money in anything, whether it be for a new toy or a winning can-opener design.

"You don't have much time for a personal life, do you?" Matteus asked. "You should make time for a boyfriend."

"First of all, for a boyfriend, I need a man who is interested in me." And *interesting* to her, too. "Second of all, I have to be interested in him."

"What's wrong with the men in Redlands?"

"Absolutely nothing. Between getting my store up and running and getting my toy line off the ground, I don't have much time for anything else. I'm young. Someday, my prince will come and he won't be an action figure in a cellophane box. What about you?"

"I needed to devote time to finishing law school and the time to getting my practice off the ground. In fact, this is the first date I've had in months."

"This is a date?" she said in surprise. "You need to work on your skills."

"I didn't think I would be dating again," he said.

She touched his hand. "I'm so sorry." But at the same time, she was glad he was with her.

He took a sip of his wine and sat back studying her. "Don't be sorry. I haven't been happy in a long time, but I'm happy being here...with you."

She smiled at him, joy filling her heart. "You're a strong man and I'm happy to see you moving forward."

"I'm not sure I'm moving forward, but I am moving." His fingers tightened around hers.

"That's all anyone can do."

If only he would move forward with her.

Chapter 9

The drive to Staples Center turned out to be an easy one. Lennox watched the scenery. She loved the grace and beauty of Redlands and hated the starkness of Los Angeles. Few trees dotted the landscape, and driving down into the LA basin beneath a pall of yellow haze always made her skin itch.

Staples Center was huge. The toy convention was in a small hall at the south end of the center. Booths lined the hall in long rows. Signs hanging from the ceiling clearly marked different sections: Antique Toys, Old Favorites, Collectibles, Dolls, Trains, Toy Distributors, Educational, Toddler.

Lennox pulled out her phone and glanced at the list of toys she was looking for.

The hall bustled with noise, chatter and the sound

of children's laughter, along with the dings and chimes of thousands of toys. She loved toy shows. Everything about them brought back all the happy memories of her years as a toy tester.

"Where do we start?" Matteus asked, glancing around, looking a little overwhelmed.

"You want to take a walk down memory lane or head straight for the future?"

"This is huge," he said, looking around. "I don't have a clue where to begin."

"ToyFest West is even bigger," she said. "Let's start with memory lane." She took his hand and led the way toward the section marked Toy Distributors. "What was the one thing you always wanted as a kid and never got?"

"A BB gun," he said.

"What a surprise," she replied, trying not to sound sarcastic. What was it with guys and their guns?

"If my parents had gotten me a BB gun, I would never have become a cop. I'd have gotten my love of firearms out of my system when I was ten."

"Why?"

"When I was a kid, one of the neighborhood boys shot my mother's cat, Clarence, with a BB gun. I wanted one to protect my family."

What a nice thought. Matteus made her feel safe. He protected the people he cared about.

She stopped at a booth with vintage Red Ryder BB guns and watched a longing appear on his face. He picked one up, caressing the stock.

"Be careful," she said with a nudge of his arm, "or you'll shoot your eye out."

He laughed.

"You have no idea how long I've been wanting to use that line."

"And I bet you watch *A Christmas Story* every Christmas."

"Of course. What's Christmas without a daylong viewing of that movie?"

"What toy did you want that you never got?" he asked, putting the BB gun down.

"I wanted a junior chemistry set," she admitted reluctantly. "Blowing stuff up sounded like so much fun."

"You constantly surprise me. I thought you were going to say some sort of doll."

"I seldom played with dolls. When I tested toys, I was assigned to the boy toys to see how girls would respond to them. So I played with GI Joe, Transformers, Tonka trucks, video games and Micro Machines. As for the chemistry set, I tested one and had too much fun. My parents were worried I'd set fire to the house or blow up my school. Crazy things like that."

"Would you have?"

"Probably," she said. "I loved experimenting and the joy of a new discovery."

They wandered down the aisle looking at each booth. She saw one with vintage Transformers and stopped. She pointed at the row of figures in their original boxes. "I tested the second generation of Transformers that came out from Hasbro. I was six or seven years old and had the time of my life with them. They had all these nifty gadgets. One of the boys in my group was actually jealous."

"Cars, robots and weapons, all in one package," he said, admiration in his voice.

"A kid's dream," she said with a sigh. She'd loved the way the toys felt in her hands, even loved the plastic smell of them.

"When you weren't testing toys, what did you play with?" he asked.

"Legos were my favorite. I built a small village of them." They wandered down an aisle with vintage Madame Alexander dolls.

"If you weren't that interested in dolls, why is your new line of toys dolls?"

"I wanted a doll that looked like me with my face, skin, eye coloring and hair texture. Dolls have always been one size fits all. If I'd had a doll that looked just like me, I could've pretended it was my little sister."

"So you're saying you wanted a sister. You can have Nina anytime."

"I'm over that. But, thanks, I'll be happy to tell Nina you wanted to loan her out."

"I loaned her to all my friends, mainly because most of my friends were terrified of her."

"That's because she wouldn't put up with shit from anyone, especially boys."

"Dad made sure both Nina and Lola had that attitude," he replied.

A group of children were clustered around a remote-controlled robot. They all squealed as the robot went in circles, performing acrobatic tricks.

"There's a lot to see here," he said as he watched the robot. "Who knew there were so many different types of toys?"

"The toy industry is one of the most profitable in the world. Just in the US in 2014, over twenty-four billion dollars was spent on toys. That's a big chunk of change." And one she wanted to be a part of, despite the stiff competition.

They wandered down another aisle, and for a second she didn't quite comprehend what she was looking at until she realized she was staring at her old boss, Ben of Talbert Toys. Usually Ben and Bernice had one of the most expansive booths at the show, but today they had a booth a quarter the size of what they usually rented. Business must not be too good.

Ben was crouched down on the floor talking to a little girl. He held a doll in one hand and was showing the little girl all the things the doll could do. After a few moments, the girl's mother simply smiled and tugged her daughter away.

At that moment Ben glanced up and saw Lennox. He stood. "Lennox!"

Like he was surprised to see her at a toy convention.

"Hello, Ben," Lennox said. If she could have turned away, she would have, but she never backed down from a challenge.

Ben Talbert's gaze slid over her and Matteus in surprise. He was a handsome man in his early forties, tanned and toned, always conscious of his appearance. His hair was styled in a casual tousle that could only be created with a four-hundred-dollar haircut. She remembered a slight receding of his hairline, but he'd had obviously a good hair transplant since she'd last seen him that had taken care of that.

"Lennox," he repeated, his tone cool.

"Ben, this is Matteus Torres," she said. "He's my lawyer."

Ben's face tightened. "I heard you hired a lawyer. You know you're wasting everybody's time."

"It's my time to waste, thank you." She wanted to say something hurtful, but being polite was too ingrained in her.

"You don't have a chance against me."

Matteus's eyes narrowed. "That's for the court to decide."

Ben gave Matteus an up-and-down look, signaling a level of derision that made Lennox want to slap him.

"Assuming it goes to trial." Ben gave her a smug grin.

She lifted her chin. "You may have been handed Talbert Toys by your dad, but I'm not giving you my dolls. You'll have to work for it. The same way I had to work for everything."

Bernice came out from behind the display. Bernice Wagner was as well-groomed and as well taken care of as her husband, even though she was seven years older. She'd had a facelift recently. Her face was too unlined, too smooth for her age, and her slim figure was the too-perfect result of even more cosmetic surgery.

"Hello, Lennox," she said.

"Hi," Lennox replied. "This is my lawyer, Matteus Torres."

Bernice gave Matteus a brittle smile. "You could

spare yourself the time and stress by doing the right thing and turning over all your documents."

Lennox leaned over the counter. "Not without a fight."

Bernice drew back. Lennox ran a practiced eye over their toy displays. Not one original idea appeared in any toy on view, except for the largest display showcasing the line of toys she'd developed for them, which was exhibited prominently. She smiled as children gravitated toward that display and ignored the other toys.

"We shouldn't be talking to you," Bernice said stiffly.

"Exactly," Matteus said, tugging Lennox away. "I've been in touch with your lawyer. He'll be letting you know what we discussed soon enough."

"Enjoy the cheap seats," was Lennox's parting shot as they went to the next booth, all the while aware of Bernice and Ben staring angrily at her.

A moment later, while they were at the next booth, Nate appeared next to her. "Lennox, I hoped I might see you today." He turned to Matteus and said quietly, "Hi, I'm Nate Talbert."

"Mr. Talbert," Matteus said politely. They shook hands. "We really shouldn't be talking to you either."

"I've been doing some snooping and I do not like what I'm learning. I'd like to make an appointment to see you."

Matteus eyed him warily. He reached into his pocket and pulled out a business card. "Call and set up a time to meet."

Nate pocketed the card. "Thank you." He smiled at

Lennox. "Go have some fun," he told her. "I know how much you love toy conventions." He turned and headed back to the Talbert booth.

"Come on, I want to check out some of Ben's competition," she said.

"Seems to me that would be everybody," Matteus replied.

"You do have some snark in you. I like that." She grinned at him, glad he'd come with her.

"What did you mean by cheap seats?" he asked.

"Normally they rent one of the largest booths at this show. That booth back there is a quarter the usual size, which has to mean business isn't as good as they want others to think."

"Which could be the reason they want your new toy line," Matteus said with a backward look.

"They have to keep the money rolling in because keeping a house in Turks and Caicos isn't cheap." She'd visited their lovely home right on the beach, with the blue Caribbean ocean only steps away from her patio. She had been impressed when they bought a house on the island but not impressed with the brash display of their wealth. "I'm more resolved than ever to find my notebooks."

"Matteus," a voice called.

Lennox turned to find Nina and Lola bearing down on them. Nina was dressed in a chic pantsuit while Lola wore jeans and a T-shirt with a wolf's head under the caption *Little Wolf's Journey*.

"Lola, Nina," Matteus said, hugging and kissing each of them. "What are you doing here?"

"Background work," Nina said. "Making contacts."

Matteus looked at them fondly. "Contacts for what?"

"For the movie Dylan and I scored," Lola added.

"I've been researching toy manufacturers for the action figures that tie in to the movie," Nina continued.

"But the movie doesn't come out for another two years." Matteus said.

"Which means we're two years behind." Nina held an iPad in one hand.

"That's in Nina years," Lola said.

Lennox burst out laughing. "I'm hungry. Have you two had lunch yet?"

They left the convention room for the concourse and eateries. Matteus found a table while Lennox, Nina and Lola studied the menu on the wall behind the concession-stand employees. They ordered and then received their food all settling at the table.

"When I found out about what you did, Lennox, I used to pretend to be you," Lola said.

"How could you pretend to be me?" Lennox asked in surprise.

"I used to tell my kindergarten friends that I couldn't play with them today because I was having lunch with My Little Pony and a paycheck." Lola broke off laughing.

"Yeah, that was pretty much my whole childhood," Lennox said as she took a bite of her hot dog. Relish squeezed out on her hand and she licked it up.

"I can just see Dylan's niece doing something like that. She'd have a blast with anything to do with horses. How do I sign her up?"

Lennox said, "Most toy manufacturers outsource to companies that specialize in providing the children. I can give you a couple of names."

"That would be terrific."

Lennox turned to Nina. "You're researching toy manufacturers? Why?"

"The producers of *Little Wolf's Journey* hired me to do the publicity for the movie," Nina said, "and asked me to research toy manufacturers for the action figures tie-in. And I've been contacting them one by one. Is there anybody you would know? Who can I eliminate from the list?"

She held out her iPad to Lennox, who glanced through the list on the screen. Talbert Toys was on it. "You talked to Ben and Bernice."

Nina frowned. "Yes, I talked to them." Little enthusiasm came through in her voice. "They tried really hard to impress me, but I told them one of my criteria was that the toys needed to be manufactured in the United States. They agreed, but then I found out they outsource to China for everything."

"A lot of things changed when Ben's dad retired," Lennox said. Nate would never have outsourced. He believed American toys should be made in America.

"I've already eliminated them." Nina wiped her hands on her napkin. "They just seemed too eager. And I didn't like the look of some of the action figures they developed."

Lennox finished her hot dog and started on her sweet-potato fries. Sweet and salty—her favorite combination of tastes. "The toy business is highly competitive."

"They are a little too litigious for my comfort," Nina said. "They've had too many lawsuits in the last few years. And I'm not hearing anything good about them."

Lennox studied the iPad. "Unless Kanvers Toy Company has changed their direction, they would be a good start. But they've always specialized in educational toys, though they do have a line of action figures with another movie tie-in. While some of their toys are manufactured in China, a lot are made here."

"I'll research them next," Nina said.

"And try Integra Toys. They have a good track record with movie tie-ins. And they're based here in Los Angeles. All their toys are manufactured in the United States."

"Maybe I should take you with me when I talk to these people."

Lennox shook her head. "I have a lot on my plate right now."

"Don't I know." Nina glanced at her brother. "What kind of questions should I be asking these companies?"

"I'll put together a list for you."

They finished their food and parted ways, Nina and Lola heading in one direction, with Matteus and Lennox going in another.

"You were awfully quiet during lunch," Lennox said as they went back to wandering the booths.

"I was puzzling out why Nate wants to meet with me," he admitted.

"I can't answer that, but I can say Nate is one of the

most ethical people I've ever known. Maybe he's found something that will help me."

"Maybe, but Ben is still his son, and you're challenging his son and his legacy."

"You'll find out eventually," she said. "Stop thinking about the lawsuit. Let's just enjoy the day." She knew she was going to enjoy being with Matteus and she could think about the lawsuit tomorrow.

Chapter 10

Desmond Shane had a small legal practice in Garden Grove. Matteus wouldn't be here, ready to track the man down, if he hadn't refused every phone call Matteus had made over the last week.

His office was located in a strip mall and was flanked by a Vietnamese restaurant and a dry cleaner. Matteus had no idea what the rest of the stores were, since all the signs were in Vietnamese. The parking lot was pitted with potholes that Matteus could barely maneuver around. He parked in front of Desmond Shane's office and got out of his car. The day was blistering hot. An air conditioner in the wall above a window wheezed as though it had asthma. Signs in the windows on either side of the door announced that he specialized in patents and inventions.

The office was full of low-end Ikea furniture, with a desk for the receptionist, two uncomfortable-looking chairs and a scuffed tile floor. A few mass-produced paintings hung on the walls.

His receptionist was a tiny, wizened-looking Vietnamese woman with black hair pulled into a bun and dark black eyes whose accented English was hard to understand. Matteus repeated his request slowly, and the woman nodded and finally pointed at a closed door with Desmond Shane's name inscribed in gold script on the dark wood.

Desmond Shane was a tired-looking man with dark brown eyes, fading blond hair and soft hands.

"Sorry about Chou. She's filling in for her daughter who is sick today."

Desmond's handshake was limp. His dark blue suit fitted him loosely, as though he'd lost a great deal of weight.

"Thank you for seeing me," Matteus said.

Desmond shrugged. "Did I have a choice?"

Matteus was taken aback. "I had the feeling you were avoiding me."

Desmond waved to a vinyl-covered chair. Matteus sat down, aware of the cracked vinyl held together with duct tape.

"The Talbert Toys case was not one of my proudest moments," Desmond said.

"We've all lost cases," Matteus replied as he shifted on the hard chair, trying to find a comfortable spot.

Desmond shrugged. "Gillian Smith wasn't the most cooperative client I've ever had."

"But the phone apps she designed were her life's work." Matteus studied the man. Desmond was nervous. He clasped and unclasped his hands and avoided looking Matteus straight in the eyes.

"She had no way of proving she'd developed the apps after she left Talbert Toys. Along with no paper trail, the only notes she had were undated. She had no choice."

"You sound like you didn't believe her." Matteus was starting to not like this man. His cop senses went on to high alert.

"I believed her, but we were up against a well-oiled machine." Desmond drummed his fingers on the worn surface of his desk.

Matteus thought that Desmond wasn't up to the task. Despite the script on his window stating he specialized in patents, he had the feeling Desmond wasn't as well versed in what he did as he should be.

"Listen," Desmond said, "I know you came all the way from Pasadena, but there isn't much I can say about the case. Ben Talbert won and Gillian Smith lost."

"Any advice you can give me about what I might need?"

"A client who has his crap together," Desmond said with a short laugh.

"I do have a client who has it together," Matteus said, irritated with the other man.

"I hope it's all dated."

"It is," Matteus replied, sending a small prayer into the ether that Lennox could find those notebooks. They needed to step up their timeline. Matteus knew he might have to hire outside help if they had a chance of getting through all the stuff in the attic. He might even have to enlist more help than just his mother. At least one brother should be free on a Saturday. Moving some of the heavier pieces of furniture Lennox's mother decided she wanted to keep really required two strong men.

"That's in your favor," Desmond said. He stood and started toward the door.

Matteus realized the interview had ended. He hated to leave, though. He wanted to keep pushing Desmond. The man was hiding something.

Desmond opened the door and gestured for Matteus to exit. Reluctantly, Matteus allowed himself to be ushered out. He didn't leave immediately, however, but sat in his car making notes about the interview. Something was wrong, but he had no clue what.

"Something is bothering you," Lennox observed as she stood in front of her tiny stove stirring noodles. She and Matteus had spent all day in the attic while Naomi watched the store. Matteus had said he'd tried to get one of his brothers to help, especially in moving the large pieces of furniture, but none had the weekend free. They'd unearthed a lot of stuff during the day, but not one notebook.

"I've gone over and over it in my head, but somehow and some way, Gillian's attorney threw her under the bus."

"That's a pretty heavy accusation." She gave the spaghetti sauce a couple of stirs.

"And I don't have one shred of proof, just a gut feeling. But I always listen to my gut." Matteus took a bite of his spinach salad.

"Desmond needs to be punished," she said. "What do you think he did?"

"I think he tanked the case. Though I don't know how."

"But you already said Gillian couldn't prove her ownership." Lennox poured the noodles into the colander.

"I know, but something isn't right."

"What, like someone can smell guilty?"

"Once a cop, always a cop. You never leave that training behind." Matteus reached for a breadstick. "And yes, I can smell guilty, I can smell hinky, I can smell lies. Doesn't mean I can prove anything, but I can always tell when someone is lying. And Desmond Shane is lying to me, telling me Gillian was at fault for lazy documentation."

"So what are you thinking?" She dumped the noodles in a bowl and added a splash of olive oil and garlic salt.

"I'm thinking of taking Gillian on as a client after I finish with you."

"Why?"

"I hate bad lawyers. They're supposed to help you, stand up for you and fight for you. Bad lawyers are worse than criminals."

"I always thought lawyers are like cops—they protect their own."

"Not this one," Matteus said.

"What are you going to do then?"

"A little area in my brain is reserved for that very question."

She poured the sauce into a bowl and set it down with another helping of warm garlic bread. While she put salad on her plate, Matteus helped himself to the noodles and sauce.

"Technically, what can you do?" she asked.

Matteus had brought a bottle of wine, and he now poured the richly colored burgundy into their wine goblets. "I can take my suspicions to the right people."

"Will you?"

"Yes," he answered. "Without even a second thought. We don't need bad lawyers."

"What are we going to do now?"

"After dinner I'll get a motel room. There's no way I'm driving back to Pasadena tonight. I intend to get a good night's sleep, and then tomorrow, it's back to work on the attic."

"You don't need to get a motel room. I have a guest room."

He hesitated. "I don't want to put you out."

"Please, don't worry about that." She held her breath while he considered her offer.

"Then I accept."

Lennox knocked on the guest-bedroom door. She'd had a shower and wore a silk kimono over her nightgown. She gripped several towels tightly against her chest. She'd had men stay overnight with her before, but Matteus was different.

A few seconds later the door opened, and Matteus

stood there wearing nothing but jeans. His chest was broad and smooth and her throat went dry. Behind him, his overnight case sat on the bed with neatly folded jeans and polo shirts inside.

She shoved the towels forward. "I—I...had my shower. The bathroom is free. I brought you extra towels. I didn't..." She stopped herself, distracted by the wide expanse of his torso. She let her gaze travel down his mocha-colored chest to his perfect six-pack abs. *Stop staring,* she ordered herself. But her eyes refused to obey. *Stop staring, she tried again.*

"Thank you." He reached out for the towels and his hand touched hers. She jumped at the electrical charge generated by his touch.

She couldn't seem to let go of the towels. "I... Matteus..."

She was really trying to get out some words that made sense. How could she be so tongue-tied with a man she'd known almost all her life?

Then she noticed he wasn't moving his hand either. Something broke in her, and she knew this was her chance. All the years of longing for him, of loving him, coalesced. She leaned forward and kissed him. Not like the tame kisses he'd offered before, but a woman's kiss filled with years of yearning.

His lips were warm and inviting on her mouth. He didn't pull away—instead he pulled her closer. Lennox began to shake and she dropped the towels. Heat stirred through her as he pulled her to him. His warm skin burned through her silky robe. She gripped his shoulders, molding her body against his.

Oh God, this was better than she expected. This was heaven. He was so beautiful, so sweet and so kind. He had always been everything she wanted in a man. Who was she kidding? He was the only man she'd ever really wanted. Every other man in her life, except for her father, had been a poor imitation.

His skin was silky smooth under her touch. She wondered if he knew how he'd captivated her.

Matteus watched her with his dreamy chocolate eyes. "I dream about you."

She let out a long breath. She wasn't sure how to respond. She'd dreamed, fantasied, probably hallucinated about him. Now that he was back in her life, she couldn't stop thinking about him.

He kissed her again, his mouth opening and his tongue pressing against hers.

Lennox ached for him. She began untying her kimono, letting it slip off her shoulders.

Matteus groaned. He slid his fingers down her back to cup her bottom and pushed against the hem of her nightgown.

He set her on fire. And only he could put out the flames.

Matteus lifted her, his arms tight around her waist. He carried her to the bed, where he flung his suitcase onto the floor and pulled back the spread and blanket. He laid her on the cool sheet and slid onto the mattress next to her.

He pushed the narrow straps of her nightgown down, exposing her breasts. Her nipples peaked to hard buds.

He gently ran a thumb over each one. Lennox gasped. Deep down at her core, a growing ache spread.

"Let's get this pesky nightgown off," he half growled.

She had no objection. She sat up and raised her arms, and he pulled the nightgown up over her head, tossing it over his shoulder.

He pushed her back down against the pillows and kissed down her neck, gently licked her nipples. His mouth and hands left a trail of fire on her skin. He took her nipple in his mouth, rolling his tongue around the sensitive skin.

No man had ever turned her on so quickly.

He lifted his head. "I need to get a condom," he said, his voice silky and hot.

Lennox's eyelids drifted close. Was she dreaming? No, this was not a dream.

He leaned over the side of the bed and dragged his suitcase to him. She listened to his quick movements as he searched through the suitcase with one hand but kept the other flat on her stomach, as though he thought she'd run away.

Heat danced over her skin.

"Open your eyes," he whispered.

"No."

"Why?"

"Because a part of me is afraid this is all a dream, and I don't want it to end."

He chuckled. "I'm here. For real." He slid his hand down her stomach to the hidden core between her legs. His finger gently stroked her.

Lennox groaned. He went back to kissing her nipples and she finally opened her eyes. Was he really here making love to her? She touched his head. It sank lower as he kissed his way down her stomach to her hidden nub. She vibrated beneath the intensity of his tongue on her as he gently parted the folds of skin to ease his fingers inside her. He stroked in and out while his tongue caressed her clitoris.

Her muscles clenched. He pulled out and eased his way back up her body, licking and kissing her skin until he reached her mouth. He kissed her hard and deep.

She shuddered. She felt his erection against her hip and realized somehow he'd taken off his jeans without her noticing. She giggled.

Matteus lifted his head. "Are you laughing at me?"

"No. At myself."

He skimmed a thumb over her lips. "I've— I've wanted to… I don't know what I wanted. I know I've been thinking about this for weeks." The words stumbled out of him. Then his kiss was hard and demanding.

She slid her hands around his broad shoulders, his hot naked skin burning her. This felt so right. Part of her couldn't believe that finally, after so many years of wondering what kind of lover he was, she was really going to find out. This was her fantasy come to life.

A moan escaped him as his lips glided over her skin, down her throat to the hollow between her neck and shoulder and back to her breasts.

He nudged her legs apart and positioned himself between them, then slowly slid into her.

She wrapped her legs around him, holding him tight inside her. "You feel so good. Make me yours."

"Oh yes," he said.

She traced her fingertips down his muscular back. Her body flooded with wetness and she cried out. With her legs entwined around him and holding him tightly to her, she lifted her hips as he thrust deep inside her.

She couldn't tell where she ended and he began. Her body was on fire, pulsing with pleasure and desire. Her skin was slick with heat that consumed her. And when she couldn't take any more, she shattered as the orgasm ripped through her.

"Thank you," she whispered against his lips.

"No. Thank you."

And in that moment, her world changed forever.

Chapter 11

Naomi opened the door to her apartment and glared at Lennox, who had one hand up, ready to knock again—harder.

"Do you know what time it is?" Naomi looked sleep rumpled, with her hair standing up and her eyes still glazed.

Lennox pushed her way into the apartment. She went to the small kitchen and started the coffee. "Too early for anything of substance. That's what time it is."

The aroma of coffee filled the kitchen. Lennox stood in front of the coffeemaker urging it to hurry, a mug clenched tightly in her hand.

"So tell me why I'm trying to wake up at 7:00 a.m. and why you look so bright eyed and bushy tailed."

Naomi held her own mug, her eyes half-closed. "And the reason better be damn good."

Lennox opened the refrigerator and peered inside. She grabbed an egg carton, a package of mozzarella cheese and some mushrooms. She had spinach and onions in her own refrigerator. "I'm making a breakfast omelet for Matteus and I'm out of eggs."

"Is he here already?" Naomi groaned, rubbing her eyes.

Lennox smiled at her cousin. "He never left."

Naomi's eyes snapped open. "Oh." She stared at Lennox, suddenly wide awake. She put a hand over her mouth. "Oh!" She leaned toward Lennox and whispered, "How was it?"

Lennox looked around the room, wondering why Naomi was whispering when they were completely alone. She leaned toward her cousin and whispered back, "Fabulous."

"OMG. OMG!" Naomi stared at Lennox. She half collapsed onto a kitchen chair. "Where do you go from here?"

Lennox shrugged. "That's the problem. I don't know." For the moment, nothing mattered except cooking him breakfast. She went back to the refrigerator. Good. Naomi had bacon, too.

The coffeemaker spluttered to a stop. Naomi held her mug out, and Lennox filled it for her and handed it back. Then she filled her own mug and leaned against the counter, holding the mug in both hands and pulling the aroma of fresh coffee into her lungs. She needed the caffeine.

"Do you think pancakes would be too much?" she asked as she opened the cabinet and pulled out a box of mix and a bottle of pure maple syrup.

"Depends on how much energy you spent last night. Do you have to fuel up for the day?" Naomi sipped her coffee. "I just read an article about some restaurant that puts pancake batter in their omelets to make them fluffier. You could try that."

"I do need the fuel," Lennox said, adding the pancake mix to the growing pile of food on the counter.

"Then you better get back and start cooking, girlfriend. Because he's going to have a huge appetite when he wakes up." She blew on her coffee. "Way to go, cousin." She gave Lennox a thumbs-up. "Now I'm going back to bed for another hour."

Lennox headed back with the food cradled in her arms. Her own apartment was quiet. Matteus must still be sleeping. Though a few minutes later, she heard the water turn on in the shower. She needed to get busy.

By the time Matteus came out, Lennox had finished the bacon. The omelet was cooking nicely, and it did look fluffier with the added pancake batter. Pancakes sizzled lightly on the griddle. She grinned at him happily, warmth flooding through her at the sight of him.

"Breakfast is almost ready." She poured him a mug of coffee and handed it to him as he sat at the table. *Please don't let him freak out,* she prayed. Last night had been so perfect.

She slid his omelet onto a plate and added three slices of bacon. She set it in front of him and stood back, waiting. He hadn't said anything. In fact, he was avoiding looking at her. Deflated, she turned back to the stove, worried she'd done something wrong.

She layered pancakes on another plate and pulled the bottle of syrup out of the microwave. She set the plate and syrup on the table and sat down across from him. She smiled at him. He still hadn't said anything. He was simply staring at the omelet. Maybe he wasn't a morning person.

"About last night…," she started.

"Give me a couple of minutes," he said, his voice gruff. "I need to eat and then we can discuss what happened last night."

Lennox could hardly contain herself. She dug into her own omelet, watching him. He continued to avoid her gaze. He was embarrassed. Something was wrong. As happy as she was, she realized he wasn't.

"About last night," she began again. She shook her head. Obviously, he wasn't having the same emotional reaction she was. Did he regret sleeping with her? If that was the case, she'd let him off the hook. She tried not to be hurt, but last night she'd thought their relationship had changed, and this morning she could see it hadn't.

"Lennox…," he said, finally looking her in the eye, "last night was a mistake."

"I'm already getting that vibe," she said in a flat tone, trying to contain her disappointment. "You don't want to move forward in your life. That's okay. If you want to stay miserable, that's your choice. I thought we shared something. But all I need from you right now is to finish this lawsuit and then we can both go our separate ways."

"You're hurt," he said.

"It's not the first time," she said flippantly, "and it won't be the last."

"What can I do?"

"Nothing," she said, standing up. She took her plate to the sink and threw the food down the garbage disposal, her appetite gone. "I'm going to take a shower." *And maybe cry a little.*

After she left the room, Matteus picked at his food. Call him clueless, but he had the feeling she was mad at him. The problem was, he really liked what happened last night and he wanted more. He hated that she had walked away from him. She'd looked so happy, so relaxed, and he'd hurt her. He should have talked faster, but the words just wouldn't come out. He wanted her. Last night had been the best thing.

She expected the worst from him. She didn't even give him a chance to talk. How was he going to fix this?

The feel of her skin and the sweetness of her mouth had left him wanting so much more. Not once had he thought about Camille, and for the first time since her passing, he felt good and he wanted to keep feeling that way.

He was stunned. Being happy like this had seemed so far away not that long ago. Lennox had made him feel alive again, and he wanted to keep feeling alive.

What should he do? Without another thought, he stood and walked to her bedroom, shedding his clothes. He opened the bathroom door and listened—to the sound of her crying. Then he opened the shower door and stepped inside behind her, sliding his arms around her and pulling her back to lean against him.

She stiffened.

"You didn't let me finish," he said.

"Okay, give it your best shot."

"In fact, you didn't let me talk at all. I'm not always at my finest in the morning." He cupped her breasts in his hands. They felt heavy and firm against his palms. "This is how I feel about you." He nuzzled her neck, becoming delighted when her breasts peaked. He slid one hand down her slick skin, across her stomach and then lower, to that secret place between her legs.

She moaned and leaned back against him. Her skin was slick and silky. His fingers slipped inside her, and she suddenly pushed him away and turned.

"What do you want?" she asked.

It took a couple of seconds for the words to come out. His heart raced at the sight of the water cascading down her body. She looked so sexy and sweet all at the same time. "To apologize."

"Accepted. Now…" She inclined her head toward the door.

"I haven't actually said I'm sorry."

"I got the gist. We're cool." Yet she didn't look like she was okay.

"I felt guilty." Okay, he had gotten it out, but he still felt like an ass. "I loved Camille deeply and sleeping with you felt like a betrayal of her." Even at the end Camille had always been cheerful and optimistic.

"I won't compete with a ghost. You have a choice to make." She kissed him firmly and deeply. She raised an eyebrow. "Aren't you lawyer types supposed to know when to stop talking? I wanted to take a walk on the wild side. So, you don't have to feel bad." She pinned him with a hard stare and then looked at the door again.

He got the hint; he just wasn't taking it. "Lennox…"

"What? You said your piece, so go."

"I don't want to." The time had come to let Camille go. He realized he wanted to be with Lennox.

She let out a long breath. "Why not?"

"I didn't want to feel anything for you. For anyone. But I do."

"You—" she held up her hands and made quotation marks "—'feel something for me'? So?"

"More than something. I like you. I like being with you." She reminded him that he was still alive.

"What am I supposed to do with that?"

"Give me another chance."

"To what? To hurt me again?"

"To make love to you, to get it right. To get us right." He hoped he'd said the right thing the right way. He wanted her again, desperately. He was ready to move forward with his life. But only if it was with her.

She didn't say anything. The shower water had started to cool.

He could see the struggle on her face. Did she want to give him a second chance? God, he hoped so.

Lennox let out a long breath. "Don't blow it this time."

He grinned. "Let's get out before we turn into shriveled vegetables."

She looked down at his erection. "We wouldn't want that," she said softly.

She turned off the water and stepped out of the shower. He picked up a towel and started to dry her skin. His hands moved up and down, caressing her through the towel. He heard a sound from her. Suddenly, he was on his knees in front her, his tongue circling her navel and moving slowly downward.

She fell back against the wall, groaning.

He stood and led her back to his bedroom.

After he slid the condom on, he settled between her legs, his erection pushing at her inner folds.

Lennox kissed him, her lips warm and firm. His tongue tangled gently with hers. Her breath was sweet and slightly minty. Her skin smelled of lavender soap. He caressed her bare thigh, massaging her skin until the heat rose and she lifted her hips toward him, inviting him to do more than just touch her.

He could feel her readiness for him. He thrust inside, wetness and heat surrounding him.

Matteus ground himself against her. "Touch me."

"Anywhere I want?" She ran her hands up his back. Her hands were warm and soft.

His muscles contracted under her touch. His nipples hardened. She was intoxicating and he loved the way she made him respond. He laughed against her mouth. "Good."

"Love me," she said.

He had to catch his breath.

"Now," she whispered, her breasts hard against him. She wrapped her legs around his hips.

The heat overwhelmed him.

She shifted her hips to take him all the way inside of her. Damn, it felt so good to be in her. In that moment he was complete. He braced himself as she arched her back to get him all the way inside. He gave hard, slow thrusts.

He loved being in her, their skin touching, mouths kissing. He'd never get enough of her. Her excitement grew as he deepened his thrusts. His pleasure was almost at the breaking point. Her head fell back and he buried his mouth in her neck.

"You feel so good," he whispered against her skin.

"Harder." Her voice came out in a harsh whisper.

Matteus felt her vagina clench around him and his body tense, and a second later he felt her come. He bit down on her shoulder as his own orgasm came to life. For the first time in a long time, he felt at peace.

Chapter 12

Roger Baker was in his late forties, with black hair streaked with gray. He was neatly dressed in gray trousers and a dark blue jacket. His shirt matched his pants and was open at the throat.

"Thank you for meeting with me," Matteus said as he stood and shook the man's hand.

Roger lived in San Diego and had agreed to meet with Matteus if they could find a halfway point. Matteus had chosen a small coffee shop in Temecula just a few blocks from the freeway.

Roger sat down. "I agreed only because I want to see Ben Talbert get what's coming to him," he said bitterly. "Because of him, I had to leave the toy business. I couldn't continue designing toys knowing that bastard is making millions on my toy designs."

"But you settled with him," Matteus said.

"At the time I was going through a nasty custody battle with my ex, and I just wanted this lawsuit to be over."

"I can understand that."

"My cousin was my lawyer," Roger continued. "She came to me and suggested I just drop the whole thing."

"Why would she do that?"

"Because Ben tried to bribe her into throwing the case."

Matteus sat back in shock. "Can she prove this?"

"No," Roger said. "The offer was very subtle and very good. And when she said no, they threatened to destroy her, me and everyone I love. I felt I had too much to risk for a long drawn-out fight. And I didn't want my cousin in danger, too."

"And you were okay with your decision?" Matteus asked.

"I loved that job, but I wasn't about to lose everything. I have a good job now working as an engineer for the navy. And I'm happy. My ex-wife is happy. My kids are happy. I'm not going to do anything to destroy that."

"You have to protect your family," Matteus said. "I understand that."

"Feel free to talk to my cousin Dianna." He pulled his wallet out of the inside jacket pocket, extracted a business card and handed it to Matteus.

"I will," Matteus said, pocketing the card. He'd met Dianna Rowland over another case and had been impressed with her.

They finished their coffee and Roger walked out to his car. Matteus sat for a moment thinking. He wondered if Ben had bribed Gillian Smith's lawyer, too? His old detective gut said yes. What he needed to do now was head back to his office and talk things out with his partner—but before that he wanted to talk to Camille.

He sat on the grass next to Camille's grave, his arms braced on his knees, hands dangling. A short distance away, a woman knelt in the grass cleaning a grave and then arranging flowers in a vase tucked into a metal frame anchored in the ground.

He knew all of Camille's neighbors. He occasionally cleaned up the graves around her since it seemed no one else was interested.

He'd put tulips across her tombstone. Usually when he came he felt she was with him, but not today. He stared out at the ground and the freeway snaking its way toward Los Angeles.

"So, Camille," he said as a preamble, "I slept with Lennox." He waited for the guilt he'd felt in the past, but nothing came. He realized he felt happy and peaceful for the first time since Camille's cancer diagnosis. "And I liked it. I like being with her. I like the way she smells. I like the way she thinks. I like her spirit. She doesn't seem like she's tough on the outside, but she is."

Lennox was so different from Camille, he was surprised at how much he was attracted to her. Her playfulness mixed with eccentricity charmed him. She didn't just exist; she lived. That was the one aspect of her that mirrored Camille. Camille, for all her seriousness, had always been so alive. He'd been attracted to her because of that.

"I wish I knew where this was going." Emotionally, Lennox didn't need him. She was her own person who knew what she wanted out of life and wasn't afraid to fight for it. Ben Talbert may intimidate her, but she wasn't backing down.

"Please understand, I'm not being unfaithful to you and I will never forget you, but I think I need to move forward. Nina is all up in my face about getting on with my life. She tells me that while I'm advancing in my career, I'm stalled in my love life." He had always liked being a cop, but he liked being a lawyer even more.

The woman finished tidying up the grave, knelt down and folded her hands in prayer. After a few minutes she stood, wiped bits of grass from her dress and turned away. She walked down the slope to the road turning toward the parking lot and climbed into a dark blue sedan parked next to Matteus's Honda.

"You'll always have a spot in my heart." He knew he was finally saying farewell to her and he felt sad. He stood up and stared down at the tulips. His heart felt heavy in his chest. "I'll be back again. You take care, sweetheart."

His phone rang as he walked to his car. His mother's name popped up on the display. "Mom, what's up?"

"I woke up this morning feeling like I needed to make oatmeal cookies. Why don't you stop by and help yourself?"

He found himself smiling. Oatmeal cookies were code for the fact that she knew he needed her. The last time she'd made oatmeal cookies was the day Camille's doctor told them about her cancer.

"Forty minutes," he said.

"See you then," she said and disconnected.

Matteus found himself whistling as he got in his car.

Grace bustled about the kitchen. Years ago, Matteus's father had stripped the original kitchen down to the studs and replaced it with an industrial kitchen large enough for a dozen cooks. Four built-in ovens, two countertop stoves and an extra-large industrial refrigerator and freezer gleamed, the stainless steel polished to a bright shine.

Matteus sat at the snack bar munching a cookie while his mother brewed coffee.

"So what's bothering you?" Grace poured coffee into two mugs and set one in front of him.

"I was visiting Camille when you called," he said between bites.

Grace smiled at him. "I know you visit her a lot."

"Yeah, but this was different."

She leaned an elbow on the snack-bar counter and cupped her chin in her hand. "How so?"

"I think I was trying to say goodbye."

"As in you're not going to visit her anymore?"

Matteus sighed. "I don't know. I slept with Lennox."

"About damn time," Grace said. She shoved the platter of cookies closer to him.

"Excuse me?" he said, surprised. Had his mother just said what he thought she said? She constantly surprised him.

"She's been in love with you since she was a little girl."

"I know, but she was just so young."

Grace smiled fondly at Matteus. "I admire the fact that you never took advantage of her affection for you. A lot of men would have used her to their own end."

"I would never have done that to Lennox."

"Of course not, because then I would have had to hurt you," Grace said calmly. "I've seen everything. I've seen seventy-year-old men with nineteen-year-old brides. I've seen fifty-year-old brides with twenty-one-year-old grooms. The six years between you and Lennox is a drop in the bucket. Ten years ago, I would have told you to wait because age is the equalizer. Six years when you're a child is a lot, but six years between two adults is nothing."

Matteus took another cookie and bit into it, digesting what his mother had just said. When he was with Lennox, he never thought about the six years' difference in their ages. He'd stopped thinking about her as a child from the first moment he'd laid eyes on her again after so many years. She'd walked right up to him like she owned the moment.

"Do you remember Roy Anderson?" Matteus asked.

"You were friends in college. He came home with you one time."

"Yeah, for Thanksgiving. Lennox and her parents came for dinner. Roy told me she was hot. And that I was out of my mind for not taking advantage of that because even he could see she was attracted to me, and if I didn't want her, Roy was going to do her." He paused. He hadn't thought about Roy in years.

"And?" Grace prompted.

"I beat the shit out of him," Matteus said. "When

we got back to school, I told him I didn't want to see him again."

"Well, you probably shouldn't have resorted to violence. But even then you were protecting her."

"She was a beautiful girl who needed to find out who she was."

Grace patted his hand. "Lennox always knew who she was. And trust me, she would never have let Roy near her."

"Roy seemed like he wasn't going to give her much of a choice."

"He wouldn't have gotten far. Don't you remember all those years she did tae kwon do? She would have handed his head to him." Grace chuckled as though the idea appealed to her.

Matteus had forgotten Lennox had taken classes in martial arts. Her parents had been big on her knowing how to handle herself in any situation. Maybe he should have let Roy make his move and get his head handed to him. Even at sixteen, Lennox hadn't suffered fools gladly.

"What do I do?" he asked his mother.

"What do you want to do?"

"I don't know. I'm a grown man asking his mother's advice."

Grace patted his hand again. "You're a grown man who is talking to his mother about his problems because I'm your mother and I have to listen. And I probably have the right answer."

"So what do I do?"

Grace stood and wrapped her arms around him.

"What does your gut tell you? Of all my sons, you have the best-developed instincts."

"My gut tells me to go for it." He was so attracted to her that just talking about her made him ache to drive back to Redlands simply to be near her.

"Then go for it. Lennox is an amazing woman and you won't go wrong with her."

He leaned his head against her shoulder and took a few deep breaths. "Thanks, Mom."

She patted his head as though he were still six years old. "That's what moms are for."

At the store, Naomi dusted the shelves and displays while Lennox waited on customers. She tried to sound perky and enthusiastic as she interacted with them, but inside she felt oddly emotionless.

During a midmorning lull, Naomi tucked her feather duster under the counter and perched on a stool. "I'm sorry I couldn't help yesterday." Her summer classes had turned into time hogs with all the papers she had to write.

"It's cool," Lennox said. "Right now, these notebooks are turning into an urban legend."

"We'll find them," Naomi said confidently. "But what about you and Matteus?"

Lennox sighed. "He's conflicted. I don't think he knows what he wants."

"He either likes you or he doesn't. Boys are just dumb. They worry about stupid things."

Lennox smiled. Her cousin had always been her

champion. "I think he's having a hard time letting go of his wife."

"Maybe I don't understand because I've never loved anybody that much."

"You're having too much fun playing the field."

"Well, yes. I'm young."

"You're twenty-six."

Naomi shrugged. "And I have plenty of time to make decisions about my personal life. Right now I'm focused on my doctoral thesis, which is way more important in my life than romance. Romance is nice, but I want my degree, because it will be my accomplishment before I have to share my life with anyone else."

"But I'm ready," Lennox said. Having Matteus in her bed had made her realize that she wanted to be married; she wanted someone to love who would love her in return. "I'm going to give him one more chance, and if it doesn't work out, I'm done."

"Are you sure about that?"

Lennox nodded. "He either gets with the program or he gets gone."

"Okay, Beyoncé."

"I've done enough waiting," she told her cousin. "If I lose this lawsuit, I'll come up with something else. I'll survive because that is what I have to do."

Naomi hopped off her stool and hugged Lennox. "I love that you are so in charge of your world."

"If you don't mind," Lennox said, "I'm going to look in the attic for a while."

"You go ahead. I'll be nice to the customers."

The door opened and a man entered the store. He was

tall and distinguished looking with blond hair, blue eyes and a pleasant smile. He appeared to be in his mid- to late-thirties. He looked around and Naomi grinned at him as he approached the counter.

"Hi, can we help you?" Lennox asked politely.

"I understand that you have vintage Steiff teddy bears." He smiled at Lennox. He had a slight accent, which she recognized immediately as German.

"We do." She turned around to show him the bears.

"Why is that one in a glass case?"

"It's for serious collectors." Lennox hadn't put a price on it because she didn't want to scare people off.

The man opened his briefcase and pulled out a catalog of Steiff teddy bears. "I'm a serious collector. I'd like to see that one." He nodded at the bear in the glass display case.

"It's in excellent condition."

Naomi reached up for the glass case and carefully set it on the counter. Lennox opened the hinged door. From under the counter she pulled out white cotton gloves, put them on and picked up the bear.

"How much?" he asked calmly, though his eyes shone with excitement.

"Twenty-five thousand," she said calmly, even though her heart was pounding with nerves.

He looked it over carefully, minutely examining the seams and the ear button. "Seventeen thousand."

She looked at him. Was he really a serious collector? "Twenty-two."

He studied her intently. "Twenty grand, and not a

penny more." He whipped out his American Express Platinum.

"Sold," she said, trying not to tremble with excitement.

"What about the two turtles?" he asked.

"You really are a serious Steiff collector, aren't you?" Naomi said, batting her eyes at him. "For fifteen hundred we'll throw in the turtles."

"Okay, a teddy bear, two turtles and your phone number." He grinned at Naomi, who gave him a flirty smile.

"Sold," she said. "I have a class tonight. It ends at seven and I plan to be very hungry."

"I will see what I can do to alleviate that hunger," he said with a laugh.

"Can I see your driver's license or other form of ID?" Lennox asked politely.

He pulled a driver's license out of his wallet and handed it to her, along with the credit card. She compared the name on the driver's license with the name on the card. They matched.

He'd forgotten all about her in his quest to impress Naomi.

"My name is Hans Knapp." He held out a hand to Naomi.

"German?" Naomi asked.

"Austrian, actually," he said with humor in his voice.

"I'm Naomi Martin."

Lennox ran the card and it came up approved. She'd almost been afraid that it wouldn't be. Naomi carefully wrapped the bear and turtles in acid-free paper and then bagged the purchases. Lennox photocopied his driver's license and the card as a precaution. Naomi handed him a paper bag with the store logo on it.

Naomi tucked her hand around his elbow and walked him to the door, her dark head tilted up to his. She opened the door and he walked out. Seconds later she returned to the cash/wrap desk, looking ecstatic.

Lennox stared at the signed credit-card receipt. If she successfully proved the RealKidz idea was hers, she would be able to pay Matteus some money and still afford her 3-D printer. She'd tried not to feel too optimistic, because she did need to be prepared for the worst.

Naomi snapped her fingers. "And that's how you get a date."

"And make me some money at the same time."

"Break out Google," Naomi said, tapping the laptop and bringing it back to life. Quickly, she typed in Hans Knapp. In seconds his photo appeared with the caption World-Renowned Architect Wins Bid on Dubai Skyscraper.

"Oh my," Naomi said as she read the first article quickly. "He lives in San Francisco and is a world traveler."

"Be careful. He looks too good to be true."

"I think I'm in serious like," Naomi said.

"Looks more like serious lust to me," Lennox said.

"I'm okay with that." She read another article. "Look, he owns his own jet. And he's a pilot, too. Lust at thirty thousand feet."

Lennox rubbed her forehead. "I'm not scrubbing that image from my brain anytime soon."

Naomi just laughed.

Lennox frowned at the article. "Check to see if he's married."

"Divorced," Naomi said. "No children."

Lennox found herself shaking her head. "Naomi, you are unique."

"I know. He's good-looking, he's rich, creative, tall and wears Brioni. Italian tailoring at its pinnacle."

"Enjoy your date, but don't let yourself get crazy. Now, I'm going up to the attic for a bit while you watch the store and fantasize about your date."

Naomi just nodded, a dreamy look already on her face.

Chapter 13

Lennox sat at her kitchen table trying not to be discouraged. Her mother sat across from her, looking as dusty and tired as her daughter.

"I'm never going to find those notebooks." Lennox poured herself a second cup of tea.

"Of course you will," Dorothy said. "I think you just need a diversion."

Lennox rubbed her tired eyes. "Like what?"

Dorothy reached for her purse and pulled out her wallet. "Why not call Matteus and invite him to the final concert of the Redlands Symphony?"

"I don't know how he feels about the symphony."

"You don't think he hasn't been? Trust me, with Grace and Manny for parents, he's been exposed to all forms of music."

The final concert of the season was the highlight of the summer. The *1812 Overture* with fireworks had always been Lennox's favorite concert. The perfect ending to a perfect season. Lennox hadn't attended too many concerts the last couple of years, and she wanted to go to this one.

Her mother patted her hand. "How are things going with the lawsuit?"

Lennox told her about Matteus's talk with the other designers and their lawyers. She skipped the part about sleeping with him. So much hinged on finding the notebooks, and she was starting to feel panicked the further into the attic she searched, since she had still found nothing.

She hesitated a long time after her mother left before she finally called Matteus. "I need a break," she said when he answered his phone.

"What kind of break?"

"I have two tickets to the symphony at the Redlands Bowl on Friday."

"I haven't been to the symphony in years."

"Do you want to go?"

"Yes, I do."

"Okay, then Friday."

Matteus read and reread the deposition in front of him. But his mind wasn't on it. His thoughts kept drifting back to Lennox and how comfortable he felt around her. She was easy to be with, and he found himself telling her more about himself than he'd ever told anyone else, except Camille. Yet she was so different from Camille, whose drive and determination had led her to a career in law.

Matteus found Lennox as intriguing as her toy store. When she'd been a kid, the last thing he'd pictured for her was a career in toys. She'd always done the unexpected. She was never greedy about sharing her toys. And she always had the most interesting ones—the same type of toys currently in her store. She still had the popular toys but tucked into the odd spaces in her store were the unexpected toys, as well. Her store was like a treasure hunt, and he found that he wanted to spend more time exploring the store, because he knew that once he understood the store, he'd understand her.

"Mr. Talbot is here," Matteus's receptionist said from the doorway.

Nate Talbert pushed his way into the office. He looked tired and worried. "I need to talk to you," he said.

Nate closed the door and stood in the center of Matteus's office. "You said you wanted to talk to me."

"Yes. I'm leaving tomorrow, but…" His voice trailed away. He studied Matteus intently. "I found some disturbing information that I don't know what to do with."

Matteus leaned back in his chair, waiting. One of his interview techniques from his cop days had been to stay silent when questioning a suspect. No one likes silence, and eventually people would fill the emptiness with talk.

Nate started to pace back and forth. "I think my son bribed Annette Conklin's lawyer."

Matteus sat up straight. "Do you have any proof?"

Nate shook his head. "I overheard my son talking about you on the phone and wondering how much you were worth. Ben then said you were unlikely to take a bribe. He ordered someone to start looking for your vulnerabilities. I think he was talking to a private investigator."

"That's interesting." Matteus doubted a PI would find anything on him. He'd led a pretty clean life. Still, he needed to alert his family about the possibility of being approached by a stranger searching for information. "I appreciate you telling me this."

"I can't believe he cheated. I brought him up to be honest and hardworking. I know business can be cutthroat, but I paid people what they were worth so I could live with myself." Nate finally sat down, looking every one of his seventy-plus years. "He broke the law."

Matteus had been researching industrial espionage and theft of trade secrets. He could see Nate was furious with his son.

"And," Nate continued, "Lennox's previous assistant, Carrie Breen, has been spying on all the toy designers. She keeps tabs on them after they leave. I think she's been telling Ben about everyone's projects. Especially if she thinks it's going to make Ben money."

And she probably made some money for herself out of that. "Do you think this Carrie is having an affair with Ben?" If she was stealing toy designs from other designers and giving them to Ben, they had to have an ongoing intimacy. He wondered if Ben's wife knew.

Nate shrugged. "I don't know. I don't want to know. I'm ashamed of my son. He's ruining people's lives.

Roger Baker was one of the brightest, most creative minds that ever worked for me. He shouldn't be working for the navy. He should be making toys. Gillian Smith created genius apps for children. He forced them out of the business to find a plan B for their lives. And now he's trying to do the same thing to Lennox." Nate rubbed his face. "I love my son, but I'm ashamed of him."

Matteus understood the other man's sadness. "I'm sorry. I can't imagine how hard telling me this must have been for you."

"Telling you was the right thing to do," Nate said.

Matteus had no idea what else he could say to ease Nate's pain. Family didn't turn on family unless they were trying to avoid trouble. Nate was hurting. He was mad.

"I think you need to go back to Florida and be as far away from this as possible."

"But I want to help Lennox," Nate said.

"Don't worry about Lennox."

"How am I going to explain this to my wife? She'll be devastated to hear about Ben's lack of—" His voice broke.

"I will keep you out of this. I'm not going to let you carry the weight of this. I have Lennox's best interests at heart. You don't need to worry about her."

"What are you going to do?"

"The less you know, the better." Matteus stood up and walked to the door. "Please, Mr. Talbert, you need to go home and let me take care of this."

Nate stood reluctantly. "Protect Lennox."

"I will," Matteus promised.

Nate shuffled out, and Matteus watched him go thoughtfully. He needed to think about what to do next.

The Redlands Bowl was one of Lennox's favorite places. As a child, her mother had brought her to workshops designed to introduce her to the different forms of music. Lennox thought about how rich her childhood had been with all the experiences she'd been exposed to.

Matteus spread a blanket over the grass and gestured for Lennox to sit on it. They could have chosen seats on the benches closer to the stage, but Lennox nixed that. Her favorite place was lying on the grass, where she could close her eyes and just listen to the music.

Matteus held the program to read from it. "We're in for a musical evening of selections from Rimsky-Korsakov's *Capriccio Espagnol*, Stravinsky's *The Firebird Suite*. Ending with the *1812 Overture*."

"And fireworks," Lennox said happily. She loved fireworks. The best fireworks in Southern California were at Disneyland on New Year's Eve and the Fourth of July.

Matteus settled next to her. He looked good in jeans and a white polo shirt. The memory of their night together, with the next morning sequel, brought a flush of heat to her cheeks. He stretched out on his side and took her hand.

"I would never have guessed you like fireworks," he said.

"When I was a kid we took a road trip to the San

Manuel res to buy fireworks that resulted in a two-month restriction."

"What happened?" Matteus asked.

"Let's just say the ex-arson investigator is still on my mother's Christmas-card list."

Matteus laughed. "That's gratitude. A whole different mindset."

Lennox grinned at him. "Right."

"I still remember your first cooking lesson."

"Good times." Manny had been teaching her to cook, and most of her soufflés tended to deflate into puddles of goo, but one had exploded. She wasn't certain why, but Manny had been deeply amused. The soufflé had popped and goo had gone everywhere, sort of like a class project she'd once done of a volcano. Her teacher had spent days trying to clean it up.

"Even though I had to clean the ceiling." Matteus squeezed her hand.

"You were tall enough. You're the one who left me unattended. I was only eight years old."

Matteus leaned over and kissed her. "I should have known better."

"Yes, you should have. I was a disaster in the making. Your dad was determined to turn me into a good cook."

"I wouldn't know. You haven't cooked for me."

"I made breakfast."

"Anybody can make a decent breakfast."

She punched him on the arm. "Now that's a challenge. You want a decent dinner, tomorrow is your chance."

"You're on. I consider that my reward, seeing how much time I've put in in your attic."

"And I appreciate that." Her mind was filled with food choices. She could think of a few recipes off the top of her head she did really well.

The orchestra had taken their places on the stage. The conductor stood in the center, bowing. A few seconds later, the conductor turned and tapped his podium for everyone's attention, and the concert began.

Another disappointing day in the attic had left Lennox drained. The attic, at least, was finally starting to look organized. Most of the large pieces of furniture were gone, taken on consignment at the antique store. Boxes had been searched and then labeled so that Lennox knew what was in them. Other than a couple more boxes of vintage toys, they hadn't found any more treasures, which disappointed Naomi, who opened each box with the expectation of finding a fortune in long-lost items.

The notebooks were nowhere to be found.

Matteus tried to reassure her as she spooned beef stroganoff on his plate. They'd both showered. Though they'd invited Naomi and Matteus's two brothers who'd donated their time, they had the apartment to themselves. Naomi had a date with Hans Knapp, and Matteus's brothers decided not to stay for dinner. Lennox thought Matteus had given them their marching orders, but she couldn't be sure.

"I don't think we're ever going to find them," Lennox said, trying to keep the panic out of her voice.

"We have time," he soothed.

"I don't know about that."

"Listen, I had a visit with Nate earlier this week, and he gave me some information that I'm working on."

"Like what?"

"I can't tell you right now, but my plan B is strong."

Lennox gulped her wine. She pushed food around her plate, too nervous to eat. "I'm not filled with confidence."

"I am." He took a second helping of the stroganoff. "This is really good."

"Thank you." She didn't tell him it was his mother's recipe, with a few additions of her own.

"Let me do the worrying. You keep on looking for the notebooks. Like I said, I'm working on plan B."

"Can you give me any idea what plan B might be?"

"No."

She rested her elbow on the table and cupped her chin in her palm. "Is Ben doing something illegal?"

"Hopefully," he answered.

"Do you care to elaborate?"

"Nope. The further I keep you out of it, the better."

She could almost hear his mind working away. She wondered what Ben had done and turned possibilities over in her mind, but couldn't think of anything.

Matteus pounded the keyboard of his laptop. His receptionist appeared in the open door of his office. Matteus raised an eyebrow at her.

"Felix Lawson is here to see you." She turned and went back to her station.

Matteus pushed away from his desk, trying not to show surprise. Felix Lawson had abandoned his fancy office for Matteus's modest storefront.

"Mr. Lawson," Matteus greeted him. "What brings you to my humble office?"

Felix looked as sophisticated as before in a charcoal gray suit, white shirt and black tie. He glanced around Matteus's office with its Ikea furniture and allowed the side of his mouth to curl in disdain.

Matteus indicated a chair and Felix perched on the edge, as though he would get some sort of communicable disease from it.

"You're putting up a good fight for your client," Felix said.

"That would be my job," Matteus responded, amused at the man's discomfort.

"You're a smart man. You must know you're not going to win."

"That never occurred to me."

"You lack experience, and a loss like this, at this time in your career, could devastate your future."

"I thank you for your concern." Matteus sat back, wondering what the man was leading up to.

"You're a talented lawyer and have a bright future ahead of you. I could use someone like you."

Matteus stiffened. "Really."

"Someone who wants to see his name on the door as a partner."

Matteus felt a spurt of amusement. He tried hard to keep his expression impassive but was having a hard time. "Your firm is well-known."

Felix nodded, pleased at the slight compliment. "My firm is one of the most prominent in California."

"What do I have to do to get this sweet deal?" Matteus leaned his elbows on the table.

"Work a little harder for yourself."

Matteus waited, wondering if Felix was going to spell out his bribe in more concrete detail. "I'm not quite certain what you're getting at."

Felix smiled. "I'm offering you the chance of a lifetime, but you will have to find a way to settle with Miss McCarthy."

"Are you here with an offer?"

Felix paused. "If Miss McCarthy is willing to accept five thousand dollars for her design and turn everything over to Talbert Toys immediately, then this will go away."

"And if she accepts this offer?"

"Six months from now, you'll have a door with your name on it in my firm."

"Let me consider it."

"You have until end of business on Friday," Felix said, a benevolent smile on his face.

Matteus could tell Felix was pleased. "I need to have this offer in writing."

"Not until everything is settled with Miss McCarthy."

"I will let you know."

Felix stood, the conversation over. Matteus walked him out to the front door. They shook hands and Matteus watched the man cross the street to his car, a black Mercedes.

"What was that about?" Sam stood in the doorway to his office.

"I think I've been propositioned."

"Did you let him get his hand up your skirt?"

Matteus laughed. "He was very polite about it." He went back into his office, Sam following, where he gave Sam more details of Felix's offer.

"Sounds like a bribe to me." Sam poured himself a cup of coffee.

"Me, too," Matteus said. "Though it was carefully phrased so that he can back out of it, which I suspect he will."

"What are you going to do?" Sam asked.

"I'm certainly not going to accept his offer. First off, I have too much respect for myself and for what you and I are trying to accomplish. And secondly, it's unethical." Plus, Lennox had become too important to him. His feelings for her had grown to the point where he wanted to be with her.

"You could report him to the State Bar of California, but you're going to need more than just a vague conversation and a possible offer."

"His offer was sort of a bribe, but not really."

"You need to talk to a lawyer he did bribe," Sam said.

"I think I know one." Matteus thought of Annette Conklin's lawyer. He needed to contact him, but first he needed to talk to Lennox. He was required to make the offer. "I need to know more about Ben Talbert." He picked up his phone and flipped through his contacts until he came to the private investigator they used on occasion. "I'm calling Tony."

"Good luck. I've got to get back to the Phillips case," Sam said as he turned and left.

Lennox sat at the counter. It was turning out to be a slow sales day. She'd finished dusting and straightening up the store. She'd worked a bit on inventory, but her thoughts kept returning to Matteus. He'd called and said he was on his way to talk to her. She wondered what had happened.

She checked her email. Professor Schröder had sent her a message telling her he was sending her a package and to be on the lookout for it. Sometimes the toys sold well and sometimes they didn't. But she loved the old man and his quirky sense of humor.

Matteus pushed open the door. She smiled at him.

"I hardly expected to see you today."

He loosened his tie and leaned on the counter. "I have an interesting piece of news."

"Do tell."

"How would you feel if I threw you under the bus?"

Startled, she said, "In pain. Are you planning to do that?"

He grinned at her. "No, I won't, but I'm going to pretend that I did."

"I'm totally lost here."

He told her about Felix's visit and the offer he'd presented.

For a moment, Lennox was speechless. "That— that… I don't normally swear, but a few choice words are going through my head." She stared at Matteus. "Ben's afraid."

"Afraid of what?"

"You," she said.

"Good. He should be afraid of me. But I think the real issue is that he sees your doll as being a huge moneymaker."

"And he thinks I'm going to be happy with five thousand dollars."

"And he'll tie you up in a nondisclosure agreement."

She thought for a few moments. "At the show, they took a much smaller booth than normal. I'm thinking they're having money issues and they need my idea to hit one out of the park."

The problem with toys was that what was popular one day could be dead the next. Children were fickle, which meant toy companies constantly had to come up with new ideas to keep their market share. A well-designed toy could keep them in business for decades. The right toy at the right time was priceless.

Her doll idea had more than just appeal to children, though. What adult wouldn't want a doll replica of themselves? Her thoughts churned. She knew her idea had far-reaching potential.

"I can request a look at their financials. But they don't have to share, and their lawyer will argue that their financial position isn't relevant to the case. Being a privately owned company has some advantages."

"So let's assume they are having financial troubles. That could be why they haven't paid Annette Conklin." Lennox rubbed her eyes. "Basically, you're going to let Ben bribe you so you have leverage."

"That's my plan C, but only if you don't find the notebooks."

Not finding them was turning into a very real possibility. Lennox sighed. She didn't want to think about this anymore. She wanted to grab Matteus by his tie and take him upstairs for an afternoon romp.

The door opened and a customer entered. Lennox took a moment to direct the woman and her toddler to the baby toys while her thoughts churned feverishly.

"I don't want to be thrown under the bus. Why did Ben have Felix make this offer?"

"They're hedging their bets. Hoping you don't stand up to them. If you cave, they are spared the expense of a trial."

"Do you think Felix offering you a partnership is genuine?"

"He has no intention of offering me a partnership. If you accept the settlement, Felix will find a way to get out of it. He'll probably say I misunderstood him."

A young woman entered the store. "Do you sell trains?"

"Down the hall, the last door on the right," Lennox directed her.

The woman smiled her thanks and headed toward the train room.

"You didn't have to come all this way to tell me that," she said.

"I didn't want to tell you over the phone."

"Are you heading back to Pasadena now?"

He grinned at her. "I thought I'd take you out to dinner tonight, and I did bring my overnight bag."

"I accept your dinner invitation."

"Thanks. Do you mind if I find a corner to get some work done?"

"Go upstairs and work. It's quieter. The store doesn't close for another three hours, so make yourself comfortable."

"Where's Naomi?"

"She's out with her new beau." Lennox thought it was cute the way Naomi had taken to Hans Knapp. She hoped that Hans wasn't taking her for a ride.

Matteus walked up the stairs to her apartment. She watched him, her heart pounding. Her feelings were so deep, she ached. She knew he loved her, but could he ever *fully* love her? His feelings for Camille still showed.

She thought about the offer Felix had made. Ben must be getting desperate. But why?

Something was going on, but she had no idea what.

Matteus plugged in his laptop and pulled a couple of folders out of his briefcase. He had depositions to read for another case and a brief to prepare.

His gaze fell on the business card with the name of Annette Conklin's lawyer. He realized the man's office was in San Bernardino. He could get there and back before Lennox closed the store.

Ten minutes later, he had an appointment lined up in an hour. He told Lennox he'd be back and he pushed out the door, heading to his car.

Parker Hughes's office was in a small building just off the 215 freeway. The office was neat and clean with standard wood furniture, a bar on one wall and a bank of windows across from it. Several chairs were grouped in the other corner.

Parker was a short, rotund man with round framed glasses that gave him an owlish look.

They shook hands. Parker's handshake was moist and limp.

"I represent a client," Matteus said, launching right in, "who is being sued by Talbert Toys."

Parker Hughes suddenly looked wary. "How can I help you?"

"You represented Annette Conklin in a similar case."

Parker nodded. "It was a loser from the get-go. She had no documentation to prove the toy design was hers."

"From what Annette says, you didn't put up much of a fight. You told her to settle and get on with her life."

Parker shrugged. "I did what was best for my client."

"That's what I'm trying to do for my client."

"I believe you."

"Felix Lawson visited me this morning."

Parker stiffened and he looked away. "Don't believe anything he says to you."

"So he made you the same offer?"

"Like I said, don't believe anything he says to you, Mr. Torres."

"So the offer didn't work out for you?" Matteus persisted.

Parker Hughes stood so suddenly, his chair bounced back against the wall. "Goodbye, Mr. Torres."

Matteus stood, too. "Thank you for your time."

A few minutes later Matteus sat in his car, thinking. He'd learned everything he needed to know. Felix Lawson wasn't to be trusted. Though he had already distrusted the man, like any good lawyer he'd needed to know for sure. Now he was angry.

Chapter 14

Matteus had known Tony Di Falco since their days at the academy. Like Matteus, Tony had retired after being injured on the job. He'd set up as a private investigator and now had three others working for him.

"Good to see you, Matteus," Tony said.

Matteus slid into the booth across from his old friend. "Good to see you, too, Tony."

A waitress approached with a plate of spaghetti, which she set in front of Tony. Matteus ordered a cup of coffee and the woman smiled at him.

The restaurant proudly billed itself as a home of old-fashioned cooking. And the delicious aromas coming from the kitchen made Matteus's mouth water.

"What have you got for me?"

"People with problems. All kinds of problems," Tony said. He shoved a folder at Matteus.

Matteus opened the folder. "Do tell."

"Ben Talbert is so deeply in debt, he's going to be years getting out of it."

Matteus whistled. "A quarter of a million dollars!"

"And to the wrong loan shark." Tony broke a garlic breadstick in half and munched on it as the waitress returned with Matteus's coffee.

"This guy owns a multimillion-dollar toy business. This is chump change." Matteus glanced quickly through the report. "How could he get so deeply in debt?"

"Gambling, and his wife has every store on Rodeo Drive on speed dial." Tony tucked into his spaghetti while Matteus read.

"Wow," Matteus said.

"And their house is mortgaged to the hilt. Plus that island vacation home is on the market for less than nothing."

No wonder they were willing to gamble so much on Lennox's design. "And the business isn't doing so well either."

Tony nodded. "They inherited a business that was at the top of its game, and they've plundered it down to practically nothing."

Matteus wondered how they could afford Felix Lawson. That man was not a cheap lawyer. He paged through the report and discovered that Felix was the wife's cousin.

"Also, Ben's having an affair with Carrie Breen, one

of his employees. She's just the latest in a long line of expensive affairs."

"These people are a hot mess," Matteus said.

"And then some."

"What about Felix Lawson?" Matteus asked.

"Nothing much. Family does for family." Tony finished his spaghetti, and a moment later, the waitress came to take his plate and set a bill in the center of the table.

"My client is ready for a big fight. In fact, I'm ready for a fight, too." Matteus closed the folder. This information certainly added to the overall picture. "Anything else I need to know?"

"I emailed you a more comprehensive report." Tony gestured at the folder. "This is just the highlights." Tony handed Matteus the bill. "Thank you for lunch."

After Tony left, Matteus paid and headed back to his office, thinking about the ticking time bomb inside the folder.

Sam waited at the door of their office, dressed in his court suit of black blazer and tie, gray pants and white shirt.

"How did the Gonzalez case go?" Matteus asked as they entered.

"Postponed till next month," Sam said. "Alfred Gonzalez's lawyer had a heart attack."

"Tony had quite a story for me." Matteus handed Sam the folder.

Sam sat down and perused it. "This is interesting."

"No kidding," Matteus said.

"Sort of a primer on how to screw up your life," Matteus said.

"And then some," Sam replied. "What are you going to do?"

"If Lennox doesn't find those notebooks then I'll have another level of leverage."

"Fair enough." Sam handed the folder back to Matteus. "You're going to go to the wall for this one, aren't you?"

"I am."

Sam stood. "Lennox has come to mean a lot to you, hasn't she?"

Matteus paused. "Why do you ask that?"

"Camille's photo is gone." He pointed at the empty spot in the bookcase behind Matteus where he'd kept a picture of his late wife.

Matteus gazed at Sam. "I'm ready to move forward."

"Good for you. Camille wouldn't want you to live like a hermit."

"I didn't think I'd ever have someone special in my life again." Lennox had changed him in her own small way.

"I didn't think you'd let someone into your life again."

He smiled at Sam. "Lennox barged back into my life and stayed there. I don't think I had a choice."

Sam laughed and went back to his office.

Matteus thought about Lennox and how happy she made him. He liked being with her. He liked the way she tilted her head when she laughed. And he liked the way she held his hand. The biggest surprise was the knowledge that he loved her. He could admit it now. He'd been falling in love with her since the first moment he saw her trailing behind her mother as they entered the restaurant. Her face had lit up at the sight of him, and that had been the first step back to life for him.

Saturday story hour had just ended, and Naomi was helping a customer while Lennox worked the register. After the last customer had left, she heard a heavily accented voice.

"The photos you sent me didn't do justice to your store, Leni."

Lennox whirled around in surprise. "Professor Schröder!"

Professor Schröder smiled broadly at her. He was a tall man with a full head of gray hair and a matching beard. He wore an old tweed jacket and trousers. Two large suitcases flanked him. "My Leni, I have brought justice with me."

"Excuse me?" She practically ran into his arms. During her time in Germany, he and his wife had been surrogate parents to her, always supportive and encouraging. She leaned against his shoulder, taking in the fragrant aroma of his favorite pipe tobacco.

He pulled her into a hug and kissed her forehead. She pulled out of his arms and grabbed his hand. "You are my Leni. My sweet wife says to me, 'Eric, you cannot let that child be treated that way. You go, you take care of her. My Hilda always loved you. She sends you much love. I bring you this." He opened a large satchel, pulled out a big envelope and handed it to her with a flourish.

"What is this?"

"Open it," he urged, a delighted smile on his face. His faded blue eyes twinkled with merriment.

The envelope was heavy and Lennox stared at it. Slowly she lifted the flap and reached inside. A sheaf of papers bound by a binder came out.

She said in an awed tone, "You brought me my term paper."

"Ja," he said. "And this is my grade book." He flipped it open and showed her a highlighted entry. "I can prove you developed this project in my class."

Tears slid down her cheeks. "You kept my report."

"I did." He wiped at her tears with a snow-white handkerchief. "I wanted to be able to say that the brilliant toy designer Lennox McCarthy was my student and I was there at the beginning of her career."

"I don't know how to thank you." But she knew she owed him a big one. At least she wouldn't need her notebooks anymore. And if nothing else, the attic was clean.

Naomi peered over her shoulder. "You need to call Matteus. Right now."

Lennox nodded. She paused for a second and then knelt down on the floor, opened the floor safe and put the envelope inside. She wasn't about to leave this sitting around for any reason. "Okay. Okay." She reached for her phone and cycled through her contact numbers to his name.

He answered on the first ring. "Lennox, what's up?"

"Can you come right now?" She could barely contain the excitement in her voice.

"Is something wrong?"

"No, something is right for a change."

"You found the notebooks." His tone grew excited.

"No. Something better."

"I can't leave just yet. I'll be there around four."

"That works. See you then." She disconnected and took deep breaths to calm herself before she turned back to Professor Schröder. She hooked her arm through his. "Come on, let me show you my store."

"Matteus," Lennox said. "Please meet Professor Schröder. I studied with him when I was in Germany, and he brought me a present today."

Matteus eyed her. She practically vibrated with excitement.

Matteus shook hands with the man, who looked to be in his sixties. His handshake was strong, yet relaxed.

"What's the emergency?"

She knelt down and opened the floor safe. She pulled out a large envelope and handed it to him. "Go on. Open it." She practically jumped up and down.

He opened the envelope and turned it upside down. A thick report in a binder clip slid out. A huge *A* had been written in one corner, and along the margins were notes in red pen. He flipped through the report and realized what he was holding in his hands.

Lennox handed him a book opened to a page. He realized it was a grade book with her name highlighted, the name of the report and a grade beside it, matching the *A* on the report.

His heart started racing. "Am I holding what I think I'm holding?"

Lennox nodded. "It's my weapon of mass destruction."

"I am willing to testify in a court of law," Professor Schröder said.

"And I'm willing to let you," Lennox cried.

"You have such a charming sense of humor, my Leni."

Lennox burst out laughing. Matteus grabbed her and planted a kiss on her lips. Her arms slid around his neck, her body pressed to his. When they broke apart, the professor was watching them with a twinkle in his eyes.

"This is perfect. It's a slam dunk, grand slam and triple-double all rolled into one." Matteus tucked the report back into the envelope. He couldn't wait for Monday morning so he could call Lawson and set up a meeting with him and Ben. Matteus wanted to see their faces when he dropped this on them. Lennox's doll was the design they weren't going to get.

"I'm free," Lennox said. "I have to call my parents and let them know, and then we're going to celebrate."

The conference room at Felix Lawson's office was large and ostentatious. The conference table was big enough to seat twenty people. One wall held a huge landscape painting, and the opposite wall contained a sideboard with coffee and other drinks set out on it.

Felix and Ben looked triumphant. Felix, with his slick smile and bespoke suit, gave Lennox a close-mouthed smile that contained a smugness that made her want to laugh. He had no idea what was coming. For the first time in weeks, Lennox wasn't tense or stressed.

She relaxed into the comfortable chair and waited. She was going to enjoy seeing the smarmy look slide right off his face when he realized what was happening.

"You've finally come to your senses," Felix said. "I can't say I'm surprised." His smug smile grew wider. Ben looked triumphant.

Matteus, Lennox and Professor Schröder sat opposite Ben and Felix. Lennox wondered where Bernice was.

"You could say that we came to our senses—in a way." Matteus placed his briefcase on the table and opened it.

Felix raised an eyebrow. Lennox worked to keep her breathing even.

Lennox studied Ben. He looked drawn and tired. He'd lost weight. His skin had a grayish tone to it. Was he ill? Or was something else going on?

Felix opened a folder containing a stack of papers. "I took the liberty of drawing up the contract." He slid the folder toward Matteus. Matteus didn't even look at it. "Look it over. You'll find everything in order."

Lennox grinned. She wanted to jump up and down. Matteus laid a hand on her arm. She realized she was wriggling in place and took a deep breath, forcing herself to calm down. She felt a little sorry for Ben.

Matteus reached toward Felix's folder with one finger and pushed it back. Felix frowned, watching the folder slide back toward him. He scrutinized Matteus intently, as though suddenly aware things weren't quite going the way he intended.

"Before we get too far, I think you need to look at this." He handed Ben and Felix copies of Lennox's term paper and a copy of the grade-book page containing the professor's notes.

Felix paged through the report, and as he did, the look of triumph on his face drained away. "I don't think I understand."

Matteus shrugged. "Let me introduce you to Professor Eric Schröder. He was Miss McCarthy's professor and adviser during her year in Germany. You will see that the papers you're holding are a copy of a term paper Miss McCarthy wrote while she was in Germany, a document containing Professor Schröder's corresponding notes regarding the project and the grade the paper received, which was not only documented and dated by the professor, but also documented and dated by the records department at the university.

"All of this proves that Miss McCarthy not only developed this project while she was in school, but the accompanying documentation conclusively dates it to show that her doll design was not developed during her tenure at Talbert Toys. And this—" Matteus slid another document toward Felix "—is a copy of the professor's sworn statement supporting the documents."

Ben looked sick as he paged through the papers. "I don't believe this. These documents were falsified."

Felix shrugged. He started reading, paging through slowly. A couple of times he looked up, his gaze sharp and challenging as he studied the professor. Professor Schröder looked relaxed and calm, as though he had not a care in the world. His tranquil manner contrasted sharply with Ben's agitation. Ben's mouth hung open in surprise.

Felix gathered up the documents and slid them into the folder. "I would like to take a few days to go over all this information, and I would like the opportunity to pose questions to Professor Schröder should I find the need."

"Professor Schröder has graciously agreed to make himself available should you have more questions."

Seeing Matteus in lawyer mode left Lennox feeling like Nate was caught between a shark and a barracuda. This side of Matteus was surprising and different.

Felix and Ben stood, signaling the meeting had ended. They left the conference room and headed toward the back of the office suite, leaving a receptionist to show Matteus, Lennox and the professor out.

"That seemed to go well," Lennox said when they were in the car and heading back to Redlands. "What will they do now?"

"Felix may want to grill the professor to see if his story holds up. The problem is that the professor is a very credible witness, and Felix won't be able to rattle him."

"I do not like bullies," Professor Schröder said from the back seat.

"Then the lawsuit will go away."

"I hope so," Lennox said with a sigh. Was this nightmare truly over? She hoped so. She smiled at Matteus happily. She would have to call her parents with the good news.

Lulled by the hum of the car motor and the release of the stress she'd been under, Lennox fell into a doze. She woke up when they dropped the professor off at his hotel, and only then did she realize she'd been dreaming about Camille. In the dream Camille had spoken to her, but now she couldn't remember what she had said.

"How did it go?" Naomi asked when they entered the store. Hans Knapp jumped away from Naomi and leaned against the counter, trying to look relaxed. Naomi appeared a tiny bit disheveled, and radiant in her own way. Hans looked like a guilty schoolboy.

Lennox couldn't get the happy grin off her face. "We won."

Naomi sighed in relief. Lennox made her way up to her apartment with Matteus following.

"You won this for me. I can even pay you since I sold the Steiff teddy bear."

"No payment required," Matteus said.

"I'm not broke anymore."

"This was a labor of love," he said in return.

"What do you mean?"

"I don't have a lot of opportunities to be the white knight, riding in on my trusty steed and rescuing the damsel in distress." He pulled her into his arms.

"My hero," she said happily.

"I liked being your hero," he said.

She kissed him. "I kind of enjoyed being the damsel in distress. When I was a kid, I played with trucks rather than dolls. So this was interesting." Though if the brave knight knew how she felt, would he ride away? "You've done your job, so…" She choked on the words, releasing him.

He kissed her again. "What makes you think I'm leaving?"

"Aren't you?"

"Not unless you make me," he replied. "Are you going to make me?"

She took a step back and studied him. Her heart filled with such love for him that tears gathered in the corners of her eyes. "I've been in love with you for a long time." There, she'd said the *L* word.

He smiled and pulled her back into his arms. "I know. I was never ready for you. But I am now."

"Say what?" She'd never expected him to even think of her as someone he could love.

"These last few weeks have been the happiest I've felt in a long time. I don't know when I started falling in love with you, but I know now. I love you, Lennox McCarthy."

She took a deep breath. "I have loved you all my life."

"I'm going to love you for the rest of my life." He kissed her again. "But before we go any further, I need to take care of something."

She wondered what he needed to take care of, but didn't pry. He would tell her when he was ready. She stood at the window overlooking the street and watched Matteus back out of the parking spot. Restless, she walked back into the kitchen for a glass of ice tea.

She wasn't certain why she decided to go into the attic one more time. She stood in the center of the room. So much had been cleared out that huge spaces were now empty. Her mother had taken most of the photo albums. The one album she'd found chronicling the building of their church had been donated to the church.

Some other photos of early Redlands had been donated to the Redlands museum.

The only large piece remaining was the armoire where Naomi had found their great-grandmother's wedding dress. The armoire had been too large to safely get down the stairs, which made Lennox wonder how it had gotten up the stairs, but that was a mystery she would leave alone.

As she studied the armoire, she realized that beneath the large doors that opened to the neat piles of boxes inside, there were also two large drawers she hadn't noticed before. She sat down on the floor and opened the first drawer. It was empty except for some dust. The second drawer contained a box. When she lifted the box, something inside shifted.

She opened the box and there, inside, were her notebooks.

"Well," she said, "here you are." They had been in the very first place she and Naomi had looked.

She stood and closed the door to the armoire. Cradling the box in her arms, she took the notebooks down to her apartment. She would share her find with Naomi later. For now, she reveled in the knowledge that she no longer needed them because of Professor Schröder.

As she sat at the kitchen table looking at all her old ideas, she wondered what her future finally held.

Matteus sat on the grass next to Camille's grave. He'd cleaned away dry leaves and grass cuttings and set a bouquet of tulips on her tombstones.

"I love you," he said. "I'll always love you, and I'll

never forget our time together. A piece of my heart will always belong to you. But…" The next words were hard to say. "I love Lennox. I need her. And I'm going to ask her to marry me." Yet the words sounded sad rather than happy.

He listened, half-imagining that Camille was sad, too. "I'm never going to leave you. I'll be back." And he would bring Lennox, because she needed to know that Camille was as much a part of his past as Lennox was his future.

Epilogue

Lennox grinned at the sight of the central hallway that had been transformed, thanks to Naomi and her new beau, Hans Knapp, who seemed to be attached to her with a besotted look on his face. Streamers hung from the second-floor bannisters. Balloons attached to the cash/wrap counter swayed. A banner on one wall said *Congratulations*. A long table hugged a wall decked out in a white tablecloth and food dishes arranged by Manny and Grace Torres. The Lionel train chugged away on its track with merry little hoots.

Matteus opened the champagne, and the cork popped out with a loud bang. Dorothy held out a tray of champagne flutes and Matteus poured the bubbly liquid into them. Richard McCarthy, talking with Professor Schröder, couldn't stop smiling at Lennox, pride shining in his eyes. Even he had something to celebrate. The charity auction had netted enough donations to finish furnishing the new research laboratory her father had been pushing for.

Lennox smiled at all the people who'd come to be with her. The only hole in her heart was Nate. She ached for him and knew he was deeply disappointed in his son. She wished Nate were here so she could offer some comfort. As though a guardian angel answered her plea, the front door opened and Nate walked in with his wife.

"Nate," Lennox said, astonished to see him. "What are you doing here?"

Nate hugged her. "Matteus called me and let me know what happened. So we came to help celebrate."

"But it was your son…" She stopped. Nate loved his son despite Ben's behavior.

"Who is in need of a great deal of help," Nate said. "And I intend to help him. Especially now that Bernice has filed for a divorce."

Lennox hadn't heard about the divorce. "I'm sorry."

"Don't be," Nate said with a merry smile. "I have a solution."

She started to ask what he meant, but Matteus approached, grinning. "I didn't think you'd really come."

"I said I would. How could I miss a party like this, especially with your parents doing all the cooking?" Nate turned to the woman with him. "This is my wife, Gwen. Gwen, meet Matteus Torres."

Gwen Talbert was a sturdy-looking woman with gray hair cut short, brown eyes and a pretty smile. "Nice to meet you. And Lennox, I'm happy for you."

Lennox hugged Gwen and introduced her to her mother. Dorothy immediately showed Gwen to the buffet table.

Matteus had a strange smile on his face, and Lennox's eyes narrowed. "What's going on?" He'd been unusually secretive the last couple of days and she wondered what plot he was hatching.

"I'm going to let Nate tell you," Matteus said.

"I have an offer you shouldn't refuse," Nate said.

Lennox tilted her head, wondering what was on his mind. Nate looked excited and Matteus looked pleased. "I'm waiting."

"Ben and Bernice have decided to retire from the toy business," Nate said. "Gwen says I'm driving her crazy. I need a new hobby because golf isn't working for me."

"So you're coming back to run the toy company." Lennox felt an overwhelming joy.

"Not exactly," Nate said, looking mysterious. "Gwen and I put our house in Florida on the market and we're relocating to Palm Springs. That's a bit far for me to run the company from, so I'm giving it to you."

Lennox took a step back, too astonished to think. "Excuse me?" Had she really heard what she thought she'd just heard? "Say that one more time." She tilted her head at him, frowning.

"You and I—" Nate pointed at her and then himself "—are running the company." A huge grin spread across his face. "Me, part-time and from Palm Springs."

"Wait a second," Lennox said, shaking her head. "You want me to run your toy company."

"No, I want you to run our toy company. I'm giving

you fifty-one percent of Talbert Toys with the option of buying me out once the company is back on its feet."

Lennox stared at him, her mouth open. She whirled to face Matteus. A thousand thoughts crowded her mind. "You knew, didn't you?"

"I brought the paperwork and contract," Matteus said. "Nate contacted me a couple of days ago and swore me to secrecy."

"How am I supposed to turn down that offer?"

"You're not supposed to." Matteus slid an arm around her.

"What do I know about running a toy company?"

"I taught you everything you need to know," Nate said. "And you have the most important resource—me. I've decided I need to get back to designing toys, so that's my new hobby. I can do that from Palm Springs."

She stared at him. "I—I don't know what to say. Who's going to run my toy store?"

Nate chuckled. "You were just handed the keys to the world's biggest toy store."

She was dumbfounded. "But…" She looked around and realized Naomi was grinning at her. "What?"

"You mean I can't do this?" Naomi said, waving her hand at a toy display. "I've been working for you since you opened."

"Do you want to run this store? What about your PhD? You had all these plans…" Lennox didn't want her cousin to put her future on hold just so Lennox could run Talbert Toys.

"I can find help," Naomi said with a wide grin. "What better way could I have to show how much I've learned about business than running this toy store? Besides, working here is fun. I get to play around with all the toys. And I love the store."

Hans Knapp stood behind Naomi, one hand on her shoulder. "I can help."

"You live in San Francisco." Lennox shook her head. Everything was moving too quickly. She took a deep breath, trying to calm herself. Could she run the toy company? She could contact all the people Ben had cheated and make sure they were properly compensated for their designs, or if they wanted, she would return the rights to their designs. She wondered if Gillian Smith was willing to come back and work for her. And now that she had her notebooks, she realized she had other ideas that would work besides her doll.

"Actually, I'm thinking of moving and opening an office here. San Francisco is getting too expensive" Hans said. "Redlands could use a decent architect." He grinned at Naomi, who matched his with a silly grin of her own.

"Plans are coming together," Matteus said, rubbing his hands.

Lennox was too dazed to respond. She felt such an outpouring of love for her family.

Matteus took her hand and grinned. "Come on, I have something to show you."

"What?"

He led her down the hall to the doll room. He turned to her and put his hands on her shoulders. "I never thought I would feel this way again."

"What way?"

"Happy. In love. With you." He stared intently into her eyes. "I love you, Lennox McCarthy."

She was stunned and couldn't think of a reply immediately. She'd been hoping for this for years. "I can't remember a moment when I didn't love you." She couldn't even think of the right words to express all the emotions she felt inside her. "I love you, Matteus."

He crushed her to him. "Marry me. Live with me. Be my wife."

She pushed him away. "You're six years older than me. Don't you think you might be too old?"

He burst out laughing. "Are you going to hold the age difference over me for the rest of my life?"

"I might." She put a finger to her cheek. "Okay, on second thought, I won't. And I'll marry you even though you're an old man."

"You said you loved this old man."

"Like crazy."

"That's the best kind of way," he said.

She smiled. It was the only way she knew.

* * * * *

Soulful and sensual romance featuring multicultural characters.

Look for brand-new Kimani stories
in special 2-in-1 volumes starting March 2019.

Available July 2, 2019

Love in New York & Cherish My Heart
by Shirley Hailstock and Janice Sims

Sweet Love & Because of You
by Sheryl Lister and Elle Wright

What the Heart Wants & Sealed with a Kiss
by Donna Hill and Nikki Night

Southern Seduction & Pleasure in His Arms
by Carolyn Hector and Pamela Yaye

Get 4 FREE REWARDS!

We'll send you 2 FREE Books plus 2 FREE Mystery Gifts.

Harlequin® Desire books feature heroes who have it all: wealth, status, incredible good looks... everything but the right woman.

FREE
Value Over
$20

SPECIAL EXCERPT FROM

Completely captivated by his new employee, André Thorn is about to break his "never mix business with pleasure" rule. But amateur photographer Susan Dewhurst is concealing her true identity. Although she's falling for the House of Thorn scion, she can't reveal the secret that could jeopardize far more than her job at the flagship New York store. Amid André's growing suspicions and an imminent media scandal, does love stand a chance?

Read on for a sneak peek at
Love in New York,
the next exciting installment in the
House of Thorn series by Shirley Hailstock!

As she turned to find her way through the crowd, she came up short against the white-shirted chest of another man.

"Excuse me," she said, looking up. André Thorn stood in front of her.

"Well," he said. "This time there isn't a waiter carrying a tray of champagne."

"I apologized for that," she said, anger coming to her aid. She was already angry with Fred and had been expecting this sword to drop all day. Unprepared to have it fall when she thought she was safe, her sarcasm was stronger than she'd expected it to be. "Please excuse me."

She moved to go around him, but he stepped sideways, blocking her escape.

"Let me buy you a drink?"

Susan's sanity came back to her. This was the president of the company for which she worked. Susan forgot that she could leave and

KPEXP0519

get another job. She knew what it was to be an employee and to be the owner of a business.

"I think I've had enough to drink," she said. "I'm ready to go home."

"So you're going to escape my presence the way you did at the wedding?"

Her head came up to stare at him. Instead of seeing a reprimand in his eyes, she was greeted with a smile.

A devastating smile.

It churned her insides, not the way Fred had, but with need and the fact that it had been a long time since she'd met a man with as much sexual magnetism as André Thorn. No wonder he fit the bill as a playboy.

"I guess I am," Susan finally said. From the corner of her eye, she saw Fred sliding out of the booth. He should know who André Thorn was, but if he planned to put his arm around her in front of another man, he would be making a mistake. "Excuse me," she said and hurried away.

Susan stood in front of the bathroom mirrors. She freshened makeup that didn't need to be, stalling for time. Why had she reacted to André Thorn that way? Embarrassment, she rationalized. She'd run into him at her friend Ryder's wedding. Judging from where he'd sat in the church, he must know Ryder's bride, Melanie. He would. Frowning at her reflection, she chided herself for the unbidden thought. It was a total accident that she'd slipped and tipped the waiter's tray filled with champagne glasses. André had reached for her, and the comedy of flying glasses and fumbling hands and feet would have made her laugh if it happened in a movie. But it had happened to her—to them. And there was nothing funny about it.

Too embarrassed to do anything but apologize and leave, Susan had rushed away to try to remove the splashes that had hit her dress and shoes. She hadn't returned.

She'd never expected to see the man again, so their eyes connecting across the orientation room had been a total surprise, but the recognition was instant. And now she had to return to the bar where he was. Snapping her purse closed, she went back to her group.

Don't miss Love in New York
by Shirley Hailstock, available July 2019
wherever Harlequin® Kimani Romance™
books and ebooks are sold.

Love Harlequin romance?

DISCOVER.

Be the first to find out about promotions, news and exclusive content!

 Facebook.com/HarlequinBooks

 Twitter.com/HarlequinBooks

 Instagram.com/HarlequinBooks

 Pinterest.com/HarlequinBooks

ReaderService.com

EXPLORE.

Sign up for the Harlequin e-newsletter and download a free book from any series at **TryHarlequin.com.**

CONNECT.

Join our Harlequin community to share your thoughts and connect with other romance readers!
Facebook.com/groups/HarlequinConnection

HARLEQUIN®

ROMANCE WHEN
YOU NEED IT

HSOCIAL2018

Need an adrenaline rush from nail-biting tales
(and irresistible males)?

Check out **Harlequin Intrigue®**,
Harlequin® Romantic Suspense and
Love Inspired® Suspense books!

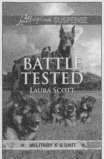

New books available every month!

CONNECT WITH US AT:

Facebook.com/groups/HarlequinConnection

Facebook.com/HarlequinBooks

Twitter.com/HarlequinBooks

Instagram.com/HarlequinBooks

Pinterest.com/HarlequinBooks

ReaderService.com

H HARLEQUIN®

**ROMANCE WHEN
YOU NEED IT**

SGENRE2018R

Reward the book lover in you!

Earn points on your purchase of new Harlequin books from participating retailers.

Turn your points into **FREE BOOKS** of your choice!

Join for FREE today at
www.HarlequinMyRewards.com.

Harlequin My Rewards is a free program (no fees) without any commitments or obligations.